Dark Water

Dark Ship

Dark Horse

Dark Shadows

Dark Paradise

Dark Fury

Dark Hunt

Dark Path

Dark Prey

Dark Fraud

Dark Drone

Dark Country

Dark Order

© 2022 Evan Graver

www.evangraver.com

ISBN-13: 979-8-9850448-7-4

Cover: Wicked Good Book Covers

Editing: Novel Approach Manuscript Services

This is a work of fiction. Any resemblance to any person, living or dead, business, companies, events, or locales is entirely coincidental.

Printed and bound in the United States of America

First Printed June 2022

Published by Third Reef Publishing, LLC

Hollywood, Florida

Your Free Book Is Waiting

———

The elusive bomb maker, Nightcrawler, is targeting Coalition troops in Afghanistan. Ryan Weller's U.S Navy EOD team is sent to find him. But Nightcrawler has plans of his own—a deadly ambush with long lasting consequences.

———

Get a free digital copy of the prequel *Dark Days: A Ryan Weller Thriller* here:

https://evangraver.com/free-book/

DARK ORDER

A Ryan Weller Thriller

EVAN GRAVER

THIRD REEF
PUBLISHING LLC

PROLOGUE

September 30, 1944
U-1226 Type IXC/40 submarine
Oslofjord Inlet, Norway

Obersturmbannführer Wolfgang Poske tore open the manila envelope stamped *Top Secret*.

He'd received the envelope from Heinrich Himmler himself, in the Berlin office of the *Reichsführer-SS* where Himmler controlled the whole of the paramilitary group known as the *Schutzstaffel*, or SS.

Poske was a member of the Waffen-SS, a lieutenant colonel who had been involved in many of Himmler's special operations, including leading an extermination squad to wipe out Communist commissars and Jewish settlements following the 1941 invasion of Russia, planning counterassaults to the D-Day invasion of Normandy, and, less openly, conducting Himmler's relic searches to find proof that the German people were the definitive Aryan race. Poske didn't believe in all that mumbo jumbo, but he *was* a loyal soldier and, as such, had been rewarded with this mission; the final act he would perform in the service of the Fatherland and his Führer.

The *Reichsführer-SS* had picked Poske for many assignments because he felt Poske fit the Aryan ideal—six feet, four inches tall and blond with ice blue eyes—excellent breeding stock and a poster boy of the *Schutzstaffel*.

"What does it say?" August-Wilhelm Claussen, the captain of the U-1226, asked, anxious to find out the destination of the U-boat's second—and unbeknownst to him, *final* —patrol. They had already left the dock at their home port in Horten, Norway, heading for the North Sea.

Poske read the orders and then handed them to Claussen. "We are to go to Hamburg, where we'll dock at the Fink II U-boat bunker."

Claussen read the orders several times, Poske's eyes tracking those of the captain as they moved up and down the page.

"It seems a strange request," Claussen commented, handing back the slip of paper. "But with the SS aboard, I shouldn't wonder at the nature of our mission."

"No, Captain, it's not your place to question the orders. They supersede any you may have received from the *Kriegsmarine*," Poske stated flatly, meaning even Admiral Karl Dönitz, the commander-in-chief of the German Navy, couldn't override the SS orders in Poske's hand.

Turning to the navigator, Captain Claussen ordered him to set course for the mouth of the Elbe River. Once they cleared the marine traffic in the inlet, they increased speed, racing across the surface of the Skagerrak Strait at fifteen knots, ready to crash dive at any moment should the lookout spot Allied aircraft or warships. This deep into the war, the Allies commanded the skies above Europe and their bombers and fighters actively ranged over the North Sea and Norway, seeking juicy prey like a U-boat cruising on the surface.

Entering the North Sea, the submarine submerged, and their speed slowed to a moderate six knots with the snorkel extended. The twin MAN diesels continued to hum, providing the U-boat with a longer range than battery power alone.

The executive officer, Lieutenant Ludwig, stepped onto the submarine's cramped bridge. "Weather's taking a turn, sir. Recommend retracting the snorkel and going to battery power, lest we ingest some water."

"Keep an eye on it," Claussen replied. "I want to run on diesel for as long as we can."

The XO nodded and left the bridge.

"What does he mean by 'ingest some water'?" Poske asked. The lieutenant colonel was a land-based officer and had little working knowledge of submarines. In fact, this was his first trip aboard such a craft. It unnerved him to be in a vessel that had been designed to sink on purpose.

"The snorkel," Claussen explained patiently, "is a device we use to vent the boat while running submerged. It consists of two tubes: an intake and an exhaust. Air is drawn into the boat forward of the engine room to give us all clean air to breathe, and to feed the diesels. Exhaust gases flow out just below the water's surface, to prevent any smoke from being spotted by enemy aircraft or ships. The intake pipe has a check valve in it to keep water from flowing down the pipe and flooding the boat. Occasionally, the check valve will stick."

"Is that bad?" Poske asked.

Matter-of-factly, Claussen replied, "It can flood the boat and kill us all."

Poske felt a prickling sensation at the back of his neck. As an SS officer, he was used to being shot at while leading a squad of commandos, or sitting in the back seat of a staff car dictating orders, or watching his men execute as he liked to say, "those filthy Jews." There, on land, he was in control. Stuck in the U-boat, Poske was forced to sweat it out with the rest of the crew.

He swallowed hard to control his nerves. Though Himmler might have thought Poske had ice water running through his veins, Poske knew the truth about himself. He was willing to do whatever was needed to get ahead, but he also had a cowardly streak that helped to preserve him.

He wasn't above concocting a scheme to make himself rich, either.

"Does the check valve stick often?" Poske demanded.

"Only when the waves are at a certain height," Claussen stated. "But don't you worry, *Obersturmbannführer*, we have plenty of work-arounds."

That didn't reassure Poske. Sweat ran down his forehead. Despite the cold of the North Sea leaching through the steel hull, the interior of the sub seemed incredibly warm. The SS officer chalked it up to the heat generated by the diesels and the close confines of forty-nine men. Already the funk of body odor wafted through the boat, on its way to the surface through the snorkel.

Poske didn't know if he would make it to the completion of their mission without going crazy.

———

Two days later, the U-1226 docked inside the Fink II U-boat bunker off the Elbe River in Hamburg, Germany. The massive bunker had four slips and spanned five acres with its ugly concrete exterior.

The Fink II's interior was dimly lit by naked lightbulbs in small wire cages. Fumes of welded metal, diesel exhaust, and battery acid soured the air. The water that sloshed around the submarine smelled like rotten garbage to Poske and was black with motor oil and spilled fuel.

Poske shoved his hands into his black calfskin gloves and then into the pockets of his greatcoat as he exited the submarine. The bunker's reinforced concrete was thick enough to retain a bitter chill despite the warmth of the fall sun. He strolled down the gangplank to the pier and walked briskly toward the Mercedes staff car that sat idling at the head of the slip, adding its noxious fumes to the already choked air.

All around the four submarine pens, crews worked tirelessly on the U-boats assembled there, getting them ready to return to the sea and hunt in wolf packs for the American merchant vessels that carried a steady stream of supplies to aid the Allied war effort. Hammers rang off metal, grinders showered the air with sparks, and men shouted at each other, trying to make themselves heard over the din.

Reaching the gleaming black Mercedes, Poske opened the door and slid onto the hand-tooled black leather seat. His superior sat across from him in an immaculately pressed uniform, wire-rimmed glasses glinting in the low light of the overhead lamp. Himmler, though diminutive and bespectacled, was not a man to be trifled with. He was more ruthless than Hitler and confidently believed he would eventually ascend to the position of *Führer* and lead the Third Reich.

But the Reich's dreams of global domination were coming to an end, and quicker than any had envisioned. While Hitler still believed his Master Race would win the war and bring the world to its knees, his officer corps was adjusting to a more practical reality.

With the Allies advancing on Germany, and the Wehrmacht losing the war, it was time to decamp and live to fight another day. Plans were in place for German officers to escape to Buenos Aires, where Himmler's operatives had established a headquarters in the presidential palace. Argentinian dictator Juan Perón was an enthusiastic supporter of the Nazi regime and had already welcomed members of the party as they made their escape along "ratlines" through Scandinavia, Italy, Belgium, and France.

"How was your journey?" Himmler asked.

The junior man shrugged his shoulders. "It was fine," Poske lied. He couldn't complain, could he? Himmler didn't care for anything but the shipment of gold. Whatever hardships his officers had to endure were not his problem, and in truth, Poske had hated every minute of the underwater nightmare. More curious to Poske was why Himmler had chosen to come to the submarine pen himself instead of sending a low-level minion while he waited in the safety of the SS offices.

"Your orders," Himmler said, handing over another manila envelope stamped "Top Secret." "Read them now."

Poske tore open the envelope and read the contents. He was to load the U-1226 with gold and head for Buenos Aires via the northern route. Poske knew that to avoid Allied detection, this route would take them close to Iceland, and he dreaded the longer journey.

As he continued reading, he saw he was to report mechanical issues off the coast of Iceland. *Easy enough*, he thought, keeping the problematic snorkel in mind. From Iceland, he was to make maximum revolutions for Argentina, where he would meet a man named Reinhold Schultz. Schultz would then take charge of the gold, while Poske was to return to Fink II with the U-boat to repeat the process.

The *Obersturmbannführer* folded the orders and placed them in the pocket of his greatcoat. The shipment of gold was payment to Juan Perón for his loyalty and to aid in the relocation of Nazi Party leaders. With wealth and the protection of the Argentine government, the fleeing Nazis could live out their lives in peace—or plot the next World War.

"You understand?" Himmler asked.

"Yes, *Reichsführer*," Poske replied. He now understood the importance of the mission and why Himmler was overseeing the delivery of the orders and the gold himself. While the officers of the SS could be trusted with carrying out the orders of the Reich, the temptation to steal the gold could be overwhelming. By appearing in person, Himmler was ensuring his survival.

"Where is the gold?" Poske asked.

"There's a convoy of trucks waiting outside. You're to remove the mine-laying equipment from the U-boat and use that space to store the gold."

Poske reached for the car's door handle.

"Do this for me, Wolfgang, and I will see that you, too, have a place in Buenos Aires."

"Thank you, sir," Poske replied, then opened the door and exited the car.

He turned to find Captain Claussen standing on the pier, watching him. Poske approached and handed Claussen their new orders while telling him to busy his men with removing the mine-laying equipment. As Poske finished speaking, the black Mercedes pulled away and a large Opel Blitz, loaded with uniformed soldiers sitting atop wooden crates, took its place.

"Hurry, Captain," Poske ordered.

Claussen turned and strode to where he was abreast of the conning tower. There, he ordered the executive officer to make the necessary modifications to the submarine. More trucks pulled into the submarine berth: five in all, each bearing four crates. The soldiers fanned out to smoke and rest while the sailors cleared the submarine of its now useless mine-laying equipment before they loaded five tons of gold aboard the U-1226.

"I don't like this," Claussen said to Poske. The two men stood on the pier, watching pieces of the mine-laying equipment being carried away as sailors used oxy-acetylene torches to cut apart the equipment so they could carry it up through the submarine's small exterior hatches.

Poske smiled. "Think of it this way, Captain. We're preserving the Reich. We're a part of history."

———

October 23, 1944
Atlantic Ocean south of Iceland

"RAISE THE SNORKEL," Claussen ordered.

The crewman sprang to his duties, ensuring the U-1226 was at the proper depth before pressing the button to hydraulically raise the twenty-nine-foot snorkel. Once it was locked into position, the crewman reported to the captain that all was well.

"Engage the diesels," Claussen responded.

The first MAN diesel started, followed immediately by the second, initiating a low rumble through the submarine's hull.

"Make your speed five knots. Prepare to send and receive radio messages," Claussen said.

The crewmen on the bridge quickly complied, reporting back when all was as ordered.

They were 150 miles off the coast of Iceland, some 7,500 miles from their destination in Buenos Aires. It had taken weeks to get this far, and Poske was going to go stark raving mad before they reached land. The submarine was a confining oven of sweating, stinking humanity, with a palpable cloud of fear hanging over every man on board.

Claussen dictated a message for the Commander of Submarines. "U-1226 position: south of Iceland. Stop. Am having mechanical issues with snorkel. Stop. Will proceed to hunting ground when operational. End."

The radioman encrypted the message and sent it flashing through the airwaves toward Berlin.

As if Claussen's orders were a portent of things to come, the check valve on the snorkel, designed to prevent water from coming down the tube, suddenly slammed shut. With the check valve shut, the engines were forced to rapidly draw air from the interior of the boat. The sudden reduction in pressure inside the hull made Poske clamp his hands over his ears. His head rang and his chest ached. He felt as if he couldn't breathe.

Glancing around, Poske saw crewmen bleeding from their ears. One had fallen unconscious, slamming his face against his console. Blood poured from his shattered nose and streamed down the control panels, coating the instrument glass in crimson.

The U-boat shuddered as one of the MAN diesels died, and chaos reigned in the boat. Men ran on and off the bridge to the sound of Claussen's shouted orders, and medical personnel tended to the wounded.

Poske kept his hands over his ears. He'd had a raging headache for days. The medical officer had told him it was because of the buildup of carbon dioxide inside the boat, and had given him painkillers to lessen the effects, but no painkillers could combat the intense pressure he felt inside his skull now.

If losing the first engine hadn't been enough to cause a panic, the second diesel engine finally quitting gave everyone on the boat just cause.

U-1226 was dead in the water.

Silence enveloped the crew for a moment, then the chaos began anew. Poske wondered what the fuss was all about. Then it dawned on him as he listened to Claussen scream new orders. If the crew wasn't able to fix the check valve and get the engines back online, the sub was a sitting duck, ripe for the American planes patrolling the North Atlantic.

"Water coming down the snorkel!" someone shouted.

It sounded to Poske as if they were inside a sink drain, with all the water swirling right down on top of them.

"Battery power—*now!*" Claussen barked. "Four knots."

The sound of water rushing past the hull replaced the sound of water entering it.

We're going to sink! Poske thought.

Minutes ticked by while Claussen continually eyed the battery bank gauges. Poske couldn't make hide nor hair of them, but he found himself watching them, too. The little needle on the amp meter flickered lower and lower with each passing second.

"We need to surface, Captain," the XO reported.

Claussen swore fiercely, then gave the order. The submarine slowly rose to pitch and roll in the steep waves, and Claussen dispatched crewmen out the conning tower hatch to repair the defective check valve.

"How long can we stay exposed like this?" Poske asked once he and Claussen stood in the conning tower.

Lookouts glassed the sea and the night sky with binoculars, frantically awaiting the enemy.

Claussen shrugged. "For as long as it takes to complete the repairs—or until we get sunk by the Yanks."

"Comforting," Poske muttered. He glanced at his Glashütte Chronograph, a watch he'd traded for with a Focke-Wulf Fw 190 fighter pilot. In exchange, Poske had given up a prized Colt 1911 pistol, picked up from the body of a dead American in France.

Fifty minutes later, the crew had the check valve repaired and the engines restarted. Claussen ordered the hatches secured and the sub dove immediately back to snorkeling depth, to run on diesels.

————

THE CHECK VALVE continued to operate flawlessly until they were approaching The Bahamas.

Poske had urged Claussen to follow the eastern coast of Africa, but the captain had vetoed that, claiming too many American ships were loitering off Morocco. The Allies had almost the entire Atlantic bracketed with picket lines and convoys, so the only option available was for the submarine to thread its way through them.

And the U-1226 would need fuel. Himmler's orders hadn't specified a particular refueling stop, but Claussen knew of a sympathetic Englishman in The Bahamas who was known to arrange refueling and replenishment operations.

Claussen had zigzagged through the worst of the Allied traffic. Now, they were within sight of Great Abaco, running on the surface at night to recharge the batteries.

"Two small boats approaching rapidly from the east," the radarman reported.

"Dive! Dive! Dive!" Claussen shouted.

Immediately, hatches clanged shut, and the boat's nose tucked under the water, heading for the soundless depths of the Atlantic. With the snorkel slowly retracting, Claussen counted on the check valve to keep the water from flooding his boat. The valve worked perfectly, but the helmsman had revved the engines too quickly, speeding the boat past ten knots. The snorkel tubes bent backward under the pressure of the surging water, just enough to keep the snorkel head from seating fully in the hull.

"Seventy feet," the helmsman called.

The first underwater detonation set Poske's teeth on edge. The second and third knocked out the submarine's lights.

"Hand grenades," Ludwig observed in a harsh whisper.

The lights came back on. Word passed quickly up and down the boat that they were taking on water from the damaged snorkel. Claussen swore again before giving an order to make a hard port turn out to sea. Soon, they had lost the marauding fishing vessels that acted as coastal watch for the Bahamian Defense Force.

Poske shivered—not from the cold, but from the fear that he might never set foot on dry land again. He *hated* this submarine.

Claussen moved through the boat, with Poske on his heels. They stopped where the snorkel trunk entered the hull. The twin tubes had retracted as far as they could, but water sluiced down around the thick rubber gasket—the only thing keeping the sub from flooding.

"We're in trouble, Poske," Claussen declared. "We'll have to make repairs on the surface. Let's hope the rumors about the Englishman are true."

Poske was more than ready for a break. He wanted nothing more than to get out of this damned boat and go ashore. They were only halfway to Argentina, and he couldn't believe Himmler wanted him to make this run again.

Living in a steel tube was insanity. Everyone aboard had headaches and was nauseous from the diesel fumes, and to make matters worse, their provisions were running dangerously low.

Fuel was another matter. It would take hundreds of gallons of diesel to top off their tanks for the last desperate run to Buenos Aires and, with the snorkel damaged, their chances weren't looking good to make it.

Returning to the bridge, Claussen ordered a course change for the six-thousand-foot-deep channel south of Cat Island. From there, they would cross the Exuma Sound, heading for the Englishman's estate on Big Darby Island. If they could find shelter in one of the sea caves there, they could repair and fuel the vessel. It was the only way to save the boat and its precious cargo.

———

THE THREE-HUNDRED-MILE JOURNEY to Big Darby took four days, running at dead slow and eking out every amp from the batteries. Claussen contacted the Englishman via the wireless, who arranged for a boat to meet the U-1226 just east of Little Darby Island and guide them into sheltered waters.

At 2 a.m., the Type IXC/40 submarine surfaced in Exuma Sound to a moonless sky and heavy cloud cover.

Poske was the second person up the ladder to the conning tower. He closed his eyes and breathed deeply of the warm, tropical night air, smelling the coming rain. The breeze on his face wicked away the sweat from his brow, but not the stench from his body. He'd grown accustomed to the body odor secreted by himself and the other men, just as he had grown used to the smell of diesel fuel, the taste of stale crackers, and warm desalinated water with a hint of salt. He contemplated jumping ship in Buenos Aires.

If only there was a way to take the gold with me and not give it to Juan Perón.

Moments later, a pinprick of flashing light broke the gloom to the east. The signalman interpreted the flashes emanating from the rocky coast and returned the prearranged signal. Out of the darkness, a rowboat bearing a sturdy black youth and an older white man appeared, its oars creaking in the silent night.

Poske visualized the water dripping from the wooden oars with each stroke. As a young boy growing up along the Rhine outside Düsseldorf, he'd been mesmerized by the way the sun had sparkled off the droplets that dangled from the oars as his father had sculled them along the river.

Claussen and Poske climbed down the ladder from the conning tower to the slick hull, kneeling close to the water-line to catch the rowboat's painter. The Englishman remained seated in the stern of the rowboat as the two German officers quickly explained their predicament.

They decided to submerge and wait for first light, then the Englishman would guide them through the channel between the Darby Islands and Rudder Cut Cay into protected water, where the submarine could be fueled and repaired, utilizing the Englishman's extensive machine shop.

Poske napped in his bunk until dawn, then returned to the conning tower to watch the sun break the horizon behind them, illuminating the coral heads and the riffs in the current. The Englishman, who had introduced himself as Guy Baxter, knew the course well and expertly guided them through before having the submarine turn in a wide basin just north of Big Darby. With the maneuver complete, Baxter advised nosing the sub up to a large cement pad with a metal ring studded into its center, which would hold the U-boat in place. Baxter seemed to have thought of everything.

As the sun rose higher, the crew of the U-1226 began to tackle the repairs needed to fix the snorkel.

While they struggled to bend the snorkel tubes back into place with block and tackle winched tight against the conning tower, Poske dressed in civilian clothing—tan slacks and a short sleeve casual dress shirt. Claussen donned his dress uniform. Baxter took Claussen and Poske on a tour of his island and fed them lunch on the veranda of what he called his "Green Castle," perched high on a hill. Poske admired the radio installation in their host's bedroom on the second floor.

Baxter's mistress, Ellen, was a sturdy beauty with black hair, wearing britches and a man's work-shirt. She did as much work as their employees, whom Baxter referred to as slaves, joking he could work them to death and pay them a pittance of what they were worth.

Despite receiving the man's help and hospitality, Poske didn't care for Baxter. The Englishman was a traitor to his country by aiding the German High Command with its war effort.

But Poske knew he was no saint himself. He'd killed plenty of people and had little compunction about it. That trait had helped him rise in rank, eventually being trusted enough to move Himmler's gold to Argentina.

As Poske stood on the upper balcony of the Green Castle, overlooking the lush plantation Baxter had established, it occurred to him that he could do the same. An idea that had been percolating in the back of his mind began to take shape.

Here, in this wild and remote place, Poske could be a free man. No one knew he was a high-ranking member of the Waffen-SS, nor did they need to. With the end of the war in sight, he felt sure the Allies would hunt down those who had committed war crimes and make them pay, especially the brutal members of the SS leadership.

Meaning they'd eventually come for *him*.

Poske excused himself from Baxter's company and made his way down the hill to the dock in the channel between Big and Little Darby. There, he had a man row him to the submarine, and once aboard, Poske inspected the work being performed on the snorkel. Large sections had been disassembled to straighten the intake and exhaust tubes.

Coming up on the chief engineer, Poske asked how the repairs were going.

"Not very well, sir," the engineer admitted. "The force of the sea at ten knots is greater than the force we can exert on the tubes with the block and tackle."

"Can it be repaired?" Poske asked, his hands behind his back as he inspected the work.

"If we can get the snorkel to retract back into the well, we can sail for Buenos Aires. If we make it there, we'll have to remove it from the submarine and overhaul the unit."

Poske nodded. He didn't like the sound of that. Going to South America no longer fit with his plans.

Later that night, as the enlisted men slept, Poske climbed down from his bunk and made his way to where the snorkel trunk fitted into the hull.

When the snorkel mast was raised into the "up" position, as it was now, two rubber gaskets fitted against the machined surfaces above and below the air outlet through which the mast passed. The gaskets were designed to create a tight seal against the external pressure of the sea. Without them, it would be impossible to use the snorkel while underway.

Poske began to hack at the internal gasket with a pair of pliers and a knife. It didn't take long to completely shred the rubber seal.

With his sabotage complete, Poske dumped his tools into the bilge and returned to his bunk.

On the way, Ludwig blocked the tight corridor ahead. The executive officer questioned what Poske had been doing out of his rack.

Poske held his finger to his lips, sensing the opportunity to place the blame for the damaged seal on someone else. "I'm going topside to piss. Come with me. I'd like to discuss the repairs."

Ludwig followed him up the ladder through the aft

deck hatch. While Poske stood near the waterline and urinated into the sea, Ludwig sat on the hatch coaming, his feet dangling into the ladderwell. They spoke quietly and were soon joined by the roving watch, a thin, blond youth named Witt who carried an MP 40 submachine gun on a sling around his neck. Secreted in their Bahamian hideaway, no one was expecting trouble, least of all the executive officer.

Poske waited for the roving watch to turn his back, then viciously kicked Ludwig in the back of the head. The XO flew forward, his forehead slamming into the coaming, and his body tumbled limply down the ladderwell, to lie in a lifeless heap on the grating below.

Witt turned at the sudden noise, his right hand resting on the top of the submachine gun, his left holding a freshly lit cigarette.

"Quickly!" Poske ordered. "Lieutenant Ludwig has slipped."

Witt flicked his cigarette into the water and hurried toward the hatch. As he bent, Poske slammed the edge of his hand into the back of Witt's neck, driving the youth to the deck. Poske pulled his Mauser pistol from beneath his shirt and fired a round into the back of Witt's head.

The loud bang of the pistol reverberated off the steel, bringing the crew on the double. Captain Claussen pushed through the crowd until he stood over his dead crewman, then turned and looked down the ladderwell at the body of his executive officer.

"What happened?" Claussen demanded.

Poske moved forward, having quickly holstered his pistol after shooting Witt. "I came up on deck to relieve myself when I saw Witt and the XO speaking in hushed voices. Ludwig was sitting on the hatch coaming. Witt suddenly kicked him, and he fell through the hatch. I couldn't let this insubordination go, and seeing Witt was armed, I had no choice but to shoot him."

"Did anyone else see this happen?" Claussen demanded, for, by now, the entire crew was standing on deck, gaping at the scene in morbid fascination.

No one spoke.

Claussen shook his head as if he wasn't buying Poske's story. "I guess we'll have to take your word for it, *Obersturmbannführer*," saying the SS rank as if it were poison in his mouth.

Poske kept his mouth shut but was ready to reach for his pistol if Claussen decided he wanted to toss him into the brig until he could convene an investigation. Instead, the captain ordered everyone back to their bunks.

Poske felt sure that by staging the executive officer's murder by Witt that it would throw suspicion on either one of the two men for the damage done to the snorkel seal.

Morning brought news of the sabotage, and word soon spread that either Witt or Ludwig was responsible for it. Theories about the two men working together spread even quicker. Poske waited for the verdict from Claussen, who broke the news while they were eating lunch on Baxter's veranda.

"The bottom seal of the snorkel is beyond repair, but we can still steam for Buenos Aires. We will just have to run on the surface. Fortunately, the farther south we go, the fewer Allied patrols we'll encounter."

"But the seal keeps out the water, doesn't it," Poske said.

"Only when the snorkel is in use. When the snorkel is retracted, seawater flows freely around it," Claussen explained.

"But what if it can't retract?" Poske asked, fearing his work had been for nothing and they would still have to run the gauntlet of Allied patrols.

"Then we'll need to revise our plans," Claussen said.

Poske's hopes hinged on the snorkel not being able to retract. He would have to sabotage it some more.

After lunch, Claussen excused himself to return to the boat. Baxter and Poske relaxed with glasses of wine and Cuban cigars. Poske asked Baxter what he planned to do if Germany lost the war.

"Stay here, of course. Why would I leave?" Baxter replied.

Poske decided he should trust Baxter. After all, the man was risking everything to help them. He told Baxter about the shipment of gold aboard the submarine and asked if there was a place to hide it on the island. Baxter's eyes lit up and he immediately stood, ordering Poske to follow him.

The two men walked down an overgrown trail to the entrance of a sea cave between the dock and the rocky northeastern point of the island. There, Baxter showed Poske the cave's interior, suggesting it would be perfect for hiding the gold. They could split it, making them both wealthy beyond their wildest dreams.

Returning to the submarine, Poske checked on the repairs. The snorkel had been lowered, but it would not slide all the way into its recessed position in the hull. Combined with the damaged seal, the submarine was no longer seaworthy.

Overjoyed, Poske immediately set about offloading the crates of gold, ordering the crew to set up a hoist above the submarine's aft hatch and then transferring one crate at a time to Baxter's creaky rowboat. The crates were then stacked as far back in the cave as the crew could get them. The weight of five tons of gold caused an unseen crack in the limestone beneath the crates.

"What will we do with the submarine?" Claussen asked Poske as the last crate was being hoisted overboard.

"You'll take her out to sea and scuttle her," Poske

ordered. "The *Kriegsmarine* already believes we had technical issues off Iceland and does not know our current position. If we sink the boat, no one will ever know what became of us."

Claussen nodded, but Poske could tell the man was disgruntled at the thought of losing command of his precious *Unterseeboot*. "We can disappear, Claussen. The gold will be ours for the taking. We can live as free men."

Again, Claussen just nodded.

"Take her out tonight when the tide is high."

"Yes, *Obersturmbannführer*," Claussen replied glumly. He left Poske standing on the deck and descended the ladder into the submarine.

Poske went below himself, moving quickly to his cabin, where he had several bags stowed. He removed the one at the bottom of the pile and opened it. Inside were plastic explosive charges and British pencil detonators.

Poske set the first delay timer to midnight, then inserted a detonator into a block of plastique and placed the charge under the deck grating against the hull. He carried the second charge into the forward torpedo room and nestled it amongst the long, shiny cylinders. The ordnance was designed to sink enemy vessels, but when the plastique detonated, the pressure wave of the explosion would ignite the hexanite in the heads of the torpedoes and blow the bow off the U-1226, sending it to a watery grave.

Confident in his plan, Poske carried his bags off the submarine and placed them in one of Baxter's guest rooms. He informed Baxter of his actions, then suggested the Englishman leave the submarine as soon as he had helped to navigate it into deeper waters.

AT PRECISELY 11 P.M., the U-1226 got underway for her final voyage.

Poske and Ellen, Baxter's mistress, stood on the balcony of the Green Castle, watching the submarine slide like a shark out into the Exuma Sound. It slowed to disgorge Baxter into his rowboat, then continued on into the night. Claussen planned to take her into the Atlantic, open the sea cocks to flood her, and while the U-boat sank, the crew would paddle ashore in the lifeboats and disappear among the islands.

An hour later, an explosion blossomed on the horizon as Poske, Baxter, and Ellen looked on.

The trio raised their wine glasses and toasted their newfound wealth.

———

THE FOLLOWING EVENING, as the three co-conspirators dined on the veranda, the black youth who had rowed Baxter to and from the submarine suddenly appeared from the dark jungle.

"Mista Baxta, I don't wanna alarm you, but a large group of my people have gathered at de dock and are on der way here."

"What for?" Baxter demanded.

"I'll let dem tells ya." The man disappeared into the night as quickly as he'd come.

"Are you armed?" Baxter asked his guest.

Poske nodded, lifting his shirttail to display the butt of the Mauser he'd kept on him since killing Ludwig.

Baxter retrieved two hunting rifles from inside the house, handing one to Ellen.

The crowd of islanders appeared, carrying torches. Flicking fire cast dancing shadows across the trees and onto the veranda. A tall, well-built Bahamian stepped forward.

"What do you want, John Andrew?" Baxter demanded.

"Mista Baxta, we've come to tell ya dat you are no longa welcome here. We don't take kindly to you helping de Germans. You is an Englishman, just as we are. What you be doing is treason. Leave, or we will kill you."

Baxter laughed in amusement at the man's threat. "This is *my* island. I'll do whatever I please. Now, leave before I shoot every one of you." He leveled his rifle at the crowd.

"This be your only warning, Mista Baxta," the spokesman stated. "Tomorrow night, we'll have your answer, or we'll hang all three of you."

The crowd filtered off the manicured lawn at the front of the house.

"Can you get a boat large enough to take the gold to America?" Poske asked once the islanders were gone.

"Not by tomorrow," Baxter stated. "We'll have to take some with us on my boat and come back for the rest."

Poske spent a restless night in Baxter's guest room. Finally accepting he couldn't sleep, he retreated to the screened porch to stare into the darkness. His plans were rapidly evolving. With the gold, he could start a new life anywhere he chose. He just needed a way to take it with him. But without a sizable vessel, they couldn't take it all.

———

BAXTER JOINED his new German friend as the sun was rising. All the servants had deserted the house and grounds, leaving the place eerily silent other than for the bleating of the occasional sheep or goat.

The two men decided to load as much gold as they could carry aboard Baxter's forty-foot motor vessel and head for Cuba. There, they could convert the gold into cash, then cross to the Florida Keys.

Ellen fixed them a simple breakfast of eggs and toast before they loaded the yacht with supplies for the trip. It was arduous work trudging up and down the path from the house to the dock, but by midday, they had everything aboard they would need. The only thing left was the gold.

As they ate a cold lunch of bread, cheese, and leftover lamb chops, Ellen excused herself, saying she wanted to walk through her beautiful home one last time. After finishing his meal, Poske retrieved his bags from his room and went to find Baxter and his mistress.

Stepping into the master suite, Poske saw Ellen fitting a brick back into the fireplace surround. "What are you doing?" he asked inquisitively.

Ellen held up a small velvet bag. "This is where I kept my valuables. One can never trust the natives."

The three companions made their way down to the cave beyond the dock and pried open the first crate they came to. Poske carefully lifted out the small bar of gold.

Each bar measured four inches long by one-and-three-quarters wide. The half-inch thick bar would fetch twelve hundred dollars on the open market; less, where Poske would have to sell it to stay off the Americans' radar. The gold bars carried the *Reichsadler*—a spread eagle with its beak facing to the eagle's right—over a laurel wreath that encircled a swastika. Under the national symbol of Germany were the words "*Deutsche Reichsbank*" and "One kilogram Feingold 999.99." At the bottom of the bar was a serial number.

Baxter hefted a bar in each hand. "We may have to melt these into ingots to get rid of the Nazi symbol. I can't imagine it will be very popular with the fences we'll need to work with."

"I agree," Poske said. "Let's take as many as we can carry and get out of here before the natives come back."

Baxter and Poske bent to their task and were busy filling

satchels with gold bars when Ellen suddenly silenced them. They listened to the wind moaning through the gaps in the rock, heard the sea crashing against the shore, and animals lowing.

"What is it, dear?" Baxter asked at length.

"I thought I heard something," she replied. "It sounded like rocks falling."

"Probably just the sea. It sounds different in here," Baxter assured her.

The men turned back to filling their bags.

Without another warning, the cave floor gave way beneath them, overweighted by the gold.

The three thieves tumbled through the chasm as crates of gold fell atop them, driving them down to the bottom of the pool of water beneath what had once been the delicate floor of the cave.

Poske struggled to push off the crate so he could swim to the surface, but it pinned him in place as the surrounding cave collapsed in on itself, forming a glistening blue hole on Big Darby Island.

CHAPTER ONE

Ryan
Present Day
Bay of Campeche, Mexico

It was an all-hands-on-deck effort for Dark Water Research.

Every available diver had been shipped into Progreso, loaded onto crew barges, and sent to the Zama oilfield to work the joint effort between Pemex, the Mexican state-run petroleum corporation, and Talos, the private oil exploration and development company that had discovered the deposit and had estimated it to contain between 1.4 and two billion barrels of oil.

After Pemex forcibly took over the project in 2017, Talos had fought to regain control. In the end, the Mexican government simply didn't have the capital to drill wells and implement the infrastructure needed to make the field produce. When Pemex had finally turned the field back over to Talos, the Texas-based company had been ready with capital and labor. One phone call to Dark Water Research, and the crews had quickly deployed. With energy production in the U.S. at record lows due to the current presidential administration's policies, there were plenty of men ready to spring into action to work the Zama field.

Ryan Weller stood on the seabed some two hundred feet below the dark surface of the Gulf of Mexico. Above him, DWR's pipe-laying barge, *Midkiff*, named for a dried-up oil town in Texas, was ablaze with lights that shone down through the water. The illumination backlit Ryan's work, but for the close-up view of the nuts and bolts he was tightening to assemble the flange of the subsea manifold, the diving contractor relied on the twin lights mounted on his yellow Kirby Morgan dive helmet. A hiss of gas accompanied each inhalation, and exhaust bubbles vented from the side of his rig. Sweat ran down from his brown hair and blurred the vision of his green eyes. Unable to wipe it clear, Ryan blinked away the water and twisted the knob on his demand regulator a little farther open to help cool his face.

An umbilical, consisting of a breathing hose, a pneumo-fathometer hose—used to measure depth—and a fiber-optic communications cable wrapped around a nylon line, was clipped to the rear of Ryan's dive harness, bringing breathing gas from the compressor laboring on the surface. High above him, the crewmen in the *Midkiff*'s viewing room could watch the real-time feed from the camera mounted on his helmet and his tender could communicate either through the comms gear or via a series of prearranged tugs on the umbilical.

Ryan reached into the pouch on his side and extracted a one-inch diameter bolt. He pushed the bolt through the hole on the pipe flange connected to the U-Haul truck-sized mani-fold. Submerged pipelines from multiple wells ran to the manifold, bringing oil from the rigs that would then travel through the line Ryan and the DWR team were currently constructing to an onshore collection point some thirty miles away, at the Puerto Dos Bocas refinery.

Next, Ryan withdrew a nut and spun it onto the bolt he'd just inserted. He continued to work his way around the flange, connecting the first section of the pipeline to the manifold. After spinning on each nut finger tight, Ryan reached for the pneumatic driver and fitted its large socket to the first nut. The bolt head on the rear of the flange seated into a hexagon cup to prevent it from spinning, which meant Ryan didn't need to hold both a wrench and the impact gun.

Triggering the gun, Ryan watched in disbelief as the nut spun backward off the bolt and shot out the end of the socket, disappearing into the sediment-laced water below.

"Way to go, butterfingers," Stacey Wisnewski commented from her perch in topside control. "We're all standing around waiting for you, and you can't even get the direction of the gun right."

Fortunately, Ryan carried extra nuts and bolts. It wasn't the first time he'd made such a rookie mistake. He'd lost more than his fair share of nuts and bolts in the mud over his years beneath the waves. But in truth, this whole trip, he'd felt like a newbie. Since he didn't work full time as a commercial diver, Travis, Stacey's husband and the diving supervisor aboard the *Midkiff*, had treated him like a pariah.

Ryan fished out another nut and threaded it on, then ensured the impact wrench was toggled to rotate forward and pressed the trigger to tighten the nuts. He worked his way around the flange in a star pattern, tightening all sides evenly so the flange didn't warp under pressure. If there was even the slightest deviation, the flange might leak and cost Talos more money and time to send divers in to repair Ryan's screwup.

"All right, I'm done," he reported to Stacey.

"Good. Move to the far end of the pipe."

Ryan hooked the pneumatic driver to his harness with a carabiner, then trudged through the mud along the pipe. Each step stirred up plumes of sediment that hung in the water column before slowly settling back to the seafloor, a blank slate of gray muck running uphill toward shore.

As he trudged through the water, Ryan decided that the next time Greg Olsen, the owner of Dark Water Research and one of his best friends, called him to work a diving job, he'd flat out refuse. While Ryan was an accomplished commercial diver, he had left that life behind and was applying his skillset to other endeavors. Lately, those had been lying on his boat and drinking margaritas. Since Ryan had come aboard the *Midkiff*, he'd had to brush the rust off his diving skills and that hadn't been easy.

Twenty feet later, Ryan halted at the end of the pipe which was also fitted with a flange so the next piece of pipe could be attached to it.

The barge Ryan worked from was equipped with a welding shop, while a second barge was alongside to feed pipe into the welding shop. The pipe ends would be welded by a computer-controlled rig, then ultrasonically inspected for defects. With the weld complete, a conveyor would feed the pipe through the stinger, a special boom hanging off the end of the barge, laying a continuous pipeline from the manifolds controlling the wellheads to the refinery on land.

"I'm here, Stace," Ryan said, reporting his arrival at the next flange.

"Cool," she said. "Travis is on his way down to help you align the pipes."

"Roger that," Ryan replied, feeling the fatigue of the long hours underwater. He glanced at his dive computer. He'd spent fifteen minutes getting the first flange bolted into place, so he now had twenty minutes of total bottom time on this dive.

Travis landed on the seafloor beside Ryan. The two men worked together to wrap a sling around the free end of the barge-fed pipe so they could hook the barge's crane onto it and use the barge to pull the pipe into place before bolting the two pipes together.

Ryan's breathing had quickened with the pace of the work, air now hissing through the regulator. A low, continuous ring of tinnitus played in Ryan's ears. He had grown to ignore it for the most part, but sometimes it was just annoying. Too many unmuffled gunshots, explosions, and working around heavy machinery and power tools had all taken their toll.

"We got it in the sling," Travis reported into his comms gear. "Slack up two feet."

Flexing his hands, Ryan tried to work the stiffness from his fingers caused by holding the sling in place.

The slack went out of the crane cable and increased tension on the pipe. This was the most dangerous aspect of the job. They had to properly align the two sections of pipe without getting their hands caught between them. Losing a digit or a hand was something neither man could afford.

The flange on the pipe Ryan had secured to the manifold had small alignment pins built into it. They just needed to align the holes on the pipeline side and insert the gasket, then bolt everything together. Seemed simple enough.

"Move the pipe forward a foot," Travis instructed.

The crane operator nudged his boom a fraction of an inch through its arc, and the two pipes nearly collided.

Ryan installed the gasket on the alignment pins and withdrew his hand so Travis could make the next move. While he waited, he saw the holes and the pins were off by a quarter of an inch and pointed to the problematic alignment just as Travis called for the next movement of the crane. Ryan snapped his hand out of the way just before the pipes kissed together.

"Hold, Johnny," Travis said to the crane operator.

"We need the chain bar," Ryan observed.

Travis agreed, calling for Anthony, the standby diver, to enter the water and bring down the tool they needed. A couple of minutes later, the St. Croix native was standing on the seabed beside the other two divers. They wrapped the chain around the pipe and cinched it tight, careful not to crush the outer ring of the dual layer pipe. The outer hull delivered hot water to the manifold to keep the oil warm and flowing while the oil moved in the opposite direction.

As Ryan and Anthony manned the eight-foot-long chain bar, Travis stood by to push home the first bolt.

"Heave, Ant," Ryan directed.

The two men applied their body weight to the bar, forcing the pipe to twist.

"A hair more," Travis said.

Grunting with the effort, Ryan and Anthony applied more force until Ryan began to feel his hand moving on the bar. "It's slipping!" he warned.

Travis tried to hammer the bolt home but lacked the fraction of an inch needed to slide the bolt smoothly through the two holes.

"Come on," Travis begged.

"I can't hold it," Ryan shouted.

"One more heave," Travis yelled back.

The bar slipped from Ryan's hand, smacking him in the side of the helmet and cracking the heavy-duty fiberglass. Water began to rush in as Ryan tried to shake off the effects of the blow.

"Get Ryan up *now*!" Travis shouted into the comms unit. "His helmet's flooding."

The tenders instantly responded, heaving on the umbilical

to race Ryan to the surface. Water continued to gush through the widening crack, covering Ryan's mouth. He twisted the knob on the regulator all the way open to increase the amount of air coming through the line and blast out the rising water.

But even with the regulator operating at maximum capacity, it couldn't ventilate the helmet as fast as the water was coming in. The comms unit shorted out with a screeching buzz.

With the water surging around his head, Ryan tilted it back to fight for one last breath. As the tenders dragged him to the surface, Ryan exhaled a stream of bubbles to prevent his lungs from swelling like balloons and bursting inside his ribcage.

Two minutes later, Ryan was on the deck of the *Midkiff*, being stripped of his gear. Once he was down to his underwear, the tenders moved him quickly into the recompression chamber and repressurized him down to working depth.

Stacey peered through the chamber's portal at Ryan. "You okay?"

"Yeah. Just got my bell rung. Other than that, I'm all right. Are Travis and Ant okay?" Ryan asked, looking up at Stacey's head of purple hair. She'd dyed it like that for longer than Ryan had known her.

"They're fine. What happened?" Stacey replied.

Ryan rubbed his temples with his fingertips. "The bar slipped out of my hand."

Stacey patted the tank. "Rest up. We'll get you checked out when you get out of the chamber. In the meantime, we'll keep an eye on you."

Ryan flashed her the "Okay" sign by circling his index finger to his thumb and holding up the other three fingers. He lay down on the thin pad that covered the bench and rubbed his eyes with the heels of his palms. While he hated being in the "Iron Cadillac," the chamber was a necessary evil of commercial diving. Divers worked long hours underwater and couldn't afford the time it took to decompress in the water, especially when the weather turned nasty and the waves built, meaning they would be bounced around like a yo-yo on a string and not capable of holding a steady depth.

Closing his eyes, Ryan allowed his mind to drift. His wife Emily was in Hollywood, Florida, staying with her mother and brother while Ryan worked offshore. He didn't have to be there. He didn't need the money. He didn't need to take the risks associated with one of the most dangerous professions in the world—but there he was, feeling like a "muppet." In diver parlance, he was someone who just couldn't get anything right. It seemed every time he went into the water on this job, something went wrong.

On account of the escalating number of accidents, Ryan was beginning to dread going back under. This time, his helmet had been the only thing to break.

The next time, he feared it would be a lot worse.

CHAPTER TWO

When the door to the recompression chamber opened almost four hours after he'd gone in, Ryan slipped out and stood in the freshening breeze. Kyle, his tender, a young kid right out of commercial diving school, handed him a pair of coveralls, which Ryan slipped on before wedging his feet into steel-toed work boots.

A sleek Bell Jet Ranger helicopter sat on the landing pad constructed above the *Midkiff*'s pilothouse.

"Whose paraffin pigeon is that?" Ryan asked.

Kyle shrugged. "Don't know. Flew in here about an hour ago."

Ryan stretched and went across the deck to the other recompression chamber, where Travis was having the nitrogen squeezed from his body. When a diver breathed compressed air, tiny nitrogen bubbles made their way into the diver's tissues. If the diver didn't ascend slowly through the water column, or, as in this case, utilize a recompression chamber, the nitrogen bubbles would either expand and lodge in their joints, or try to push out through their skin, or ride the bloodstream to the brain, causing painful and debilitating injuries—and sometimes death.

He pressed his face to the porthole to see Travis. The younger man lay stretched out on the bunk, his eyes closed and arms crossed. Not wanting to disturb him, Ryan made his way to the galley to find something to eat. Diving always made him hungry, and the chef kept a ready supply of sandwiches and diced fruit as snacks for the crew.

"What's up, Cookie?" Ryan asked the chef, a heavyset man in his forties.

"Just another day in paradise, brother."

"Amen to that," Ryan replied.

"Sandwiches are in the cooler, but you might want to hold off. One of the welders caught a mess of grouper. I'm whipping up some fish tacos for tonight's meal."

"Count me in," Ryan said hungrily. "But I need something to hold me over."

Stacey came into the galley as Ryan was unwrapping a ham and cheese sandwich.

"There's a guy here to see you," she said to Ryan.

Ryan glanced up at her. "What?"

"I said—"

Ryan cut her off. "I heard what you said. Why is he here to see me?"

She shrugged. "You'll have to ask him yourself."

Ryan had a gut feeling that the guy, whoever he was, was there to ask him for a favor. His reputation as a troubleshooter had grown since he'd led a team to rescue missionaries being held hostage in Haiti.

"Is Travis out of the chamber yet?" Ryan asked.

Stacey glanced at her watch, an enormous Garmin unit that monitored her heart rate and breathing. She also used the timer function to monitor Travis' chamber rides. "About ten more minutes."

"When he gets out, have him meet me here and we'll go talk to this guy together."

"Are you sure?" she asked.

"Why wouldn't I be?" Ryan responded. "Trav is my boss. Whatever the rich guy in the Jet Ranger has to say, he can say to both of us. Besides, you know how Trav gets when Greg pulls me away to work a troubleshooting contract."

Stacey rolled her eyes. "He wasn't wrong. You've left us in the lurch plenty of times."

"Yeah, well, we all work for Greg Olsen and when he says jump, we ask how high."

"I get that," Stacey said, "but we've got a time crunch with this job, and we need every available man even if you are a freaking muppet."

Ryan chuckled. "No argument there. I'm almost scared to go in the water. It feels like I'm jinxed."

"Everyone goes through it, Ryan. You haven't worked underwater in a while, so it's your turn."

Ryan heard the accusatory tone in her voice, but he chose to ignore it, no matter how true her inference was. He hadn't worked as a commercial diver since he'd been part of the crew aboard the *Peggy Lynn*, a converted trawler Ryan, Travis, Stacey, and a group of others had used to traverse the Caribbean, performing whatever jobs Dark Water Research had assigned them. Ryan would frequently leave the boat to run operations for Greg Olsen or at the request of Floyd Landis, a DHS agent Greg and Ryan worked with. It always agitated Travis to be left shorthanded and he'd given Ryan an ultimatum the last time he'd been aboard *Peggy Lynn*—commit to working as a commercial diver full time or leave their crew for good. Ryan had left. But on this operation, Greg had stuck him with Travis, thinking Ryan would mesh right back into the old crew.

Stacey left the galley, leaving Ryan alone. He bent to eat

his sandwich, chewing quickly to get it all down before Travis got out of the chamber. Ryan had forgotten how hard the work of commercial diving could be. There was a weariness in his bones, and the constant wonder of what would go wrong next had seeped into his brain, causing Ryan to doubt everything he knew about working underwater.

Travis arrived just as Ryan was finishing his snack. "You're a real piece of work, Weller. Everything you touch turns to shit."

"I'll take that as a compliment from you, Travis."

"It wasn't." Travis retrieved a bottle of water from the fridge. "Do you know who this guy is that flew out here to meet you?"

"Not a clue. I figured since you're the boss, you should be privy to the conversation. Just what you always wanted."

Travis snorted in derision. "Let's go."

Ryan rose from his seat and dropped his sandwich wrapper and empty soda can in the trash. Together, the two men made their way to the bridge, where Captain Stewart stood watch over the barge's broad deck with his arms crossed. As Ryan and Travis stepped into the captain's domain, Stewart nodded to them before raising a soda can to his mouth and spitting a stream of tobacco juice into it.

The captain angled his head toward the rear of the bridge. "Your guest is in my cabin."

Ryan thanked Stewart and led the way to the captain's cabin, just behind the bridge. The cabin was the most luxurious on the vessel, but even it was bare bones, consisting of a small sitting room with a desk, a chair, a love seat, and a hanging closet. Stepping through the second door in the room would lead to a five-by-ten space that contained a bunk, another hanging closet, and the all-important ship's safe.

Sitting in the love seat was a man in his mid-sixties with thinning, light brown hair, going gray at the temples and combed over to hide his crown. He stood and straightened his long sleeves. To Ryan, the man appeared to have purposely dressed down in his fishing shirt, khaki pants, and boat shoes, but all of them were brand name and high dollar.

Ryan introduced himself and Travis. As they shook hands, the older man said, "I'm Steve Carlton."

"What can I do for you, Mister Carlton?" Ryan asked, leaning his butt against the captain's desk and crossing his arms as Carlton returned to his seat.

Carlton glanced at Travis. "Could you excuse us?"

"Travis is good to go," Ryan said. "Say what you came to say."

"I find myself in need of a troubleshooter," Carlton said succinctly. "Your name keeps coming up when I ask around."

Ryan wondered who this guy had been talking to. He tried to keep his name out of the news and even used a fake passport when traveling for some troubleshooting jobs.

Travis asked for him. "Who have you been asking?"

"I happen to know Greg Olsen personally. I knew he used to own a PMC, so I called him when I started having trouble. He recommended Mister Weller and mentioned I might have seen his handiwork in extracting those kidnapped missionaries from Haiti."

"Whatever you need, Ryan's your guy," Travis quipped.

"I realize you're under time constraints here, but I wouldn't have come all this way if it wasn't crucial," Carlton stated.

"We can spare him," Travis replied.

"I'm glad to hear you say that," Carlton said, relieved.

Ryan cocked his head. When these situations had cropped up before, Travis had always been reluctant to let Ryan go and had even tried to convince him to stay to finish their diving job. Now, he was pushing for Ryan to leave. Part of Ryan understood Travis' position. He was a clumsy diver on this trip and things would probably go faster without him.

"What's the job?" Ryan asked.

"I recently purchased Big Darby Island in the Exumas."

Travis whistled. "I heard that place had a forty-five-million-dollar price tag."

"I paid less than that," Carlton said matter-of-factly.

Ryan snorted. Rich people problems. Money bought power, and power corrupted.

"Blah blah blah. I'm rich. I bought an island," Travis said, spinning his finger to get Carlton to speed up his tale of woe. "So why do you need a troubleshooter?"

"I would kindly ask you to rein in your impertinence, Mister Wisnewski. I'm a businessman, a husband, and a father. There's more to me than money. Please restrain yourself or leave."

Ryan wasn't exactly feeling amicable to Carlton's difficulties, either, but he motioned for Travis to keep quiet. "What's the problem, Mister Carlton?"

"I mention my family because I purchased Big Darby for my daughter, Diane. She wants to rebuild the Green Castle there. It's a spectacular mansion built in 1938 by Sir Guy Baxter. Anyway, she wants to run it as a bed and breakfast."

Carlton went on to tell Ryan and Travis some of the island's history. After King George VI had gifted Big Darby Island to Baxter, the Englishman had run a self-sufficient farming operation that included goats, cattle, and sheep, as well as growing cotton, palm oil, and various fruits. Baxter exported the fruits of his labor from his deep-water dock in the channel between Big and Little Darby Islands. He'd also carved out an airstrip and multiple walking paths on the 554-acre estate.

When World War II broke out, Baxter had conspired with the Germans, believing the Nazis would defeat the

English. He'd installed large concrete pilings in nearby sea caves on Rudder Cut Cay and around his own dock to resupply U-boats. As the war wound down, it became clear Hitler would not be the victor, so Baxter had disappeared, leaving the island's facilities to fall into a state of disrepair.

Ryan had been to Big Darby Island just over a year ago. He and Emily had ignored the "NO TRESPASSING" sign with its ominous warning that lawbreakers would receive their passports back at their trial and had walked the island's overgrown paths, explored the livestock pens formed in the rocky inland caves, and stood on the balcony of the decrepit Green Castle. Situated on a ridge a mere eighty feet above sea level, the seven-thousand-square-foot mansion still retained a sense of its former self, with mahogany floors, tile in the bathrooms, and antique furniture in some of the rooms.

Carlton's first priority, he told them, had been to clear the runway and regrade it. Once completed, he could fly in supplies to rebuild rather than using the runway on Little Darby and having to ship everything across the channel. A backhoe and a track steer were brought in by barge. After the local Bahamians had commenced work on the runway, Carlton had flown over from Nassau to check on the progress, but the landing strip had only been partially cleared. The pilot had landed the helicopter on Little Darby, and after a thorough search of Big Darby, Carlton could find none of the workers he'd hired. It seemed they had fled without even taking any of their personal effects from their tents.

"I called the construction company," Carlton said. "The foreman informed me the workers had caught a ride on a passing boat and stated they would never return because the island was haunted."

Ryan and Travis glanced dubiously at each other.

"So, you need my help because your island is *haunted?*" Ryan asked in disbelief.

Ignoring the troubleshooter's question, Carlton continued with his story. "I took it upon myself to clear the strip. I flew in, squared my camp away, and started on the runway. I was pushing the trees into a pile near the north end of the runway with the track steer when someone began shooting at me. I ran for cover and hid in the mangroves. After being eaten alive by mosquitoes for two hours, I saw no one, so I returned to clearing the land, and encountered no more further problems that afternoon. The next morning, I awoke to the smell of smoke and stepped outside to find my backhoe and track steer were ablaze.

"I ordered a second set of equipment to be brought in. Once the machinery arrived, I towed the damaged vehicles aboard the barge and continued with my work. The next morning, I found sand in the fuel tanks. I drained them and cleaned the tanks the best I could. I still needed to clear another two hundred feet of runway, but again, someone took potshots at me. I found rifle casings on the roof of the Castle." Carlton reached into his pocket and then held up a brass cartridge.

"Someone doesn't want you on that island," Ryan said, impressed Carlton would choose to get his hands dirty doing a job he could easily pay others to do and for not being scared off by the gunshots and the destruction of his equipment.

Ryan extended his open palm and Carlton dropped the cartridge into it. Holding it up to catch the light, Ryan examined the butt. "Standard 5.56 NATO round. The DAG on the headstamp means it was manufactured by Dynamit Nobel AG in Germany. Saw a lot of these over in Iraq." He tossed the casing back to Carlton. "What you need to do is hire a squad of PMCs and sweep the island stem to stern, eradicate your boogeymen, and move on with your life."

"I did that. I called Academi," Carlton said, meaning the world's foremost private military contractor. "They sent over six men, armed to the teeth and ready to fight, but there was no one on the island. With them encamped, I finished clearing the runway, then smoothed and packed it. The Academi team called in a twin-engine Cessna, and we all flew out to Miami. A week later, I returned to find the landing field had been sabotaged, with massive holes blown in it."

Carlton took a deep breath. "Which brings me to you, Mister Weller. I want you to sneak onto Big Darby and find out who is destroying my property."

"I've got work to do here, sir," Ryan asserted.

"I just told the man that we could spare you, muppet," Travis said.

Ryan ground his teeth together. He wanted to punch Travis in the face every time he called him a muppet. He knew he was a muppet, he just didn't like Travis riding him. Sure, he'd been clumsy on this project, but he and Travis had worked other jobs together where things had gone off without a hitch. Be that as it may, the men still regarded each other with a fair amount of animosity—partly because, as Stacey had once said, they were so much alike. Ryan chalked the guy's recent round of bullshit up to the fact that a Chinese submarine had torpedoed *Peggy Lynn* out from under Travis and his crew over a year ago, and Travis blamed Ryan for it.

"Pack your kit," Travis said curtly. "You and Mister Carlton can take his paraffin pigeon back to wherever he came from. I'll do what I always do—have Greg send me a *competent* diver."

Ryan took a deep breath and pursed his lips. It took every ounce of self-control to restrain himself from punching Travis in the throat and then dumping his body over the side of the barge. Damn, this kid infuriated him. Always had. It would be good to get off the *Midkiff*.

Straightening from his position against the desk, Ryan

said, "I'll need a half hour to pack my gear, Mister Carlton. I'll meet you on the landing pad."

The older man smiled. "Thank you."

Travis led the way out of the captain's cabin. Ryan headed for the berthing to collect his clothing, then he'd go up to the gear shack to pack his diving equipment.

When Ryan stepped out of his berthing, Travis was waiting for him in the passageway. As they walked along the corridor to the stairs up to the deck, the lead diver said, "You know you don't belong here, right?"

Ryan ignored the verbal jab. Travis wanted a fight, and as much as Ryan wanted to put him in his place, he knew it would only cause more trouble than it was worth.

"I mean, you're not a bubblehead," Travis added. "You *pretend* to be a diver. It's a game to you, not a job."

Ryan stopped and dropped his bag on the deck. He turned to face Travis. "You want to take a swing? I'll let you have one free punch. It's what you've always wanted."

Travis puffed out his chest, stretching his smaller frame to match Ryan's six feet. Ryan stared down at the man's blue eyes and boyish face, but Travis didn't make a move.

A moment later, Ryan bent and picked up his duffel. As he straightened, Travis punched him in the jaw, swinging his right hand from shoulder height. The blow snapping Ryan's head around. His jaw ached, and fury burned inside him.

Rubbing his jaw and working it around its hinges, Ryan kept his temper in check. "Is that all you got, Wisnewski?"

"Get off my boat and never come back," Travis hissed through gritted teeth.

"Next time you throw a punch, don't aim at the jaw. Aim beyond it and punch through it." Ryan picked up the duffel he'd dropped in surprise at being punched and headed for the gear locker. Over his shoulder, he added, "Swing from the hips, too. Puts more power behind the punch."

Travis held up both middle fingers. "Get off my boat!"

THIRTY MINUTES LATER, Ryan was staring out the window of Carlton's airborne Bell Jet Ranger, watching the pipelaying barge recede into the distance and wondering what his future held.

"Where to, Mister Weller?" Carlton asked, drawing Ryan's gaze from the helicopter's window. "After we change to the jet in Coatzacoalcos."

Ryan centered his thoughts with a couple of slow breaths, his mind still working through the encounter with Travis. He hoped the kid had finally gotten whatever it was out of his system. Yeah, it sucked that *Peggy Lynn* had been torpedoed, but she'd been on her final voyage to Miami to be scrapped anyway. Ryan had even told Travis that he thought her sinking was quite poetic, that the old gal had received a proper burial at sea instead of being chopped up to make razor blades.

"Where to?" Carlton asked again.

"Wilmington, North Carolina," Ryan replied, rubbing his jaw.

"What's there?" Carlton asked.

Like it or not, Travis had saddled Ryan with this mission, and part of Ryan was grateful to be off the barge and back in the deadliest game.

He was going hunting.

Ryan turned to look at his new employer. "The gear I need to do my job."

CHAPTER THREE

From Coatzacoalcos in the dip of the saddle between mainland Mexico and the Yucatán Peninsula, the flight to Cape Fear Regional Jetport was just under fifteen hundred miles, easily within the range of Steve Carlton's twin-engine Embraer Phenom 300 jet. Ryan dozed on the flight, catching up on some of the sleep he'd lost while working twelve-hour shifts on the diving job.

Crossing over the long, swampy Florida peninsula, the sky was darkening to the east while the west was still brightly lit by the sun, providing a surreal contrast of dark and light. Green and blue. Land and water. Good and evil.

From a mile high, the world had a pristine feel to it, like a woman hiding her acne with makeup. Sure, the scars were still there, but from a distance, it was hard to see them.

Ryan had seen and created more than his fair share of scars on the earth. But time had a way of dealing with scars. Nature had a way of rightfully reclaiming what was hers, just as the human brain had a way of suppressing bad memories and highlighting the good. Ryan had his share of scars, too.

Time and love had healed quite a few, but there were still wounds in him just as raw as a strip mine looked.

He could see the glow of lights along Florida's east coast, from Stuart to Homestead, lit up like daytime against the blackness of the Everglades. Emily was down there. She was definitely his better half—more kind; more patient; more of everything Ryan would never be. *Could* never be—because of the darkness in his soul.

He was the hammer sent into the world by men like Carlton. He had to be forged from steel to meet evil head-on. Some called him a mercenary; others called Ryan Weller a private military contractor, although he had no military to back him up. His fictitious friend Travis McGee referred to himself as a salvage expert. Ryan preferred the term "troubleshooter."

Because wherever Ryan Weller went, there was always trouble—and always a good deal of shooting. Men died. *Friends* died. Ryan carried the names of those men around in his heart, to remind himself of what he was capable of and what his line of work had cost him.

He knew he should call Emily and let her know he was off the *Midkiff* and about to commence a wild goose chase to an island in The Bahamas, but he didn't pick up the phone. His wife was with her family, and her worrying about him diving was better than her worrying about him getting shot at. Ryan figured he was more likely to be eaten alive by the mosquitoes and the no-see-ums before these supposed "ghosts" appeared on Big Darby Island.

But he was wrong about that.

———

THE PHENOM TOUCHED down in North Carolina three hours after leaving Mexico. While in the air, Ryan had called Scott

Gregory, who was staying at Ryan's house along the Intra-coastal Waterway, to come pick them up. Scott met the plane at the jetport in a new Ford Bronco Raptor. The six-foot-three former Navy SEAL shook hands with the two men. Ryan introduced his tattooed houseguest to his new client.

"You can stay here with the plane, or you can come to the house," Ryan said to Carlton.

"I'll come with you," Carlton replied. "We can get a fresh start in the morning."

After Carlton gave instructions to his pilot, the three men loaded into the Bronco and Scott hotfooted it across the Cape Fear River and through Wilmington to Ryan's Blue Shores estate, an hour away.

Pulling up to the house, Scott shut off the Bronco. Ryan glanced over at the garage where his groundskeeper, a buddy from high school who was now a detective with the Pender County Sheriff's Office, lived in the upstairs apartment. Kyle Fowler's old red Ford pickup was absent from its usual parking spot, so Ryan figured he was at work.

Inside the Craftsman-style house, Ryan showed Carlton to a bedroom where he would be spending the night. Carlton dropped his Dopp kit on the bed and turned to face Ryan who was leaning on the door jamb.

"You have a nice place, Ryan."

"Thanks, boss. My house is your house. Help yourself to whatever you need."

"I'm just going to freshen up. It's been a long day of travel."

Ryan retreated to the living room where Scott handed him a beer as he sat down on the sofa.

"What's the job?" Scott asked.

"Someone's running amok on Carlton's new island. He wants me to dissuade them from continuing."

"Sounds eerily vague," the ex-SEAL commented.

Ryan explained the job and the island, informing Scott that Carlton was in elite company. Illusionist David Copperfield owned Rudder Cut Cay—the island just north of Big Darby—and the eleven islands surrounding it, which included a high-end resort on Musha Cay.

"They must throw some wild parties," Scott surmised.

"They're actually pretty quiet," Carlton interrupted, returning from his room. "They own islands for the privacy they afford."

"Maybe these ghosts want some privacy of their own," Scott said. "Why do you think they want to keep you off your island?"

"Do you mind if I grab one of those beers?" Carlton asked.

"In the fridge," Ryan said. "Help yourself."

Carlton went to the fridge and returned with a beer. "I think there are a number of reasons why they don't want me around. First, they live somewhere on the island and don't want to lose their home. Second, they're searching for something, and me being there interferes with their progress. Or third—which is the most likely—they're using the island as a waypoint for trafficking drugs."

"How do you think these people are evading your search?" Ryan asked. "Obviously, they're using boats to get on and off the island, but how are they doing it unseen?"

"That has me baffled as well. As you pointed out to Mister Gregory, the islands around Big Darby are owned by wealthy individuals, but none of them live there full time. They employ locals to care for the property, so maybe the men I'm dealing with are friends or family of those workers, coming and going as they please."

"If they had drugs stashed on the island, I assume your PMCs would have found them," Ryan ventured.

"The report from the Academi team said nothing

appeared to have been disturbed," Carlton said, "but they have no idea what the place looked like before or after their arrival. The tropical vegetation reclaims everything quickly."

"I assume you've searched the island yourself?" Scott said.

"I have, but I don't really know what I'm looking for. I'm a businessman, not a smuggler. Working to clear the airstrip was the first time in decades that I've been in the field. My father was a heavy equipment mechanic, and as a boy, I used to help him. I was running dozers and excavators by the time I was fourteen. I worked with my hands enough in my childhood to know it wasn't how I wanted to spend my life. My father worked hard. He paid for me to go to college, and I founded an engineering firm in Maryland. We hold multiple patents revolving around the heavy equipment industry, which is how I made my money. I'm not opposed to getting my hands dirty, but mucking around in the dirt isn't the best use of my time or the easiest way to make money."

"I guess that's where roughnecks like me come into play?" Ryan commented. "Speaking of making money, I'd like to discuss my fee."

"I'll pay you double what you would have made on the diving job," Carlton offered.

"While that's tempting," Ryan said, "troubleshooting rates are a bit different."

"I understand," Carlton replied.

Ryan wasn't so sure that he did. Greg Olsen had used a complicated algorithm to factor the price of contracts when he'd run his former PMC, Trident. He'd account for the number of men needed, the time on ground, if rounds were exchanged, and a host of other aspects to determine the going rate. Ryan boiled it down to a number in his mind and gave it to Carlton, adding that the proposed fee didn't include expenses.

The old man let out a low whistle.

"You've already spent a great deal of time and money on this project," Ryan said by way of justification. "And it hasn't worked. You came to me for help, and this is what I need in return. And while I'm risking life and limb, if there is something worthwhile to be found, I'd take a fifty percent split of the take."

Carlton pondered the steep price tag while sipping his beer. "You think there's something worthwhile on my island?" he asked.

Ryan spread his hands as if to say he didn't know. "My fee is non-negotiable," he continued. "The asset recovery fee is only in place in case I come across something of value. I don't expect to find anything on your island, so as a businessman, fifty percent of zero is a risk you can afford to take. That said, if it's drugs, we burn them. If it's a ghost, we exorcise them." Ryan's face broke out into a wide grin. "If it's *treasure*, we split it."

Carlton drained his beer and set it on a coaster on the coffee table. "I knew you were the right man for the job, Weller," he said, then excused himself and headed upstairs to bed. At the base of the steps, he added, "Right man or not, you're my last hope of making these people see that it's futile to continue their efforts to dissuade me from getting what I want. Which is full control of that island. Put a contract in writing and I'll sign it tomorrow before we leave."

Ryan nodded and watched Carlton disappear up the steps.

A moment passed before Scott asked casually, "Can I go with you?"

"We just had a whole conversation with Carlton. If he didn't invite you to the party, then I'm not going to, either."

"Come on, bro," Scott pleaded. "I'm going a little stir-crazy sitting around here, and I am *not* working offshore. That shit is *nuts*. Besides, we both know how a typical Ryan Weller operation goes: Ryan gets in over his head and calls someone to save his ass. All I'm asking is that I'm the guy you call."

Ryan snorted. Scott's words rang true. He *had* needed help on a lot of previous contracts, but he didn't think this was going to be one of them. Still, he'd been in the game long enough to know that it wouldn't hurt to have backup standing by. "I'm not sure what I'll find down there, but I'm gonna take the sat phone, and I have you on speed dial. If I need you, you can mount up as a quick reaction force."

"Then I should take a vacation to The Bahamas to be close to the action," Scott decreed. "If I've learned anything over the years it's that when Ryan Weller thinks it will be a simple job, that's when the shit hits the fan." He nodded to himself in affirmation then stood. "A little fun in the sun sounds about right to me."

"Let's get packed up," Ryan said with a roll of his eyes. "Then I need a good night's sleep without having to listen to some kind of engine running all night. No matter where I went on that damn barge, I couldn't get away from the noise."

Ryan and Scott stepped out to the garage. The last time Ryan had been at the property, he'd constructed a small weapons and gear room in one corner. He used a digital keypad to unlock the heavy vault-style door, then swung it open.

From the gun rack, Ryan pulled a KRISS Vector SMG complete with folding stock and suppressor, then added a Glock 19 Gen 4 pistol and suppressor to his loadout, along with batches of magazines for both weapons. While Ryan preferred his Walther PPQ M2 pistol, the Glock magazines fit both the pistol and the submachine gun, streamlining the loadout. A chest rig with internal ceramic plates, a medical blowout kit, a couple of fixed-blade and folding knives, and some camping gear rounded out the duffel.

"What's the accommodations like on Carlton's slice of paradise?" Scott asked.

"A house that's been abandoned since World War II and a couple of caves."

"Sounds palatial."

"The last time I was there, the place was overgrown with palms and mangroves," Ryan said. "Emily and I spent a couple of days exploring its fourteen beaches and diving in the shallows for grouper and king conch, but I never saw anything worth killing for out there."

"Most Bahamians I've met don't give a rat's ass about what someone else is doing as long as they have some fish and some rum."

"Which leads me to believe it's not Bahamians. Besides, whoever was shooting at Carlton was using German-made 5.56 ammunition."

"Could be anyone with a NATO weapon," Scott reasoned.

"Carlton said his adversaries were like ghosts. There are only two ways on or off that island: by plane or by boat."

"Or they've gotten religion and learned to walk on water," Scott suggested.

Ryan chuckled. "It's more likely they're using silenced outboards or even row boats. Kayaks aren't out of place down in the islands either."

"Well, whatever they're using, there's only one way to find out," Scott replied, hoisting his Springfield M1A Loaded Precision 6.5 Creedmoor sniper rifle to his shoulder and peering through the scope. "A good old-fashioned stakeout."

CHAPTER FOUR

Hermann
Big Darby Island
Exumas, The Bahamas

Hermann Ziegler rested on the starboard pontoon of his black inflatable boat, holding an apple in his left hand. He carefully sliced off a wedge with a knife, then ate it straight from the tip of the razor-sharp blade. The lanky German wore a wetsuit peeled down to his waist, exposing the broad slabs of muscle that comprised his torso and shoulders.

His mother, a fashion consultant for many of the leading German newspapers and women's magazines, had declared her son the perfect candidate for an underwear model. Hermann had gone to two fashion shoots before deciding he hated standing around waiting on photographers and lighting and being told he couldn't sleep with the female models, so he quit the fashion industry and joined the *Bundespolizei*,

Germany's federal law enforcement agency. After two years on the force, he'd applied to the GSG 9, the *Bundespolizei's* counterterrorism outfit.

Craving action and adventure, the elite police tactical unit had provided just what Hermann was searching for. Upon completion of the five-month selection course, he'd attended sniper school and then learned underwater hand-to-hand combat, achieving high marks in all his training.

On one occasion, Hermann had returned to Berlin on vacation from the GSG headquarters in Sankt Augustin, and his mother had tried once again to lure him back to the fashion world. Her son was incredibly handsome and, in her eyes, the archetypal Aryan. He shared his mother's wavy blond hair and deep blue eyes. The son was several inches taller than his mother at six-two, and he had a physique chiseled from the same block of marble as Michelangelo's *David*. Mother and son were often mistaken for brother and sister. And Hermann's elder sister was their mother's doppelgänger.

More than once, Katrine had commented on her son's rugged handsomeness, strong jawline, and well-defined cheekbones, making Hermann highly uncomfortable because it almost felt like she was hitting on him.

Looking around the small inflatable boat, Hermann listened to his men joke and laugh during their lunch break on the beach under the shade of tall coconut palms. They had worked hard all morning and Hermann allowed them these moments of levity—encouraged them, even—on the understanding that it sharpened their focus when the work began anew. He commanded their respect and would accept nothing less than their very best in the field.

To his left sat Robert Meyer, the only member of Hermann's team who was not former *Polizei* or military. A professor at the Free University of Berlin, Meyer might have been thin and pale, but he had worked tirelessly beside the others, leading their exhaustive search for the missing U-boat.

Like the others aboard the inflatable, Meyer was a member of The Paladin Group—a devotee of Nazism and the rise of a Fourth Reich. Noticing Ziegler's stare, the academic paused in midbite of his cheese sandwich to grin at him.

A year ago, Hermann could never have imagined himself being allied with a man with such ideology, but there they were, literally in the same boat. Their motivations, however, could not have been more different. Hermann didn't care about returning the Nazis to power. In fact, his training with the GSG had dictated the exact opposite, pushing the fight against the rise of right-wing extremism, and he wanted nothing more than to put Germany's past where it belonged: firmly in the past.

But Hermann loved his mother, and she had begged him to help. But, in truth, it hadn't been her pleading or political ideology that had driven him to lead this crusade. No, Hermann Ziegler cared only about the adventure of searching for a lost *Unterseeboot* full of Nazi gold.

The former member of the GSG continued to trim slices off his apple until it was gone, chewing the delicious fruit with slow deliberateness. It was the last apple in their supply, and they were hard to come by in the outer islands of the Exuma chain. Hermann had always loved apples, having picked the fruit at his grandfather's farm when he was a boy and gorging himself until they'd given him diarrhea. Soon, the salvage vessel *Leopard* would resupply them, and Hermann would have fresh apples.

Tossing the apple core into the trash bag in the center of the boat, Hermann ordered his men to quickly finish their lunch. It was time to get back to work, searching Big Darby Island by the grids Meyer had laid out so they could use ground-penetrating radar to see through the sand and rock.

While they cleaned up, Hermann returned to the cave where Sir Guy Baxter had once corralled goats, sheep, and cattle. He examined the high arched ceiling of rock, noting the way tiny sinkholes in the cave's roof allowed shafts of sunlight to filter through. Wayward tourists had left trash in some areas—plastic bottles, faded candy wrappers, and sandwich bags—marring the natural beauty. Hermann wasn't a rabid environmentalist. He just believed people should pick up after themselves, hence the trash bag in his boat.

According to Meyer's research, Nazi U-boats had stopped at the Baxter estate to refuel before heading to Argentina. Where the fuel had come from was another unsolved mystery, but Meyer had found a diary penned by Wilhelm Falkner, a crewman aboard the lost U-1226, in a Bahamian museum that told a different tale of intrigue. According to the wilted pages, the U-1226 had left Norway, picked up a consignment of gold in Germany, and then proceeded across the North Atlantic to Iceland. There, they'd reported a mechanical issue with the snorkel, which was to be their last communication with Submarine Command. Meyer had then searched the *Kriegsmarine*'s records and found the U-1226 had been listed as missing in action after no further communications with the submarine.

Falkner had written in his diary that Captain Claussen had run straight for The Bahamas, avoiding the roving fleet of American warships before docking at Baxter's estate to fix the snorkel. Tired of being cooped up on the boat and fighting a war he thought unjust, Falkner had waited until the U-boat had berthed at Big Darby Island and then slipped overboard, hiding on Rudder Cut Cay until the U-boat left the tiny harbor. He'd watched the repairs for a day or two, noting the removal of twenty crates of gold from the boat, before making his way south until he could flag down a native, who took him by boat to George Town. From there,

Falkner had moved to Freeport, married a native, and fathered five children. After his death in the mid-1990s, one of Falkner's daughters had donated his diary to the Sir Charles Hayward Library, where it had yet to be cataloged in the new electronic system, which had enabled Meyer to pilfer it without much notice.

Hermann cocked his head, hearing a single-engine plane racing across the water, the sound growing louder as it approached the island. He dashed for the cave entrance to peer up at the white Cessna with red floats as it flashed overhead, so low its pontoons almost clipped the treetops. Hermann had seen that plane before. It was the new owner returning to the island, but there was something different.

He'd never flown so low on approach before.

A gut feeling told Hermann that this time, it wouldn't be so easy to evade the owner or his efforts to run him off the island.

CHAPTER FIVE

Ryan
Big Darby Island
Exumas, The Bahamas

"Bombs away," Ryan called from the passenger seat of the white Cessna 185 floatplane.

He watched the heavy duffel containing his battle gear and weapons fall past the red pontoons and tumble through the air before a small parachute blossomed open, carrying the waterproof duffel toward the shallow saltwater pond. A flock of Bahama Pintail ducks rose as the bag smacked into the brown water, then sank beneath the surface.

The Bahamas, as Ryan was well aware, had a strict policy against undeclared firearms. In fact, the Royal Bahamian Defense Force, or RBDF, arrested anyone found in possession of a firearm without declaring it upon entry or possessing a license for it. While Ryan didn't want to go to jail, he definitely didn't want to be alone on a deserted island with people indiscriminately shooting at him.

"Damn, Mister Carlton! You get any closer and we'll be trimming treetops," Ryan said into his headset as he closed the door.

"Nah." Carlton laughed. "We had a good six feet of clearance." Like Ryan, he wore a headset so they could communicate inside the airplane and talk to ground control in Nassau.

In his line of work, Ryan had met several billionaires, most of whom were down-to-earth people, but some could be complete assholes. Typically, those were second- or third-generation characters who'd grown up with a silver spoon in their mouths and had never had to roll up their sleeves and actually work for their money.

Ryan had figured Carlton for the latter when they'd first met, but Ryan was changing his assessment of the man as he spent more time with him. Carlton had spine, persisting with clearing his landing strip on Big Darby while under fire and not flinching when his equipment burned to the ground. A lesser man would have tucked tail and run.

Moments later, Carlton radioed Nassau Control to inform them the Cessna was on approach to Little Darby Island, rising in the air to align with the dirt strip below. Looking out the portside window over Carlton's shoulder, Ryan could see the Green Castle, centered on the larger of the two Darby Islands.

The second story of the dilapidated building poked high above the surrounding landscape that was slowly overtaking what man had wrought. It reminded Ryan that nothing in life was permanent. If Guy Baxter had intended to build a legacy, then he'd done a poor job of it by abandoning his homestead, but he'd left behind a mystery about what his life had been like before and after his time on Big Darby. There was little recorded information about Baxter before King George VI had supposedly gifted him Big Darby, just rumors about what he'd done on the island, and no trace after disappearing. Ryan was starting to wonder if the man was a myth, conjured up to explain the fact that someone had built a great house and subsequently left it to rot.

Carlton lowered the wheels on the floats and touched down on the dirt strip, raising a cloud of dust and sand in their wake. He turned the plane in the open lot at the north end of the strip and shut down the engine.

Peeling off his headset, Carlton hung it on the hook mounted to the cockpit roof and, with a wide grin, said, "Thank you for flying Steve's Seaplane Service."

The two men disembarked and walked to a small compound of luxury homes informally called The Drifts Lodge that overlooked Darby Channel, the channel dividing Big and Little Darby Islands.

Ryan had sailed his catamaran *Huntress*, a Fountaine Pajot Saba 50, up that channel a year or so ago when he and his wife had been island-hopping down the Exumas. It was unusual not to see several sailboats anchored in the channel or off Rudder Cut Cay. When Ryan commented on their absence, Carlton told him the ghosts had run the boaters off as well. "You're a cruiser. You know how word spreads when pirates abound."

Ryan nodded, knowing exactly how the cruisers would set the radio waves ablaze with news of gunshots and ghosts. He'd heard it before, in Trinidad and off the coast of Nicaragua.

A middle-aged Bahamian woman with nut-brown skin and black hair pulled into a severe bun atop her head greeted the two men at the front door of the main lodge. She introduced herself to Ryan as Alice, then showed the men to their rooms before bringing beers to them on the screened veranda.

"Have you scouted the islands by plane to see if there are

any encampments nearby?" Ryan asked Carlton as they settled into the wicker couches.

"I did after these bastards blew holes in my landing strip, but, again, I didn't see anything except the usual houses. They could have rented a house, but I have a feeling these guys don't want to leave a paper trail."

"Do you own Little Darby, too?" Ryan asked.

"No. It's owned by a private corporation. David Copperfield owns Rudder Cut. Johnny Depp is north of that. Tim McGraw and Faith Hill own Goat Cay, directly to the south of Big Darby. They custom-built their estate there, and it's a nice setup. Diane is hoping to eventually turn Green Castle into a luxury retreat like theirs."

"Do you mind if I ask you a question?" Ryan said.

"Go ahead," Carlton replied warmly.

"What's a *billionaire* doing opening a B&B? Seems kinda off-brand from your engineering company."

"I told you, my eldest daughter wants to run the place. She's about your age, and after working for me for the past couple of years, she came to me with the idea of building a retreat on Big Darby. She'd even prepared a business proposal, had a budget, and a potential profit and loss statement."

"Well, I hope she's quadrupled the budget from her original estimate," Ryan said. "Getting work done in the Out Islands is tough and bringing in materials can be a real pain in the ass since everything has to come by ship or plane."

Carlton snorted. "I don't think she accounted for someone trying to run us off the island, or factored in your salary, but I'm confident that we're going to get back on track now that you're aboard."

Ryan nodded. Tomorrow, he would cross the channel, find the ghosts, and get these good folks back on track. It couldn't be that hard.

As Ryan was finishing his beer, Alice appeared and asked if the two men would like another.

"Two more," Carlton instructed.

Alice came back several minutes later with fresh beers for the men. "Dinner will be served in thirty minutes."

"Can you sit for a minute, Alice?" Ryan asked her. "I'd like to ask you some questions."

The woman sat and smoothed her dress over her thighs. She kept her eyes cast downward.

"Have you seen anything or anyone suspicious on the island?" Ryan probed.

Alice shook her head.

"Have you heard gunshots?" Ryan asked.

"Yes." Alice nodded.

"Do you know anything about who might be trying to run Mister Carlton off Darby Island?"

"No, sa," she replied. "This be a peaceful place. I be working here nigh on seven years. Never a once have no trouble."

"So, you don't know who's shooting at Mister Carlton, or who might have burned his construction equipment?" Ryan asked.

"No, sa." Alice smoothed her uniform dress again.

Seeing as she was less than forthcoming, Ryan tried a new tack. "You married? Got kids?"

"Married fifteen years now. Got two boys," Alice replied with a smile.

"Where does your husband work?"

"Rafi works for a construction crew. They go most islands. Stay till the job's done. He come home on de weekends mostly. I practically raise dem boys by myself, you knows?"

"I bet they're a handful," Ryan said, remembering how he and his older brother, Mike, had terrorized his mother until his father had put them to work on his construction crews in

Wilmington. It had been like trying to break wild horses, but the hard work had done the trick. Ryan was now a troubleshooter and Mike helped run the old man's construction company.

"They good boys, though," Alice was quick to point out.

"Rafi been around lately?" Ryan asked. "Does he know about what's happening on Big Darby?"

"Oh, everyone know what's happenin' on Darby Island. Mista Carlton, he want to build a big resort. Rafi, he be a good man for you, Mista Carlton," Alice insisted.

"When the time comes, I'll talk to him," Carlton promised.

"Where's Rafi working now?" Ryan asked.

"Musha Cay. He up there with Coffee's crew."

Ignoring the fact that he had no idea who Coffee was, Ryan asked, "Your boys get out and about? They see any suspicious men or activity?"

Alice shrugged. "Dem boys go traipsing all over. I never know where dey be."

"Do you know where they are now?" Ryan asked. "I'd like to talk to them—ask them if they've seen anything."

"Let me ring dem." Alice removed a cell phone from her pocket, hit a number on the speed dial, and held the device to her ear. When the recipient answered, Alice instructed them to come to the big house and to double-time it. Carlton explained for Ryan's benefit that a new cell company, Aliv, had been putting up towers across the Out Islands and cell coverage had greatly improved in the past couple of years.

Ryan leaned back in his chair and sipped his beer as he peered through the darkness at the island on the other side of the channel. Cell coverage was great, but it also meant the bad guys could communicate just as effectively as everyone else, or like him, they could be carrying an encrypted satellite phone. One thing he'd learned from all his years of military service and independent contract work was that communication was key for any operation.

Another thing he'd learned early on while watching cartoons as a kid: there were no such things as ghosts. Scooby Doo had taught him that.

Ten minutes later, Alice's oldest boy, RJ—short for Rafi Junior—sat on the veranda with his mother, Ryan, and Carlton. RJ was a skinny youth with no shoes on his calloused feet. He wore ragged cutoff jeans and a faded Nirvana T-shirt, leaving Ryan to wonder if the kid liked to rock out to "Smells Like Teen Spirit." Approximately fourteen in Ryan's estimation, the boy's dark eyes looked as though they'd seen their share of economic uncertainty and pain. Ryan tried to compare his own childhood to the boy's. He had never known poverty or hunger, nor had his father ever been away for long stretches of time, but he figured they had at least one thing in common—a love of the sea.

"You fish?" Ryan asked, trying to break the ice.

"Yes, sir." RJ's face brightened, but his eyes remained wary. "Made myself a pole spear out of a lignum vitae branch and an ol' inner tube. I can hold my breath for four minutes." He held up four fingers in pride.

"Amazing," Ryan said.

"My pole ain't de best. My papa promised me a new one, but ..." RJ shrugged.

"I assume you know your way around these islands and have explored most of them," Ryan said.

"Yes, sir."

"Have you seen a group of men you don't recognize hanging around Big Darby? They may be searching for something, or they may be transporting something through the islands."

The youth leaned back in his chair and cocked his head up and to the right, his eyes flickering as he thought.

Ryan wanted to press him, but he knew kids could clam up if they thought an adult was acting like "the man."

"Go on, tell Mista Wella what you know," Alice urged her son.

"There be a camp on Prime Cay," RJ offered hesitantly. "I sees it two days ago. Dem look like dey put de fix on me."

"Da 'fix' be a voodoo spell," Alice interpreted for her son.

"Why did you think that?" Ryan asked.

"Just de way dey look. White men. Big like you. Five or six, maybe."

"Anything else you can remember?" Ryan pressed.

The boy pursed his lips together and shook his head.

"Hold on." Ryan held up a finger. "I've got something for you." He got up and went to his room, where he opened his bag of dive gear and pulled out a new Cressi three-piece pole spear. He'd packed two just in case one broke because he planned to live off fish and conch as well as eat the supplies Carlton had left—*if* they were still there.

Returning to the veranda, Ryan handed the pole spear to RJ. "Be sure to stone some big fish for your mother."

RJ's eyes widened and a huge grin spread across his face as he took hold of his gift. He immediately screwed the aluminum shafts together and then ran a hand along the six-foot length of black anodized tubing, before testing the rubber sling.

"I can have this?" RJ asked.

Ryan smiled at the boy's enthusiasm. "Absolutely. It's yours."

Alice started to protest, but Ryan held up a hand to silence her. "Don't fuss about it. He gave me information I needed and I'm happy to pay for it. Now, how about dinner?"

Alice stood and hurried off as Ryan sipped his beer. He'd known all along the ghosts were just humans.

And thanks to RJ, he had the location of their camp.

CHAPTER SIX

The sun was barely up as young RJ ran Ryan around the south end of Big Darby Island in his brightly painted wooden panga, its ancient outboard coughing out a haze of two-stroke exhaust fumes behind them.

From every side of the island, Green Castle dominated the view, sitting high atop its bluff, waiting patiently for its previous owner to return. It was easy to see how Baxter had used it as a makeshift lighthouse to lure in submarines for resupply by turning on the house lights at night. The locals who could remember that far back said Baxter had even had a high-powered shortwave radio and telegraph system installed to communicate with the subs, perhaps even the Fatherland. Ryan guessed it was most likely for calling Nassau in case of an emergency, but the truth was always stranger than fiction.

"You ever go up there?" Ryan asked RJ over the noisy outboard, pointing toward the abandoned house.

"Not no more," RJ replied. "Dem ghost put de fix on de house."

Ryan nodded. Being in that spooky old house would give anyone the creeps and the Bahamians, being a superstitious lot, could conjure up all kinds of ghost stories to justify their reasons for staying away.

As RJ rounded the tip of Betty Cay, a triangular-shaped, acre-sized chunk of rock about twelve hundred feet offshore of Big Darby, Ryan pulled his wetsuit over his upper body and zipped it up.

Once in the lee of the island, RJ idled the motor while Ryan donned his fins, mask, and snorkel, then slid over the side of the boat into water that barely came up to his shins.

RJ laughed. "You not be needin' dat getup."

Ryan rolled his eyes. "Thanks for the heads-up."

"Good luck, Mista Wella." RJ roared away in his panga, slicing through the clear, shallow water and still laughing about Ryan's outfit.

Ryan snorted at how silly RJ must have thought he looked, but he wasn't planning to wade to the island. He was going in on his belly and he would need the neoprene suit to protect his skin against the rough coral and whatever else awaited him in the salt pond when he went in to collect his dry bag. He hoisted his backpack to his shoulders and waded through the water to the rocky shore of Betty Cay. He climbed the short cliff face to the top and made his way down the slope on the other side through dense scrub, careful to avoid the massive spider webs that often blocked his path with strings as thick as bailing twine and banana spiders the size of his hand.

On the eastern side of Betty Cay, Ryan sat cross-legged on the sand beside a boulder and watched the far shore of Big Darby for any movement. He wanted to slip onto the island unnoticed and be a ghost walking amongst the ghosts.

Twenty minutes later, the only movement he'd seen other than Carlton flying off in his seaplane was the tall coconut palms swaying in the breeze and the gentle lap of the sea against the shore.

Ryan rose from his spot on the sand, brushing away his tracks with a palm frond as he made his way to the water. Tossing the frond back into the brush, Ryan submerged himself in the water that was less than two feet deep at high tide. The plan was to stay low, but as he pulled himself along with his hands, his head, shoulders, and the roundness of his buttocks frequently broke the surface.

Once Ryan made it to the beach on Big Darby, he shed his fins and carried them in his right hand as he entered the grove of fifty-foot-tall, non-native, coconut palms that had been planted by Guy Baxter as an export crop. They frequently dropped their dry fronds onto the ground, blocking vegetation from growing. A low stone wall ran east, delineating the palm grove from the rest of the island. Ryan examined the natural stone wall, wondering where the workers had found all the rock needed to construct it and the similar walls that traversed the island.

Although Ryan wanted to linger and examine everything now that he had permission from the owner to be on the island, he had a job to do. He wasn't immune to the idyllic tropical setting after living for so long on his sailboat and traveling throughout the Caribbean. In fact, he thanked God every day that he got to live his dream—a good woman, a sailboat, and a mission.

He stopped short in the palm grove. Instead of concentrating on where he was going, Ryan had been thinking about his life. What had caused him to stop so abruptly was the realization that his priorities had changed. The order had always been a sailboat, a woman, and a mission, but in his methodical mind, the cards had shuffled. His wife was now the first marker, followed by the boat. The missions came as they came, but without Emily, the rest of it was meaningless now. All the tropical vistas would be dull and pointless without that big, beautiful blonde beside him.

Suddenly, Ryan wondered what the hell he was doing on Big Darby Island, chasing ghosts when he should have told Steve Carlton "Thanks, but no thanks," and hopped a silver bird to Fort Lauderdale, and right now be snuggled into a comfortable bed with Emily. His mouth watered at the thought of the heavenly meatloaf his mother-in-law had fixed before Ryan had flown to Mexico to work offshore.

"I've gotta wrap this up quick," Ryan muttered to himself, then continued toward the salt pond.

The stone wall led to a narrow land bridge between a small triangular section of the salt pond and the main body of water. Ryan paused to watch a startled iguana scurry into the water, swimming beneath the surface with quick, quivering flicks of its tail, and stood stock-still as he listened to the surrounding environment. Everything was quiet, alerted by the sudden movement of the iguana.

Glancing down at the muck near his feet, he saw three evenly spaced tracks from what appeared to be mountain bike tires. The thick tread had left imprints in the mud beside boot prints. Squatting to get a closer view, he remembered seeing tracks like that earlier in his walk but had no clue what type of machinery had made them, but he rightly assumed they'd been made by the ghosts.

Ryan opened the tracking app on his phone. The onscreen icon showed the bag he'd dropped from the plane was close to the middle of the pond. With no idea how deep the water was, he tried to triangulate the bag's location using landmarks he could easily identify on the overhead map and by visually scanning the pond. One of the biggest landmarks appeared to be a T-shaped dock extended about a hundred feet out into the water. Pocketing the phone, he made his way around the southeastern edge of the pond to the dock, walking quietly through the woods.

At the head of the dock, Ryan discovered it was underwater. While the structure could be seen from overhead on Google Maps, it was difficult to see when standing at the verge. Ryan found a stick and poked at the water to find the head of the dock. Careful to stay on what felt like stone slabs, he moved out along the dock until the stick no longer tapped rock but instead dropped into open water. Ryan was thankful he didn't have to wade through the surface caramel layer formed by evaporating water that left behind the crusty salt along the edges of the pond. He wondered if old Guy Baxter had used these ponds to gather salt, like so many other Bahamian salt ponds had been farmed.

Donning his fins and mask again, Ryan took one last look at the tracking app, triangulated the bag again, and then stowed the phone in the waterproof backpack he'd brought with him from Little Darby. He sat in the shallow water covering the lip of the dock and prepared to dive for the duffel bag containing his gear. At least there were no crocodiles in The Bahamas, but Ryan's heart rate still raced at the need to go into the murky pond. While this wasn't the first time he'd dove in a low visibility setting, the fear of what might be lurking in the darkness below was sometimes almost as great as the fear of facing an enemy force of Taliban fighters.

Ryan pushed himself off the dock into the warm water and swam toward the triangulated coordinates. When he reached where he thought the bag had landed, Ryan dove below the surface, holding his breath with the snorkel out of his mouth. There was no need to potentially inhale something nasty.

He could barely see his hand in front of his face in the murky water, and his hand found the bottom of the pond before he saw it. Forced to trail his hands through the mud to keep contact with the bottom, Ryan swam a makeshift spiral box search pattern as he hunted for the bag.

A half hour later, Ryan was about to say, "screw it" and forgo the search for the weapons duffel when he struck gold. Tracing the outline of the bag, his hand clutched the webbed handle and tried to pull it free of the muck, but the bag was laden with heavy weapons, ammunition, and body armor. The whole kit probably weighed close to forty pounds, and the mud had formed a suction hold on the bag. There was no way he could remove it from the pond while swimming with it.

Ryan put his foot on the bag and pushed himself straight up to the surface. He spun in a circle, orienting himself to the lay of the land again and fixing reference points in his mind, then swam back to the dock. There, he opened his backpack and removed a length of climbing rope. He closed his bag tight, tied one end of the line to it, then swam back to where he figured he'd left the sunken duffel. Diving down again, he found it on the first try. After securing the free end of the line to the duffel, he cut the small parachute loose so it wouldn't cause more drag.

The troubleshooter returned to the stone dock and used the climbing rope to pull the weapons duffel to shore. He was steaming hot inside the three-millimeter wetsuit. Sweat ran down his face and back. As the neoprene dried quickly in the hot sun, it rubbed against the insides of Ryan's armpits and chafed at his thighs.

With the duffel in hand, Ryan peeled the wetsuit down to his waist and mopped his forehead. He coiled his rope and lashed it to the exterior of the backpack, then shouldered the pack and carried it and the duffel into the trees.

Ryan tore off the wetsuit and stood in his Speedo, letting the sweat dry on his skin. From his backpack, he removed a hand towel, tan rip-stop cargo pants, and a long sleeve fishing shirt. After drying off, he got dressed and then pulled on socks and tan combat boots to complement his shirt and pants. The last piece of equipment he strapped on was the thigh rig complete with spare mag carrier to holster the Glock 19.

His next objective was to traverse the island to where Carlton had established his base camp. Hopefully, there would be a supply of water there, as Ryan had just chugged one liter of the four that he'd brought with him from The Drifts Lodge as he'd unpacked his duffel. With no natural source of fresh water on the island, it was imperative that Ryan obtain whatever he could from Carlton's camp, otherwise he'd have to swim back to Little Darby and hit up Alice for food and water. From the last time he'd visited, Ryan also knew there were three cisterns under the Green Castle, reportedly able to store 125,000 gallons of water, but Ryan figured whatever was in them now was probably not fit for human consumption after seventy-seven-years of neglect.

From the salt pond, the land rose toward a ridge that ran almost the entire length of the island. At the top, Ryan stood amongst a cluster of white mangroves. From his vantage point, he could see the freshly cleared landing strip. Strategically blown at the beginning, middle, and end of the runway were three craters twelve feet across and at least two feet deep, down to the limestone bedrock. A yellow JCB 4CX backhoe loader and a matching 300T track loader sat side by side. Neither appeared to have been tampered with, but that wasn't Ryan's area of expertise. Even though he'd driven a few track loaders, he'd never worked on their engines or hydraulic systems. Ryan would leave that for Carlton and his construction crew once he'd exorcised the ghosts.

The heavy equipment sat facing the runway at the end closest to Ryan. Right behind them stood a wall tent of green canvas with a stove pipe jutting through the roof. Figuring it was the base for Carlton's work camp, Ryan made his way down the hill, avoiding the spiderwebs, tree roots, and low hanging limbs.

He knelt in the trees behind the tent and removed the KRISS Vector from his pack. In the sand around the tent were impressions of combat boot treads. It was hard to tell how many men had been here because the boot prints all looked the same.

Leaving his bags behind in the trees, Ryan shouldered the KRISS and peered through the holographic sight. Easing forward along the length of the tent, he counted off four paces, guesstimating the tent to be twelve feet long. At the front, Ryan spun around the corner and swept the area clear with the barrel of the SMG. He was as alone as the moment young RJ had motored away.

So far, this mission had been a cakewalk.

With his back to the tent, Ryan figured his next step was to investigate the interior and inventory the supplies.

But before he could turn around, he heard the slide on a pump-action shotgun being racked.

CHAPTER SEVEN

Ryan's blood ran cold and his whole body tensed in anticipation of having a slug slam into his spine.

"Put the gun down," a female voice instructed.

Slowly, Ryan extended his arms out from his sides and let the KRISS Vector fall into the dirt.

"Now the pistol."

Again, Ryan complied, slowly removing the Glock from its holster with his fingertips and dropping it beside the SMG.

"Turn around," the voice ordered.

Ryan pivoted, moving with exaggerated deliberateness until he faced the woman holding the shotgun. Dressed in khaki shorts, a long sleeve T-shirt, and hiking boots, the woman couldn't have been more than five feet tall. The shotgun looked too damn big for her diminutive figure, but she held it like she meant to use it.

"Who are you?" she asked.

"I'm Ryan Weller. I'm here on behalf of Mister Carlton, the owner of this island."

The woman cocked her head, her hair catching the sunlight, highlighting its glossy blackness tucked into a tight French braid. "Why are you here?"

Ryan could see the hardness in her blue eyes. "I'm here to investigate the destruction of Carlton's equipment."

"How did you get here?"

"I flew into Little Darby last night with Mister Carlton and waded ashore this morning. Can I ask who you are?"

"How can I be sure that Carlton sent you?"

Ryan racked his brain for something to tell her. He hadn't expected to find anyone on the island except for the people antagonizing Carlton's progress. For all he knew, this woman could be one of them, but then again, she could be Carlton's daughter. She had the same determined look on her face that Carlton had worn when talking about Big Darby. With a shrug, he said, "Carlton hired me. Want to call him? I've got his number in my sat phone."

"Let me see." The woman held out her left hand, keeping her right index finger on the shotgun's trigger.

"The phone's in my backpack, just inside the tree line."

"Go get it. No tricks."

"Can you take your finger off the trigger? I'd hate to have you trip and shoot me in the back."

With a wry smile, the woman slid her finger off the trigger and put her left hand back on the slide, then motioned with the barrel for him to get moving.

Ryan led the way to where he'd left his backpack and duffel, hands still raised. When he reached the backpack, he squatted beside it and unzipped a side pocket. He withdrew the sat phone and scrolled through the contacts until he found Steve Carlton's number, then handed the phone to the woman.

She hit the button to dial Carlton's number, putting the phone on speaker.

Ryan heard Carlton answer with, "I didn't expect to hear from you so soon, Mister Weller."

The woman said, "It's me, Daddy."

Ryan's mouth fell open.

"Diane!" Carlton barked, in just as much surprise as Ryan.

"Did you send this Ryan Weller guy to the island?" Diane asked.

"Yes, I sent him, but why are *you* there?"

"Apparently for the same reason he is. This is my future, Daddy. I'm not going to let some random locals run us off *our* island."

"Diane, honey," Carlton pleaded. "Please go to Little Darby and let Mister Weller do his job. He's there to find out who's been impeding our operations."

Without saying another word to her father, Diane ended the call and handed the phone back to Ryan.

The phone rang in Ryan's hand. It was Carlton. Ryan held his phone to his ear. "Hi, Mister Carlton."

"I had no idea my daughter would be on the island," Carlton stated. "With that being said, she's as stubborn as I am, Mister Weller, so she won't leave unless you hogtie her and drag her out of there."

"That's not my job. You want her off the island, you come get her."

"I'm not asking you to drag her away, Mister Weller. I want you to look after her—protect her."

"This is an investigation. You didn't hire me to be a bodyguard," Ryan reminded him.

"I'll double your fee," Carlton said in exasperation.

"Works for me," Ryan said, though, for the record, he would have done it without the pay increase. Even though he'd just met Diane, he admired the woman's spunk.

"Just protect my daughter."

"Yes, sir." Ryan ended the call and shut the phone off to

conserve battery power. He shouldered his pack and asked Diane, "Can I pick up my guns now?"

She waved him forward. Ryan carried his bags into the tent, then retrieved his firearms from the dirt, brushing the sand and debris from their exteriors. Back inside the tent, Ryan moved aside several cups and plates from a table, then set his firearms on it before disassembling them and cleaning their actions and barrels before reseating the magazines and feeding rounds into their chambers.

While he worked, Ryan asked, "Have you seen anyone else on the island?"

"You mean other than you?" Diane replied, watching him intently.

Ryan felt her gaze on him, aware of her thick dark lashes above light blue eyes. Her delicate hand rested on the table, finger and wrist bones defined under deeply tanned skin, as if she spent many hours outdoors. She sported no rings, and the only jewelry he saw was in her ears, which she'd pierced with multiple diamond stud earrings set in silver.

He glanced around the tent to distract himself. It was tidy, and supplies seemed to be abundant, but there was an almost magnetic quality about her that kept drawing his eyes back to her.

"Other than me?" he clarified.

"No. I came in two days ago," Diane said. "I wanted to work on the runway."

"Your dad said the machines have sand in the fuel tanks, but that's not my area of expertise."

Diane crossed her arms, pressing her small breasts upward like a push-up bra. "And what *is* your area of expertise?"

Ryan concentrated on his guns. "I'm a troubleshooter."

"Like, 'have gun, will travel?'" she asked.

"Something to that effect."

With his firearms ready for action, Ryan took a quick inventory of the stacks of bottled water, cans of food, and the small pile of firewood beside the cooking stove. He opened a bottle of water and guzzled it down, the heat and humidity on the island making him thirsty.

"All right, troubleshooter, what's next?"

"I want to look at the Green Castle," he said.

"There's not much up there. I haven't seen any signs of people there."

"Your dad found a shell casing. Whoever is trying to run you off used the building for a sniper hide."

Ryan opened his weapons duffel and pulled out his chest rig. He carefully inspected it for damage and then checked the magazines he'd preloaded with nine-millimeter hollow points. Between the extended mags for the KRISS and the shorter fifteen-round Glock mags, he was carrying almost five hundred rounds. If there was a shooting contest, he wanted to have plenty of ammo.

With his gear checked, Ryan donned the chest rig and strapped it into place.

"You toting that scattergun?" he asked Diane.

"I take it with me everywhere on the island, plus I have a Smith & Wesson Airweight." Diane lifted the hem of her shirt to show Ryan the black butt of the chrome .38 Special on her hip, and he couldn't help but notice her skin there was just as brown as her hand.

"Got any extra rounds?" he asked.

"In a box over there." Diane pointed to a plastic tote as she dropped her shirt back into place.

"Let's hope you don't need them," Ryan said.

———

FROM THE CAMP, Ryan and Diane patrolled along the edge of the clear-cut landing strip. At the far end, the opening in the trees afforded them a clear view of the turquoise water of Rudder Cut and the little islands and atolls between Big Darby and Rudder Cut Cay.

About halfway along the landing strip, Diane motioned for Ryan to turn onto a path leading up the hill toward Green Castle. "Across the strip, the path takes you to a dock on the west side. When the first set of the workers arrived, Dad had them cut the brush back along this path from that dock to the Castle and then down to the dock in Darby Channel, but the rest of the paths are still overgrown."

"At least he cleared the most critical ones," Ryan said.

"No cobwebs to fight or snakes to scare away," Diane said.

Ryan stiffened.

"*Uh-oh*," Diane's singsong voice teased. "The troubleshooter doesn't like spiders."

"Spiders are fine. The snakes can all die."

Diane laughed.

"All right, cut the chatter," Ryan growled, leading the way up the path. "We don't need the whole island to know we're coming."

"Don't you think they already know we're here?"

"Not if we can help it. Now, be quiet."

They made the climb up the ridge to the abandoned house. It was easy to see why the building was called the Green Castle: the exterior had been painted a light green, and each corner of the house was a rounded turret with three large inset windows per floor to provide expansive views of the island and its surrounds. Darkly stained wood trimmed the windows and doors.

The place looked much the same as it had when Ryan had last seen it a year ago. The mahogany floors were peeling up and covered in plaster that had fallen from the ceiling. In places, whole sections of the floor had caved in. With each step, the floorboards creaked beneath his weight. Old cast iron sinks still clung to tiled walls in the bathrooms, and arched doorways led into each room.

Ryan made his way up the rickety staircase, careful not to step on loose boards or fall through openings. At the head of the stairs, only two of the ornately carved balusters remained, connecting a long section of handrail to the weathered top step.

The flooring on the second story was just as bad as on the first. Ryan moved along the walls, trying to put his weight on the joists. The top floor was one large master suite that Sir Guy had constructed for him and his mistress. A large brick fireplace encased in more extravagantly carved wooden trim stood ready to warm the main room.

Together, Ryan and Diane stepped out onto the balcony that dominated half of the upper story. A knee-high, cast-concrete wall ran around the lip of the balcony, cracked and crumbling from neglect and age. They faced northeast, looking out upon a stunning view of the cut between Big and Little Darby, the protected anchorage to the south, and Rudder Cut Cay to the north. This was the view most people braved the overgrown island and the decaying house to see, and it was prominently featured in the YouTube videos of trespassing boaters.

From the northwest corner, the balcony didn't provide an angle for Ryan to see where Carlton had claimed he'd been shot at.

Ryan turned to face the door they'd just come through. Above it was an eyebrow window, with two arched windows flanking the door. At one time, twin light sconces had also flanked the door, but they'd been torn off and the electrical wiring ripped from the wall, leaving a large brown upside-down-U-shaped groove in the green plaster above the door. Farther along the walls, nearer the corners of the building, were two more rectangular windows, and a chimney stood on the right-hand side.

Stepping back to the door, Ryan shed his chest rig and KRISS Vector, laying them in the shade, then he walked to the edge of the balcony, pivoted, and dashed full speed at the wall. Diane looked on in amazement as Ryan put his right foot on the open windowsill and pushed himself up and to the left, setting his left foot halfway up the slope of the chimney and using his momentum to jump up and grab the lip of the roof. Bracing his left foot against the chimney again, Ryan levered himself up and over the parapet.

On hands and knees and breathing hard, Ryan looked down at Diane. "You want to come up?"

She shook her head in amazement, then said, "Yes, but I'm not a spider monkey like you."

Ryan lay on the roof and extended his hand down to her. Diane used the windowsill as a step while holding Ryan's wrist, and he pulled her up high enough for her to get a leg over the parapet and then roll onto the upper roof.

As she stood and brushed off the seat of her shorts, she said, "Remind me to buy a ladder."

From the top of the Castle, they had a view of the whole tree-covered island. Just north of the house, a blue hole sank deep into the earth, surrounded by lush green trees. The ridge the house stood on crested a little higher to the south before dropping quickly to the edge of the largest of the salt ponds from which Ryan had retrieved his weapons duffel. The land surrounding the bottom of the ridge between it and the water looked almost tabletop flat beneath a cover of scrub, but from experience, Ryan knew it wasn't.

The two salt ponds appeared a greenish brown in the

sunlight, and the surrounding Atlantic was navy blue to the east before varying in shades of turquoise as the depths shoaled through narrow channels and across broad sand and coral flats.

Below Ryan and Diane were two outbuildings, one of which contained the rusted remains of two Lister generators that had powered the old plantation. Along the path to the large concrete quay in Darby Channel was another two-story building. Diane claimed it had housed Baxter's machine shop, wicker furniture factory, and slaughterhouse.

Ryan walked over to a white plastic barrel laid on its side on two rusty I-beams. "This doesn't look original."

"It's not. The previous owner installed it when he thought he was going to renovate," Diane informed him. "Not only does the water in the barrel get boiling hot in the sun, but the height also provides pressure."

Bending down, Ryan looked under the barrel where he found and retrieved another 5.56 shell casing. The roof was an ideal position for a sniper layup, facing the expanse of the runway with excellent views of the camp while the tank, at the proper angle, provided some shade from the sun.

"What's that?" Diane asked as Ryan straightened.

"Shell casing like the one your old man found." He tossed it to her, then cocked his head.

The sound of an outboard purred far off in the stillness of the afternoon. Ryan pulled a pair of small binoculars from the pocket of his cargo pants and scanned the horizon. He centered them on a black inflatable boat with a large silver motor. He counted six men aboard.

"You ever see that boat before?" Ryan asked, handing the binoculars to his companion and pointing across the island at the small craft heading through Rudder Cut.

Diane fitted the binos to her eyes and adjusted them while Ryan kept an eye on the boat as it rounded Little

Darby Island and headed south, bucking through the Atlantic swell.

"I've never seen it before," Diane replied when she handed the binoculars back.

Ryan lifted his sunglasses and peered through the optics again, tracking the boat as it sped past Lignum Vitae Cay, where he lost track of it behind the island's hills.

"It looked like it came from the point just across the bay from us. Do you know what's down there?" Ryan asked.

"There's a sea cave on the far side, but nothing else I can think of," Diane replied. "We get a lot of cruisers who come through the islands to stop and take pictures of the Castle or snorkel over the reefs, especially that stainless-steel piano Copperfield sank off Rudder Cut. Could be one of those?"

Ryan wanted to believe it was a cruiser checking out the sights, but he knew most cruisers didn't use military-style inflatable boats. "What's the quickest way to the cave?"

"It's a rugged half mile across the island if we walk, but I have a boat down at the dock," Diane said. "We can use that to get around the point."

"Let's go." Ryan slid over the edge of the roof and dropped nimbly to the balcony below.

Diane peered over the edge and shook her head. "Freaking spider monkey," she muttered.

"You coming?"

Diane levered herself over the edge of the parapet and hung by her fingertips. Ryan caught her around the legs, feeling the smoothness of her bare thigh against his cheek and the lightness of her frame before lowering her to the balcony floor.

"Enough manhandling me, Tarzan. Get your play toys so we can go."

Ryan shouldered into his chest rig again and picked up the KRISS Vector.

They made their way out of the house and walked down the path to the dock.

"You guys need some ATVs," Ryan said, thinking all this walking was going to get old. The island might have been only a mile and a half long by three-quarters of a mile wide, but trudging up and down the sandy paths would soon become tedious.

"They're on the list," Diane replied.

At the dock, Ryan chugged some more water and appraised the twenty-three-foot Carolina Skiff with a molded fiberglass cover on the T-top. Diane jumped to the wheel and started the muscular Suzuki outboard motor while Ryan tossed off the bow and stern lines. Once he was aboard, Diane drove them around the point, careful to stay in deeper water.

The sea cave was hollowed-out limestone, the basic rock that formed The Bahamas. Water had found a crack in the hump of rock on Darby Island and, over eons, the crack had widened and eroded into the shape of a bread box, fifteen feet high and thirty feet wide, with smooth, round corners. Rock had fallen from the ceiling and landed in the shallow water, slowly turning into sand as the water continually lapped away at it to build a beach. When the tide was low— as it was now—Ryan could see the seawater had undercut the entire length of the cliff, leaving an inverse shelf of rock over-hanging the water.

Diane let the boat drift in close, but neither saw any sign indicating that someone had been there.

Ryan pointed at the beach that ran the length of the northwestern coast. Angling the boat in that direction, Diane idled them through the shallows, then nosed the boat up on the sand beside a smooth spot presumably left by the black inflatable.

Boot prints just like Ryan had seen beside Diane's tent led

into the trees. Ryan climbed over the skiff's gunwale and followed the tracks. They led through the sabal palms and mangroves to the edge of the blue hole. There, shallow limestone walls rimmed the light blue water, whereas the center of the pool was a much deeper shade of blue. At the eastern end, a high hump of rock rose up to block the surface of the pool from the ocean, suggesting there was passage somewhere below, connecting the pool to the sea.

There was something curious about the rock formation, but Ryan couldn't put his finger on what it was.

Returning to the skiff, Ryan pushed it off the beach and hopped aboard. He was quick to notice Diane had shed her shirt in favor of a blue bikini top, revealing a silver stud in her belly button. "You got any pressing plans?" he asked.

Diane shrugged. "I was thinking about having a hot bath and a glass of wine before dressing for dinner in Paris."

"Don't let me hold you up," he said. "In fact, I think I should drop you on Little Darby so your dad can come get you."

With a puff of air, Diane blew a strand of hair out of her face and placed her hands on her hips. "I'm not going anywhere. This is *my* project, and I'm going to see it through. I have a shipment of construction materials arriving next week."

Ryan met her eyes. "Look, these guys are obviously dangerous. Please consider going to Little Darby or anywhere else for that matter and let me do my job."

"I'll repeat this slowly so your lizard brain can understand it," Diane said truculently. "I'm. Not. Going. Anywhere. If you want to earn whatever my father is paying you, then you're going to have to take me along."

Ryan clenched his teeth together, flexing his jaw muscles. He took a deep breath to relax his body and blew air out through puffed-up cheeks. "Fine. Move over. I'm taking the wheel."

"Excuse me. This is *my* boat."

"Yeah, and I'm driving. You want to go along for the ride, then scoot over, Princess Di."

Their eyes met over the windscreen. He could see the dislike of her new nickname by the furrow of her brow.

"How do I even know you can drive a boat?" she asked.

"Watch and learn," Ryan said, stepping behind the wheel and casually bumping her out of the way with his hip. He quickly navigated them into the deeper water of Rudder Cut before throwing the throttle forward to race the boat out into Exuma Sound.

Ryan figured the black inflatable had come from the camp RJ had seen on Prime Cay. Running parallel to the waves rolling in from the east, the little skiff was taking a beating, so Ryan ducked into the channel between Little Darby and Salt Cay. He slowed and watched the shadows of the reef under the water ahead and the depth sounder mounted on the skiff's dash as they skirted Lignum Vitae Cay.

The next cay in the chain was Prime Cay. Consulting the chartplotter, Ryan saw the island was a mile-and-a-half-long misshapen chunk of rock with a small hook-shaped lagoon in the center, before the land widened out to form a C-shaped bay at the southern end which was where Ryan figured the owners of the inflatable would be camped.

Diane signaled for Ryan to head across the flats before turning back through the cut between Prime and Bock Cays. According to Diane, the co-founders of Fry's Electronics owned Bock, Prime, Lignum Vitae, Melvin, Neighbor, and Woody Cays. They planned to open a private golf resort complete with a helipad and a marina. Diane had been in contact with the manager and was trying to work out an agreement for her future guests to use the golf resort's facilities.

Before them in the C-shaped bay was what looked to Ryan to be a converted tug. It was, he guessed, close to one hundred feet in length, with a gleaming hunter green hull and forward white superstructure. About thirty feet of open aft deck had been outfitted with cranes and canvas sun covers. The black inflatable floated just astern of the bigger boat.

"How in the hell did they get that thing in there?" Ryan wondered aloud, thinking the vessel's draft was too deep for the cut.

"They must have come in at high tide and be sitting over a deeper hole," Diane observed.

Ryan wondered if RJ had been mistaken about a campsite, but then, as the skiff drifted in the current, he saw a tent and a fire ring nestled in the mangroves. Because of the shape of the bay and the density of the trees, an observer had to be almost straight across from the camp to see it. He guessed the ship had come in to resupply the campers.

"At least now we know where they've been living," Diane said.

Ryan pulled out his sat phone and snapped a picture of the ship, then, as they continued to drift, their skiff swung around so they could read the name on the stern of the converted tug: *Leopard*.

Ryan put the skiff's outboard in drive and eased the throttle forward, heading for the open ocean, passing right by the well-equipped salvage vessel. He appraised her with the eye of a commercial diver. A salvage vessel in Bahamian waters could mean a couple of things, but, to Ryan, it confirmed these men were looking for something.

Gold was the first item on the list. There were lots of old Spanish treasure galleons sunk by hurricanes in The Bahamas as they headed for their homeland. Drugs were the next thing that came to mind. Ryan wondered if a plane had gone down en route to the States and if these men had been sent to recover the load. Of course, the *Leopard* could just be doing legitimate salvage work, but given the black inflatable tied to her stern, he doubted it. That boat screamed mercenary.

"Who do you think they are?" Diane asked.

"Ghosts," Ryan replied.

CHAPTER EIGHT

Thirty minutes later, Ryan and Diane were back in Steve Carlton's tent at the end of the damaged runway on Big Darby Island.

Ryan sat at the table, drinking from another bottle of water.

"What's your plan, troubleshooter?" Diane asked.

"I need to figure out what these people are after. There's got to be a reason they want the island clear of anyone who might interfere with whatever they're doing."

"This island has had cruisers and tourists traipsing all over it since Guy Baxter disappeared in 1944, and the islanders ransacked the house and outbuildings decades ago. What could be left?"

"You got Internet access out here?" Ryan asked.

"On Little Darby. They're hooked to the local wireless service."

As Ryan stood, he said, "Good. Let's take another trip."

On the way out of the tent, Ryan picked up Diane's shotgun and stuffed it into his waterproof duffel along with his KRISS Vector and the Glock.

"What are you doing?" Diane asked.

"Caching the firearms. If the crew from the *Leopard* comes back, I don't want them to run off with my gear."

"What about my Airweight or Dad's compound bow?"

Ryan's eyebrows rose. "Compound bow?"

"Yeah, he's got a PSE Stinger with about a dozen arrows. He uses it mostly for target shooting, but he told me he wanted to hunt a hog if one came over to Darby."

"You're dad's an interesting guy."

"He's something," Diane responded quietly. She threw clothes into a bag while Ryan examined her father's weapon of choice. "While you're using the Internet, I'm going to take a bath and get Alice to fix us dinner."

"Sounds good," Ryan agreed.

Carlton had stowed the bow in a plastic case which Ryan set on the table and opened. The Stinger had a detachable quiver, fiber-optic pin sights, and a trigger release. Ryan tossed the spare shotgun shells into the bow case, then carried the case and his waterproof duffel into the brush behind the tent, to a small depression he'd spotted on his way into the camp earlier. Ryan pushed them into the depression and covered it with sabal palm fronds and dead leaves.

"Paranoid?" Diane asked as she watched him sweep away his tracks with the leafy end of a tree branch.

"Just taking precautions." Ryan tossed the branch away, then asked for her Airweight.

Diane crossed her arms and cocked her hip. "I know how to use it."

Ryan held out his hand and motioned for her to hand it over. While having two people carrying firearms might have been better than one, he didn't really know if she could shoot the small pistol, and he didn't trust her judgment or know how she would react should they get into a shooting match with the crew from the *Leopard*. "I figured you know how to use it, but I'm a trained professional. Let me carry the gun, please."

Diane shook her head and rolled her eyes. "Some professional you are. I got the drop on you."

"So, I made one mistake today. Let's not compound it."

"Boy, you've got some ego," she muttered as she unclipped the Airweight from the small of her back and handed it to him. Ryan took a moment to check the small revolver over before reseating it in the holster and clipping it to his waistband in an appendix carry.

"Come on, Princess. Let's go to Little Darby." Ryan headed for the boat again, his legs tired from walking so many miles over the sandy terrain.

Once in the boat, they puttered across the channel to Little Darby, tied up at the dock behind The Drifts Lodge, and walked up to the main house, where they found Alice in the kitchen. The Bahamian cook was bent over the oven, checking the appliance's temperature while a large snapper lay on a pan, its eyes staring glossily out at the world. Ryan's stomach rumbled, and he realized he hadn't eaten anything since before sunrise.

"Miss Diane, what be you doing here?" Alice cried in surprise and delight.

"Just came to take a bath while the spider monkey uses the Internet," Diane said.

Alice looked puzzled for a moment, not understanding the inside joke, but then quickly recovered. "I was just fixin' supper for me and the boys. I'll get the other snapper out of the fridge for you two. RJ used his new pole spear and shot two fine snappers. Stoned 'em straight away, he did."

"I knew he'd put that pole spear to good use," Ryan said.

"I'll fix dis one for you and de other for my family," Alice said.

"Thank you," Ryan replied. "I don't want to take food off

your table."

"Nonsense," Alice replied. "We have plenty. Now, will ya be staying de night?"

"Yes," Diane replied for Ryan and herself. "We could use a good night's sleep before heading back to Big Darby."

"Da rooms be all made up. Just chose whateva ones ya like."

"Thanks, Alice. Come on, Ryan, I'll show you where the computer is."

Ryan followed Diane out of the kitchen and through the house to an office. He, too, felt the urge for a shower and decided to skip the research and clean up first. Trailing after Diane, he entered the bedroom, where she was rummaging through her bag of clothes.

"You need something?" she asked.

"I'd like to take a shower, too. Point me in the right direction."

"You make it quick and you can use mine."

Ryan entered the bathroom, stripped down, and stepped under the hot water, letting it pound his skin and wash away the dirt, sweat, and salt before putting on clean shorts and a T-shirt from his pack. Less than ten minutes after closing the door, he opened it again to find Diane holding two cold beers. She handed him one, biting her bottom lip as she looked him up and down.

He took a long swig, then said, "It's all yours. Thanks."

Diane nodded and watched Ryan leave the room, closing the door behind him. He went to the office and sat before the large screen of the HP all-in-one computer. Taking out his phone, he looked at the picture he'd snapped of the salvage vessel. The name *"Leopard"* was clear, but there appeared to be smaller lettering beneath, designating a home port. He used two fingers to enlarge the photo and saw in stenciled letters the word: "Paladin."

"Where the hell is 'Paladin'?" he whispered aloud.

Ryan's first Internet search for "paladin" netted a Merriam-Webster definition, meaning "trusted military leader or a leading champion of a cause." Wikipedia said the term came from Old French, derived from the Latin *comes palatinus*, or count palatine, a title given to close retainers—men who were confidants of kings and emperors. In more modern times, the term had come to mean a knight-errant. Ryan smiled. A knight-errant wasn't far off from how he saw himself, roving the land in search of adventure.

Included on the first search pages were various companies with "paladin" in their names, but none that Ryan thought would operate a ship in The Bahamas. Then, there was Richard Boone's character in the old television western series, *Have Gun – Will Travel.*

When he'd been typing "paladin" into the search bar, he'd seen the term "Paladin Group (a fascist organization)" appear in the autogenerated search terms, so he clicked on it and began to read. The Paladin Group was co-founded in 1970 by former Waffen-SS Colonel Otto Skorzeny and a rogue CIA special operations officer, Colonel James Sanders. Both were members of the ODESSA network, a covert operation designed to smuggle Nazis out of Germany in 1946. Together, the men had run paramilitary operations and political warfare using former SS personnel and civilian right-wing nationalist organizations, but the group's efforts ended in 1975, when Skorzeny had passed away.

Leaning back in his seat, Ryan crossed his arms. Paladin had been created by former Nazis. Sir Guy Baxter had aided Nazi U-boats. Ryan couldn't ignore the likelihood of a connection between the two, especially when added to the fact that the shell casings he and Carlton had found on the island came from *German*-made ammunition.

Hoping to learn more, Ryan kept clicking on links, but

only found himself going down rabbit holes as he sipped his beer. He learned that Ian Fleming had used Skorzeny as the prototype for his villain Ernst Stavro Blofeld, even down to the facial scar Skorzeny had received in a fencing duel. Blofeld had managed his own ODESSA network named SPECTRE, and even comic book legend Stan Lee had used ODESSA as a template for Hydra, Marvel's fictious terrorist group. Both imaginary organizations were even identifiable by a similar octopus logo.

"Hey!" Diane rapped on the desk to get Ryan's attention.

He glanced up from the computer. "What's up?"

"You've been on that thing for an hour. Dinner's ready."

He glanced at his watch. Time moved fast when he was engrossed in learning history.

"Find anything interesting?" she asked.

"Just strange rabbit holes with no real context as to how they fit together with Darby Island, if they do at all," Ryan replied.

"You'll have to shelve it for now. Alice sent me to get you. She gets upset if dinner gets cold."

"Let me make a phone call first, and then I'll join you."

"It can wait," Diane said. "I'm famished, and I'm sure you are as well."

Ryan agreed and stood to follow her, taking in the short yellow sundress she wore, offset by her tan skin and black hair still woven into the French braid.

On the way to the dining room, he could smell the freshly baked fish, and again his stomach growled. Padding barefoot down the hall, his feet scuffed over the polished hardwood and soft area rugs. He rarely wore shoes, preferring to go barefoot on his boat or wear sandals when running errands. By contrast, the combat boots he'd worn for the past few hours had felt heavy and constricting, but he'd wanted the ankle support and heavy tread for hiking across the island.

They took seats at the table and Alice came into the room, carrying a dish of peeled, boiled potatoes. She placed it on the table beside the whole snapper, a platter of conch salad, a bowl of pigeon peas and rice, and a large pitcher of switcha—a tart, lemon and lime drink similar to lemonade.

"Ya call me if ya need anyting else," Alice said, then retreated to the kitchen.

Ryan glanced over at Diane, who had positioned herself across from him. In the fading light of the sunset, he saw the glow of her skin, the flush of her cheeks as she felt his gaze upon her, and the slow way she curled her bottom lip in to bite it before smiling shyly. Ryan hadn't known her to be shy. She'd been ready to pump him full of lead earlier that day and had given him sass ever since.

Without waiting for another invitation, Ryan started heaping his plate with food. He made short work of Alice's wonderful cooking.

"You know it's not a race, right?" Diane asked, her plate still half full.

"Force of habit," Ryan replied. "I was the youngest kid growing up, then I did a lot of single-handed sailing where I needed to eat quickly."

"Here, I thought it was the military who taught you to eat fast."

Ryan chuckled. "I had it perfected before I joined."

"What did you do in the ... what ... Army?"

"No," Ryan said flatly, with a snort of derision. "I was an EOD tech in the Navy. We're sort of a jack of all trades, but our expertise is disarming any type of explosive, from underwater mines to nuclear weapons."

Between bites of fish and conch salad, Ryan went on to explain about his years of training, not just in bomb disposal but in hand-to-hand combat, parachuting techniques, small unit tactics, and how he'd qualified on just about every small caliber weapon in the Navy's arsenal. At one point, Navy EOD had been the only EOD techs to deploy with Special Forces and, consequently, they had many of the same skill sets as those hardened warriors. Since leaving the Navy, Ryan had also attended combat and firearms training at various civilian schools to keep his perishable skills sharp and to keep abreast of the latest bomb disposal techniques.

"I'm confused, why did my father hire you? I haven't seen any bombs on my island," Diane said.

Ryan put his hands on the table and pushed back, tipping his chair up on two legs. "You'll have to ask him."

"Huh?" Diane mused, wiping her mouth with a white linen napkin.

Ryan could list a bunch of reasons as to why Steve Carlton had hired him, but he wasn't one to brag. He would let his work speak for itself. Tomorrow morning, he needed to start in earnest. Today, Ryan had gotten the lay of the land, something he had figured on doing anyway, but he hadn't counted on being accompanied by a partner.

He lowered the chair legs to the floor and stood. "Now, if you'll excuse me, I have some more work to do in the office before I turn in."

Making his way through the house, Ryan admired the handsome finishings, the watercolor paintings of striking Caribbean settings, and the way the interior designer had taken a modern approach to traditional Bahamian culture and architecture. Along the way, Ryan acquired a glass of rum from the sideboard in the office and sipped it as he sat before the computer again. This time, he used satellite terrain maps to recon the small islands around Big and Little Darby, then he used open-source nautical charts to view the water depths around those same islands.

Reaching for his sat phone, Ryan stepped outside onto

the veranda and dialed the number for Ashlee Williams at Dark Water Research's headquarters in Texas City.

When she answered, Ryan cut off the sarcastic remark he knew she would make by saying, "I know, I know. I only call you when I want something. So, here's what I need. I'm going to send you a picture of a boat, and I need you to tell me more about it."

"Yes, Ryan," Ashlee said in an exasperated tone.

Ryan could practically hear her eyes rolling. Ashlee had remote access to a bespoke program at MarineSat AI which was capable of locating boats anywhere in the world. He texted her the picture of the *Leopard*.

"Should be pretty easy," Ashlee said.

Making small talk, Ryan asked about her husband, "How's Don?"

"He's good, as far as I know. He's down in Mexico with the rest of the crew, working that Zama job. Speaking of which, I thought you were down there, too?"

"I still am. I just want to know about a ship that's been hanging around the oilfield. It looks suspicious."

"Somehow, with your track record, I don't believe you."

"I really don't care what you believe, Ash, I just want you to tell me about the ship."

"You do know I could ping your phone and find out where you are, right?"

"Do you *like* your job?" Ryan said, his voice dropping an octave to underline the seriousness of his question.

"I love my job. Why?"

Ryan let the question hang for a moment.

"You're not a bastard, Ryan. Don't act like one," Ashlee said, irked by his threat to have her fired.

"Then don't poke your nose into my business. All I need to know about is the ship."

"Fine. Does Emily know where you are?" Ashlee insisted.

Ryan gritted his teeth, trying not to bite his friend's head off. He took a breath, deciding to end this line of questioning by being honest—and because Ashlee was probably pinging his phone as they spoke. "Thank you for being concerned, Ash. I'm not in Mexico. I'm on a troubleshooting gig."

"See? Was that so hard?"

"Apparently as hard as you giving me the information I need about the *Leopard*," retorted Ryan.

"Keep your pants on, Ryan. Okay, let's see here ... Uh, it says the *Leopard* was originally constructed as an oceangoing tug and converted to a salvage vessel before being purchased by Werwolf Group." She spelled out "Werwolf" for Ryan's benefit. "They're a German company, but the ship is registered in the Cayman Islands. A quick search for Werwolf with that spelling gives two main subjects. The first is *Führerhauptquartier Werwolf*, or however you say it—I probably butchered those words. Anyway, it was Hitler's Eastern Front military headquarters, north of Vinnytsia in Ukraine. The second is in reference to a German resistance group intended to carry out clandestine attacks on Allied Forces at the end of World War II."

"Everything keeps circling back to the damned Nazis," Ryan complained.

"What does?" Ashlee asked, intrigued.

Having already divulged to her that he was on a mission, Ryan decided to confide the rest to her, hoping Ashlee could help make sense of the things he was trying to piece together in his mind. He gave her an info dump about where he was and why he was on Big Darby. He still didn't know what the men who had destroyed Carlton's equipment wanted, but he figured that if he could find out, he would be a step ahead.

As Ryan talked out his problems, a plan started to form in his mind.

CHAPTER NINE

After ending his phone call with Ashlee Williams, Ryan powered down his sat phone and took a seat on the veranda. The breeze carried a hint of rain, and far in the distance, streaks of lightning blistered the night sky, causing the low rumble of thunder. He counted off the seconds between flashes of lightning and the sound of the thunder, then divided by five, giving an estimated six miles between Little Darby and the storm. The light and sound happened at the same time, but since light traveled faster than sound, it gave the appearance of the thunder happening after the lightning flash had superheated the surrounding air, expanding it so quickly that it produced a shockwave.

A smile eased across Ryan's lips as he thought of his grandfather. The old man had always said thunder was caused by potatoes falling out of God's potato wagon. Grandpa Flynn had been a hoot. He could sail upwind with one foot on the rudder and a glass of wine between the toes of his other foot, arms spread across the gunwale, completely at ease. And he could grow the biggest, juiciest tomatoes Ryan had ever seen, just by tucking a tomato plant into a five-gallon bucket of dirt.

Another brilliant flash of lightning illuminated the sky, pushing the shock wave of thunder outward. As the storm drew closer, the wind increased, knocking palm fronds against tree trunks and scraping bougainvillea bushes along the veranda's screening.

In a sudden roar, the rain came, beating down with a fury that made Ryan glad he was inside the house and not on Big Darby, sleeping in the tent or out in the jungle.

With a yawn, Ryan leaned his head back against the chair, sliding lower to stretch his feet out to the veranda railing. He closed his eyes, pretending the rain was rattling off the canvas sun dodger on his sailboat. Ryan missed being aboard his sailboat. He'd grown up on the water, learned to sail with Grandpa Flynn, worked at a marina through high school, then left to sail around the world at eighteen, before joining the Navy two years later upon his return to Wilmington.

Since becoming a contractor for Greg Olsen, Ryan had bounced around the Caribbean on his boats. *Sweet T* had been shot out from under him by pirates in the Gulf of Mexico, and *Windseeker* had been set ablaze by a drug thug on St. Thomas. *Huntress* was his third vessel and the best of them.

He prayed nothing happened to his precious Fountaine Pajot Saba because Emily was talking about settling down somewhere, maybe Fort Lauderdale, near her mother. Ryan wasn't ready to settle into suburbia just yet. He had too much knight-errantry left in him.

Ryan liked his lifestyle, sailing and exploring and working missions as they came. Truthfully, when Carlton had brought his problem to him, Ryan had been more than delighted. It meant he had built a reputation as a man who could get the job done.

He finished the rum and stood, making his way to the

bedroom. Making use of the brilliant flashes of lightning instead of turning on a lamp, Ryan undressed and crawled between the sheets. He hadn't realized how tired he was until he'd sat down on the veranda to sip his rum. He'd almost dozed off twice. Closing his eyes, he took slow, deep breaths, concentrating on the air flowing in and out past the tip of his nose, and was soon fast asleep.

As tired as Ryan was, the lizard part of his brain knew he was sleeping in a strange room, and it wouldn't let him fully drift into REM sleep. The thunder startled him awake, rattling the light fixtures. He rubbed his face as his heartbeat slowly came back to its resting rate. He'd been dreaming but couldn't remember what about. He presumed his mind was trying to make sense of what he'd learned about who might be at work on Big Darby Island. Ryan wasn't sure how it was all connected, but there seemed to be a dark order lurking in the shadows.

A dark order with Nazi roots.

Lying in the dark, Ryan tried to go back to sleep again. He focused on his breathing, and while he was able to relax, he couldn't induce sleep to return. With a final deep breath, he threw his feet over the edge of the bed and stood. He stretched his lanky frame, feeling the stiffness in his muscles and the aches in his bones. The glowing hands of his watch said it was just past one a.m.

Knowing Alice lived in another house on Little Darby and that Diane was the only other resident of the main house, Ryan padded to the office in his boxer briefs, pulling on a T-shirt as he walked. There, he turned on the floor lamp near the window above the side table, fixed himself another drink, and sat on the veranda, thinking about how he would execute his infiltration of the *Leopard*. He figured that when the inflatable carried away the search team, only the boat's crew would stay aboard the salvage vessel, and it would be the perfect time to have a look around.

As he sipped his rum, Ryan noticed a shadow flit across the veranda. Diane moved into the light, wearing dark magenta silk pajama shorts with a matching tank top. She carried her own drink and stood by the screen, peering out into the darkness while taking the occasional sip. The rain had slackened to a gentle drizzle, but more was on the way, as evidenced by the coming thunder and lightning.

Ryan took a good look at her standing there in her short shorts, a hint of cheek tantalizingly exposed when she cocked a hip. Her calf muscles knotted and bunched as she stretched and rose on tiptoes. She'd combed her black hair out of the French braid, and it fell in one solid sheet down to her mid-back. When she turned, he noticed she wore no undergarments.

In that moment, his tired and alcohol-addled mind wondered how soft her kisses were and how her lips tasted. He wondered how her body would react to his touch, the feeling of his calloused hands whispering over her soft, smooth flesh. There was a time in his life when he wouldn't have hesitated to act on the attraction he felt for Diane. However, now that he was married, he had to curb his impulses.

But now he was basically alone on an island with this driven young woman, and he was strangely attracted to her. The thing was, Diane wasn't his type at all. He preferred blondes, and she was just too short—a whole foot shorter than his six feet—but there was something about her that he couldn't put a finger on. Diane had a mysteriousness that attracted him, but at the same time, warning bells clanged in the back of his mind, telling him she was dangerous.

It was dangerous for him to even contemplate this line of thinking. If he acted on the impulse and jumped into the sack with Diane, then he'd never be able to get that image out of his head. He'd think about it every time he climbed into bed with Emily. Every time he made love to her, Diane would be there—a guilt deep inside of him. So, Ryan forced his mind back to the mission that lay ahead and would put him in harm's way, a situation he could handle with less stress than dealing with the attractive woman before him.

Suddenly, Ryan remembered exactly what his dream had been about. He hadn't been focusing on his current danger, but rather, a past one. He'd been wrestling with Tree Trunk again, the giant Haitian bodyguard who had tried to drown Ryan on his previous mission to Haiti. It had been an intense struggle that had taken months to recover from. Tree Trunk's blows had damaged Ryan's ribs and bruised his muscles. Ryan and Emily had spent the time in the protected anchorage off Samaná, in the Dominican Republic, exploring the area when he felt well enough to venture out. He fixated on those memories now and tried to put his lustful thoughts for Diane out of his mind.

But it wasn't that easy. She came over and sat beside him on the long glider, crossing her legs beneath her. The pajama bottoms rode up to show the full length of her legs, and Ryan could see the crease of her skin where thigh met hip. Diane leaned forward to put her elbows on her bony knees and looped her loose hair back over her ears. The row of tiny diamonds set in silver studs from her earlobe to the peak of her helix glittered in the low light coming from the lamp inside the house.

"What are you thinking about?" she asked, the light casting shadows over her face, making her high cheekbones infinitely more striking.

Ryan couldn't tell her what had just occupied his thoughts. It was forbidden territory. His attraction to her felt like Pandora's box. When opened, it couldn't be closed.

"What do you like to do for fun, Diane?" Ryan asked, trying to get his thoughts out from a place they didn't belong.

"Well, I like to sail and ski and dive, and I like to ride motorcycles fast along twisty, curving roads."

Though he didn't show it, her answer made Ryan desire her all the more, knowing they shared so many common interests. With the exception of skiing, which he'd done several times as a kid, but never as an adult, Diane had described things Ryan derived pleasure from. He instantly chided himself for thinking that way.

His mind swirling with distracting thoughts of Emily, he said, "So, besides the call of the water, what brought you to the Caribbean?"

"I lived in Colorado for a long time after I graduated from the University of Colorado Boulder. I started to get my mechanical engineering degree but found I liked to ski and ride motorcycles too much to concentrate on my studies. So, I switched to Business Administration, figuring one day my father would offer me a job. After college, I bounced around Colorado, taking jobs in marketing, communications, and public affairs in places that had the best skiing and riding, like Telluride and Aspen.

"Then Daddy asked me to come back to Maryland and work for his company as a marketing director. A couple of years there made me realize it wasn't what I wanted to do with my life. So, here I am, trying to start this bed and breakfast and combine all the things I really like to do."

"Not too many roads to ride motorcycles on around here," Ryan commented.

Diane laughed. "Daddy said the same thing. I still have my bikes in storage out in Colorado. I figure I can fly out there and ride whenever I have a chance. Sort of a break from the island."

"You said 'bikes,' plural?"

Diane nodded, the excitement visible on her face, two tiny dimples appearing in her cheeks as she smiled. Her wide smile made Ryan mirror it. "I have a Ducati Monster for riding on the street and a BMW F650 adventure bike for the dirt. Do you ride?"

"I haven't been on a bike in a long time, and honestly, I don't have a motorcycle license."

"I figured a man of action like you would have one tucked away somewhere."

"Nope. I live on a sailboat, and I don't even own a car."

"Really?"

Ryan almost said his wife owned a Jeep Wrangler, but he didn't let that piece of information slip. He wore no wedding ring and had no tan line on his left ring finger, so Diane wouldn't know he was married unless he told her.

He changed the subject. "What's keeping you awake tonight?"

Diane leaned back and ran a hand through her hair, tilting her head back to expose her delicate throat as she did so. Ryan was torn between wanting to kiss the hollow at the base of her clavicle and punching her in the windpipe so he could run away screaming for help, but he did neither, sitting placidly on his ass, watching her every move.

With a sigh, Diane answered his question. "It's this whole situation, honestly. I thought Daddy was lying to me when he said those men had shot at him, but then you found that shell casing, and now I'm starting to get worried. Do you really think those men are dangerous?"

Ryan contemplated the question for a moment, then said, "It all depends upon what they're after. If it's something valuable, my guess is, they wouldn't lose a night's sleep if they killed you over it. But maybe they just want to drive you off the land. Shots fired is a good way to do that."

Diane looked startled. "I don't know what could be on my island that's so important to them."

Ryan scratched the back of his neck, forcing himself to look out into the darkness. "That's the question we need to answer. In order for us to do that, it's going to take some detective work."

Diane took a sip of her drink, then asked what he meant.

Ryan debated about how much he should tell her about his plan. Honestly, he didn't think she'd want him snooping around on the bad guy's boat, but he'd never know her opinion unless he told her. Maybe the attractive lady beside him had larceny in her heart, too.

She leaned forward again, placing a warm hand on his thigh, her voice warm and soothing. "I can see you're thinking about something, Ryan. Tell me what it is, because the sooner we get rid of these guys, the sooner I can get back to building my new life."

"We'll take care of it." He put his hand on hers to reassure her.

Ryan saw the glint in her eye. She started to lean forward. Her lips parted slightly as if she meant to kiss him. He squeezed her hand and took a sip of his drink, using it to block her advance.

Diane stood and walked to the screen, staring into the darkness with her back to him.

"Why didn't you buy Cave Cay?" Ryan asked. "The work there is almost done. You'd have a marina, a hotel, a landing strip, and cabanas for less than what your old man paid for Big Darby."

"Because I've been captivated by the island's history since I first learned about it as a little girl. Can you imagine the marketing campaign I can run?" She spread her hands majestically. "Come explore where Sir Guy Baxter once resupplied the deadliest vessels of World War II. Relive history on this beautiful island paradise."

"Honestly, it doesn't do it for me," Ryan said. "But I'd love to come back and check it out when you're done with the renovations."

Diane turned to face him. She was biting her lower lip again.

A bolt of lightning struck nearby, shattering their world with a crack of thunder so loud that it made them both jump. The floor lamp winked out, and the low hum of the generator died.

"Oh, *great*," Diane muttered.

Ryan sipped his drink, thinking he should make a quick exit under the cover of darkness. When the next bolt of lightning brightened the sky, he saw he was too late. Diane was lifting her shirt over her head, then her weight settled onto his lap as she straddled him. He gulped as Diane's lips brushed his stubbly cheek.

Her breathy whisper over his ear set his skin atingle. "I can't wait for you to come back."

Before Ryan could move her off him, Diane's lips found his. They were as soft and warm and hungry as he'd imagined, tasting of a hint of switcha.

Ryan stood swiftly, dropping Diane heavily to the floor.

The lightning exposed her look of surprise and fury as she stared up at him, sprawled on the veranda floor.

"I'm sorry, Diane. I ... I can't do this. You're ... I'm ... I can't."

Ryan turned and fled to his room, locking the door behind him before falling onto the bed face-first and burying his face in the pillow. "Why didn't you just tell her?" he muttered. "Why didn't you just tell her you're married?"

But Ryan knew the answer to his own question, and he hated himself for being so weak. He had wanted to know how he would react if Diane made an advance. He hadn't encouraged her, but he hadn't exactly discouraged her, either. He'd wanted it to happen.

He felt like a foolish child. He'd played with fire, and he'd gotten burned.

"You're a stupid, weak idiot," Ryan chastised himself.

"Ryan?" Diane asked softly as she knocked on the door.

Dammit, woman, Ryan screamed in his mind. *Take a hint.*

He chose not to answer the door, wrapping the pillow around his head and willing her to go away.

"Ryan?" Diane called through the door again. "I'm sorry. I didn't mean to startle you. I just ... I wanted ..."

After a few moments of silence, he heard her pad softly away on bare feet. Ryan lay awake, determined to atone for his sin. He would tell Emily about the kiss—after he told Diane about his wife.

Ryan recalled looking at the weather radar on the computer. The line of storms promised to clear around three a.m. He glanced at his watch. It was almost two now. He rose and began to dress.

It was time to get back to work.

CHAPTER TEN

The *Leopard* lay at anchor in the sheltered cove at the southern end of Prime Cay, where Ryan had last seen her. She was dark save for the white anchor light atop the masthead and the soft glow of red lights on the bridge. Ryan imagined someone was standing watch in case the tug dragged anchor, or the storms forced the vessel to have to get underway.

The troubleshooter had gotten dressed quickly and then thrown his pack into Diane's skiff while the generator was still off, and everything was pitch-black. From Little Darby Island, Ryan had motored south, slowly making way and picking out the channel with a spotlight until he was close to Prime Cay. There, he had to take the chance that he could negotiate the skinny water at the mouth of the fishhook cove.

Fortunately, luck was with Ryan. He made it through the shallows and beached the skiff out of sight of the cove entrance, then made his way overland through a half-mile tangle of mangroves and spiderwebs in the darkness.

By the time he reached the campsite of the "ghosts," the

false dawn was tingeing the eastern sky. Ryan wanted to flail his arms to get the last wisps of spiderweb off his face, but he managed to corral his irrational agitation and methodically pick off the strands until he could no longer feel them on his skin.

Staying well back inside the cover of the sopping wet trees, Ryan settled into a seated position with his back against the trunk of a lignum vitae tree, the arching canopy of which sported blue blossoms. Ryan's clothes were soaked, from bucking through the waves in the skiff and then from traipsing through the jungle, so he pulled on a camouflage poncho to trap in his body heat.

He drew his legs up under the thin plastic and observed the camp. Checking his watch, he found the time to be just past five. Another hour, and it would be dawn. It had taken much longer than he'd anticipated to get into his hide.

With the heavy storms sweeping through the islands, Ryan figured the "ghosts" would have spent the night aboard the *Leopard*. He was glad he'd waited to approach the camp because shortly after he'd ensconced himself under his poncho, Ryan saw movement inside the tent. At first, he thought it was just the wind moving the heavy canvas, but then a light came on inside the small structure. Without warning, a man rounded the corner of the tent and headed straight for Ryan. He was bare-chested, and in the early morning light, Ryan caught a glimpse of a black swastika tattooed above his navel.

Ryan froze, willing the man to turn away. Slowly, Ryan lowered his chin toward his chest to hide the whites of his eyes, for he'd already polished his face with some mud he'd picked up amongst the black mangrove roots. He kept his eyes on the camper as the man stumbled through the trees and came to a stop not ten feet away. The man unzipped his pants and urinated on the trunk of a tree, humming a tune Ryan didn't recognize.

With a grunt, the man shook off and zipped up his pants. He returned to the campsite, where he moved a hissing kerosene lantern from inside the tent to a folding table, then busied himself with making coffee on a portable stove. The smell of the strong brew caused Ryan's stomach to grumble. He'd left Little Darby in a hurry, not bothering to grab anything to eat from the kitchen because he hadn't wanted to see Diane again. There was an MRE in his backpack, but he was loath to eat it. He'd had a gutful of the instant meals while humping through Iraq and Afghanistan.

When the "ghost" had his coffee brewed, he sat at the table and smoked a cigarette while sipping from a tin cup. The sound of an outboard motor starting made Ryan glance toward the beach a dozen yards away. He could see the *Leopard* swinging on her anchor as the sun gathered itself to lurch above the horizon.

The inflatable arrived with a complement of five men. Ryan picked out the leader immediately. He was tall, blond, and strikingly handsome. The man spoke to his compatriots in what Ryan thought was German. He recognized a few words, but the man spoke too fast for Ryan to catch much. Grandpa Flynn had spoken German, a language he'd learned from his mother after they'd immigrated to the United States.

Now, sitting under the tree and watching the big Aryan move about the camp, readying weapons and gear to set off in the inflatable, Ryan was reminded of all the references to the Nazi Party he'd come across during his research last night. Just because these dudes were speaking German didn't make them Nazis—other than the dude with the swastika tattoo—but Ryan couldn't help but think these men were searching for something left by the Nazis on Big Darby Island or one of the surrounding cays.

Ryan's stomach grumbled again. It felt like it was trying to turn itself inside out as it demanded food. He worked up a mouthful of spit and swallowed hard, trying to convince his body that he'd ingested liquid. Licking his lips, he tasted the tartness of switcha. He knew it was just his imagination. Diane's kiss had been scrubbed off by the wind and waves on his way to Prime Cay.

He remained seated and still, observing the camp as the Germans readied themselves to leave.

———

AT FIRST, Ryan didn't know how long he'd been asleep. He checked his watch. More than two hours had elapsed since he'd sat down by the tree. When he saw no guards or movement around the camp, he slowly stretched his legs straight out, relieving the cramping in his muscles.

He'd let his guard down, and fortunately, he hadn't paid a price for it. When his muscles loosened, Ryan gathered his legs under him and stood.

After shedding the poncho and stowing it in his pack, Ryan moved cautiously forward, trying to stay out of the line of sight of anyone keeping watch aboard the salvage vessel. He walked through trees still damp from the rain until the tent was between himself and the boat, then he crept inside.

The tent was similar to the one Carlton had erected for his base camp. Constructed of green canvas, the tent had six-foot-high walls held in place by aluminum poles and a sloping roof designed to shed snow or rain. Under his feet was a platform of wooden grids designed to allow water and grit to filter between the slats. Movement of the men within the tent had compacted the grids into the sandy soil, with only one or two rocking awkwardly as Ryan moved toward the table in the center. Along both walls were collapsible bunks of aluminum and canvas, and at the rear of the tent were storage boxes and a custom-built unit that acted as a kitchen and pantry with a fold-out stove and sink basin.

Ryan saw a stack of granola bars in the pantry and helped himself to two of them, shoving the wrappers into his pocket as he munched on the German-made snack. While he ate, he studied the map laid out on the table. The Germans had sectioned off Big Darby Island into fifty grid squares. At least thirty of them had a red X through them. Ryan took this to mean they'd searched the southern and middle portions of the island already, saving the house and sea caves for last.

Some of the unsearched grid squares had notes scribbled in grease pencil, but Ryan couldn't read German any better than he could speak it—which was not at all. He settled for taking pictures of the map and close-ups of the notes, then sent them through the ether for Ashlee Williams to decipher.

The rest of the tent revealed little about who was conducting the secret search of Big Darby. The only new piece to the puzzle was the confirmation that the men were German.

Ryan left the tent and walked down to the water, squatting in the shade to watch the salvage vessel through his binoculars. Occasionally, men roamed around her deck, but there was no pattern to their movement. Only one carried a sidearm that Ryan could see.

He debated with himself about the need to go aboard the *Leopard*. There was a greater risk of being seen by the crew, and he doubted these guys would leave information about what they were searching for just lying around. The map was one thing, but research materials, journals, photographs, or other paperwork would be locked in a safe for operational security.

The problem for Ryan was that he was feeling dangerous.

Since his encounter with Diane, he'd felt the need to exorcise some of his own demons, and that usually meant he did something stupid, hoping the adrenaline and shock would cleanse him. It rarely absolved him of his sins and usually damaged his body. Perhaps Ryan should have known better by now—and he did—but he still fancied himself a singleton asset—a John Wick type, but in reality, Ryan knew he was more of a bumbling Don Quixote.

Carlton coming to Ryan directly for help had inflated his ego. What he figured he should do was pull out his sat phone and get Scott Gregory on the horn. At least with the two of them operating together, they had a better chance against the six-man search team and however many crewmembers were aboard the *Leopard*.

And Scott would provide a buffer between Ryan and Diane.

"Damn your idiot eyes," Ryan muttered to himself, then immediately wondered why he was talking like a pirate. Diane had thrown him off his game from the moment she'd gotten the drop on him at her father's base camp.

Ryan ran a hand over his bristly brown hair. He'd cut it short, almost to the scalp, because it was easier to deal with while diving and living on the *Midkiff*. His brain told him to retreat and dial for help, but the energy in his body wanted to propel him into the water to creep aboard the *Leopard* and take his chances with the crew.

"What would Emily tell you to do?" Ryan asked himself. He focused on his wife, trying to sort through the emotional strain he'd put himself under, but his mind kept drifting back to Diane. Well, he knew what Emily would say to him. He could hear her chiding him now. "Don't be stupid. Call Scott."

After one last look at the salvage vessel, Ryan retreated into the mangroves, bypassed the Germans' camp, and headed for the skiff. Once there, he pushed the boat off the sand and idled out of the cove, careful to avoid the coral heads and sand bars that would beach him until high tide in another six hours.

Clear of the cove and into the deeper water, Ryan motored between the two massive pillars of rock that stood between Prime and Lignum Vitae Cays, forming three distinctive channels through the cut. To his right, the water that surged through the narrow opening was choppy and formed whitecaps for nearly a quarter of a mile out to sea. To his left, the water swirled in tiny eddies and whirlpools, sweeping north along Lignum Vitae. The rush of water through the cut moved like a freight train at ten knots or better. The outgoing tide shoved the little skiff forward, lifting her stern as if in following seas.

Ryan let the swift water carry him out into Exuma Sound and then turned north. This time, he raced across the flat sea toward Cave Cay. It took him less than fifteen minutes to traverse the eight miles to the well-protected and aptly named Safe Harbor Marina.

As Ryan was tying up the skiff, a heavyset white man with a long beard appeared on the dock. Shark had been the owner for better than a decade, but now he was trying to sell. He eyed Ryan with a look of suspicion, then smiled. "I remember you. You were here in a big catamaran with a blonde." Shark snapped his fingers as he looked up and to the right. "Emily was her name. And the boat was *Huntress*. A Fountaine Pajot Saba."

"You've got a good memory," Ryan said, impressed. "I need to talk to one of your guests. Can you top off the fuel tank while I do that?"

"Cash only," Shark replied, sliding his hands into the pockets of his shorts.

Ryan patted his backpack. "I've got it."

"Deja can help you up at the front desk."

Ryan walked off the dock, then followed the curve of the road as it rose from the marina to the boutique hotel. The exterior was clad with pale yellow siding under a blue metal roof, while white railings with intricate, inset square patterns fenced in the rocking chairs on the wrap-around porch. Bougainvillea vines, blossoming in vivid pinks and purples, laced up diamond-shaped lattice and sprawled out across the top of the hill, intermingled with the seagrass.

From the porch, Ryan could see the straight, sandy length of runway and the parking ramp constructed of ancient, faded, and potholed asphalt. Across the island, hidden amongst the mangroves and Australian pines, were small cottages, big fuel and water tanks, and heavy construction equipment. At the long stretch of dock, several large yachts and sport fishing vessels rode easily without tugging on their lines.

Safe Harbor was a beautiful piece of property, and Ryan wished he could afford it, but he knew that if he spent his life's savings on the island, he'd be shackled to it just as it anchored Shark. Ryan had no desire to be a gas jockey, boat mechanic, plumber, electrician, landscaper, property manager, ass kisser, people pleaser, or whatever else the job required on an hourly basis. He wondered what fascinated Diane about the idea.

He wondered why *she* fascinated him.

In the hotel lobby, Ryan ordered a cold Kalik beer. He walked over to the small desk with the bartender following him. She was a thin Bahamian woman in her early twenties, whose name tag read: Deja.

Ryan turned the guest log around so he could read the names, scanning them quickly for the one he knew would be there. He tapped it with the tip of his right index finger, then slid his finger across the page to the room number that had been carefully penned in by the clerk.

"I'd like you to ring Cottage Three, please," Ryan told the girl.

CHAPTER ELEVEN

Deja, the hotel barkeep and desk clerk, picked up the phone and dialed the number for Cave Cay Cottage Three. When the man at the other end answered, the girl said, "Mista Gregory, there's someone in the lobby ta see ya."

Ryan didn't hear the response but knew Scott had hung up and was on his way. Shortly before leaving North Carolina, the two men had decided Scott should fly to Cave Cay in case Ryan needed to call in the cavalry, and he assumed Scott had a duffel bag full of weapons stashed somewhere, including his favorite sniper rifle.

The former SEAL came bounding up the porch steps and entered the lobby through the hurricane-strength French doors. "I'm ready when you are," he said after bumping fists with Ryan. "All I need to do is grab my gear and check out."

"Where you goin', Scott?" Deja asked.

"Big Darby Island," he replied.

Ryan would have preferred to keep their destination a secret, but he figured the islanders had their own grapevine and Deja would probably know where they were headed before they'd even made it to the skiff. He also wasn't surprised that his friend was on a first-name basis with the pretty young Bahamian.

While Ryan was a good-looking guy, people sometimes found his demeanor off-putting, and he could come across as grouchy and standoffish, but Scott was built differently. The guy was ruthless and could torture an enemy for information without a second thought, then walk into a bar and chat up a pretty girl like nothing had happened. Maybe it was his personality or maybe it was the blond hair, the wide grin, and the sparkling blue eyes, but people were drawn to Scott— women, especially—and Ryan could see that Deja was clearly smitten.

"You be careful," Deja said, placing a hand on Scott's arm. "Der's nothing on dat island but an old house."

"We're camping," Scott replied. "Nothing to worry about."

"De owner runs people off by shooting at them," Deja added. "He be a scary man."

"You know Mister Carlton?" Ryan asked.

"Mista *Carlton*?" the young woman replied, confused. "No, de new owner is a German man. Big, blond, very handsome— but he not be as handsome as you, Scott." Deja smiled as if to regain Scott's good graces and he grinned back, encouraging her to continue. "He said his name be Ziegler. It was difficult for me to understand his accent. He come here to see my Great Uncle Clivon."

"About what?" Ryan asked.

"De man wanted to know about de history of Big Darby. Uncle Clivon worked for Guy Baxter."

"No shit," Scott muttered. "Well, we'll be extra careful, so I can come back to see you."

A shy smile crept across the girl's face as she gazed up at Scott.

Ryan cleared his throat to interrupt whatever moment

Deja and Scott were sharing. "Is your uncle around? I'd like to speak to him, too."

Deja's smile faded as her focus shifted back to Ryan, and then she shrugged. "I'm sure he'd love ta talk ta ya. He's almost blind, and he don't get many visitors." She picked up the phone and asked for someone named Patty to come to the check-in desk. "She'll be here in about fifteen minutes," Deja said after she hung up the phone.

Ryan led Scott outside to sit in the rocking chairs on the porch. He quickly outlined what he'd seen, done, and learned during the last day and a half, minus the encounter with Diane.

Ryan gulped as he remembered Diane, backlit by the flash of lightning, lifting her shirt to expose her ... He shoved that memory aside. This was not the time to revisit it.

"You okay, bro?" Scott asked.

Ryan nodded. "Yeah. This job is more complicated than what I figured it would be."

"Sounds about par for the course," Scott replied.

A few minutes later, Patty arrived in a golf cart. She was nearly sixty, had short, graying brunette hair, and wore khaki shorts and a collared shirt adorned with the Cave Cay logo. Threads of blue varicose veins trailed down her spindly legs to her sturdy work boots. Patty stubbed out the cigarette she'd been smoking in an ashtray as Deja came out the door.

Deja introduced Patty as Shark's mother, then said to the older woman, "I'll only be a moment."

Patty grunted and headed inside while Deja led Ryan and Scott to the vacant golf cart. The three piled aboard and, with Deja driving, careened across the island on one of the dirt roads that crisscrossed Cave Cay. She pulled up to a cottage nestled among willowy pines, coconut palms, and mangroves. The cottage was part of a larger compound that served the needs of the island caretakers and hotel service personnel.

Deja took them into a bright and airy front room bedecked with polished pine on the floor and white shiplap on the walls. The windows had recently been upgraded and had yet to be trimmed out, an oversight Ryan figured was partly due to the speed of the installation and the cost of finish carpentry which probably took money away from other projects. Still, Ryan found the work to be shoddy. His old man would have balked at leaving a job half done and the senior Weller's work ethic had rubbed off on his son.

"Uncle Clivon! Ya got more visitors," Deja called out, then headed for the small kitchen to pour glasses of switcha for the three men.

Ryan and Scott stood beside the wicker furniture and held their sweating glasses as Deja left one glass on the counter and disappeared into another room. Several minutes later, she came back out, holding the elbow of an elderly man. He was bent at the waist from age, his hands gnarled and almost clawlike. He wore tan utility coveralls and canvas boat shoes that Ryan guessed were to protect the old man's feet in case he accidentally kicked a chair leg or some other piece of furniture. The Bahamian's wiry hair was almost completely gray, and his eyes had a milky white cloudiness over the pupils, but he had a bemused smile on his face.

"Sit here, Uncle Clivon," Deja said, guiding him to a wicker rocking chair.

When the old man was comfortable in his chair, Deja fetched his glass of switcha and directed Ryan and Scott to sit across from her uncle in a wicker loveseat. Ryan introduced himself and Scott and then explained the reason for their visit.

Clivon looked thoughtful, his wrinkled mouth turning

down. His voice was shaky as he questioned his visitors. "Are ya friends with Mista Ziegla?"

"We know of him," Ryan replied, thinking of the leader of the ghost search team. "He told you he was the owner of Big Darby Island?"

The old man turned his face toward Ryan's voice, but his eyes had a vacant, glassy stare that was creeping Ryan out.

"He say he represent de owner of de island. He's wantin' to rebuild de ol' house," Clivon said.

It was a plausible story and obtaining the history of the island would be important to potential visitors. "You worked for Guy Baxter?" Ryan asked.

Clivon nodded. "When I was a boy."

Ryan wanted to jump right into whether Baxter was resupplying German U-boats but decided to wait for Clivon to tell his story.

"What did you do for Baxter?" Scott prodded.

The old man leaned back in his chair and sipped from his glass of switcha.

Deja waved to get Ryan and Scott's attention, then motioned she was heading back to work, closing the screen door softly behind her.

Ryan turned back to listen to Clivon telling his tale.

In 1942, Clivon, just a ten-year-old boy, had moved with his parents to Big Darby so they could work on the plantation. Baxter had assigned the youth to help in the livestock pen, feeding the cows, goats, chickens, and sheep, cleaning the caves of their manure, and helping to shear the sheep and butcher the livestock while his parents worked to construct many of the stone walls that crisscrossed the island. The workers used native limestone rock, either plundered by collecting loose rock or quarried when creating the large cisterns under the house.

When not tending the livestock, young Clivon would

work in the machine shop, established by Sir Guy in a two-story building between the main house and the dock constructed in the dredged channel between Big and Little Darby.

"How did Baxter supply the U-boats?" Scott asked.

Clivon turned his vacant stare on the former SEAL. "Ya got no time for de stories of an ol' man?"

"I'd like to hear about the U-boats," Scott replied. He was about to say something else when Ryan cut him off with a touch on his hand.

"Boy, dem was the days! Dat island was so damn buggy, we had to leave every night. Most workers took boats about three miles up island to Lansing Cay and slept on the rocks on de southern point. It was like campin' every day. Wore on a body. My knees is shot, and my eyesight is fadin'. I can see der's two of yas but can't see no detail. What I can see is peoples lookin' for tings dat ain't der."

"What do you mean by that?" Ryan asked.

"Dat other fella, Ziegla. He asked about U-boats, too. Dat be all anyone cares about. Well, let me tell ya someting." Clivon leaned forward. "Sir Guy be a tinhorn, skimpin' on wages and not payin' on time, but he employed more people dan anyone else in de islands at de time. I's got no call stirrin' up memories of a man dead."

"What about the story that the island's workers confronted Baxter and drove him away for helping the Germans?" Scott asked.

Ryan glanced at his friend. Scott had obviously been doing some research about the island's history. There wasn't much about Big Darby Island or Sir Guy Baxter on the Internet. Many of the articles repeated the same information Carlton had given Ryan back on the diving barge in Mexico. A brief scan of the Internet articles took only a few minutes, and there was a plethora of commercial real estate advertisements for Big Darby, mentioning a castle built by a Nazi sympathizer. Sir Guy's disappearance was explained only by the islanders confronting him about aiding the Nazis and asking him to leave.

"Dey ask him," Clivon confirmed. "Der be a long story to get to dat point."

"We've got plenty of time," Ryan said, not eager to return to Big Darby.

Clivon sipped his switcha, and his eyes seemed to stare out the screen door. "I tended de livestock, as I's told ya. One night, Sir Guy come out ta de cave. He seemed agitated and kept pacing around, rubbin' de back of his neck and just actin' jumpy, givin' us de cut eye. My friend James asks de boss what he wants. Sir Guy ordered James to butcher four cows—three more than normal." Clivon held up three gnarled fingers. "James asked me to stay an' help. It took us most of de night with dat ol' man standin' right over us de whole time."

Scott glanced at Ryan with a grin, as if they were finally getting somewhere. Ryan didn't know what Scott was so pleased about. The troubleshooter watched the old man take a long drink from his sweating glass. In the stillness of the house, Ryan could hear a clock ticking and the branch of a tree rubbing against the siding. He picked up his own glass of switcha, tasting the bitter sweetness of the lime drink. Despite it reminding him of his kiss with Diane, it was growing on him, and he made a mental note to look up a recipe for how to make it himself. Why he hadn't drank more of it while cruising through The Bahamas, Ryan wasn't sure. He reckoned it was because of the ready supply of Kalik that, when cold, went down just as easily as water.

Clivon cleared his throat. His eyes seemed to bore straight into Ryan's soul. "I's be wonderin' why two groups of men show up at me doorstep within days of each other ta ask me de same damn ting?"

"A fellow by the name of Steve Carlton purchased Big Darby Island a few months ago," Ryan said, then related the trouble Carlton had been having while clearing the airstrip. "I think the man you spoke to is the one causing trouble for Carlton."

Clivon nodded, sipping his drink.

"Please, Clivon, continue with your story about butchering the cows," Scott said, interrupting the silence in the room.

Clivon cleared his throat and then coughed. "I's be gettin' old. Too old for rememberin' all dis nonsense." He shook his head in dismay. "James and I worked through de night to get dem cows skinned, gutted, and cut up. Two of de carcasses we quartered, den wrapped in butcher paper and took down to de dock. On de way back up de path, I sees a boat come up and de crew load de two cow carcasses into it.

"When James and I got back to de slaughterhouse, Sir Guy asks us if we'd seen anyting while down at de dock. James said no and give me de cut eye. I's no idiot. I's know when ta keep my mouth shut. Two days later, James and I was down in de pens when a policeman came to see us. He wore no uniform but had a badge."

"He was undercover?" Scott clarified.

"Dat's wat ya call it. He undercover. He ask about de beef. I tell him I sees de little boat. James got upset and told me to keep my mouth shut. I say it was like I sees it: de men in de boat took de meat."

"Where did they take it?" Ryan asked.

"De policeman, he tells us dey took it to a German U-boat. Word get around de island, an' de workers be angry. We English no like de Germans. Sir Guy was usin' dat big radio to talk to de submarines. James told me he cut up lots of meat, and de men in de boats come from de submarines. James say de submarines hunt Americans. My parents quit workin' for Sir Guy soon after, an' we went back to Nassau."

"Have you been back to Big Darby since you left with your parents?" Ryan asked.

"Once," Clivon said.

"Did anything change?" Ryan asked.

"Lots be changin'," Clivon stated. "Thirty years of neglect change most everyting."

"Anything in particular?" Ryan pressed. "You said you worked in the caves. Did they change?"

Clivon frowned, lost in thought for a moment. "Come ta think of it, where de pond is on de north end, der used to be a cave. Big'un, too."

Ryan remembered seeing the boot prints that led to the blue hole. Thinking the search team might have been looking for an entrance into the old cave, Ryan asked Clivon, "Did you tell Ziegler about the old cave?"

Clivon shrugged. "Sure."

"What do you think happened to it?" Ryan asked.

"Who knows," Clivon said with another shrug. "De sea reclaims what de sea reclaims."

Ryan pondered that statement. The chances of anything valuable being in the old cave were probably zilch because there wasn't anything of value in any of the other caves. Ryan drained his glass of switcha and stood. "Thank you for your time, Clivon."

"Ya be careful on dat island," Clivon warned. "Dey says de ghost of Sir Guy and his mistress, Ellen, still haunt de ol' house. Dey put de fix on ya."

"I'm not worried about ghosts," Scott said nonchalantly.

Clivon leaned forward in his chair, his chin jutting out toward Scott. "De ghosts ain't be de ones dat need heedin', boy. It's dat Ziegla fella ya needs to worry about. He's a man ya don't wanna cross, hear? I can't see worth a damn, but I's know der someting evil 'round dat man. Whatever he be searchin' for ought ta be left alone."

"I don't know what Ziegler's looking for, but he's keeping the new owner of the island from taking up residence," Ryan said.

"Stay away," Clivon warned.

"I can't do that," Ryan replied.

Clivon sat back in his chair, rocking gently and staring into space.

To Ryan, it felt like an ominous warning from a man who had seen many things in his life. Sure, Clivon might be almost blind, but his other four senses had taken over, giving him a heightened awareness, a hypervigilance, that keyed him into certain emotional and psychological traits that others might have missed.

"Did Ziegler threaten you?" Ryan asked.

"No." Clivon slowly shook his old head. "No. He didn't threaten me. It was just de words he say and de way he say dem."

Ryan nodded for Scott to follow him.

When the bigger man stood, Clivon seized his arm. "Yous be careful. I's tell ya, dem men is *evil*."

CHAPTER TWELVE

The two troubleshooters walked briskly back toward the hotel, both feeling the weight of Clivon's ominous warning.

Ryan had known going into this job, as he did with every gig, that danger was close, yet he was compelled to keep going. He needed the thrill of solving other people's problems and of being of service. Yes, he had plenty of cash in the bank, a beautiful wife, and an oceangoing catamaran with which to escape from the worries of the world, yet if he were to sail away and spend days either at sea or at anchor, he would go stir-crazy. His dreams of dead friends lost on previous missions would return, and he'd become bitter and angry. It was always that way. Here, on the prowl for trouble, fixing a problem others couldn't resolve for themselves, was where Ryan felt most alive.

On every contract, there was a point where Ryan wanted to turn around, run back to his boat, and forget about whatever he was doing, but he always kept plowing through to the end because he couldn't turn his back on someone in need. Diane and her father needed to run Ziegler and his men off

Big Darby, so that's what Ryan would do, despite Clivon's warning.

The motivations of men boiled down to two things: money and sex. There weren't any women on Big Darby Island before Diane showed up, so whatever Ziegler was after had to do with money.

Interrupting Ryan's train of thought, Scott asked, "How did you get here?"

Ryan pointed to the skiff he'd pilfered from Diane.

"Let me grab my bags and check out," Scott said. "I'll meet you back here."

He took off, jogging up the hill toward the cottages, disappearing quickly amongst the riot of bougainvillea.

Ryan walked down the dock to where Shark had the cover off an outboard motor and was changing the spark plugs.

"Two hundred dollars," Shark said as Ryan approached. "Tank took thirty gallons. You was almost empty."

Ryan pulled two one-hundred-dollar bills from his pack and handed them over. "I'll need a receipt."

Shark harrumphed and wiped his hands with a rag before using his shirt sleeve to wipe the sweat from his brow. He waddled up the dock to the floating two-story office. Inside, he scribbled the number of gallons and the dollar amount on a slip of paper and handed it to Ryan.

"You ever see a big, converted tug called the *Leopard* come in here?" Ryan asked.

"Can't get nothing with a draft over ten feet up the channel. How big is the *Leopard*?"

"A hundred feet, at least."

"Won't fit. Draft is too deep," Shark reiterated. "Besides, we don't have enough fuel on the island to fill up a ship like that."

"Is fuel harder to get now?" Ryan asked.

"Used to get two shipments a week. Now, we're down to

one. And last week, I only got half of what I asked for. It's getting to be so a man can't do an honest day's work without it being a giant pain in the ass." Shark clamped his teeth together and his jaw muscles flexed, then he pulled off his ball cap, wiped his forehead, and reseated the hat. "Where's that lovely catamaran of yours?"

"Down in the DR," Ryan replied. "I'm helping out the new owner of Big Darby."

"That German guy? He didn't seem so bad, but those other two he had with him gave me the creeps. Guess he talked to Clivon for about two hours."

"He wanted the history of Big Darby," Ryan explained.

"Not much to know," Shark replied. "It was an overgrown island some British yokel thought he could tame. If I didn't bust my ass twenty-four/seven, this place would be just as overgrown as Big Darby in two weeks."

"Is that why you're selling out?" Ryan asked.

"Living the dream ain't always what it's cracked up to be. Know what I mean?"

Ryan *did* know what Shark meant. The dream often turned out to be a daily grind of monotonous chores, filing paperwork, letting Big Brother steal from you by levying taxes, and then suffering through inflation as the Federal Reserve printed more money in one day than half the nation paid in taxes each year. Ryan wondered what the point of it all was. Working hard to get ahead was like as the old saying went—one step forward and two steps back. Ryan worked because he needed something to do with his life. He felt better when crafting something with his hands or when helping people solve their problems. Whatever dreams he'd had as a kid of the life he'd lead as a grownup hadn't materialized. They'd changed so much that the kid would barely recognize them.

Scott trotted down the dock and set his bags in the skiff.

He kicked off his flip-flops and climbed aboard, sitting at the leaning post behind the wheel. Ryan walked over, tossed off the bow line as Scott started the motor, and then released the stern before stepping aboard and pushing the craft away from the dock. Ryan glanced back to see Shark leaning against the side of his floating workshop, his hands in the pockets of his shorts. Ryan wondered if he, too, was dreaming of motoring away from the island.

Once past the narrow channel leading out of the protected bay of Cave Cay, Scott turned the skiff south. Ryan pointed for Scott to stay close to the western side of Musha Key and the entrance to a five-foot-deep channel of water that ran along the length of David Copperfield's holdings. At the south of Rudder Cut Cay, they stayed between it and Guana Cay, having to increase throttle to battle the current sluicing through the cut.

Once clear, Ryan had Scott motor into the Atlantic. They ran above the shelf that sloped out from the islands to fifty feet of seawater, then dropped steeply into the abyss. Today, the ocean's surface resembled a sheet of hazy sapphire glass. The only wind came from the movement of the boat, whipping past them at fifteen knots. It was a slow cruise down island, taking in the sights and acting like a couple of gawking tourists out for a lark.

"I think we missed your island," Scott called over the noise of the engine as they passed the Darbys.

"I want you to look at the *Leopard*. Tell me what you think of her and if we can board her."

"Don't you remember how that worked out for us last time just the two of us boarded a boat?" Scott asked with a shake of his head. "You got your ass kicked, and we had to be rescued. Don't get me wrong, it was fun, but we got no backup here."

"Let's just check it out and we'll go from there," Ryan replied.

Scott gave him a thumbs-up, and the two men settled back to enjoy the ride through the picturesque islands. A pod of dolphins joined them, racing just under the surface before broaching to arc through the air, sometimes twisting in circles before crashing back in. Ryan smiled as he watched the dolphins play, enjoying the moment and remembering times when he'd been joined by dolphins when sailing. After a few miles, the dolphins veered off to chase a school of small fish that were rippling the surface farther out to sea.

"We've got a couple of nice-looking fishing poles aboard," Scott said. "That looks like a great place to wet a line."

"Sure does, but we're not here to catch fish," Ryan said.

"You take the fun out of everything—but I guess that's what makes you a good team leader."

The skiff continued on, and Ryan looked out across the endless expanse of blue water ahead of them. If truth be told, he hated being the team leader. He could deal with the decision-making and the mission planning, but it was dealing with the consequences that always got to him. Men got hurt. Men died. They haunted his dreams. He preferred to operate like this, as a singleton or in a two-man team, where there was less chance of something going wrong and if someone did get hurt, it would most likely be him. Pain wasn't weakness leaving the body, as his boot camp DIs and EOD instructors had shouted so often. It was atonement for past mistakes.

And Ryan had a lot of mistakes to atone for.

CHAPTER THIRTEEN

Hermann

T he German team leader crossed another grid square off his map.

Surveying the ground was taking much longer than they'd anticipated. Hermann felt their best chance of finding the lost gold was at the north end of the island, either around the crumbling structures built by Sir Guy Baxter or in one of the caves, but Professor Meyer insisted on examining every square inch of the island in a methodical, scientific search to eliminate guesswork. To that effect, Hermann's crew took turns pushing and pulling the compact ground-penetrating radar device housed in a three-wheeled cart. He thought the GPR looked remarkably like the jogging strollers he'd seen women pushing in parks as they tried to eliminate their baby fat with hours of exercise.

While the GPR cart shared some similarities to the jogging stroller with its off-road tires and push handle, what set it apart was the radar device slung from the undercarriage and the electronics nestled into the carrier where the baby would sleep. Atop the handle was a tablet displaying real-time results of the scan. To maneuver the GPR over tree roots, up the steep hills, over limestone rocks washed with seawater, and everywhere in between, one team member pushed from behind while another wore a shoulder harness to pull from the front.

Robert Meyer wiped sweat from his forehead with the back of his hand as he leaned over the tiny computer screen. "The limestone here is dense, and the radar cannot penetrate it so easily."

"You keep saying that," Hermann lamented. "So, why do we keep pushing this thing around?"

"Yeah, let's go to the caves," one of the team piped up. "Surely, the gold is there."

"*Nein*," Meyer admonished in a low growl. "We do this the right way. If not, we'll miss something."

"This island isn't big enough to hide a U-boat," another team member remarked.

"The U-1226 is only seventy-seven meters long," the German professor stated. "This island could easily hide a boat twice that size."

Miffed at the men he'd been saddled with because they were shooters, not explorers, Hermann grabbed the towline for the GPR and started up the hill through the tangle of tree roots, limbs, spiderwebs, wildflowers, and mosquitoes that swarmed every inch of visible skin. Sweat poured off his body as he yanked and jerked the heavy piece of equipment up the slope, cursing it all the way.

Two hours later, Hermann crossed another grid square off his map. They were closing in on the more promising areas of the island, but there was more punishment to be had, as each man took a turn in the GPR's harness with another pushing.

Meyer studied the readout on the tablet as they walked, watching for anomalies under the surface, hoping they would find a cave large enough to hold a submarine.

During one of his breaks, Hermann perched himself on a small stone outcropping and pulled out his map to study it as he sipped water from his canteen. He was glad the *Leopard* had shown up the day before to resupply his little camp. They'd almost been out of food, water, and his favorite apples. With the ship at hand, it would make things easier once they found their objective because she had all the recovery gear aboard the team would need.

Hermann doubted the whole submarine was buried beneath a mountain of limestone rubble. Someone would have remembered a cave that large or have seen the entrance being closed with dynamite. The crewman's diary gave no indication of what had happened to the submarine. That left two possibilities in Ziegler's mind: the sub had either succumbed to snorkel problems and lay on the bottom of the sea somewhere between The Bahamas and Argentina, or the U-boat was hidden somewhere on the island. Only the ancient Bahamian, Clivon, had talked about the collapse of a sea cave at the north end of Big Darby, but he'd said the cave had been landlocked and was in no way large enough to accommodate a submarine the size of the U-1226.

Ziegler was under no illusion that the whole exercise could just be a wild goose chase, but that was what made it so much fun. He closed his eyes and thought back to how he'd gotten drawn into the expedition.

———

HERMANN HAD BEEN on vacation when he'd first heard of The Paladin Group.

He'd been lounging around his mother's penthouse apartment near downtown Berlin, reading magazines and sleeping with the young models who dropped by the house to visit Katrine. It was a relaxing time for the young policeman, but his mother wasn't happy about his lifestyle choices.

One evening, as Hermann was preparing to go out, his mother handed him the business card of a club owner and told him to speak to the man. He'd almost thrown the card away but then decided he might receive VIP treatment from the club owner, which meant free booze and access to the prettiest girls. So, he'd bounced from one bar to the next, until he found himself drawn to the one listed on the card his mother had given to him.

The bar was what was referred to as a *rathskeller*, a beer hall in the basement of a city hall. It had been decades since this building had been a seat of government and had long ago been converted to mixed-use. It was easy to see, from the age of the wood paneling, the worn vinyl on the barstools and booth seats, and the smoke-stained ceiling, that the *rathskeller* had escaped the attempts at modernization.

Hermann ordered a beer and sat at one of the stools at the bar, watching a couple of young women sway to the beat of the music pouring out of hidden speakers. Given it was a Friday night, Hermann had figured the place would be hopping, but there were only a handful of patrons. Disappointed in his mother's choice of drinking establishments, he almost decided to forgo speaking to the owner, but curiosity got the better of him. Hermann hailed the bartender, a gruff-looking, older man with a graying beard, and presented the business card. "Is Herr Fischer around?"

The bartender eyed young Hermann for a long moment as he wiped out a beer stein. He set down the heavy mug, flicked the towel over his shoulder, and examined the card by holding it under a light above the cash register before handing it back to the patron. Using his chin to point the way, the bartender said, "Go past the restrooms and through the door marked 'PRIVATE.' Show the card to the man there."

Hermann, now feeling like he was on a clandestine operation, did as instructed, presenting the card to a squat man in a leather trench coat that obviously concealed a firearm. As a policeman, Hermann knew the man shouldn't be carrying a firearm, but didn't want to ruffle any feathers by demanding the man surrender it, so he casually mentioned to him that he should do a better job of concealing his pistol after he had the business card back in his pocket.

The guard told Hermann to go screw himself, then motioned for him to go through the swinging door. A man with a deeply lined face and thinning white hair swept back off his forehead looked up from his desk as Hermann entered. The GSG officer introduced himself and handed the man the business card.

"Where did you get this?" the older man inquired, flicking it with his finger.

"My mother, Katrine Ziegler, gave it to me."

The man's eyes danced. "Ah, I know your mother well. How is she this fine evening?"

"She was well when I left her. She said I should speak to you."

Herr Fischer asked about Hermann's background, his current work situation, and what he was doing in Berlin, but Hermann soon got the impression that Herr Fischer knew all about him already.

Once Hermann had answered the older man's questions to his satisfaction, Fischer asked, "Are you happy at GSG 9?"

"I enjoy what I do," Hermann replied.

"What if there was something more you could do for your country?" Fischer asked.

Intrigued, Hermann asked, "Like what?"

Fischer scribbled an address on a slip of paper and handed it over to the police officer. "Go there. Enjoy yourself, and we'll talk more."

The secrecy ratcheted up Hermann's curiosity, so he took a taxi to the address Fischer had given him. It was a stately old manor in Charlottenburg, one of the wealthiest neighborhoods in Berlin. Hermann didn't bother to ring the doorbell because a party was clearly in full swing, with music blaring in the background.

As he stepped inside, Hermann wondered why the *Polizei* hadn't been called, before remembering *he* was *die Polizei*. He could shut this rave down but decided to enjoy himself instead, keeping his badge tucked safely into his pocket in case he needed it for later.

Hermann found a plethora of scantily clad beauties and half-dressed men. It wasn't long before he had a drink in his hand and a woman on each arm. He was about to steer them toward an unoccupied bedroom when he saw his mother. She spotted him at almost the same instant and waved, beckoning him to follow her.

With a roll of his eyes, Hermann groaned. He didn't like the mysterious look on her face.

Then, Herr Fischer appeared, and Hermann suddenly found himself being separated from the blondes and escorted to the home's basement.

The rickety stairs led to a dark hovel of a utility room, but there was a secret door recessed into a shelving unit. Behind it was a much larger, well-lit space, adorned with memorabilia from the Third Reich. Two Nazi flags hung from the far wall, with a portrait of Hitler featured prominently between them.

In another photo, a much younger Fischer wore a Waffen-SS uniform even though the man was too young to have been in the war.

A foolish man in a foolish costume, Hermann thought.

But then he spotted another picture that made his blood run cold: his mother and sister standing beside Fischer in their own SS uniforms.

"What is this?" Hermann asked, outraged. The display of memorabilia sickened him. Seeing his family dressed in Nazi regalia made him want to throw up.

"This is one of our secret meeting locations. Upstairs is a party being thrown in your honor, Herr Ziegler," Fischer explained. "It is to celebrate you joining our cause."

"And what is your cause?" Hermann asked, fearing the answer.

"The rise of the Fourth Reich, of course," Katrine stated boldly.

"Mom? You don't believe in this crazy shit, do you?" Hermann asked incredulously.

Katrine placed her hands on her son's cheeks. "I am so proud of you, Hermann. You have become such a wonderful man and an excellent policeman, but it is time for you to join us—your *true* family."

"*No*," Hermann said, his eyes scanning the room, fully taking in all the Nazi propaganda. "My job is to protect the German people from shit like this."

"You don't understand, Hermann," Katrine said earnestly. "Your grandfather was *Lebensborn*. He was born in Norway to a German soldier and a Norwegian mother. In 1943, he was sent to Germany to be raised by good Aryan parents and be educated in the ways of the National Socialist German Workers' Party. He later joined The Paladin Group as a teen, where he met your grandmother, who was also a product of the *Lebensborn* system. I am their daughter, making you *Lebensborn,* too. You spent many days of your youth in daycares run by other members of The Paladin Group. Whether you like it or not, this is your destiny, as it has been ours."

"You keep saying '*Lebensborn.*' What is that?" the GSG operative asked.

Fischer cleared his throat before explaining. "It was a program started by Heinrich Himmler and run by the SS to build a master race. Young women with certain Aryan traits were encouraged to birth as many children as possible. The Nazi Party declared whether those children were racially pure. If not, they were killed. Those they certified as pure were raised, as your grandparents and your parents were, to have socialist ideology."

"My father is a Nazi?" Hermann asked his mother, not remembering the word Nazi being used, but plenty of their socialist rhetoric being spoken during his youth.

"Yes. His parents were also *Lebensborn.* The Paladin Group matched us—Herr Fischer himself—to produce *you*, the fine physical specimen of a man that you've become. It only took three generations, but you and Petra are as pure of Aryan blood as a German can be. Please, Hermann, listen to what we are proposing to you."

"We are asking you to join The Paladin Group," Fischer said. Help us to return our party to prominence."

"And Petra?" Hermann asked, thinking about his older sibling, who could have been his mother's twin with her stunning looks. He pointed to the photo of her in uniform. "I can't believe she's part of this."

"Yes, dear," Katrine replied. "Petra is one of us. She's on assignment, otherwise she would be here to welcome you into the fold."

Aghast at the stunning revelations, Hermann backpedaled toward the door. He couldn't believe that anyone, let alone members of his own family, would willing associate themselves with the Waffen-SS, Hitler, or the Nazi Party. But there he was, in a living nightmare, standing in a room full of Nazi bullshit and learning his whole family was a bunch of diehard believers.

Hermann had always thought that the whole of Germany wanted to shun their shameful past as part of the German collective guilt—a theory born of Allied invention that all German people, not just the SS, were responsible for the Holocaust and the world war. The collective guilt theory had protected many of the former SS rank and file who had escaped prosecution for their war crimes.

Evidently, it had also allowed The Paladin Group to thrive.

If word got out that Hermann had allied himself with Nazism, then his career was over. The men he worked with hated the far right. Everything within him screamed to put as much distance as possible between himself and The Paladin Group and forget all about the harsh revelations about his family and their preposterous beliefs. Hitler was nothing more than a mean little man who had spread hate and discontent. Hermann couldn't think of one positive thing about Hitler other than his death.

"I'm *not* a Nazi," Hermann replied staunchly.

"Listen, my son," his mother said, taking hold of his biceps with both her hands and drawing him away from the door and back to the center of the room. "Forget about politics for now. We want you to help us with another project. One I believe you'll enjoy."

Hermann looked dubiously at his mother's pouting red lips and searching blue eyes, smelling the familiar lemony perfume she always wore.

She placed a hand on his cheek and stroked his high, sharp cheekbone with her thumb, then leaned up and kissed him tenderly on the lips. "I love you, son. I wouldn't ask you to join us if I didn't believe it was the right thing for you."

Her affection had never disgusted him before, but now he

wanted to vomit. In most households, the parents' political ideology influenced the children, but Hermann had been given free will, and his school-age peers had helped him decide the radical right should never be allowed to come to power again. He swallowed hard and gritted his teeth. He couldn't believe he had missed all the signs that his parents were Nazis.

"Come, Hermann," Fischer said authoritatively, sensing the younger man's reluctance as he motioned Hermann to a table laden with maps and documents. "This is the job we have planned. Have you heard of the gold that went missing at the end of the war?" Fischer asked, ignoring Ziegler's statement.

Gold? Now, Hermann's interest was definitely piqued, despite his virulent opposition to joining The Paladin Group.

"Sure. There are lots of myths about what Hitler did with all those Jewish teeth," Hermann said, making light of the fact that the Waffen-SS, who'd overseen the extermination camps, and had often pulled the gold fillings from the teeth of the dead and melted them down into gold bars stamped with the Nazi eagle and swastika. He wondered if his joke was the result of his dark humor, forged from hanging around the men of the *Bundespolizei,* or if it was some deeply ingrained hatred instilled in him by his parents or one of The Paladin Group's nannies.

Herr Fisher smiled. "Some of that gold was put on a submarine bound for Buenos Aires, to help finance the escape of Party members to South America. One submarine in particular, the U-1226, disappeared with five tons of gold aboard. Our researcher, Professor Robert Meyer, has narrowed down where we think it went missing. We have a salvage vessel ready to head for The Bahamas and a group of ex-*Polizei* and military to help search for it. All they need is a leader. Someone with *your* expertise."

"You want me to lead a search for missing Nazi gold?" Hermann asked, glancing between his mother and Herr Fischer.

"Exactly," the older man replied.

Hermann felt a stirring in his soul and in his loins. Hunting for Nazi gold would be the adventure of a lifetime. Upstairs, two blondes awaited his prowess between the sheets. *This night might turn out to be all right, after all.*

"Of course, you'll need to resign from the GSG," Fischer said.

Disappointment coursed through Hermann at having to leave his position with the elite unit. It had taken many years of back-breaking work to achieve his dream.

His mother smiled at him, flashing that infamous grin he'd never been able to resist. She was a classic beauty, and Hermann had taken to bedding blondes because, as Doctor Freud would have put it, he had an Oedipus complex. The sad part was that Hermann knew it. He couldn't help but return her grin.

He didn't give a rat's ass about resurrecting some oppressive regime that desired to take over the world, but searching for gold on an all-expenses-paid junket was the opportunity of a lifetime.

"How soon do we leave?" Hermann asked.

———

"HERMANN!" Meyer shouted.

The team leader struggled to his feet. His leg muscles were rubbery from the arduous task of dragging the heavy GPR through the underbrush on Big Darby. He scrambled down the hill to where Meyer hunched over the GPR's tablet, with the team gathered around him.

"What is it?" Hermann asked, hoping for good news.

"The GPR shows there is a cave below us," the professor announced.

"Where's the entrance?" Hermann asked.

"I'm not sure. We'll need to keep searching."

Hermann glanced around at the overgrown thicket. "Stein, Kessler, keep working the GPR on its track. The rest of you, spread out and search for an entrance."

It took an hour, but the team eventually discovered an opening in the limestone karst hidden behind a tangle of vegetation. The mouth of the cave was barely large enough for Hermann to fit his wide shoulders through. He let the beam of his LED flashlight shove back the darkness to reveal a tight tunnel that sloped downward for about twenty feet before narrowing further.

Hermann pulled his head back out of the hole. Turning to Meyer, he said, "Unless there's a bigger entrance somewhere, I don't think there's any gold in that cave. It's too narrow for anyone to get into."

Meyer looked disappointed. "Then we'll have to keep looking."

CHAPTER FOURTEEN

Ryan

"I count five crewmen and, I'm guessing, a captain, because that dude in the wheelhouse never leaves," Scott Gregory said, lowering the binoculars.

"About what I saw when I was checking things out this morning," Ryan replied.

He bumped the throttle on the Suzuki motor, keeping the bow of the Carolina Skiff pointed toward the cove on the south end of Prime Cay. In between checking out the salvage vessel and keeping their skiff in place, Ryan was casting a big red-and-white Yo-Zuri lure that was already tied onto one of the spinning rods. He didn't care about catching a fish, he just wanted the appearance of being fishermen instead of two guys gawking at the salvage vessel anchored where a vessel of that size wouldn't normally be parked.

"Camp looks deserted," Scott added.

Ryan flicked the lure out, then steadily retrieved it, keeping one eye on the helm and the other on the *Leopard*.

"You said there's a team of six guys in an inflatable," Scott said. "Where do you think they are?"

"Searching Big Darby, I'm guessing," Ryan replied, wiping sweat from his brow. The sun was moving into its noonday position, and without a breeze, the air was just plain hot and exhausting.

"The guys on the boat aren't doing anything but hanging out. I don't think we're going to find any answers here," Scott said. "Let's go see what your *ghosts* are doing."

Ryan stowed the rod, then waited for Scott to move back to the leaning post behind the wheel before shoving the throttle forward and racing toward Big Darby. On the way, he wondered how miffed Diane was going to be at him for commandeering her boat.

Rounding the head of Little Darby, they motored through the cut and slid past Big Darby's enormous sea cave before beaching the boat at the head of Carlton's new runway. Scott carried the skiff's painter across the sand and tied it to the trunk of a small palm. Reaching into his waistband, Ryan checked the Airweight, slipping the cylinder out to see the brass cartridge butts winking in the sunlight, then slamming it home again. The hammer fell on the one empty chamber, leaving four rounds in the J-frame.

Scott pulled his duffel from the boat. "You want a bigger gun?"

"Nah, this is good. I've got the rest of my gear stashed near Diane's tent."

"What do you want me to do with my gear?" Scott asked.

"Let's find a place to hide it, but keep a handgun with you," Ryan replied.

Scott pulled a Springfield XD-M Elite Tactical pistol in flat dark earth from his waterproof gun case, then closed it.

"Twenty-two plus one, baby," Scott said, slipping the gun into a holster at the small of his back. "That pussy Glock you like to carry is short five rounds."

"Maybe you need to take a shooting class," Ryan quipped. "More rounds doesn't make you a better shooter."

Scott grinned. "I took a class. It was called BUD/S. More rounds equals more dead."

"If you say so," Ryan scoffed.

Scott picked out a big clump of mangroves and slid his gear into the center of them, then the two men set out for the camp at the far end of the runway.

About halfway down the strip, they heard the boom of a shotgun. Glancing at each other just as another blast rang through the air, Ryan and Scott took off, sprinting down the runway.

When they reached the tent, both men were breathing hard.

Ryan checked the interior but found no one there. He was about to say something to Scott when the former SEAL put a finger to his lips and pointed up the hill. Ryan held his breath. After a second, he could hear a woman shouting, but he couldn't make out the words.

The two men headed into the jungle, pushing through it as quickly and quietly as they could. As they approached the unseen confrontation, Ryan heard Diane shout, "Get off my island!"

The flat crack of a rifle was her answer.

Again, the shotgun roared.

Incoming rifle rounds sprayed the trees, shredding bark and limbs and leaves. Ryan and Scott dove for the dirt, getting covered in falling debris. Most of the rounds were high, and Ryan figured the shooter was just trying to intimidate Diane or provide cover for whoever she had engaged to make a tactical retreat.

Diane shot back as soon as the automatic fire fell silent.

Hell hath no fury like a scorned woman with a shotgun.

Ryan turned to Scott and whispered, "They don't know you're here. Keep quiet and stay out of sight unless we get into real trouble."

Scott flashed him the "Okay" sign with his fingers.

Wiggling forward, Ryan tried to determine where Diane was hiding. He scanned the slope, spotting a patch of blue from her jeans amongst the tree roots and trunks. He jumped up and ran hunched over up the hill to her position. The shooter must have seen him move because multiple rifles immediately joined the fray.

"You good?" Ryan asked, dropping down beside his charge.

Diane shook her head, her eyes wide. She lay on her back, holding her shotgun across her chest. She'd woven her black hair into a French braid again, but it was now littered with dead leaves. Tears streaked her cheeks.

He reached out and gripped her trembling hand. "Take it easy. You're going to be all right."

Diane nodded slightly. Ryan noticed the barrel of the shotgun had sand and twigs protruding from it. Evidently, she'd jammed it into the ground the last time she'd taken cover.

"Cease fire!" Ryan shouted to the other team. "Cease fire!"

The gunfire died away.

"Who is there?" a voice called back, the German accent prominent and heavy.

"The lady you're shooting at is the owner of this island," Ryan called out.

Again, the German voice replied, "We return fire because we were fired upon."

Ryan got to his feet, then shouted, "Let's parlay!"

"What do you mean?" the voice asked a moment later.

"We meet. No guns. No shooting," Ryan said.

The island was deadly silent for several long moments before the German voice called out, "Come down the slope. There's a clearing here."

Ryan turned to see Scott making his way toward them in a low crouch.

"Hold fire," Ryan called. "We're coming down."

Ryan helped Diane to her feet and brushed the dirt off her backside, starting at her shoulder blades and working down. She gave him a strange look as he swept his palm over her bottom. He immediately withdrew his hands and held them in the air. Again, he hadn't thought his actions through and had meant nothing other than to brush away the dirt that had collected on her clothing.

Diane raised the tail of her shirt and wiped the smudges and tears from her face. Ryan glanced down at her flat, tanned belly and the little silver stud in her belly button.

Get a grip, Weller, he chided himself. *Stop being an asshole.*

Scott arrived and collected the shotgun, opening the chamber and checking the barrel. He held the gun muzzle down and smacked the butt, knocking loose the sand and debris that had collected in the end of the barrel, then he put his eye to the breech to ensure it was clear. A few more smacks later, he declared, "Not perfect, but at least it won't blow up from a plugged barrel."

"Who the hell is *this* guy?" Diane whispered to Ryan.

"He's my backup," Ryan explained. "I warned you about these guys. They're dangerous."

"Then why are we meeting?" she asked.

"Unless we want to hunt each other until we're all dead, we need to meet and figure out what these guys want," Ryan replied.

He pulled out the Airweight from his pants and handed it to Scott. Together, he and Diane walked down the slope while Scott remained in the trees. Ryan didn't like going into this meeting unarmed, but he'd asked for this parlay and had given the terms. He figured their opposition would melt into the woods and keep their automatic weapons trained on them.

Standing in the clearing was the tall blond man Ryan had seen in the camp. Beside him was a slimmer, paler man with rectangular glasses on a rectangular head. He had thick brown hair, brushed straight back off his forehead. Like the blond, the man wore cargo pants, a bush shirt buttoned at the wrists and neck, and tan combat boots. Both men were perspiring heavily, as if they'd recently been doing hard labor.

When Ryan and Diane were within ten paces of the two men, the blond held up his hand. "That's close enough. Frisk them, Artem."

A third man, the camper with the swastika tattoo, came out of the trees armed with a submachine gun and patted them down. Finding nothing but Ryan's tactical folding knife, which he confiscated, Artem grunted something in German, then stepped back into the shade.

"You and your men are trespassing on my island," Diane said flatly.

"Miss Carlton, we have a claim to property on this island. Once we have what we've come for, we'll leave, and you can do whatever your heart desires. Until then, stand clear."

"I will *not* stand clear," Diane insisted. "I *own* this island and you cannot just do whatever you please on it."

The German gave a tired smile. "Then I will not be responsible for your fate."

"What *are* you looking for?" Ryan asked.

"That is none of your concern," the man with the glasses said.

Diane opened her mouth to respond, but Ryan held up his hand to silence her. He figured honey was better for catching flies. And besides, they had common ground. Ryan extended his hand to the taller man. "I'm Ryan Weller. My great-grand-father emigrated from the Westphalia Region."

The big blond raised his eyebrows. "You are of German descent?"

"I am, but I consider myself an American," Ryan replied. "My grandfather probably fought against yours in the war, but that's ancient history. What we need to do is iron out the situation we have here. What is it you need from us?"

The blond looked down at Ryan's hand, then he reached out and shook it. "I'm Hermann Ziegler. My men and I need another week, perhaps two, to finish our work. If you leave us be, there will be no harm. Otherwise ..." He shrugged his broad shoulders.

Based on Ziegler's past actions, Ryan figured the man had no compunction about killing them to achieve his objectives, but he wanted Diane to know he was protecting her and the island. "That's reasonable, but I'd like to stay to watch over Miss Carlton's interests."

"*Nein*," Glasses said.

Ziegler stepped forward. "You must leave the island now. Let us finish our work. When the *Leopard* leaves the area, you will know we are done."

"Listen, Chief," Ryan said, holding his ground. "You and your men are trespassing. You're in possession of automatic weapons, which I assume you didn't declare to the Bahamian government, which makes you criminals in their eyes. And you fired indiscriminately upon us, making you guilty of attempted murder. All of *those* are serious charges and punishable by years in a shitty Bahamian jail, so I suggest you guys clear off before we call the Royal Bahamian Defense Force."

"Tough charges to prove," Ziegler responded, unconcerned.

"Not so tough when they show up and find you still on the island," Ryan said.

"You're making this more difficult than it needs to be," Ziegler stated.

"No. *You're* making it difficult," Diane cut in. "Get off my island or I'll call the authorities."

Glasses appeared nervous over the confrontation. Ryan didn't think the man was a former soldier, but he'd seen nerdy-looking fellows in the military, usually doing some geeky naval rating like aviation electronics technician or information systems tech.

"I suggest you leave now." Ziegler held up a hand in signal. Five men appeared in the tree line with their submachine guns leveled at Ryan and Diane.

Ryan glanced around at the hostile men, then fixed his gaze on Ziegler's face. "Is this about a U-boat?"

A flicker of surprise flashed in Ziegler's blue eyes before being replaced with annoyance. He pointed up the hill the way Ryan and Diane had come. "Leave."

"No!" Diane shouted. "You leave. This is my island."

"Control your woman," Ziegler said to Ryan.

Diane took a step toward Ziegler, her fists balled. Ryan caught her around the waist. "Easy, Diane. We're outnumbered and outgunned."

"Let go of me!" she shrieked, lashing out at him with feet and fists.

While Ziegler and his men looked on, amused, Ryan plucked her off the ground and tossed her across his shoulder. He felt he had little choice in the matter. Diane had gone ballistic at being told to leave her island and then started battling with Ryan so she could attack the Germans.

Ryan started up the hill, hoping Scott was covering their retreat, but a shotgun and two handguns were no match for full-auto SMGs. With each step, he felt Diane's body bouncing against him, her fists pummeling his back. At one point, he took a wicked elbow to the back of the head, almost knocking him off his feet, but he kept moving. He thought that if he stopped, he would never start again because he and Diane would be cut down in a hail of bullets.

"Put me down, you asshole!"

"Calm down, Princess. We need to get beyond their line of fire," Ryan replied, continuing up the hill.

He passed the area where he had found Diane, but Scott was nowhere to be seen. Once they were safely over the rise, he set Diane back on her feet.

"What the hell were you thinking?" she demanded. "You never, ever touch a woman like that."

"You didn't leave me much of a choice. It was either cart you out of there or watch you start a fight you couldn't win and both of us would be dead right now."

Diane's jaw muscles and fists clenched and relaxed multiple times as she digested his statement. Finally, she took a deep breath, staring up at him in bewilderment. "How could you just give up like that?"

"Did you not see the five machine guns aimed at us? It was a relatively easy decision."

"Some troubleshooter you turned out to be," she muttered.

"Let's go to the tent and regroup," Ryan suggested.

Diane turned and headed down the hill toward the runway. She didn't stop until they were standing inside the tent. Ryan could tell she was still pissed at him for throwing her over his shoulder, but he didn't feel like apologizing for having her best interest at heart.

She grabbed a bottle of water and sat down in a chair. "Now what?"

Ryan got a bottle of water for himself and sat silently in a chair opposite her. He drank his water while thinking over the problem. Ziegler had a group of heavily armed men ready to take them out if they decided to stay, but the German had also confirmed Ryan's suspicion that they were looking for something related to a U-boat.

Now that he'd had an up-close encounter with their "ghosts," he knew the job wouldn't be as easy as he'd thought.

Locals making trouble was one thing. A heavily armed group of Germans was another.

———

AN HOUR LATER, Scott came into the tent, carrying the shotgun. He set it and the Airweight on the table.

"Where have you been?" Ryan asked.

"I took a little walk. While you guys were having a chat, I circled around the clearing and found some kind of cart. Looks like a baby stroller." Scott pulled his phone from his back pocket, opened the photo gallery, and showed the picture of the contraption to Ryan and Diane.

"That's a ground-penetrating radar," Diane said. "One of the companies I worked for in Colorado used it for locating underground utilities and buried pipelines."

"What are they using it for here?" Scott asked.

"Finding underground caves," Ryan answered, finally realizing what had made all the tracks he'd seen around the island. "They're searching for a lost U-boat or something the U-boat had aboard."

"What would it have left here?" Diane asked.

"Nazi gold," Scott surmised. "At the end of World War II, Hitler was shipping everything he could out of Germany to keep it out of Allied hands. Submarines full of gold and art were sent to South America to set up a new base in Argentina. If one of those U-boats stopped here before disappearing, then maybe those Germans think the sub is close by or that the crew hid a load of gold on the island. Why else would they be searching so hard?"

"Stands to reason," Ryan agreed. "When I was in their tent, I saw a map with grid squares laid out over the island. They're searching it inch by inch."

"And if they're still looking, it means they haven't found it yet," Scott added.

"So, we're going to sit back and let them do whatever they want on my island?" Diane asked.

"Technically, isn't it your dad's?" Scott asked.

"Technically, you're an asshole, just like your friend, Ryan," Diane replied, with enough snark to prompt Scott to glance at his fellow troubleshooter.

Scott held up his hands in mock surrender. "Take a chill pill, lady. I'm just here to help scare off the ghosts."

"That's what *he* was hired to do," Diane replied sternly, hooking a thumb over her shoulder at Ryan. She stalked to the opening in the tent, threw the flap back then turned to face the two men. "Now get rid of them," she ordered before leaving the tent.

"Someone's got a burr up her ass," Scott said, raising his eyebrows.

"You would, too, if German treasure hunters were tearing up your island and shooting at you."

"Fair point. Now, like the lady said, what are *we* going to do about it?"

Ryan stood, put his hands on the table, and leaned on them. Sighing heavily, he said, "I don't have the slightest idea."

"We can go Rambo and pick them off one by one," Scott suggested.

"No. I don't think that will work. I think these guys are backed by big money. An operation like this—the intensive search, the hired muscle, the salvage vessel—requires a lot of resources. Something tells me that picking off these guys would be like kicking over the hornets' nest. More will come buzzing around, making life a living hell for the Carltons. We need a plan to send them away for good."

Scott stroked his chin in thought. "The only way to do that is to find what they want first and then strike a bargain."

CHAPTER FIFTEEN

Hermann

T he Paladin Group indeed had resources spread across the world.

Those resources consisted of bank accounts in Swiss institutions and offshore holdings worth billions, carefully curated toward the end goal of funding the Fourth Reich. Those accounts were padded by treasure hunts like the one Hermann was now on and by businesses run by sympathetic collaborators. They carried many labels—the alt-right; Aryan supremacists; antisemites; totalitarianists; ultra-nationalists; and neo-Nazis, to name a few.

Hermann Ziegler didn't think he was any of those things. He was an adventurer; a treasure seeker; a hunter of relics. Herr Fischer had promised to send him on more hunts if Hermann produced the gold from the U-1226. He was determined to find it because, as arduous as the search could be at times, it was more fun to be looking for lost artifacts than training to fight terrorists. Just the thought of holding a gold bar in his hand made adrenaline pump through Hermann's veins.

"What is your plan now, Hermann?" Professor Meyer asked when they were aboard the *Leopard* and drinking cold Kalik beer. It was not Hermann's favored Kölsch, a pale ale brewed in Cologne, but it was refreshing in the heat of the day.

Hermann took another sip of beer before replying. "We carry on with the search. If the woman continues to be a problem, we isolate her."

"What does that mean?" Meyer asked.

"It means we force her to leave—or we hold her hostage until we're through."

"We're nearing the end," Meyer said, looking down at the map between himself and the expedition leader.

"For your sake, Professor, I hope your research is correct. If the gold isn't on the island, then we'll have wasted weeks of our time."

"No," Meyer shot back. "We will have eliminated one place it *isn't*."

Hermann pursed his lips. He wished he could fly back to Germany, take a long, hot shower, and bed a couple of rowdy blondes. While the adventure was fun, so was getting laid on a regular basis.

Meyer continued in Hermann's silence. "We started at the far end of the island to eliminate all possibilities. The most logical place to hide the gold is around the Castle or its outbuildings where there are underground cisterns and more numerous caves."

"Big enough to hide an *Unterseeboot?*"

"You have read the diary, Hermann. The crewman said he saw them unloading the crates of gold."

"But what if they reloaded the gold and it now sits on the

seafloor between here and Argentina? Is that not a possibility? The U-boat crew could have repaired the snorkel and reloaded the gold."

"That is a possibility," Meyer conceded.

"Perhaps there are more natives we could speak to about the island? There must be someone who saw what happened to the U-boat," Hermann said.

Meyer shrugged. "It wouldn't hurt to search them out."

Their conversation came to a halt at the sound of an approaching airplane.

A *Leopard* crewman stuck his head into the cabin. He made eye contact with Hermann. "Captain Haas wants you on the bridge, sir."

Hermann followed the crewman up to the bridge, where the captain had a pair of binoculars to his eyes and was watching a seaplane taxi smartly across the water. The pilot kept power to the engine, providing a slight lift to the aircraft, the floats just skimming the water.

"Is there a problem?" Hermann asked.

"Not for me," the captain replied, not bothering to look at the expedition leader.

"Who's on the plane?" Hermann asked. As far as he knew, they weren't expecting visitors.

The captain lowered his binoculars as the plane settled in the water and slowed to a stop. With a wicked grin, he turned to Hermann and said, "Your sister."

"Petra? What is she doing here?" Hermann asked in dismay.

"You'll have to ask her. All I know is that she is more ruthless than you'll ever be, Herr Ziegler."

Hermann considered the captain's choice of words as he watched the *Leopard*'s tender race across the water to the plane. He could take them as an insult, but he'd never known

Captain Haas to be disrespectful. *Perhaps*, Hermann wondered, *the man knows my sister better than I do*.

Petra stepped down to the seaplane's pontoon, tossed two bags into the bottom of the tender, and then stepped lightly aboard. She wore black stretch pants, three-inch heels, a cream-colored blouse, and a scarf knotted loosely at her neck. Her long blonde hair swirled in the air disturbed by the propeller.

Once Petra was seated in the tender, the crewman turned the small vessel away from the plane and headed toward the *Leopard* while the plane turned and began taxiing across the water for takeoff.

Hermann took the steps down to the *Leopard*'s aft deck, standing alongside the rail to welcome his sister aboard. Once the crewmen had the tender tied to the salvage vessel's stern and their tongues back in their mouths, Petra climbed aboard with expert efficiency and instructed the driver of the tender to take her bags to her stateroom. Then, she stepped over to her brother and embraced him.

The length and intimacy of the hug, the warmth of her body, and the smell of her jasmine perfume made Hermann feel a little uncomfortable. She was his sister, after all. When Petra finally let him go, she kept her hands on his shoulders. They were almost the same height, so they could look into each other's blue eyes with ease.

"Welcome to The Paladin Group, brother." Petra kissed him on the cheek. "I didn't think you would join us."

Hermann bit his tongue. He had joined for the adventure, not the ideology, but he was glad to see his sister again. It had been several years since they'd last spent time together, as both had been busy with their jobs and lives. While Hermann had been headquartered in Sankt Augustin, Petra had been globetrotting as a fashion model, living in an apartment with a view of Central Park in New York City. Now, she was on his boat, looking as if she had just stepped from the pages of a trendy magazine.

"To what do we owe the honor, dear sister?"

Petra threw her head back and laughed heartily. "You always were so stiff, Hermann! Is that the police training in you or is it just your natural inclination to rebel against a strong woman?"

Hermann felt his body go rigid. His sister always knew how to push his buttons. In fact, he'd never told anyone they were related when his friends had commented on how beautiful she was based on the magazine spreads she'd appeared in. His initial joy at seeing her had faltered to suspicion as to why she had decided to show up in the middle of nowhere and interfere with his search for the gold.

Because that was what she did. She took control. Just like his mother. Maybe Petra was right: Hermann did have a distaste for women in authority—especially his mother and older sister.

"The question remains, Petra—what are you doing here?"

"I'm taking charge, my dear brother. When our masters determine things are taking too long, they send me in. I'm here to ensure the mission is accomplished."

Hermann felt bitter bile rise in the back of his throat. He swallowed hard, clenching his jaw to keep from lashing out. *Taking too damned long? Have they not seen the island and the conditions we have to endure?*

"Come." Petra looped her arm in her brother's. "Let's go below so you and Professor Meyer can bring me up to speed."

Moments later, seated on the bunks in the small cabin that Hermann and Meyer shared, the two men apprised Petra of the search's latest developments.

"The new owner of the island is a *woman?*" Petra asked once the men had finished speaking.

"Her father actually owns the property," Meyer replied.

"It seems the woman is intent on converting the Castle into a high-end hotel."

Petra tapped her pink manicured nails on the tabletop that held the survey map Meyer had unrolled. "Why didn't we purchase the island?"

"I assume you mean The Paladin Group?" Meyer asked. "It's my understanding that the island had been sold to Steve Carlton just before I discovered the diary. Fischer reached out to Carlton to make him an offer, but he said the island was not for sale."

"If the gold isn't on Big Darby, it would have been a waste of resources," Hermann stated.

"And what would *you* know of our resources?" Petra asked indignantly.

"I don't. I'm just the guy leading the expedition, but it would seem the purchase of the island would be a steep price to pay for failure if we don't locate the gold on it."

"It would be a pittance compared to the market value of that gold, though," Meyer remarked.

"Exactly," Petra said. "But we can't fret over the past. We must secure our future. The gold is ours, gentlemen. It belongs to the heirs of the Reich."

Hermann snorted.

Petra fixed her cold blue eyes on his. "Something wrong, dear brother?"

"Nothing," he replied dismissively. "We have work to do. Please get back on your plane and fly back to your hidey-hole."

"The plane has left, Hermann. I'm here for the duration," Petra said with a smile.

"Then I have a broom you could use to fly out of here," Hermann muttered.

"You always were a jokester," Petra said. "I'll have to remember that one for later. Mother will like it."

Hermann turned to Meyer, and the two began plotting tomorrow's course for the GPR device. They were finally nearing the house, meaning the search would be complete in the next few days, if all went well.

When Meyer left the cabin to find dinner in the galley, Petra leaned across the table and smiled at her little brother. "From what I can see, you've been doing excellent work."

"But?"

"But ... we need to make faster progress. This meeting you had yesterday with the owner was not a smart move."

Hermann's eyes widened, betraying his surprise that she knew about the meeting. Obviously, someone on his team was reporting back to headquarters.

"Don't be alarmed, Hermann. I have informants everywhere. On your team, and even on this ship."

The team leader remained silent. Betrayal was a bitter pill to swallow, but then again, he should have known someone— Meyer, even—was reporting back to Fischer.

"Do you know the history of our organization?" she asked.

"I met with Mother and Herr Fischer. She told me we are *Lebensborn*. They begged me to join The Paladin Group, but she didn't tell me anything else."

"Then I shall set you straight, dear brother." Petra unbuttoned several of the buttons on her blouse, fanning the shirt in and out. "Is it always this hot in here?"

"It's hot everywhere in this cursed country," he replied.

"Get me something cold to drink," she instructed.

Hermann retrieved several bottles of beer from the galley. Upon his return to the cabin, he handed her the beer, then sat on his bunk.

After Petra downed several long swallows of her Kalik, she sat opposite him and began her tale. In the early 1940s, the SS realized the war might not end the way Hitler had hoped. He was driving the army—and Germany, by extension

—to destruction. Members of the SS founded an organization called ODESSA to help spirit themselves safely out of the country.

Juan Perón, the then president of Argentina, provided them with seven thousand blank passports for foreign travel. Thousands of SS men traveled the ratlines into neutral Spain, or over the Alps to Rome, where they were aided by the Catholic clergy there. ODESSA also set itself up comfortably using the ill-gotten gains of mass murder, raping their prisoners of property and money. Flush with resources, the network sought to establish a new Fourth Reich in Argentina, but their organizers soon realized it was impossible due to the ferocious opposition to anything Nazi.

When the new Republic of West Germany was established in 1949, the members of ODESSA set five goals for themselves. First, they reintegrated members of the SS into German society, taking positions across all levels of civil service, using their power and influence to help former SS members escape prosecution and placing them in jobs where they could continue to implement Nazi ideology.

The second goal was to penetrate the political system, organizing at the grassroots level and taking posts in low-level positions inside the ruling party. These men quietly subverted investigations and the prosecution of crimes committed by their comrades. They were aided greatly by the general populace, using the collective guilt syndrome in that as much as one of them was guilty, they were all guilty for allowing the SS to commit their war crimes.

Third, ODESSA used its stolen wealth to place its people in business, commerce, and industry. In the thriving economic boom of the 1950s, those businesses flourished, enriching ODESSA's coffers. With money, they had power and influence.

ODESSA's fourth tenet was to provide top legal defense

for any SS man who stood trial, paying for even the poorest member to have the best legal minds at work on his case.

Hermann wondered how the German people had allowed all this to happen, but he wasn't surprised. ODESSA was probably funding his expedition to find the gold. He gritted his teeth and listened as his sister continued.

"The fifth leg of the stool was propaganda. ODESSA worked tirelessly to enact statutes of limitations for SS crimes and to convince the people that the members of the SS were patriotic soldiers like their comrades in the Wehrmacht. They used advertising dollars to pressure journalists, newspapers, and magazines into looking the other way when it came to investigating former SS and funded propaganda to keep the Nazi ideology alive."

"Wait." Hermann held up a hand, like many he was a student of the second world war. "The Wehrmacht and the SS hated each other. The SS executed thousands of Wehrmacht when they pulled back from fighting the Russians on the Eastern Front, and they killed five thousand after the Wehrmacht tried to assassinate Hitler and take over the country under Operation Valkyrie. How can the men of the Wehrmacht and the men of the SS live side by side?"

"*That* is the real success of ODESSA," Petra said proudly.

"So, how does The Paladin Group fit into this?" Hermann asked, now confused by the tangled web of deceit perpetrated on the German people by the continued efforts of the SS.

"The Paladin Group took over ODESSA assets, including financing and personnel. ODESSA succeeded in their goals, but their primary focus was ensuring the safety of members of the SS after the war. The Paladin Group focused on the future—spreading Nazism through the world. Eventually, it took over ODESSA, setting new goals."

"And those are ...?" Hermann asked, feeling overwhelmed.

"One: that we continue the tradition of *Lebensborn*. Look

at us, brother—we're the perfect Aryan specimens. If we were not brother and sister, we would be paired together."

Hermann snorted. *Paired* with a woman? No wonder his father had slept around. Then he thought more about it. The women his father had slept with were physically much the same as his mother. "Do we have siblings? Was our father impregnating other *Lebensborn*?"

"You're catching on, Hermann. We have ten stepbrothers and sisters. Do you remember Josie?"

"Of course, I do," Hermann replied. How could he forget her? She had been the first girl he'd ever kissed. He remembered fondly the tender moment they'd shared together outside the schoolhouse after much flirting when they were both fourteen.

"She's the oldest of our stepsisters."

Hermann almost gagged. Gone was the precious memory of that intimate moment.

Petra laughed at his distress, causing his cheeks to redden further. She settled quickly and continued with the goals of The Paladin Group.

"Two: we continue to spread propaganda. We have a strong foothold in America. Many of their politicians are democratic socialists and are already pressing our agenda. Three: population control. Hitler started it with the Jews, and we have enlisted many of the world's elite to our side. The Earth cannot support the billions of people who live on it. Four—which goes hand in hand with three—implement our 'One World Government.' We *Lebensborn* will be the rulers. The conspiracy theorists think it's the Rothschilds and the Illuminati, but it's just us: the Nazis. *We're* in charge."

"*Mein Gott!*" Hermann blurted. "Are you insane?"

"No. Absolutely not. Remember, Hermann, you're a part of this now. You're one of us. We work together. We have each other's backs. We're a fraternity of brothers and sisters, just like your police department. In fact, we are more. We are *family*."

"What about my men? Are they all *Lebensborn?*"

"No. They're mercenaries hired to help you. They're expendable once we find the gold."

"Even Meyer?"

"He is *Lebensborn*. Not a big, strong man like you, but privileged nonetheless."

Hermann swallowed hard. He wasn't sure what to make of these new revelations. He had jumped at the chance to hunt for Nazi gold while not understanding the complete picture. He wished he could turn back the clock, to say no to Fischer and his mother and still be employed at GSG 9 to fight these Nazi bastards. Instead, he found he was now one of them.

But he could never go back. He had made a choice. His mother and father had always preached family and unity—and now he understood why. His family was *Lebensborn*. Nazis.

Hermann glanced up from his clasped hands. "What do *you* do for The Paladin Group?"

"I ensure things run smoothly," Petra said matter-of-factly. "And I'm here to ensure this operation stays on course. Now, brother, tell me everything. Especially about this woman, Diane."

CHAPTER SIXTEEN

Petra

Petra Ziegler listened intently to her younger brother. People had always found her easy to talk to, and she put it down to her classic beauty, open smile, and her ability to ask the right question at the right time. It made her an asset within The Paladin Group, but as charming as she was, Petra had a ruthless streak just beneath the surface that she liked to feed by interrogating, humiliating, and then killing men.

When her brother finished his account, culminating with the parlay in the clearing with Diane Carlton and the sturdy fellow of German descent, Ryan Weller, Petra smiled. "It seems, dear brother, that you were too lenient on these people."

"So far, we have been able to do our work without interference," Hermann replied, standing firm. "Killing them would only draw more attention to our work."

"True, but you have yet to find the gold."

"You need to talk to Meyer about that," Hermann said. "He says we need to be methodical, so we don't miss anything."

Petra nodded. She ran a hand through her thick blonde hair that fell to her mid-back. It was hot in the cabin and sweat trickled down her neck and between the cleft of her breasts. She plucked at the shirt again, generating some air movement, then she pulled it off altogether and tossed the silky fabric onto the table bearing the map. She eyed her brother to gauge his reaction. He must have grown used to seeing women in their bras after spending time in the fashion industry and while sating his legendary appetite for blondes. At least he had good enough sense to stay away from brunettes. If he was to father a child, it would be blonde and beautiful and wholly Aryan.

She sat back on the bunk and contemplated the story he had told her about the parlay. It was obvious that the Carlton woman and her friend would be a problem. They weren't going away any time soon, and her brother's "best efforts" had done nothing to scare them off. They needed to get them off the island so Hermann's team could continue the hunt—although Petra was seriously considering putting the professor in charge since her brother seemed to still have the ingrained police instinct to protect civilians.

"The man Diane Carlton was with. What was his name again?"

"Weller. Ryan Weller. He said he was of German descent."

Petra smiled mirthlessly. "Maybe we can use that as leverage."

Hermann shook his big head. "He told me his grandfather fought against the Nazis."

"Against *us*, Hermann," Petra reminded him. "We need leverage to force them off the island, but for that, I need to do some research. Get your men ready to go to Big Darby in the morning to continue the search with the radar device."

Hermann stood and headed out of his cabin to ready the troops while Petra remained, moving closer to the air-conditioning vent to let the trickle of cooler air blow across her sweaty skin. After a moment of standing under the vent, she moved to her own cabin. Her two bags lay atop the single bunk. She changed out of her travel clothes, pulling on a white bikini and terry cloth shorts before slipping her feet into four-hundred-dollar Valentino Garavani sandals she'd purchased at Harrods during a sale. A girl had to shop, right?

Making her way up to the bridge, she found Captain Haas standing with his arms folded across his chest. He wore white uniform shorts, a pressed white shirt with captain's epaulettes on the shoulders, white shoes, and white knee-high socks. He looked more like the captain of a luxury cruise liner than that of a salvage vessel, but his background had been thoroughly vetted and he'd come highly recommended from SMIT International, a Dutch offshore salvage company. Poaching him had cost The Paladin Group a small fortune, but they needed the best money could buy. At least the captain was living up to his end of the bargain, even if her brother wasn't.

Petra had read the dossier of every man aboard the *Leopard* and in her brother's crew, including Hermann's, most of which she knew already. While she had gone off to boarding school at thirteen to be trained by the *Lebensborn* as a covert operative and had then gone on to work in the fashion industry at eighteen, she had kept tabs on her not so "little" brother.

Standing in the shade on the steps outside the bridge door, Petra closed her eyes and relished the wind whipping around her body, cooling her superheated skin. When she felt sufficiently refreshed, Petra dialed a number into her satellite phone. After several long moments, she heard a male voice on the other end of the line, a researcher in Berlin who was part of The Paladin Group.

"I want you to gather all the information you can about a man named Ryan Weller," Petra instructed.

In the background, a keyboard rattled. "There are many Ryan Wellers on the Internet. Do you have any details that will narrow my search?"

"He claimed his ancestors were from the Westphalia Region, and his grandfather fought in the war."

"Hold, please."

Petra waited impatiently as the silent moments ticked passed.

Finally, the researcher came back on the line. "Ryan Weller was born in Wilmington, North Carolina. He served as a member of the U.S. Navy on their Explosive Ordnance Disposal teams. After his military service, he began working for Dark Water Research, a commercial dive and salvage company. After a short stint there, he dropped off the radar until almost two years ago, where his name appears on a marriage certificate in Broward County, Florida."

"Anything else?" Petra asked.

The analyst clicked on his keyboard. "Oh, here's something. He was involved in the rescue of missionaries being held hostage in Haiti six months ago."

Petra's interest piqued. Weller could be a formidable foe.

"I'll have to do more digging. I'll email you a complete dossier by the end of the day," the researcher stated.

"Thank you," Petra said, then terminated the call.

She placed both hands on the railing and stared out at the two large rocks that jutted from the sea in the narrow channel. She thought more about the man who had faced off against her brother. Weller was ex-military, and he knew salvage, so he could be either an asset or a hindrance.

The key, she thought, *is to turn him into an asset. So, how do I do that?*

Petra would have to wait for her researcher to compile his data and forward it to her. Until then, she would look over Meyer's notes to see if they had missed anything. She had read the diary of the U-1226 crewman, as well as Meyer's other research into the missing submarine, while preparing to take over the search for the gold.

She, like Meyer, felt confident that the crew of the U-1226 could not have repaired a damaged snorkel with Guy Baxter's limited facilities. Falkner's diary had said the crew had unloaded the gold from the submarine onto the island, but he hadn't stuck around to see if the gold crates had been reloaded. If they had, Hermann's team would have to search half an ocean between Big Darby and Buenos Aires, but if not —and this was The Paladin Group's hope—the gold was still on Big Darby and easily salvageable.

That hope was waning with each passing day.

Without much else to do, Petra retreated to the ship's stern, slipped off her sandals and shorts, then dove overboard. The water was still warm, but it cooled her body further, relaxing her as she swam toward the beach.

Petra knew the effect she would have on the team of mercenaries when she walked out of the water. They didn't disappoint her, immediately stopping to stare. She walked past them to the tent and entered to find her brother and Meyer poring over a laminated grid map.

Placing a dripping finger on the Green Castle, she said, "Forget the rest. Start here and work north, to the old live-stock caves."

"But we might miss something," Meyer objected. "There's a lot of ground to cover between where we stopped today and where you want us to start tomorrow."

"I've seen your data from the GPR unit," she persisted.

"It's useless. The limestone prevents you from seeing deep into the ground, and the cracks and fissures you've found haven't been big enough to conceal the gold."

"How do you know this?" Hermann asked angrily.

"Because Professor Meyer uploads his data to The Paladin Group servers every night," Petra replied smugly.

Hermann crossed his arms, clearly perturbed. "I agree with Meyer. We need to be methodical."

Incredulously, Meyer said, "*Now* you agree? You've been pushing to search that area since we arrived."

"It's the most logical place to look, based on the number of crates Falkner reported seeing," Petra said. She felt Hermann's siding with Meyer was a way to test her authority. She had no time to waste dealing with pettiness. "Stop bickering. Tomorrow, I'll go with you. I want to see this Carlton woman's campsite."

———

STANDING outside Diane Carlton's tent at the end of the runway on Big Darby Island the next morning, Petra Ziegler took in all the details with a practiced eye. It looked to her as if the campsite was still in use, but no one had spent the night there.

"I think they return to Little Darby every night," her brother said. "Diane Carlton has a runabout she uses to go back and forth."

"I wouldn't want to sleep in that tent, either. It's hot as hell out here," Petra said, fanning herself. Just traversing the half mile of runway had left her sweat-soaked and thankful she hadn't been on the island for the same amount of time her brother and his team had been there.

The conditions were primitive—the air-conditioning nonexistent, the sand gritty, the water salty, and the air too humid. Her hair was starting to frizz, and Petra had to pull it back into a ponytail to keep it off her neck. She rarely wore her hair any other way than down because men found that to be sexier, and her job was to make men weak in the knees to extract as much information as possible. That was why she had pulled the stunt in the white bikini, coming out of the water like a vision that made the mercenaries' jaws drop.

She could feel their eyes on her now. Petra never said "no" outright to any man, always leaving the door of possibility slightly ajar, but she also kept one hand firmly on the knob, ready to slam it shut. Her brother's teammates were all wrong for her, but she wanted them to think they had a shot. If they thought that, it meant they would do anything for her—including taking a life.

Turning to two of the mercs, she ordered them to stand guard at the tent and report back if Diane Carlton or Ryan Weller showed up, then she told her brother to lead the way to the Green Castle.

Like so many visitors before her, Petra walked through the crumbling structures and tried to imagine what the place had looked like when Guy Baxter had lived there. The kitchen was sparse—a white cast iron sink set into faded wooden cabinets reminiscent of old farmhouses. Here and there, pockets of beautiful handmade tiles lined the walls. Petra ran the tip of her finger over the ornate flower designs, feeling the layers of hand-painted blue under the baked-on glaze.

While she explored the house, Hermann's team located the covers of the three large cisterns situated near the Castle. When they uncovered the first one, Petra walked over to look down into the black hole. One of the mercs shone a light onto the oily surface of the water below.

Petra had figured the cisterns would be full to over-flowing and had insisted the men hike in scuba equipment, but this one was only partially full. Without waiting for orders, the man she knew as Steiner zipped himself into a black drysuit, then pulled on the harness that held a silver air tank. He donned a full-face diving mask before the rest of the team lowered him into the cistern via a climbing rope.

Attached to Steiner's mask was a video camera and sending unit that beamed what he was seeing to Meyer's tablet. Petra and her brother looked over Meyer's shoulders at the screen. The big beam of light from the diver's hand-held illuminated the interior of the cistern with ease.

Sir Guy had lined the cisterns with concrete, much like a swimming pool, but the mixture must have been tainted with either too much lime or too much sand. The concrete had completely flaked off the limestone on the eastern wall, allowing groundwater to seep in.

Steiner waded carefully around the bottom, testing each footstep before declaring the cistern devoid of anything but mud and debris that had fallen in over the years. The team hauled him out and moved to the next cistern, leaving the grate off the top.

Neither of the other two cisterns held crates of gold; just a collection of random trash dropped by tourists, old construction debris, tadpoles, and dead leaves. Petra tried to contain her disappointment. She knew it would be too easy for the gold to be hidden in the cisterns, and she feared that someone else might have already found it. However, there was no sign of wooden crates or packing material, though, as Meyer had pointed out to her, the wood would have deteriorated into mush after being submerged in water for seventy plus years.

"Where to next?" Hermann asked as Steiner took off his dive gear and guzzled water.

"I think we split up," Meyer said. "I'll take three men and continue the search with the GPR, and the rest will search the caves. This means we need to pull the guards from the tent. Our priority is the gold, not Diane Carlton."

"I agree with Meyer," Hermann said. Turning to Petra, he added, "It's the best way to continue this hunt. Searching for treasure is about being methodical, checking off the boxes. It's a lot like police work."

"Fine," Petra replied, lips pursing as she drew in a deep breath. They were right this time. Splitting the team was the best way to go. But she was scheming over how to add a third element to the mix—Weller and his salvage expertise.

While Hermann and Meyer recalled the two men she'd stationed outside the tent and then divided the team, planning to swap out at intervals to keep the men pulling the GPR unit from becoming exhausted in the heat, Petra climbed the rickety stairs to the second-story balcony of the Green Castle. Down at ground level, the trees blocked the wind, but above them, the gentle breeze cooled her. She stared out at the island, slowly turning, trying to imagine everything as it had been in Sir Guy Baxter's day.

"Where did you put it?" she whispered into the wind.

As Petra took in the island's beauty, she heard an outboard engine start. From her perch, she could see a center console leave the dock behind The Drifts Lodge and idle across Darby Channel. She couldn't tell how many people were on the boat because the T-Top blocked her view, but she figured it was the Carlton woman and her boyfriend, Weller.

Earlier that morning, Petra's researcher had emailed her a file on the former EOD tech. Weller was a capable foe, one she would have liked to have gotten to know more intimately under different circumstances. He had been trained to disarm explosives and had experienced war firsthand, deploying to Iraq and Afghanistan and other hot spots around the globe, fighting America's interventionist wars. After ten years in the Navy, Weller had gotten out and spent time as a carpenter, then joined his friend Greg Olsen at Dark Water Research as a commercial diver.

Petra knew his real job had been to work with the Department of Homeland Security.

Later, Weller had distanced himself from both entities, but he'd remained an independent contractor, operating all around the Caribbean. His legend had grown following several high-profile cases. Despite using aliases and trying to keep his name out of the papers, Weller had been associated with stopping an explosive-laden ship from detonating its payload in Fort Lauderdale, and the word on the street was that he'd tangled with Chinese Special Forces in Jamaica while recapturing a top-secret U.S. satellite.

But Petra was more interested in Weller's ability to find people. The story she had heard about Haiti was that not only had Weller led the team that saved the missionaries, but he'd also uncovered a conspiracy to commit voter fraud in the country and had tracked down the elusive man behind the scheme. If that was true, then Weller would be an excellent asset to put into play.

If Weller wanted to do his job and protect Diane Carlton, then Petra would use that as leverage to force him to help her find the gold.

As Petra watched with her hand shading her eyes, the center console made a wide arc around the northern end of the island, then stopped on the beach at the end of the runway. She borrowed her brother's binoculars and zoomed in on the two figures clambering over the gunwale.

Petra was delighted to finally lay eyes on her two foes. They made quite the pair, him a full foot taller than her. She focused on Weller's face, seeing the animation in it as he spoke, explaining something to Diane.

For a married man, Petra thought Weller appeared awfully chummy with a woman who wasn't his wife. She'd seen that look before. She'd been the object of that puppy dog expression many times, and Petra had used it to her advantage before.

Just as she would use it now. *Motivation*, she thought.

Men did stupid things for women, even those who weren't their significant other. An elderly gentleman who had served on the Senate Armed Forces Committee and had shared government secrets with Petra after bedding her had tried to explain it as chivalry, the dying art of protecting the weak and a quixotic notion that men must polish the armor, sharpen the sword, and ride forth on the white steed to fight for the fair maiden and to protect the kingdom.

Petra had preyed many times on the fantasies of those knights-errant, allowing them to partake in their delusions and bed the fair maiden before playing them like the useful idiots they were. She had made full use of the technique to get information, national secrets, and encrypted passwords, and in Ryan Weller's case, she would use it to find their missing gold.

Petra knew other men like Weller. They had a yearning for adventure, the desire to serve their country and fellow man, and they used their quick wit and eager smiles to win approval—much like her brother.

Before this was over, Petra would test her brother's resolve and his dedication to the cause. While her mother and Herr Fischer thought highly of Hermann, she wasn't convinced of his loyalty to The Paladin Group.

And while she ensured her brother's compliance, she would test Weller's resolve, too.

CHAPTER SEVENTEEN

Diane

Climbing over the gunwale of the skiff, Diane pulled the bow line across the sand and tied it off to the same palm tree as Scott had the day before, then she stood in the shade, waiting for Ryan to join her. She was still royally pissed about him carrying her up the hill away from the Germans, but she also understood his reasoning. When she'd stepped toward the team leader, her intent had been to gouge his eyes out.

She was also angry that he'd taken her skiff yesterday morning, but she also understood he was only trying to do his job. In some way, she knew he was also trying to put some distance between them after she had thrown herself at him. When he'd dumped her on the floor and fled to his room, Diane's first thought was that he might be gay, but she had also seen the animal hunger in his eyes after she'd removed her top.

As Ryan approached her now, Diane noticed he was looking at her differently. His gaze had a stoic flatness to it. He was good at bluffing, but not good enough to hide the combination of pain and desire that hid behind his hooded eyes.

"I have something to confess," Ryan said when he reached her position.

Diane kept her mouth shut, wanting to hear what he had to say since they hadn't had time to speak privately with Scott around last night.

"I'm married," he said. "I should have told you that right away."

Yeah, she thought. *You should've. Then I wouldn't have made a fool of myself.*

"Why don't you wear a ring?" she asked. "That would be a dead giveaway."

"Rings are a hazard in my line of work. I've seen too many men get their fingers ripped off because of them."

"They make special rubber ones now," Diane replied.

"I know. I just ..." Ryan trailed off, then started walking up the runway.

Diane had to quicken her pace to keep up with his longer strides. Together, they walked silently through the sand, avoiding the big holes blasted into the earth to prevent a plane from landing. It still irritated her that Hermann and his men had caused so much destruction.

She found herself breathing hard in the humid air. The going should have been easy for a woman who prided herself on staying in shape, but the soft sand sapped her strength quickly.

"So, what's the plan?" she asked, choosing to focus on business rather than probing further into the awkwardness between her and Ryan.

"Scott will stay in the shadows. He's an asset as long as

Ziegler and his men don't know he's here. Our goal is to find the gold they're searching for first."

"Finders keepers," Diane added.

"Something like that."

"Is that why you put the contingency clause in the contract with my father? You knew there was gold on the island, and you wanted your share?" Diane asked. She had spoken to her father yesterday and he'd explained his reasons for hiring Ryan and had emailed her a copy of their contract to look over.

"It's a standard condition I put in all my contracts when doing this sort of work."

"Did you know who you would be facing before you arrived?" she demanded.

"Diane," he said tiredly, "until we walked into that clearing yesterday and met Ziegler and his men, I had no idea who we were up against. Quite frankly, if I'd known this was some sort of military-style operation, I might not have taken the job."

"So why did you bring Scott?"

"Because every operator needs backup, and Scott is the best there is."

"Does your wife know you're here?"

"No. She thinks I'm still in Mexico, working a commercial diving job," Ryan said.

Seems it's not just me he's been lying to, she thought sullenly. "Why didn't you tell her?"

"Because I thought it would be easier for her to worry about me on a barge in the middle of the ocean than it was to worry about me possibly getting shot at."

"Speaking from a woman's point of view, she's going to be pissed."

"Maybe."

Diane kept pressing as they neared the tent. "Are you going to tell her about kissing me?"

"*You* kissed me," Ryan stated with conviction.

"Semantics. Our lips touched, ergo a kiss. And if I remember correctly, you hesitated before dumping me on the ground."

"I don't want to talk about it," he said flatly.

She smiled, victorious. Diane knew the truth, even if Ryan was lying to himself. He had kissed her back, if only for an instant before his better judgment took hold. Now that she knew he was married, Diane understood his reaction, but she still had a bruise on her ego and one to match on her tailbone.

Diane didn't know why she took such joy in poking the bear, but it delighted her to see the color rise on Ryan's cheeks and enjoyed hearing him stammer as he tried to palm their kiss off as something she had done alone. She had gotten a reaction from him, whether he liked it or not. When they'd been sitting on the porch, surrounded by those brilliant flashes of lightning, she had seen the lust in his eyes. It had been quite a while since she had wanted anyone as much as she had desired Ryan. Knowing he was married didn't switch off her hormones, but she could chalk it up to her biological clock ticking away.

Ryan came to a stop just outside the tent and pointed to fresh tracks in the sand.

Diane pushed past him and tossed the tent flap aside. After a quick survey, she saw nothing out of place.

"I don't know why they're searching around here," Diane said.

"They're probably keeping an eye on us. You threatened them pretty good yesterday."

"Not well enough," she replied, crossing her arms. "They're obviously still on my island."

She watched Ryan grab a bottle of water and asked him to hand her one. He slid it across the table before opening his own and taking a long drink. Diane did the same, the water warm but still refreshing.

"Where do we start looking?" she asked when she'd lowered the bottle from her lips.

The tent flap opened, and a six-foot-tall blonde entered. "That's an excellent question, Diane."

Diane immediately wondered who this woman was and at the same time felt intimidated by her. It wasn't just the height—Diane knew plenty of taller women—it was her physical beauty and the way she carried herself. She had a resounding self-assurance that seemed to ooze out of her, as if she knew every man wanted her and every woman wanted to be her.

Hermann Ziegler entered the tent next.

Diane immediately saw the family resemblance between the siblings, registering their slim noses, high cheekbones, penetrating blue eyes, and the way they stood, poised as if ready to walk down the catwalk. Diane had seen this woman before. *What the hell is her name?*

"I'm Petra," the woman said, answering Diane's unspoken question. "You've already met my brother, Hermann."

Suddenly, Diane knew exactly where she had seen her: Petra Ziegler had graced the cover of a prominent fashion magazine last fall. Diane rarely paid attention to those rags. In her mind, they catered to the lower class, who had nothing better to do than scour the articles for beauty tips or the latest celebrity gossip. However, she'd been at a doctor's office in Baltimore for a yearly checkup and had picked up a copy of *Vogue* because she was bored. Petra had been blowing a kiss from the magazine cover in a stunning red sheath dress, bright red lipstick, matching high heels, and windblown hair.

Diane had resented the woman then just for her smug

good looks. She hated her now for her smug arrogance. The nerve of this woman, walking into *her* tent on *her* island!

"What can we do for you, Petra?" Ryan asked, bringing Diane back to her original question.

Diane had a feeling that whatever Petra said, it wasn't going to be good. She wondered if Ryan knew Petra was a model, which also made Diane feel there was something incongruous about Petra suddenly appearing on her island. Since she was with Hermann, Diane could only suspect it was for nefarious reasons.

Her jovial mood at teasing Ryan slipped into a glower that puckered her bottom lip and furrowed her brow. She glanced at her troubleshooter. His face was open and his expression blank, despite the smile on his lips being completely plastic, and his eyes had changed from a sparkling amazonite at being teased to hard malachite at the unfolding danger.

Diane shivered. Until that very moment, she had doubted Ryan's ability to scare off these people, despite her father's assurances that Ryan was one of the toughest men he could have hired. The look she now saw in Ryan's eyes scared her.

Petra stepped closer to the table separating Ryan and Diane. "What you can do is vacate this island until my team and I have finished recovering what we came for."

Diane's hackles were already up, but Petra's demand made them stand on end. Slowly, she rose to face Petra, trying desperately to keep her anger in check, unlike their first encounter with Hermann. She didn't know why these people brought out such hatred in her. "Listen here, you bitch— everything on *this* island belongs to *me*. You have no business being here, and neither does your brother. I want all of you to *leave*."

Petra used the tip of her right forefinger to wipe away a speck of spittle from the side of her nose. Her demeanor immediately shifted from neutral to hostile. The skin above her collarbone flushed red, and a vein pulsed in her neck.

Diane sensed a malevolent violence ready to spring forth from Petra as the German model leaned forward to bring her nose within an inch of Diane's face. A hint of jasmine wafted off Petra's sweaty skin.

"*I* am in charge here," Petra growled, her voice low and menacing. "You will do everything I say. If you do not, I will not be responsible for what happens."

"And what will happen?" Diane asked, fists balling.

"Your father will mourn the loss of his daughter," Petra replied dispassionately.

Diane wanted to recoil, but she stood her ground, staring right back into Petra's cobalt blue eyes. She noticed tiny flecks of gold in the German woman's irises.

"We're not leaving," Ryan declared, inserting himself between the two women and breaking their staring contest. Diane breathed a sigh of relief as Petra backed out of her personal space. Ryan's hand on her shoulder was reassuring, but the look of warning from him helped curb the burning desire to claw the model's face and scar her for life.

Without looking at her brother, Petra snapped her fingers. Hermann held open the tent flap so everyone could see the contingent of armed men standing in the clearing. He spoke a few words in German, and three of his men entered the tent. They searched Ryan, taking the Airweight from his belt and a new tactical folding knife from his pocket that he'd gotten from his gear bag to replace the one Artem had confiscated before their parlay. The men then searched Diane, their rough hands groping her body. She felt thoroughly violated.

"Take them to their boat," Petra ordered.

The thugs used their gun barrels to prod Ryan and Diane out of the tent. Petra scooped up the Airweight on her way out as her brother gave an order to one of his men. "Search the tent for the shotgun she had yesterday."

Diane felt her heart sink. Now, they were going to tear apart her living quarters. She was starting to think the island was cursed, just like some of the older Bahamians had told her, and that she should just forget the idea of turning Big Darby into a resort. There had to be a reason why no one else had purchased the island when islands up and down the chain had already been snapped up by wealthy individuals and corporations.

The small procession marched down the runway to Diane's skiff. Petra and her brother climbed into the boat beside Ryan and Diane. Petra ordered the gunmen to push them off the sand, and once they were in deeper water, she turned to Diane, issuing another order. "Drive to Little Darby."

With no alternative, Diane motored them across the narrow cut. Looking over her shoulder, she saw a man with an automatic rifle standing on her concrete quay. Petra must have posted guards to ensure that Diane and Ryan wouldn't return to Big Darby.

At the dock behind The Drifts Lodge, Petra told Ryan and Diane to get out of the boat. Before she and Hermann motored off in it, Petra said, "Don't come back to Big Darby until you hear from me. There will be consequences if you interfere again."

When the skiff was out of earshot, Diane cried, "That bitch just took my boat!"

"It's okay," Ryan said calmly, placing a reassuring hand on her shoulder. "We'll get it back."

Diane looked at him curiously. She was burning with anger at the gross violation of her human rights—she'd been rejected, groped, robbed, kicked off her own property, and had her life threatened. The troubleshooter's face, however, was still stoic, but she could see the maniacal gleam in his eye.

"What are you going to do?" she asked.

With a smile that turned Diane's insides to ice, Ryan replied, "What I was hired to do."

CHAPTER EIGHTEEN

Ryan

It was just past ten p.m. when Ryan crawled out of the water and up the beach to the tree line on Big Darby. He crouched in a thicket, allowing the stout breeze that howled up from the southeast to dry the saltwater on his skin. As he waited to see if anyone had noticed him, a light rain began to fall.

Suspecting the Germans had retired to the *Leopard* to wait out the coming storm, Ryan figured it was the perfect time to slip back onto Big Darby and check on Scott. The former SEAL was probably holed up somewhere, waiting for the blow to pass.

Ryan donned the clothes he'd brought along in a dry bag, pulling them up over his Speedo. While the bag had saved them from the ravages of the ocean, they quickly dampened in the rain.

After lacing up his boots, he started across the island,

finding the going easier along one of the stone walls that ran up and over the ridge to the largest of the salt ponds beyond.

At the crest of the ridge, Ryan left the comfort of the wall and headed north, tracking the hulking shape of the Green Castle against the lighter night sky. The going was tough through the overgrown foliage. Deciding the risk was worth the reward of not breaking a leg, he turned on his flashlight. He'd capped the lens with a red cover to aid his night vision and prevent his beam from stabbing through the darkness and giving away his position.

With the red illumination guiding his way, Ryan's travels became measurably easier. He walked along the top of the ridge toward the abandoned utility shed where he and Scott had agreed to meet earlier.

As Ryan approached the house, he paused to switch off his light. He stood there in the darkness, listening for anything out of the ordinary, but the patter of rain on the tree leaves dulled all sounds.

He was about to move when he spotted a flare of light in an upstairs window. The smoker shielded the flame, and it was replaced by the red glow of a cigarette cherry. Scott didn't smoke, so that meant the Zieglers had left a guard to stand watch overnight. The Germans were serious about attempting to keep Ryan and Diane off the island.

When the smoker moved away from the window, Ryan began a circuitous route through the foliage to reach the rear of the house. He kept his light off and crept along, placing his feet gently on the forest floor to keep from stepping on fallen branches or rolling an ankle on a rock outcropping.

It took the former EOD tech twenty minutes to make his way around the Castle to the utility room. Before rushing in, he stopped to observe the area again. If there was one guard, there was probably more. Hopefully, the rain had driven them undercover. Even professional soldiers didn't like standing out in the elements.

After another five minutes of being drenched by the rain, Ryan moved forward. He entered the old building, the rain falling through the missing roof and second-story floor to pelt him on the head and shoulders. The fat drops fell even harder now. Ryan backed up two steps to stand in the doorway, somewhat shielded by the vertical wall. Scott wasn't in the building. The ancient generator, despite its size, didn't provide the cover needed to hide a man as large as Scott.

Ryan nearly jumped out of his skin when a pebble bounced off his chest. A hushed snickering came from the bushes, and Ryan grinned as another pebble bounced off his shoulder. He glanced around the corner of the utility shed at the big house to see if any guards were present, then moved into the brush when he saw the coast was clear.

Scott rose from a crouch as Ryan approached, but the two men didn't stick around, instead following a narrow path to the entrance of the old livestock caves. Once inside, Scott switched on his own flashlight, and the two red beams provided enough light for them to avoid banging their knees on the rocks jutting up from the ground.

Inside the cooler cave, Ryan shivered in his wet clothing. He had dry clothing in the bag he'd been forced to leave in Diane's tent when the Zieglers had marched them off the island earlier that day.

"What's the scoop?" Ryan asked, using the edge of his hand to wick the water from his exposed skin.

"The Bobbsey Twins went back to their boat. They left three guards: one at the dock, one at the tent, and one in the Castle."

"I saw that one," Ryan commented.

"Where'd you come ashore?"

"Down near the southern tip. I swam across the channel."

"And you walked across the island in the dark? You're a brave man."

"Stupid is more like it, but I wanted to check on you."

"I'm good to go. I pretty much holed up here when the rain started, but knowing we were meeting at the shed, I made my way up there. What's the plan?"

"We even the odds a bit," Ryan replied. "The guards are isolated so we can easily take them out."

"And do what with them?"

Ryan shrugged. "We tie them up and keep them some-place safe until this is over, then let them go."

"We'd have to take them to another island. Little Darby would be the easiest. There's a storage shed behind the scientific station."

"Let's take the guard by the dock first," Ryan said, "then the one in the house. We can take the one in the tent last."

The former SEAL rubbed his hands together. "Sounds like a plan. I've been dying for some action."

CHAPTER NINETEEN

Ryan and Scott left the confines of the sea cave and made their way down the wide path toward the concrete dock in the channel between Big and Little Darby Islands.

They were careful to stay in the shadows, allowing the trees to mask their movements and break up their silhouettes. As they approached the dock, they paused to observe the miserable-looking guard as he huddled with his hands in the pocket of the raincoat and his hood raised against the elements.

Scott slipped off his backpack before handing it to Ryan, then motioned for Ryan to act as a decoy. Ryan concurred. His friend had a lot more training and experience at quietly dispatching bad guys, but normally the SEALs took guards out with kill shots from silenced pistols, knives slipped between ribs, or even snapping necks with their bare hands. Ryan grabbed Scott's arm before he could move off and warned him not to kill the guard.

With a roll of his eyes, Scott shook off Ryan's hand, then

motioned him forward with a crisp knife hand. When Ryan was almost to the dock, he stopped and waited for Scott to signal that he was ready.

Once Scott gave an "Okay" sign, Ryan moved forward again, purposely stepping on a large branch to alert the guard to his presence.

The sound didn't cause the man to turn.

Ryan figured the rain pounding on the guard's hood was probably blocking the sound. Scott motioned for Ryan to distract the guard.

Ryan picked up a chunk of the branch and winged it at the guard. The branch smacked the man square in the back. He spun on instinct, bringing up his SMG to aim at Ryan, who immediately threw up his hands.

Before Guard One could move again, Scott sprang into action. He swung his arm back and nailed the guard in the side of the head with a short black object.

The guard crumpled to the cracked concrete.

Ryan ran over to help Scott corral their prisoner. He saw Scott slipping a leather sap into his back pocket before rolling the guard over and stripping away the submachine gun.

From his backpack, Scott pulled out flex cuffs, put a pair around the unconscious guard's feet, and then cuffed the man's hands behind his back. Stuffing a roll of the man's shirt into his mouth to complete his binding, Ryan and Scott dragged him off the dock and into the trees.

Scott brushed off his hands. "One down. Two to go."

The two men walked up the trail to the house, deciding it was best to lure the smoker down the stairs and out the door to avoid having to wrestle among the debris inside, risking injury to themselves or the guard. Determining where Guard Two was inside the house turned out to be pretty easy. He was still leaning against the doorway that led to the balcony on the second floor, right where he'd been when Ryan had last seen him.

Ryan stood on the stoop and leaned through the open door of what would have been the kitchen at the rear of the house. He let out a shrill whistle, confident the walls of the house would contain it from traveling farther and thus alerting the third guard in the tent.

Above them, the floorboards creaked as Guard Two walked toward the stairs. He called out something in German that Ryan didn't understand.

"Hey, you wanna play?" Ryan called out softly, trying to make his voice sound eerie, thinking about the ghost stories he'd heard about Sir Guy haunting his old house and hoping the guard was thinking about them, too.

Guard Two clumped down the stairs, gun at the ready. The stocky man's face appeared white as a sheet as he stepped off the last stair. Ryan called softly to the man again from outside the house. Scott stood at the ready, back pressed against the exterior wall, sap raised high.

Ryan and Scott could hear the guard moving about and shielded their eyes from the bright beam of his flashlight. Holding his own light so it was visible in the doorway, Ryan flashed the red beam several times, then withdrew it.

The guard moved quickly toward the opening to investigate.

When the mercenary passed through, Scott smacked him on the back of the head with the sap and he toppled forward, burying his face in the dirt.

The two contractors flex cuffed Guard Two and stuffed a rag the man carried to wipe away the rain into his mouth. With the second German out of the game, Ryan and Scott had to decide how to transport him to the dock.

"Ever heard of a travois?" Scott asked.

"Is that some sort of cowboy shit you just made up?"

Scott grunted in disapproval. "No. The Indians used to use them for transporting heavy loads. It's made of two sticks bound together at one end to form a 'V.' The load is piled into a sling between the poles."

"That might work," Ryan conceded. "Let's wait to build it down by the tent. There are some poles there that might suit our needs."

"And we can make one trip hauling two men," Scott pointed out.

Ryan led the way down the slope toward the tent, carrying Guard Two's H&K UMP40. The German-made SMG had a thirty-round magazine loaded with .40 caliber hollow points and a two-shot burst mode on the fire selector switch. It was a handy weapon to have since Petra Ziegler had taken the Airweight and Ryan hadn't had time to return to his cache to rearm himself.

As they approached the canvas tent from behind, moving through the trees like wraiths, a soft glow from the interior of the structure provided plenty of illumination for the two contractors to see by. Ryan smelled something cooking and figured Guard Three had raided Diane's food rations.

Without hesitation, the two men burst into the tent. The unsuspecting guard glanced up in surprise from where he was warming a can of beef stew over a propane burner, his rifle well out of reach.

"Hands up, Kraut," Scott commanded.

The guard eyed the can of stew for a moment then sighed, as if he knew he wouldn't get to eat his meal. He slowly raised his hands. Scott moved in to cuff him but instead gave him a sharp rap on the skull with the sap. Guard Three fell to the floor.

Scott cuffed his hands and feet, then found one of Diane's socks to stuff into the German's mouth.

Ryan gathered up the other UMP as Scott shut off the camp stove and found a hot pad with which to lift the can. He also found a spoon and began devouring the warm food, blowing on each bite to cool it before chewing. With his mouth full, he looked at Ryan and shrugged. "I'm starving."

"I bet. Eat up while I'll start on the travois. There's plenty of rope in here and limbs outside."

"Screw that. I have a better idea. Let's use the backhoe. It would make short work of moving these bozos."

Ryan shrugged. "Steve Carlton thinks there's sand in the tanks."

"Figures," Scott grumbled.

"If you can get it running, we'll use it. In the meantime, I'll start on the travois."

Ryan picked up a coil of rope and headed for the tent flap. "And clean yourself up while you're at it. You dribbled stew on your shirt."

Scott glanced down at the brown stain and shrugged again before spooning in another mouthful. Ryan shook his head at his friend's antics and headed out to find poles for the travois. He couldn't blame Scott for eating the stew. He figured Scott was probably ravenously hungry after spending the day alone on the island.

Remembering where two long poles lay off to the side of the clearing, Ryan headed there, using the beam of his flashlight to find them. He soon shouldered the poles and headed back toward the tent. When Ryan rounded the heavy equipment, he saw Scott shining a light into an open access panel on the side of the yellow backhoe.

"What are you doing?" Ryan asked, peering over his friend's shoulder.

"I'm looking at the fuel separator. I see some water at the bottom, but no sand."

"Carlton said they'd been tampered with," Ryan reminded him.

Scott shone his light on the overhead console, then swept it around the interior, ignoring Ryan and preparing to work on the backhoe.

"Can I ask how you know about backhoes?" Ryan said.

"Top secret," Scott replied with a grin. "But no, seriously, my grandpa used to have one on his ranch. We worked on that piece of shit all the time."

"So, you're just going to run the engine until it quits and needs to be rebuilt because you ignored the sand in the fuel?"

"No. The sand is heavier than the fuel, correct?" Scott asked.

Ryan shrugged. "Sure."

"So, we drain the tank in the backhoe, then use diesel from the track loader to refill the tank. There are tools and siphon hoses in the tent. We just need the key to fire this beater up. Any idea where it is?"

"No, but I can find out." Ryan pulled out his sat phone from the dry bag he'd stuffed inside Scott's backpack. He texted Diane Carlton, asking for the location of the key.

Moments later, she replied that she'd buried the keys in the sand inside the tent on the right-hand side of the stove, then asked what they were doing.

Ryan texted an explanation. A moment later, his phone pinged again. He glanced at the screen, then snorted derisively. "Diane says there's nothing wrong with the equipment. Her father just told us they were out of action."

Scott shook his head. "That saves us some time, but why did he lie to you?"

"An excellent question," Ryan replied. "Probably didn't

want some hooligans messing with his equipment after Ziegler and his people burned the first two units."

Returning to the tent, Scott dug through the sand until he found the keys in a zip lock bag. He was back in the backhoe moments later, and used the key to bring the diesel to life. Scott flicked on the exterior lights and then oriented himself to the controls as Ryan watched from the tent, avoiding the still falling rain even though it had now slackened to just a drizzle. Scott spun the backhoe in circles, then zoomed up and down the runway between the tent and the first blast hole.

When Scott finally brought the backhoe to a stop by the tent, he climbed out and helped Ryan load Guard Three into the front scoop.

As they drove up the trail toward the house, with Ryan standing on the external fuel tank and holding onto the side of the cab, he had to admit it was easier than dragging the dead weight of an unconscious man up the hill on a travois.

With Guard Two in the bucket, they motored down to the dock and shut off the backhoe's engine.

"Which one of us is swimming?" Scott asked.

"I'll go," Ryan said, then stripped down to his Speedo and entered the warm water. He made the short swim to Little Darby Island, climbing out of the water behind The Drifts Lodge. He found Diane Carlton standing at the head of the dock, her arms crossed and a smirk on her face as she took in his lean, wet body.

Ryan ignored her and went for the runabout the island's owner kept at the dock for his guests to use. Diane held up the keys, twirling them on her finger.

Before Ryan could object, she was aboard the boat with him and starting the engine. He cast off the lines, knowing it would be of no use to object, and he needed to put his clothes back on. He was shivering from a combination of the cool night air, the constant dampness of the rain, and the late-night swim.

Diane brought the runabout alongside the dock where Scott waited beside the backhoe. Ryan and Scott tied off the bow and stern lines, then tumbled the guards into the boat like sacks of potatoes.

"Take us over to the research center," Scott instructed after Ryan had dressed.

Diane motored them over to the research facility, where, in the storage shed, the two contractors found a dusty, old tarp that smelled of motor oil and latex paint. Scott wedged it under his arm and helped Ryan throw some rusted junk out into the rain. Returning to the boat, they rolled the first guard into the tarp, and carried him to the shed, then repeated the process two more times. Once they had the guards stretched out on the shed floor, Scott closed the door and dropped a stick into the latch in place of the absent padlock, thus securing their prisoners inside.

"What now?" Diane asked once the men returned to the boat.

"I need a hot shower and more chow," Scott said.

"Alice can fix you something," Diane said, aiming the runabout toward The Drifts Lodge.

When they arrived at the lodge, Ryan and Scott took hot showers and changed into dry clothes before descending on Alice's kitchen for a well-deserved snack.

Diane leaned against the counter, watching the two men eat. "What's the plan now that you've taken those men prisoner?"

"We wait to see how the Zieglers react," Ryan stated flatly.

"Isn't that placing you on the defensive?" Diane asked.

"Possibly," Ryan admitted, "but we've evened the odds a bit."

But Ryan had to wonder if he'd made the right choice. The Zieglers were already pissed that he and Diane had refused to leave the island. Knocking out their guards would probably make them even more furious. Diane was also right in that he had put himself into a defensive position. The only way to stay ahead was to find the missing Nazi gold before they did.

Ryan decided he would start at first light.

CHAPTER TWENTY

Dawn was still an hour away as Ryan began preparing breakfast in the kitchen of The Drifts Lodge. Scott soon joined him, and the two men quickly ate eggs and toast, washing it all down with hot, black coffee.

As they came to the end of their meal, Scott asked about their next steps.

"The plan is the same," Ryan said. "You stay out of sight while I confront the Sauerkraut Twins."

Scott nodded. He was packing his bag with snacks when Alice came into the kitchen, looked at the dirty plates and skillet stacked neatly by the sink and then asked if they were headed back to Big Darby. When Ryan said yes, she immediately went to the refrigerator and removed two Tupperware containers. "I made sandwiches from de leftover ham. My boys like dem with mustard and lettuce. Hope dat's good for you."

"Perfect, Alice," Scott said. "I'm so happy I could kiss you right now."

"You keep your sweet lips to yourself now, sugar, we don't

need no hanky-panky in my house." She glanced at Ryan with a pointed look. "I's a *married* woman."

"For not having to eat granola bars and MREs today, I'd kiss you anyway," Scott said. "Your husband is a lucky man. A good woman like you is hard to find."

"You keep dem lips and dem lies to yourself like I's already tells ya." Alice fixed them both with a suddenly stern stare. "Now, you wants I feed dem boys you got locked in de shed?"

Ryan and Scott exchanged a wide-eyed glance.

"I know everyting dat happen on my island," Alice reminded them, turning to run water in the sink. "I'll make sure dey gets a meal."

"Leave them cuffed," Ryan instructed as he stuffed his lunch into his backpack.

"I take Rafi with me," Alice replied. "He knows how to handle hisself."

"I thought he was working on one of the other islands," Ryan said.

"He come back last night. He saw yous put dem boys in de shed."

Ryan thanked Alice for taking care of their prisoners and for fixing them lunch, then he and Scott headed for the runabout. They found RJ sitting on the dock, holding his panga in place with his feet. He grinned when he saw Ryan. As the kid babbled about shooting a large grouper with the pole spear Ryan had given him, a man walked out on the dock. He was shirtless, wearing only cut-off jean shorts. Ryan had to admire the man's tremendous physique—his stomach a washboard of abs under a broad chest. Rafi introduced himself and thanked Ryan for his son's present.

"You can repay me by taking me and my friend over to Big Darby," Ryan replied. "Just drop us at the dock."

Rafi and his son climbed into the panga, followed by Scott and Ryan, and the four men motored across the channel.

When the two contractors disembarked, Ryan shoved the boat away. "Stay away from this island and that camp down on Prime Cay," he warned Rafi and RJ. "These men are armed and extremely dangerous."

"My Alice in danger?" Rafi asked.

"She should be fine," Ryan replied honestly. The Zieglers didn't know where Ryan and Scott had stashed the kidnapped guards. Unless they happened upon them while Alice was feeding them lunch, the Germans wouldn't know she was involved.

Scott hopped into the backhoe and fired it up. He gave Ryan a lift to the Green Castle, then headed down the hill to park the machine back in its designated spot before disappearing into the trees to keep overwatch. Ryan knew Scott would replace the keys in the plastic bag, so Carlton could find them when this crisis was over.

Ryan climbed up to the balcony, checking the UMP he'd stashed there last night behind a cabinet that was half-falling off a wall. He'd left Guard One's UMP hidden by the dock, and he'd stored Guard Three's inside the engine compartment of the backhoe.

He then used the same trick as earlier to run up the wall and shinny over the parapet onto the building's roof. From his pack, he removed his binoculars and began glassing the channels between the islands, hoping for a glimpse of the Zieglers and their team on the way to the island. He wanted to see the look on their faces—from afar—when they discovered their men were missing.

It didn't take long for the black inflatable to appear. Despite the specially designed baffle on the outboard's engine, it was still loud in the morning air, alerting Ryan to its presence long before he saw the actual boat. When it appeared in the cut between Little Darby and Lignum Vitae

Cay, the boat created a wide, creamy wake in the dead calm sea of slate gray water.

On the horizon, glimpses of pink dawn sunlight appeared between thin cracks in the heavy cloud cover. The light breeze carried the smell of damp earth and had a chill to it that promised more rain to come.

A noise behind Ryan startled him, and he turned to see Scott levering himself over the parapet. The former SEAL stayed low as he moved over to where Ryan crouched behind the white plastic barrel.

"What are you doing up here?" Ryan asked.

"I'm checking out the scenery," Scott replied, taking in the surrounding island with an appraising eye. "I hadn't been up here yet, so I figured I'd see what the fuss was about." A moment later, he added, "I've been all over this island, but this is by far the best view yet. It's absolutely gorgeous. I can see why Diane wants to turn this place into a resort."

"And she can't do that until we get rid of the Zieglers and their search party."

"We have half the battle won," Scott said, "but not the war."

Ryan offered a grim smile. "You're right about that."

Scott dropped prone on the roof as Ryan continued to watch the black inflatable skim through the Darby Channel anchorage, then slow as it approached the concrete dock. Through his binos, Ryan could see the confusion on the faces of the Ziegler siblings as they glanced for the guard they'd posted last night.

The boat party disembarked to stand on the dock. Petra gave orders and three men with UMPs fanned out into the thicket to search for their missing counterpart while she, Hermann, and Meyer headed up the trail toward the house.

"Here they come, Scott," Ryan said. "Time for you to disappear."

"Ugh. Another day swatting mosquitoes and dripping with sweat. When this is over, you owe me a long vacation."

Ryan raised an eyebrow. "Don't you live in my house for free?"

"Yeah, but I could still use a vacation. Somewhere I can drink margaritas and chase *señoritas*."

"You and me both," Ryan said. "Now get out of here."

Scott bear-crawled to the edge of the roof and then dropped over the side to the balcony below. Ryan raised his binoculars again and saw Petra speaking into a handheld radio, which immediately piqued his interest. None of the guards had been carrying radios last night.

The little handheld the German used had a limited range. From experience, Ryan knew Petra would have to be standing on the roof, like he was, for the radio to have any hope of sending a transmission to the *Leopard*, especially with the salvage vessel tucked into the cove.

More interestingly, Petra had clearly taken charge, and Ryan could plainly see her little brother wasn't happy about playing second fiddle.

The little shore party continued toward the house. Hermann and his sister, whose height and beauty reminded Ryan of his own wife, were flanked by their three well-armed escorts. Suddenly, two of the men broke into a jog, bypassing the house and heading down the hill toward Diane's campsite.

From below, Ryan heard voices as the siblings mounted the stairs to the balcony. Ryan dropped to his belly and lay at the edge of the roof, listening to their conversation.

But the element of surprise offered him no advantages. As they spoke in German, Ryan couldn't understand a damn thing either of them were saying.

CHAPTER TWENTY-ONE

Hermann

Hermann Ziegler had known there would be trouble from the moment Diane Carlton had walked into the clearing with the man who'd introduced himself as Ryan Weller. The former German police officer hadn't liked the looks of Weller then, regardless of his dubious claim about being of German heritage, and now that three of his team had disappeared, he was certain the American was behind their abduction.

Petra had told him that Weller was a contractor with military experience, but Hermann hadn't believed the man would be bold enough to make a move against him and his men. They were well-armed, and Petra had openly threatened Diane Carlton's life. He had hoped Weller would have taken the hint, but it seemed the man was continuing to meddle in their business.

Standing on the balcony of the Green Castle, Hermann

gritted his teeth as his sister droned on about how she would like to murder both Weller and "that little tart." He had never seen his sister act like this before, but then again, he hadn't been around her much since she'd gone off to boarding school at the tender age of thirteen. Most of their time together had been during the holidays or for a week or two when Petra returned home during summer break.

Last night, she had told him that the boarding school had taught her how to be both a lover and an assassin, before confiding that she had twelve kills under her belt. Hermann hadn't liked the way his sister's eyes had glowed as she recounted an especially brutal interrogation and murder of an American businessman. She had confessed that the businessman had come to believe in the role The Paladin Group should play as rulers of the world but had then turned his back on her. Hermann wondered if the businessman had just been saying all the right things so Petra would take off her pants, or whether Petra taking her pants off had convinced the guy to say the right things. Either way, Hermann was seeing his sister in an entirely new light.

And it left a bitter taste in his mouth.

"Hermann, are you listening to me?" Petra asked for the third time in the last five minutes.

Hermann shook himself from his reverie and moved his gaze from the beauty of the contrasting greens and blues of the island meeting the sea to a different kind of beauty. For all his sister's exterior appeal, her insides were rotten to the core. He had taken an oath to uphold the law, and he'd promised himself that he would remain loyal to that oath, no matter what pledge he'd uttered in Herr Fischer's basement to become part of the salvage team. Listening to Petra made him want to lock her up in prison and throw away the key.

"What are you thinking about?" she asked.

He watched the wind teasing her thick blonde mane. He

had a weakness for blondes, especially his mother and sister. Hermann wondered how often he had told them he would do anything for them. Obviously, one too many times. Here he was, on this shitty island, looking for gold and being drawn into Petra's web of lies and deceit. Hermann felt like he didn't even know his own sister.

"Nothing other than where the gold might be," he replied.

Petra crossed her arms and stood with her hip cocked. "I told Mother and Herr Fischer that you were the wrong man for this job. In fact, I begged them not to tell you that you are *Lebensborn*, or about our family's association with The Paladin Group."

"I wish they hadn't," Hermann mumbled.

"You would rather be back in Germany, working for GSG 9?"

"In some ways," he replied. "Look, I signed on to hunt for gold. I didn't sign on to kill innocent people. Diane is protecting her investment, and Weller is doing his job. *We* are the ones trespassing."

"But we're taking what is *rightfully* ours," Petra insisted. "The gold on this island belongs to The Paladin Group, regardless of who owns the land. You swore an oath of allegiance to our cause. We must do our part to restore order."

Hermann rolled his eyes. "And how many years has The Paladin Group been trying to restore order? Seems to me, the people don't care for their kind of order."

Petra threw up her hands. "I knew this was a mistake! There's no talking sense into you. I told Mother to hire professionals, yet she wanted *you*. She thought this adventure would bring you around. Instead, you have squandered time when you should have killed them both."

Hermann turned his back to her, looking out over the island. He was torn between loyalty to his family and loyalty to the law he had sworn to uphold when becoming a police officer. He knew nothing about The Paladin Group except for what they themselves had told him. Truthfully, he had buried his head in the sand. He had focused on the hunt for treasure and the rewards that awaited him up those stairs in the form of alcohol and compliant women. Now, he felt like it was all coming back to bite him in his overly exposed ass.

Petra must have sensed his unease. She laid a hand on his arm, then ran it up to cup the back of his neck, her fingers slipping into his hair. Her voice shifted into a low, soothing tone. "You're a part of this cause now, Hermann. Whether you like it or not, you have a job to do. Upholding the principles of The Paladin Group must be first and foremost in your mind."

She moved even closer to him. He could feel the heat of her body and hear the sultry guile in her voice. "Hermann, do you love me?"

Petra's other hand slipped under his shirt, fingernails digging into the skin on his back, pulling him tight to her. Hermann wanted to be repulsed by her attempt at seduction, but part of him enjoyed having her so close. Resisting the incestuous call of her beauty, Hermann stepped away from his sister.

When he looked into her eyes, he could see they were not soft and wanting, but hard as diamonds. Petra was manipulating him, just as she would any other man. Hermann felt his chest swell with indignant air pulled in through gritted teeth. Petra had already decided his fate and the fate of his team. They would all be dead as soon as they set their hands on the gleaming gold bars from the U-1226.

For now, Hermann would go along with her plan. He had a job to do.

Reaching out his hand, he felt Petra place her delicate fingers in his. Wanting to appease her and save his own skin, he spoke words he hoped would make her happy. "Of course,

I love you, Petra. You're my sister. We are *Lebensborn*. It is our birthright to rule the world. We can do it together, side by side."

Together, they stood on the balcony, holding hands as they watched their men marching up the path from Diane's campsite. Meyer led the way, having checked on the GPR equipment they'd left in the woods the previous evening.

A few minutes later, the professor mounted the steps to the balcony to make his report. "There was no one at the tent. All the men we left behind are gone, and the GPR unit has also disappeared."

"What do you mean that it's disappeared?" Petra asked.

Hermann felt her hand tighten on his. She burned with anger. Secretly, he was laughing at her. Petra had taken charge of the operation, and this had happened on her watch.

"Just what I said," Meyer replied. "It has disappeared. Last night, when we left, I covered it with a tarp to keep the rain off, but the equipment is now gone. We followed the tracks left by the carriage, but we lost them on the rocks at the edge of the sea."

"Damnit!" Petra screamed. She took a deep breath to calm herself and then turned to her brother, her blue eyes showing no sign of the anger she'd just expressed. With a beguiling smile, she said, "You know what must be done, Hermann."

Even though he knew better, Hermann could feel himself being pulled under by her spell, willing to do whatever it took to please her. *This*, he thought, *must be how that businessman had felt before she tossed him away*.

Torn between his two loyalties, he felt the stronger pull of family. By pleasing Petra, Hermann would also be pleasing Katrine. He didn't want to be a disappointment to his mother. She had trusted him enough to tell him of their secret life, and he had sworn to uphold her guiding principles because he loved her.

Though he had not signed on to be a stormtrooper, willing to slash and burn and kill to get what he wanted, he was about to do just that.

Hermann summoned the leader of his remaining team, Artem Kowalchuk, a Ukrainian soldier who had served in the neo-Nazi Azov Battalion and had inked his beliefs onto his stomach. Artem came to a stop just outside the balcony door and raised his arm in a Hitler salute before coming to attention.

Involuntarily, Hermann snorted. He had never required his men to render salutes or to have proper military bearing, his only requirement had been that they worked as a team. Petra's aura had whipped them all into shape. He wondered if they all were trying to impress her so they could get into her pants. Petra knew exactly how to wield the strange power women held over men—let them think they might have a shot at bedding her and they would do anything for it. He wasn't immune to it. They all had gold and pussy fever.

"We must find Weller and Carlton," Hermann ordered. "We'll interrogate them until they tell us what they have done with the others."

CHAPTER TWENTY-TWO

Ryan

L ying on his belly at the edge of the roof and hidden
behind the low parapet, Ryan had heard the entire
conversation between Hermann and his sister.

The only problem was, he hadn't understood a word of it
except for his and Diane's names. He knew the outcome of
the conversation didn't bode well for them.

As the Germans departed the balcony and made their way
down the path toward the dock, Ryan moved across the roof
in a bear crawl, his hands hot and sticky from the old tar.
Despite the rain and the coolness of the overcast clouds, the
roof was unbearably hot, and Ryan was drenched in sweat.

From behind the plastic water barrel, Ryan watched
through binoculars as Hermann the German and his party
departed the island by boat and arrived quickly at The Drifts
Lodge. Ryan's heart sank as the armed men stepped out of
the boat and headed up the dock.

Moments later, they reappeared with Diane in tow. Two of the men held her upper arms and practically carried her to the boat, with the third bringing up the rear and brandishing his weapon at Alice, who had followed them out of the house.

Ryan knew he had to do something, but he had no long-range rifle to pick off Diane's captors. The Germans muscled her down into the boat and then zoomed away from the dock, heading south through the anchorage. Ryan kept tracking the inflatable through his binoculars. Diane turned to look over her shoulder, her black hair shining in the light, loose strands from her French braid waving in the wind.

Ryan watched the boat until it disappeared behind another island. He hadn't counted on getting tangled up with anyone other than the "ghosts" haunting Big Darby Island, but Diane had grown on him in the last couple of days. Now, he had to save her. The trouble with letting a situation become personal was that emotions had a way of clouding one's judgment.

He had to get her back. Not because of some misguided feelings toward her, but because it was his job. Diane was his principal, and Ryan had given his word to her father that he would keep her safe. He licked his lips, tasting an imaginary hint of switcha.

Ryan felt anger burning through him, not just at himself for lusting after Diane, but at the Zieglers for trespassing on the island and for taking Diane against her will. He also recognized that he and Scott had caused this situation by taking out the guards and hiding them in the shed. The Zieglers were repaying tit for tat, only instead of moving pawns off the board, as Ryan and Scott had tried to do, Hermann had gone straight for the queen.

What the German didn't know was that he'd just made a fatal error. Ryan was now out for blood.

Climbing down from the roof, Ryan tossed his backpack on the floor, then sat down beside it, listening to the wind moaning through the open windows and doors. A crack of thunder boomed in the distance.

At this point, Ryan's regular team of operators would have come in handy. More men meant a greater force with which to take the fight to the Germans, but Greg Olsen had them occupied with other assignments. Despite selling Trident, Greg still got calls from dignitaries and wealthy individuals doing business in the Caribbean, asking for his private contracting services. The DWR security forces not certified as commercial divers were tasked with those occasional personal protection details.

"Yo! Ryan! Where you at?" Scott called out.

"Up here," Ryan said, remaining seated beside the fireplace in the master bedroom.

Scott mounted the stairs and sat across from Ryan. He pulled his knees up and rested his outstretched arms on them. Ryan couldn't look his friend in the eye, afraid he'd give away his fear of what might happen to Diane. They sat in silence for a long time, both men contemplating their next move.

But they didn't need to come up with a plan.

One was provided for them.

Ryan and Scott glanced at each other as they heard an approaching outboard motor. They both recognized it as the big engine hanging on the rear of the black inflatable. Scrambling to their feet, they ran out of the house. Scott veered into the trees as Ryan jogged down the path toward the dock.

He was breathing hard when his boots touched the concrete dock. The black boat sat just out of reach, idling in circles in the teal blue water. Ryan figured the boat must have circled the islands and come back to Big Darby. Everyone sat in the same place as when Ryan had viewed them through his binoculars. His heart went out to Diane. Her face bore a plaintive expression that begged for him to rescue her.

As Ryan stepped onto the dock, the black boat came alongside it. The gunman in the bow sprang out to keep Ryan covered with the barrel of his UMP as Petra climbed up to face him. He could feel the force of her presence radiating off her. Ryan assumed most men found it so alluring that she would have them eating out of the palm of her hand in no time—but he wasn't most men. She had taken his principal and pissed him off. He had no use for her, so instead of looking away as Petra expected him to do, Ryan stared right back at her, trying hard not to acknowledge the personal involvement he had with Diane.

If Petra sensed his weakness, Ryan knew she would seize on it and use it against him.

Ryan kept quiet, letting Petra make the opening move. The clouds to the southeast were heavy and black. Thunder rolled in the distance, and lightning sizzled in the air. There was a coolness to the breeze that was almost chilling considering the ominous moment.

Petra's gaze seemed to bore through him, to understand every nuance about Ryan, but it wasn't a malevolent stare. It was an open blank that invited Ryan to spill his guts. He wondered how many men had fallen victim to her. To keep himself from talking, Ryan bit his inner lip.

Finally, Petra huffed out a sigh and put her hands on her hips. "Where are my men?"

"You let Diane go and I'll tell you," Ryan promised.

"This is not a negotiation, Weller."

"Your opening question suggested that it was," he replied.

"Let me rephrase it for you, then," Petra said, leaning forward to emphasize her point. When she spoke again, her voice had a threatening menace to it. "I want my men back."

"And I want you to hand over Diane," Ryan replied.

"I see we are at an impasse." Petra finally glanced away from Ryan's face and looked into the jungle. "What did you do with my ground-penetrating radar?"

"Your what?" Ryan asked.

"The radar device my men have been using to search the island."

Ryan glanced past Petra to her brother. She had said they were "her men" not his. Hermann kept his eyes fixed on the fast-moving storm.

Refocusing on his female adversary, Ryan figured Scott had moved the GPR that morning after they'd separated, but he wasn't about to tell Petra that. He simply replied, "I have no idea what you're talking about, Petra. I didn't move any radar device. Maybe it was the same 'ghosts' who shot at Steve Carlton or the other 'ghosts' that burned his backhoe and track loader."

"There are no ghosts on this island," she stated. "I want my men and my GPR device returned within the hour."

"And if I can't do that?" Ryan asked.

"You're a smart man," Petra said. "You're former military, a commercial diver, and a paid mercenary working for whoever will hire you, be it Dark Water Research or some billionaire like Steve Carlton. I know your type, which means I know you'll follow orders." She extended her manicured nail and poked Ryan in the chest. "Now do what I'm telling you."

Ryan gritted his teeth as she punctuated her point with another stab of her finger. He figured one of the Zieglers would have run a background check on him. Despite him wanting to leave as small a digital footprint as possible, it was next to impossible. One data scraper could find out every address he'd ever resided at, old phone numbers, family members, military service records, police reports, and credit scores. So, the fact that Petra knew his history was no shock.

He just smiled and said, "I'm a mercenary, remember? I'm loyal to the highest bidder. Since you haven't paid me a dime, I'm still the Carltons' dog."

"Is that all?" Petra said with a bemused smile. "By the way you keep glancing over my shoulder to look at Miss Carlton, I'd say you have feelings for the woman. Does your wife know?"

Ryan held himself check and spoke slowly to avoid adding fuel to the fire. "Diane is my principal. I've been hired to protect her. You're trespassing on Big Darby Island. You don't have the right to search for anything here. If you let Diane go, I'll tell you where your men are, then you can get the hell off this island and out of The Bahamas."

Petra shook her head. "No. No. No. You just don't understand." Thrusting her finger at her own chest now, she screamed, "I'm Petra. I'm in charge. What *I* want, *I* get."

"*You* can get off this island," Ryan said. He crossed his arms. "You're one superficial bitch, Petra. You think you can charm your way into a guy's heart by batting your lashes and flashing those big blue eyes but let me tell you something: your act won't work on me. I have a job to do, and no petulant bimbo is going to dictate to me how well I do it."

Hermann Ziegler smirked.

Ryan could see the cracks in Petra's carefully crafted façade. She apparently wasn't used to men standing up to her or ignoring her orders. Her querulous demand that she was in charge and her brother's reaction had emboldened Ryan to further agitate her. He stepped around Petra and offered his hand to Diane. "Let's go."

"Have it your way," Petra replied, voice trembling with barely controlled rage. "I can't convince you to leave but a bullet will. Shoot him!" She gestured angrily for the man with the UMP to kill Ryan.

Hermann gave an order in German.

Out of the corner of his eye, Ryan saw the merc lower the weapon he'd shouldered at Petra's order.

"What are you doing?" Petra cried in dismay. "Shoot him!"

Hermann shook his head.

The two siblings began arguing in German, but Hermann made a hand gesture that cowed his sister into silence, however Ryan could see the cloud of anger hovering over her red face as she stared daggers at him.

"My men are as expendable as I am, Mister Weller," Hermann said. "My sister has made that quite clear. Keep the guards and the GPR. What I want from you is for you to find the gold. Herr Meyer seems unable to locate it, and Petra has been sent to speed things along, but she's making a spectacle of herself." His voice carried a hint of sarcastic contempt as he glared up at her. Turning back to Ryan, he added, "Find the gold, and Diane will be returned to you, unharmed."

"You'll have to give me more to go on than that," Ryan said.

"Near the end of the war, a U-boat brought crates of gold ashore here," Hermann said. "We know this because we found a journal documenting it being unloaded after the submarine was deemed irreparable. It's buried somewhere on this island."

"And if I can't find it?" Ryan asked.

"We'll cross that bridge when we come to it," Hermann responded. "To save yourself some trouble, we already checked the cisterns. Now, Lukas, help Petra into the boat."

The mercenary on the dock did as he was told and held out his hand to steady the furious woman. Petra's face was a mask of fuming rage, ready to boil over at the next possible infraction. Once they were seated in the boat, the engineman twisted the throttle and the inflatable shot away from the dock.

Diane glanced over her shoulder again. It was the second time she'd given him that heartbreaking look today.

As their eyes met, Ryan renewed his earlier vow of rescue. *I'm coming for you.*

CHAPTER TWENTY-THREE

R yan rubbed his face with both hands, trying to wipe away the image of Diane's wounded look and penetrating gaze as the Zieglers' black inflatable raced away. *How am I going to find gold on an island that has already been searched from top to bottom?*

Retreating up the hill to the old sheep shearing pen and machine shop, Ryan found a place to sit as the fat drops of rain began to fall. He closed his eyes and pulled his legs in to cross them. Breathing deeply, Ryan expanded his belly to force air all the way into his lungs, then exhaled. Combat breathing had always helped to focus and relax him. The Navy taught what they called Box Breathing: take a deep breath in over a four count, hold for four, out for four, hold for four, and repeat, all while the sailors were imagining that they were drawing the lines of a box as they breathed.

For Ryan, the pattern wasn't effective. Years ago, he'd modified the process into a deep breath in for three, out for four, and repeat.

Combat breathing heightened cognitive performance by clearing the mind, allowing for greater focus and balance of the nervous system. Research conducted by both military and civilian establishments had deduced that deep breathing activated genes associated with reducing inflammation and stress, as well as shutting off the body's tendency for "fight or flight." Breathing basically reset the body's response to stress, and Ryan needed to reset and refocus.

As he sat breathing, Ryan tried to concentrate on what he knew about Sir Guy Baxter. The Nazi sympathizer had supposedly communicated with submarines to resupply them. When confronted by locals still loyal to Britain, as The Bahamas was under British rule at the time, Baxter and his mistress had fled, never to be seen again. The possibilities as to where they'd gone seemed limitless.

Ryan knew that at the end of World War II, the Nazis had made contingency plans to escape Germany. Many of Germany's armed forces had been captured by the Allies and had stood trial at Nuremberg, while others had escaped along the ratlines and lived out their lives in hiding in Europe and South America. Many believed that Hitler, instead of killing himself and Eva Braun in his Berlin bunker, had taken a submarine full of stolen treasure to Argentina, where he'd lived for the rest of his life, surrounded by his loyal subjects, ready to raise a Fourth Reich.

There were lots of rumors floating around about a treasure train buried in a tunnel in Poland, and about a sunken ship transporting gold from Tunisia to Germany, known as Rommel's Gold. People were still searching for these legendary lost treasures decades after the end of World War II, and it made sense that someone would come looking for gold on Big Darby Island.

And now Ryan was the one looking. It was his only option to save Diane.

He breathed in, filling his lungs from the top down,

swelling the abdomen to expand the diaphragm—one, two, three, hold for a beat, then breathe out one, two, three, four.

Think, Ryan. Think.

He had to assume Ziegler had searched the caves, but assumption was the mother of all screwups. *"Assume" makes an ass out of you and me.*

Standing, Ryan brushed the dirt from his hands. The rain continued to fall in heavy sheets as he began a thorough search of the machine shop. Where he had been sitting was the only dry spot in the room. Like the utility shed behind the Green Castle, the machine shop was missing its roof, and the support beams for the second floor had rotted away and collapsed. Unless the gold was buried under the dirt floor, it was a waste of time to continue poking through the debris. Ryan had been in the other outbuildings already, and they were each in a similar condition.

He wondered where Scott had holed up and decided he was probably stretched out in Diane's tent, taking a nap while the storm raged across the island.

Ryan jogged through the driving rain to the livestock pen. The cave was almost cathedral-like, with openings in the ceiling to allow the sunlight to filter through. Moss grew on the damp limestone, and the sand underfoot had been trampled by hundreds of tourists' feet and animal hooves. Ferns sprouted from craggy rocks, and the color of the stone changed from tan to white as it rose to curve overhead. Vegetation grew all around the ceiling holes, with ferns and small vines hanging down through them. Water poured through the gaps to form pools on the floor, with rivulets tracing their way through the sand on their way out of the cave.

Starting at one end, Ryan methodically worked his way through the cave system. He saw boot prints from Hermann's men everywhere he trod. They, too, had thoroughly searched the area—and probably more than once.

Frustrated at the entire situation, Ryan kicked the sand. "Damn you, Travis Wisnewski for getting me into this stupid mess."

Deciding his next search would be of the old house, just in case something had been overlooked by everyone else who had ever rummaged through the place, Ryan started out of the cave. As he stepped outside, he caught his pant leg on a paddle of a prickly pear cactus. Jerking it free of the thorns, the toe of his boot caught a tree root and knocked him off-balance. Ryan landed face-first in a muddy puddle, and he whacked the ground with his fist. "Son of a bitch! Can this day get *any* worse?"

He was sick of the island, and its mosquitoes, tree frogs, mud, sand, bugs, and human pestilence, and at having to walk long distances to get from one point to another.

Heaving a sigh, Ryan pushed his muddy body up off the ground and let the heavy rain wash over him. He scrubbed at the mud with his hands and tried to rinse it away, but all he succeeded in doing was spreading it around.

The easiest way to get clean was to jump in the ocean, and already soaking wet, it made little difference now. Ryan ran down the hill to the dock and leapt into the water. He held his breath and floated just under the surface, his heavy boots providing the weight needed to keep him under the warm water. Ryan scrubbed at his skin until he could no longer hold his breath, then rose to the surface to find he had floated south.

Ryan swam to the small beach and continued to wash away the mud. Once he was clean, he walked out of the ocean, water streaming from every inch of his body and cloth-ing. The rain continued to hammer down.

He wiped his face clean, but the water kept streaming down his skin, running into his mouth and dripping off his chin. "This has *got* to stop," he whined to himself. "This freaking sucks."

Ryan had been through worse, but right then, he was at a low point. Everything made him feel miserable. All he wanted was to take a hot shower and then crawl into bed beside his wife, but when he closed his eyes, it wasn't Emily's face he saw. Instead, it was Diane, pulling off her shirt and sitting on his lap.

Get a grip, Weller.

He jogged up to the Green Castle. Inside, he took off his clothes and wrung them out. He wished he could build a fire in one of the fireplaces so he could dry out faster, but he was afraid the place might burn to the ground. With his clothing hanging from whatever convenient piece of broken furniture he could find, Ryan walked around in his combat boots and underwear.

With a two-fold mission of finding the gold and rescuing Diane, Ryan knew he would need to be proactive in his search, but he'd been over almost every square inch of the island in the last few days and had seen nowhere to hide a cache of gold. As he pondered searching the island again, it dawned on Ryan what Hermann and his men had been doing. The map he'd seen on the table in their camp on Prime Cay had been sectioned off into grids. Starting from the southern tip of Darby, the German had marked off grid boxes with a red "X." They had been methodically searching the island using the ground-penetrating radar device that Petra had said was now missing.

Ryan reasoned that if they hadn't found the gold using high-tech equipment, it meant the gold either wasn't on Big Darby, or they hadn't looked in the right spot.

Pulling an ancient wooden rocking chair over to the fireplace, Ryan sat down, running his hands over the rough armrests devoid of polish after decades in the brutal tropical elements. He leaned his head back and closed his eyes, trying to come up with a plan for what to do next. Outside, the wind moaned in the trees and rain continued to pour down. There was no use in going out in the storm and risking injury. He kicked off his wet boots and wiggled his toes, trying to shake the dampness out from between them.

As he stared at the cold fireplace, the firebox devoid of ashes and the paint peeling from the whitewashed brick, Ryan's gaze traced the cracks in the mortar between the dark red bricks. The cracks traveled horizontally and vertically, meandering up from the floor and continuing all the way to the ceiling. He figured the cracks had appeared as a combination of the house settling and the heat generated in the fireplace during cold, rainy days such as the one raging outside.

Idly, Ryan reached out his right foot and nudged the fireplace with his big toe. He pushed against it gently, moving himself back and forth on the chair's rockers as he tried to formulate a plan.

———

AFTER TEN MINUTES of steady rocking, Ryan had yet to come up with a fresh idea. It seemed that every scenario ended with him going empty-handed to the Zieglers and Diane dying for his failure.

Ryan felt the need for action, despite the weather, but again, he knew it was foolish to go racing around the island in the downpour.

The rain continued to sheet down, and Ryan found a poncho in his backpack to use as a blanket to keep warm as the cool breeze played through the broken windows and, during heavy gusts which brought mist into the room.

Ryan had been steadily pushing against the same spot on the fireplace with his foot until a blast of thunder directly overhead startled him, making him jump in the chair. He almost fell over backward but caught himself, and when his foot landed against the chimney, it was much harder than before.

He felt something give and immediately jerked his leg back, startled again by the shifting brick beneath his bare foot. This time, the chair rocked backward beyond its limit. Ryan's arms pinwheeled as he tried to save himself, but he continued over backward. Instinctively, he tucked his chin to his chest, spread his arms, and tried to distribute his weight as his shoulders slammed into the hard mahogany floor, followed by the back of his head bouncing off the boards.

He lay there, stunned.

Ryan groaned as he extricated his legs from the overturned rocking chair. He slowly turned over onto his stomach, then rose onto all fours, shaking his head to clear the dull ache from his skull. But pain wasn't the only thing registering in his head. There was something else niggling at the back of his mind. He leaned his head down into his hands and rubbed the lump on the back.

A question popped into Ryan's mind. *Why did the brick move?*

Groaning as he rose to his feet, Ryan rolled his head in slow circles with his eyes closed, feeling the muscles stiffening between his shoulder blades from the initial impact. He stepped forward and squatted down to examine the fireplace. With the tip of his right index finger, Ryan pushed against the loose brick. Dried mortar crumbled and fell as the brick shifted.

Working the brick carefully with both hands, Ryan slowly pulled it free of the surrounding chimney. After setting the brick on the floor, he could see there was a hole behind where the brick had been. He retrieved his flashlight from his backpack and snapped on the powerful LED light.

There was something in the hole.

It appeared to be wrapped in an old cloth. Fearing spiders or snakes or spirits, Ryan examined as much of the shallow hidey-hole as he could see before sliding his hand in and retrieving the object. From its feel, he guessed it was a book. He set it on the floor beside the brick, then shone his light back inside, finding nothing other than dust and soot and crumbled mortar.

Returning the light to the object on the floor, Ryan examined it. The book appeared to be wrapped in rubberized cloth, like that of an old poncho or raincoat, with twine wrapped around it, as if the previous owner had trussed up a Christmas present. Ryan gingerly pulled the end of the string, feeling the decades-old strands part and crumble.

With the string off, Ryan unwrapped the package to find a leather-bound journal approximately six inches square and a good inch thick. The leather was still oily, but particles of it rubbed off on his fingers as he gingerly lifted the book.

Opening it to the first page, he read aloud, "Journal of Ellen Paige Carter."

The edges of the paper pages were brittle with age, but the interior near the spine turned just as easily as the day the journal had been manufactured.

Ryan set the rocking chair back on its rockers and resumed his place in it. He flipped to the last page of the book. Sir Guy Baxter's mistress had kept a journal of her time on the island, and it provided the secret to where Ryan needed to search for the gold.

CHAPTER TWENTY-FOUR

Settling into the rocking chair and pulling the poncho tighter around him, Ryan delicately turned the book back to its opening pages. Ellen Carter wrote with a fine, cursive scrawl, the letters distinctive and leaning slightly to the right.

The first entry was dated June 1937.

While still in England, she had written, *I eagerly await Guy's call. He has traveled to Darby Island to inspect it, to see if it will be suitable for the plantation he has in mind. It was so kind of King George to gift him such a large island, however inhospitable it may be. I know I will love it there, as these winters are miserable for my constitution.*

Ryan turned a few more pages, scanning the dates. Ellen had documented major undertakings in her life, the journal skipping months at a time. He wondered why she had concealed it in the fireplace instead of taking it with her. It seemed that such a valuable possession would be something she would want to pass down to her heirs.

In September 1938, Ellen had detailed the great expense of shipping brick and mahogany and the luxurious trappings needed to construct the Green Castle. Most of their supplies had come from Miami, and the Great Depression made some items nearly impossible to buy. Baxter set about purchasing machinery to set up his own woodworking and metal fabrication facilities on the island, as well as importing herds of sheep, goats, and cattle. Being self-sufficient wasn't a requirement, but an all-encompassing need.

Ryan flipped again to the end of the journal, hoping to learn more about the disappearance of Baxter and his mistress, but he ended up thumbing back toward the center of the book to get the full story.

December 18, 1944

Guy has guided in another submarine. We believe it will be the last one, as the war is ending. The Americans and the Russians are encroaching on Berlin. Soon, Hitler may have to surrender. We believe we are still safe on the island. Germany's surrender will mean little for us, other than Hitler will not be in charge. Life here will go on as it has for centuries before us. The islanders can be such a backward lot, but they are excellent at surviving. And so shall we.

Last evening, the submarine captain, August-Wilhelm Claussen, and another high-ranking SS officer, Wolfgang Poske, joined us for dinner. Claussen told us that his crewmen are repairing the submarine's snorkel tubing, damaged, he says, when they were forced to submerge too quickly. Now, the tubing is bent and will not retract into the hull.

December 20, 1944

Poske and Claussen came to lunch. Claussen reported someone had further damaged the seal around the snorkel, preventing the submarine from submerging. He kept staring at Poske as if he knew the man had something to do with the damage. Also, Poske told us he had witnessed a crewman push the first officer through a hatch and kill him. Because the crewman carried a rifle, Poske shot him.

There is palpable animosity between the crew. Many are ready to desert with the submarine no longer functioning. Guy helped unload twenty crates from the submarine and stored them in the sea cave not far from the main dock where they will be convenient to retrieve. The cave mouth is low, and one must stoop to get inside, but then it opens to almost cathedral-like proportions. It is a marvelously beautiful cave, with long stalactites forming pillars to support the cave roof.

After dinner, Claussen excused himself to return to his boat. Poske stayed on to smoke cigars and drink wine with Guy. I helped the maid clean the table and kept an ear on the conversation. Poske has moved his things into the house and asked Guy to guide the submarine through the channel tomorrow so Claussen can sink it in the deeper waters of Exuma Sound.

DECEMBER 22, 1944

Yesterday, after guiding the submarine through the channel, Guy returned to the house and the three of us stood on the balcony, watching the dark sky. Suddenly, it was lit with a tremendous explosion. We could hear the noise rolling like thunder over the water.

Poske confided in us that he had set charges on the submarine to purposely sink it. I fear for our lives. This Poske is an animal. He admits to sabotaging the submarine and to killing the first officer and the crewman. He is mad for the gold hidden in the cave, trying to convince Guy to take him to Cuba aboard our small cruiser. I pleaded with Guy not to take him. Guy has started to carry a pistol concealed on his person.

As afraid as we are of Poske, tonight has been full of surprises. The natives, led by John Andrews, one of our finest slaves, came out of the bush bearing torches and issued us an ominous warning. We are to leave the island, or we are to be hanged for helping the Germans.

They only do this because England is winning. If Germany had swept across the English Channel instead of invading Russia, we would all be happy German citizens. Instead, we are being forced to leave.

I don't know what tomorrow holds. The plan as of now is to load as much gold as we can aboard our cruiser and head for Cuba, as Poske had originally suggested. I leave my diary for someone to find. I fear that if I take it with me and it falls into the wrong hands, our past will be discovered.

I am loath to leave the island paradise we have worked so hard to build, and I pray the next owner loves it as much as we do.

RYAN CLOSED the book and put his chin on his palm, his elbow resting on the arm of the rocker. So, Baxter and his mistress had fled Big Darby in the company of a German named Poske. Ryan's gaze focused vacantly out the window at the gray storm clouds that rolled past on the horizon.

When his stomach rumbled, Ryan glanced at his watch. It was almost six p.m. Time had flown by as he'd read the incredible journal Ellen Carter had left behind, detailing her life. He wrapped the diary back in the rubberized material and used a length of paracord from his backpack to retie the package, then he carefully placed it back inside its hiding spot in the fireplace and reinserted the brick. With the crumbling mortar, the anomaly was much easier to spot, but Ryan hoped no one would be trespassing on the island to find it.

Ryan got up, pulled on his still damp clothes, and shouldered the backpack before pulling the poncho overtop. He walked down the hill toward the campsite, ready to tell his friend about his latest discovery.

As he approached the tent, Ryan called out, "Yo, Scottie!"

Expecting the former SEAL to answer him from inside

the shelter, it surprised Ryan when he didn't receive a response.

"Scott? Where you at, brother?" Ryan asked, lifting the tent flap.

The tent was empty, with no sign of anyone having been inside it recently. Ryan pulled off his poncho and hung it on a hook, then slung his backpack into a chair. He leaned against the table and studied the large topographical map of Big Darby Island. He put his finger on the concrete dock jutting into Darby Channel. Ryan saw no rock formations that would support a cave the size Ellen Carter had described.

Leaning down, he inspected the map a little closer, focusing on the blue hole. Ryan remembered Clivon's words: *"Where de pond is on de north end, der used to be a cave. Big'un, too."*

So, if there had been a big cave on the north end of the island, then it must have collapsed. The questions Ryan had to ask were: what had made it collapse, and was there another way to access it?

There had to be, otherwise he wouldn't have any leverage for rescuing Diane. Knowing where the gold might be was the only other bargaining chip he had.

What Ryan needed now was some dive gear, but since it was getting dark, there wasn't much he could do. Deciding it would be best to start fresh in the morning, Ryan geared up again and headed up the hill toward the castle. He called softly into the fading light for Scott but saw neither hide nor hair of the big man. Ryan toured the house again, then headed down to the dock. Tired and wet, he wanted a hot shower, one of Alice's home-cooked meals, and to talk things over with Scott. He was growing increasingly worried about his friend.

As Ryan stepped out on the dock, he looked across the channel to see Scott sitting under an umbrella with a tall drink in his hand. Ryan snorted and shook his head. Leave it to Scott to get a head start on relaxation. He remembered the old SEAL adage: *It pays to be a winner*. Scott knew how to play the game.

Ryan raised his hand in greeting as Scott raised his glass in salute. He took a long sip and then set it down before getting up to untie RJ's panga. Moments later, Scott brought the little boat alongside the dock, and Ryan jumped down into it.

"How long have you been over there?" Ryan asked, pointing at Little Darby.

"After they took Diane, I figured you were preoccupied, so I swam over to Little Darby to get out of the storm. Where have you been?"

"Figuring out where the gold is," Ryan replied.

Scott brought the panga up to the dock behind The Drifts Lodge, and Ryan tied it off. Scott picked up his drink as he followed Ryan into the house. "So, where is it?"

Ryan shrugged. "I don't know exactly, but I've narrowed it down."

"What's our next move?" Scott asked.

"I'm going to take a hot shower and get something to eat. We need maps, dive gear, and salvage equipment—all of which the Germans have. I'll run down to talk to them in the morning."

"You think you can trust them?" Scott asked.

"I don't trust them any farther than I can throw them, but we need what they have. If I can expedite the operation with their gear, then we'll get Diane back that much sooner."

Scott leaned against the door jamb and sipped his drink as Ryan got a cold Kalik from the fridge. "What's the deal between you and her?"

"She's the principal, Scott. I let her get kidnapped. I have to get her back."

"No. There's something else. You get all weird when you're around her."

"Because I'm trying to be professional. Now, get out of the way so I can take a shower."

Scott moved aside and Ryan headed for his room. He let out a deep breath. He had to get a grip on this Diane situation. Watching her be taken away had stirred all kinds of emotions in him. Ryan just needed to get her back safely, then collect his fee from her daddy and never see her again. It was that simple. Get away and shove those feelings down deep inside. Don't tell anyone about them. He was even thinking about keeping the kiss to himself. It wasn't something Emily *really* needed to know about.

Ryan drained his beer as he stood under the hot water.

He finally had a plan.

Get the gold. Rescue Diane. Get the hell out.

CHAPTER TWENTY-FIVE

Showered, shaved, and wearing clean clothes, Ryan used the phone in the office of The Drifts Lodge to call Ashlee Williams.

"I assume you want to talk about the pictures of the map you sent me?" she said after their usual sarcastic greetings.

Ryan told her the red Xs meant they had already searched the grids with ground-penetrating radar and not found the gold. "Did the notes have anything useful?"

"Not really. They were basic comments about the ground density, porousness of the limestone, and general survey notes. It seems the guy doing the survey was being very thorough."

"They're searching for gold, Ash—of course they're going to be thorough. What I need from you is overhead satellite views of Big Darby Island, as far back as you can get them."

"How far back?" she asked.

"1940s."

"Come on, Ryan," she said, incredulous. "You know the Landsat program to photograph the Earth wasn't started until 1972. How do you expect me to find overhead images of some obscure island in the Bahamas as far back as the 1940s?"

"The U.S. military routinely photographed the Caribbean for ongoing operations and during routine training flights. Check their archives."

"You've *got* to be kidding me," an exasperated Ashlee replied.

"There used to be a large cave on the north end of Big Darby Island. I need to see what it looked like before it collapsed," Ryan explained.

"I'm telling you, Ryan, it's next to impossible."

"But there's a chance," he said.

Ashlee sighed. "Is this about recovering some treasure?"

"Well, yeah, but there's—"

"You want me to drop everything I'm doing at DWR to dig through decades-old photos on the off chance there *might* be one of some old cave, just so you can go treasure hunting? No thanks. Does the boss know about this?"

Ryan sighed. "I haven't spoken to Greg about this job."

"Maybe you should. We're very busy over here. Why don't you call your buddy Barry?"

"Barry isn't taking my calls right now."

"I shouldn't wonder, after all the trouble you got him into on the last job."

"I'm not the one who asked him to hack the CIA. They take that shit kinda personal."

"But you *were* the one who asked him to dig around for information," Ashlee countered. "And now he's in hiding."

"We interceded for him as much as we could, but I'm not sure where he is."

When the CIA had learned Barry Thatcher had opened a back door into their computer system to actively mine data about an elusive Agency case officer named Mister Smith, they had put out an immediate arrest warrant for the hacker.

Despite stopping illegal drug operations and an attempt to rig Haiti's presidential elections by CIA-contracted personnel, the Agency hadn't appreciated Barry's efforts. Ryan, Greg Olsen, Floyd Landis, and Cori Maxwell, Scott's girlfriend at the Defense Intelligence Agency, had all made phone calls on behalf of the hacker, but still Barry and his long-time girlfriend, Carmen, had disappeared.

"So, I'm your new Girl Friday until he turns back up?" Ashlee asked.

"Sort of."

"It might be easier if you just did a Google search," Ashlee said. "I mean, you know what you're looking for."

"Maybe," Ryan conceded. He wished he could call Barry. The hacker had always come through for him, even if his rates were astronomical. He hoped Barry and Carmen weren't rotting away in a CIA black site. It would be an extreme waste of talent.

"Look, I know you like to play dumb about this computer stuff, but I know the truth, Ryan. You have a lot of advanced training in robotics and specialized computer programs for dealing with explosive devices. Doing a Google search isn't out of your wheelhouse and making me do it is just laziness on your part."

Ryan bit his lip so he wouldn't bark at her. The Navy had taught him how to use robots to defuse bombs on land, to use remote-operated vehicles underwater, and how to repair those systems, but he didn't have a degree in information technology or computer science. He could put his computer skills to use, however it always seemed easier to pay someone else to do the legwork while he was in the field, where he'd rather be instead of getting blurry eyes from staring at a computer screen.

"Besides," Ashlee continued, "most of you EOD guys are true geeks in every sense."

"Okay, so you got me. I know how to operate a computer, but that doesn't mean I know anything about hacking a database which you might have to do to find those photos."

"Listen, Ryan, I appreciate you calling me, but I've got other work to do. You're a big boy—see if you can find it yourself."

"I won't bother you anymore." Ryan slammed the phone back into its cradle. He flexed his jaw muscles, trying to figure out why he was so angry. Ashlee had always provided him with solid intel before, and he had been surprised that she'd balked at helping him now. This whole mission had been one long series of slow-motion disasters, from Travis drop-kicking him off the diving barge to Diane getting kidnapped. Ryan needed to get a handle on the situation—and fast.

"You okay?" Scott asked, setting down a fresh beer on the desk for Ryan.

"Yeah. I'm just having trouble getting tech support. I miss Barry. Has Cori had any luck tracking him down?"

"Not yet."

Ryan took a long swig of beer, then started typing on the computer.

Looking over Ryan's shoulder, Scott asked, "What are you looking for?"

"You remember Clivon saying there used to be a big cave where the blue hole is now?"

"Yeah."

"I was hoping to find old photos of it."

"You think that's where the gold is?" Scott asked.

Ryan leaned back in the chair and told Scott about finding Ellen Carter's diary in the fireplace.

"She said they stashed the gold in the cave?" Scott asked.

"She and Baxter were supposed to take off with some of

it. Apparently, Baxter had a boat they were going to take to Cuba."

"Did they make it?"

"The diary doesn't say," Ryan replied. "She left it behind so no one could use it to identify them."

Pondering this while sipping his beer, Scott finally asked, "What if they came back for the gold and took it all with them?"

"That's a question I don't have an answer to."

"You said Baxter's mistress mentioned the name of the Bahamian who confronted them, right?"

"Yeah. John Andrews."

"Suppose Alice or Rafi know who he is?"

"Worth a shot," Ryan replied, standing and picking up his beer.

The two men walked to the kitchen where Alice was cleaning up. Ryan asked her if she had ever heard of a man who had worked on Big Darby by the name of John Andrews.

Alice ran a hand over her black hair, smoothing the tangles. "Nobody 'round these parts by dat name."

"Suppose Rafi knew him?" Ryan asked.

"You can ask him. He be over in de cottage."

"Thanks, Alice," Ryan said before he and Scott headed out into the night. The sky had cleared, and bright stars shone through the patchy clouds as they raced north on warming air. At least the storm had moved on. That would make searching for the cave easier.

"What did you do with the ground-penetrating radar unit?" Ryan asked.

"I found a little cave to tuck it into, then covered the entrance with some brush and old palm fronds."

"Petra was extremely pissed that it had gone missing."

Scott grinned. "I figured that would get her spooled up. She seems a little on edge."

"With millions of dollars' worth of gold at stake, I'm sure she is."

They found the cottage shared by Alice, her husband, and their two sons. Ryan knocked on the door. When Rafi opened it, he wore the same pair of cut-off jean shorts Ryan had last seen him in. In his right hand was a sweating beer.

After exchanging pleasantries, Ryan asked the laborer if he knew of John Andrews.

"He be dead ten years now."

Ryan felt disappointment course through him.

"Any relations we might be able to talk to?" Scott inquired.

"He had a son, James. Lives up on Staniel Cay."

"Can we get RJ to take us up there?" Ryan asked.

Rafi rubbed his chin. "A little far for his boat." He motioned for Ryan and Scott to wait on the porch and went into the cottage. A few minutes later, he returned. "My friend, Rufus, he come get you. Be at de dock at eight tomorrow morning."

"Thanks, Rafi," Ryan said.

As Ryan and Scott left, the troubleshooter hoped John Andrews's son could shed some light on the situation. If the cave had collapsed with the gold inside, there might not be any way to recover it.

For Diane's sake, Ryan prayed that there was.

CHAPTER TWENTY-SIX

James Andrews lived in a small cement-block building painted a vibrant blue, with yellow trim running around the window, door, and soffits. Ryan knocked on the front door, the yellow paint bearing the dirt of a hundred handprints around the knob. Small weeds grew in the cracks of the walk leading up to the single block used as a step into the house.

The door opened slowly, and an elderly Bahamian grinned when he saw Rufus, a mid-twenties kid with dreadlocks tucked into a Rastafarian cap. The two men shook hands before Rufus introduced him to Ryan.

"Mista Wella wants to speak to ya about Big Darby."

James looked quizzically at Ryan.

"I know your father John worked for Sir Guy Baxter on Big Darby," Ryan explained. "I was hoping you could answer some questions for me."

"Like what?" Andrews asked.

"Can I come in?" Ryan held up a six-pack of Kalik. It was still early in the day, but Rufus had insisted Ryan bring the beer as a gift.

"I could use a cold one," the older Bahamian said, holding the door open.

Inside, the house was cool, the air conditioner running at full blast despite yesterday's rain and chill.

Andrews moved a colorful afghan off the couch cushions and bid Ryan and Rufus to sit, then he popped the top on a Kalik and took a long drink. He nodded toward the beer carton, and Rufus and Ryan helped themselves. With beers in hand, the two men settled onto the couch across from Andrews in a recliner.

"Do you mind if I record this?" Ryan asked, pulling out his phone. "For future reference."

With a shrug, Andrews consented. "My father was the one on Big Darby. He swore me to secrecy about what happened to him. Why are you so interested?"

"I work for the new owner, Steve Carlton. He's tasked me with tracking down the history of the island so when his daughter is done renovating the Green Castle, she can use it as part of her advertising campaign."

Andrews snorted.

"I wanted to talk to you about what happened the morning after your father asked Baxter and his companions to leave the island," Ryan probed, pushing the record button on the phone app. "I know your father swore you to secrecy, but the men we're talking about are long dead."

Andrews seemed to ponder that statement as he sipped his beer.

"It's my understanding," Andrews finally said, "that my father and a group of people who worked on the island wanted Baxter gone. He'd been resupplying German submarines and had allowed one to spend multiple days at the island's north anchorage, having repair work done. My father, being a loyal subject of the Crown, called Baxter a traitor.

"After they told Baxter to go, my father stayed up all

night, watching the house. He hated having to make them leave. Baxter had been good to him, paid him a decent wage, and provided him with a job and a place to live when many in The Bahamas were struggling. But the war turned our economy around. Baxter wasn't the only employer in the game anymore. We had a lot of British troops and sailors training at various bases, so my father knew he could find employment elsewhere. I remember those days. There was still a lot of racial tension, but things were improving.

"Anyway, my father watched Baxter make preparations to leave. There were three of them—Baxter, his mistress, and a German."

"An SS officer named Poske," Ryan said.

"My father never knew his name. He was the only one to stay behind after the submarine left. About lunchtime on the day after they were asked to leave, the three of them went into the cave at the north end of the island. He said it used to be like a fancy church inside, that God had built for Himself. Before the submarine left, the crewmen unloaded twenty crates from it and placed them in the cave."

Ryan's heart rate increased. This was anecdotal confirmation of Ellen's diary. He stayed silent, letting Andrews fill in the blanks. Rufus leaned forward, enthralled by the story.

"Just after they entered the cave," Andrews continued, "there was a loud crack. Daddy described it sounding as if the Earth had split open. The whole island trembled and, suddenly, God's cathedral shattered and collapsed. The sea rushed in to fill the gap left by the cave. When the dust settled, there was no more cave, only the blue hole."

Ryan felt all hope drain away. The collapse had probably buried the gold so deeply that it would be impossible to retrieve. It would take a colossal effort to dig out the rubble. Complicating matters would be the sea that covered everything.

Trying to mask his disappointment, Ryan asked, "What happened to the boat that Baxter was going to use to escape?"

"For many years, my father used it as a charter vessel, taking rich, white tourists fishing in the Exuma Sound," Andrews replied. "That's how I got to talking so good. They didn't like all the dems and dats. Anyway, he stole the boat and brought my brothers and I to Staniel Cay, where we altered it substantially so no one would recognize her. It was much easier to do back then—the hulls were made from wood."

"Did anyone look for Baxter?" Rufus asked.

Andrews shook his head. "There was no need. He was in the cave when it collapsed. Rock and water cover his final resting place."

Ryan finished his beer and set the empty bottle back in the carton. "Thanks for telling us your story."

"It wasn't what you expected?" Andrews asked.

"It was about what I figured. I'd heard a cave had collapsed, but I didn't know Baxter, Ellen, and Poske had been inside. It does explain their mysterious disappearance."

"How did you learn the German's name?" Andrews asked.

"I found a diary with his name in it," Ryan replied, trying to remain vague.

Andrews nodded. "I always wondered when someone would come poking around, asking questions. Nazis and submarines are powerful lore."

"There's a lot of mystery surrounding Big Darby," Ryan replied. "Your story and others like it are putting the pieces together. Thank you for sharing it."

Andrews stood with Ryan and Rufus. He extended his hand to the troubleshooter. "You're welcome here anytime. Thank you for the beer."

At the door, Rufus and Andrews bumped fists, then Rufus walked with Ryan back toward the marina.

"Where to now, Mista Wella?" the Bahamian asked as they tossed off the boat's lines.

"First, we need to stop at Little Darby, then I need you to drop me off near Prime Cay."

CHAPTER TWENTY-SEVEN

Two hours later, Ryan dove over the side of Rufus' boat and swam toward the *Leopard*. Wearing nothing but his swimming trunks and a T-shirt, Ryan sliced through the shallow water with ease.

At a rocky outcropping, he paused to survey the scene. The salvage vessel still lay at anchor where he'd last seen her. The white sand, turquoise water, and green trees provided a picturesque tropical backdrop. On any other day, Ryan would have been excited to explore the island and dive beneath the sea in search of new treasures. Today, he was swimming straight into the shark's jaws.

Two crewmen stood watch near the rear of the vessel, and, as always, the captain stood guard on the bridge. Ryan wondered if the man ever slept. As he watched, Petra came strutting out of the main superstructure in a bright red one-piece swimsuit. He had to admit there was a reason she graced the covers of so many magazines—she was gorgeous, but Ryan knew underneath that supermodel body lurked an evil heart.

And he had to make a deal with her.

Shaking his head, Ryan heaved a deep sigh. He wasn't looking forward to facing these Nazi psychopaths again, but he couldn't leave Diane with them. Now that he knew where the gold was, hopefully he could exchange that knowledge for her freedom.

Plunging forward, Ryan made smooth strokes underwater. He came up for a breath partway to the *Leopard,* then swam the rest of the way on the surface after seeing the two guards aiming their weapons at him.

When he arrived at the ladder up to the salvage vessel's deck, Ryan wiped the water from his face with one hand while holding onto the ladder with the other. He looked up at the curious face of Petra Ziegler as she stared down at him.

"Is this a rescue mission?" she asked.

"No. I came to talk to you."

"I don't date peasants," she replied.

Ignoring her barb, Ryan climbed up and stood dripping on the hot steel deck.

"What do you want?" Petra asked, hands on hips.

"Where's your better-looking twin?"

Petra arched her back to accentuate her assets, feigning a wounded expression that she intended to be provocative.

"Lady, you can't hold a candle to my wife."

"What brings you aboard, Herr Weller?" Hermann asked, stepping out of the superstructure.

Ryan glanced at the two men with their H&K UMPs, then focused on Hermann. He didn't stand a chance of taking them down without getting shot in the process.

"I came to get Diane," he said.

"I told you," Petra repeated. "First you bring us the gold and then you can have the woman."

"I know where the gold is," Ryan said nonchalantly. "Is that good enough?"

Petra's eyes sparkled. "Tell us."

"You got a map?" Ryan asked.

"Inside."

Petra led the way into the galley and told Ryan to sit while she barked an order in her native tongue to Swastika Tattoo. Soon, the man returned with a laminated map and spread it out on the table in front of them as Meyer joined them.

"Show me," Petra ordered.

Ryan placed his finger on where the entrance to the old cave had been. "It's there, buried under countless tons of rubble."

"What makes you so sure?" Petra asked, arms folded across her chest.

"Just this morning, I spoke to the son of John Andrews, the man who asked Baxter to leave the island." Ryan went on to relay the version of events as told to him by James Andrews. "Baxter, his mistress, and Poske died in the cave collapse. The gold is buried under there." Ryan put his finger back on the map, then glanced around at the strangely silent faces of the German treasure-hunting team as they digested his story. "So, can I take Diane now?"

"*Nein*," Petra practically screamed. "I told you to bring the gold, not some *Scheißdreck* story!"

Ryan raised his hands, not understanding her German, but correctly figuring she was calling bullshit.

The enraged model slapped the table, then leaned down, bringing her face close to Ryan's. "*You* are a salvage diver, Herr Weller. *You* will recover *my* gold and deliver it to *me*."

"That's going to take equipment that I don't have," Ryan said. "I'll need dive gear, air refills, and hydraulic jackhammers. Clearing that mess won't be easy. It'll take time, and I'll need help. Bring the *Leopard* to the anchorage off Big Darby."

"Hermann will help you," Petra stated.

"Are you a diver, Hermann?" Ryan asked.

"I've been trained by the best combat swimmers at GSG 9," Hermann stated proudly.

"That don't mean shit," Ryan said. "We're not doing hand-to-hand combat underwater. We're busting rocks."

"Even easier," the German replied.

"This is a salvage vessel," Ryan said. "Surely you have qualified commercial divers aboard?"

"Four," a man said from the galley hatch. Ryan recognized the captain, wearing his typical white uniform, polished shoes, and a shiny brass belt buckle, from his time spying on the *Leopard*. His mustache was neatly trimmed and combed, and his short black hair was graying at the temples.

"This is not your business, Captain Haas," Petra barked.

"But this is my ship. As long as you're aboard my vessel, you are under my authority. This man needs qualified divers to do the work he is talking about. I will supply them, along with all the equipment he needs to recover the gold. If you doubt my word," Haas said, stepping toward Petra and placing his hands on his uniformed hips, "you may call Katrine."

Ryan wondered who the hell Katrine was, but from the look on the siblings' faces, she was clearly a woman neither of them wanted to trifle with.

"Captain, we will head north at once," Petra stated. "Prepare your men to dive."

Haas left the galley and headed up the steps.

"Can I see Diane?" Ryan asked.

"Where are my men?" Hermann countered.

"They're locked in the shed behind the research center on Little Darby."

The big German nodded and called for his men. When two men with UMPs dangling from shoulder harnesses appeared at the hatch, he instructed, "Put him in the cabin with *Frau* Carlton and lock the door."

The guards shoved Ryan out of the galley, down a ladder-well, and forward to a small cabin. The one with the missing pinkie finger on his left hand unlocked the door and motioned for Ryan to go inside. Reluctantly, the troubleshooter stepped through the hatch, and it slammed closed behind him.

Diane launched herself at him, wrapping her arms around his neck and her legs around his torso as she and burying her dark head against his chest. Ryan was immediately torn between comforting her and peeling her off him.

Ryan held her close, knowing she needed the comfort. When she finally dropped her legs to the deck, Ryan pushed her away, his hands on her shoulders. He got a glimpse of the dark circles under her red eyes, evidence that she'd been crying.

He heard the diesels start and felt the deck rumbling beneath their feet.

"Where are they taking us?" Diane asked, fear in her voice.

"To Big Darby. I told them where the gold is."

"How did you find it? I mean, they've been searching for it all over the island?"

"I just put the clues together, and I had a little help from a diary written by Ellen Carter, Guy Baxter's mistress." He went on to explain about finding the hidden journal in the Green Castle and talking to James Andrews.

"How will you get the gold out?" she asked once Ryan had finished.

Ryan sat on the bunk and rubbed his temples. "I'm not sure, but I guess we'll know soon enough."

CHAPTER TWENTY-EIGHT

The *Leopard* anchored off the tip of Big Darby where Ryan supposed that decades ago, U-1226 had sheltered while the crew had tried to repair its snorkel before offloading the gold.

Ryan stood on deck with Gunther, the German diver assigned to be his minder and helper while Hermann and Klein, another commercial diver, would provide backup. Two more divers, Schuler and Bergmann, would also standby to assist.

An array of diving gear was spread out on the deck. Ryan had been able to find items that fit his frame, but his main concern was a tight-sealing mask. There was nothing worse than a leaky mask when working underwater. Fortunately, the divers aboard the *Leopard* had brought first-rate Dive Rite gear, including backmount harnesses, regulators, masks, fins, and Pinnacle wetsuits. It pleased Ryan to see the excellent condition the gear was in, but he wished he could retrieve his own bag of equipment from where he'd left it in the woods behind Diane's tent.

As Ryan geared up, he eyed the dive knife in its plastic

sheath that lay on the deck near his feet. Petra saw him glance at it, stepped over, and kicked the knife out of the way. "You won't be needing that."

The knife might have come in handy, but for now, he needed to focus on the dive.

Ryan strapped his diving harness to a steel tank and screwed the regulator into the tank valve. Once he and Gunther had tested their gear, Artem Kowalchuk, the dude with the Nazi tattoo, drove Ryan, Hermann, Gunther, and Klein across the water to the beach in the *Leopard*'s tender.

Once the divers had waded ashore, Kowalchuk returned to the salvage vessel to pick up the shooters and Petra. Everyone wanted to be on hand for the first dive of the day. Ryan, however, wasn't so optimistic. He'd studied maps and photos of the island but hadn't spotted anything resembling an opening to a cave or a flooded underwater tunnel. The seabed rose from the shallow channel between the islands in a gentle slope covered in less than a foot of water in most places. The seawater was so clear, it would have been impossible not to spot a cave entrance submerged beneath it. Of course, the entrance could be covered with sand, in which case it would be next to impossible to dig out, so Ryan's best bet was to start in the blue hole and search beneath the water there.

In the back of his mind, Ryan plotted a way to rescue Diane at the first opportunity. He wasn't sure how he would make it work, but he knew that given the chance, he would act. At some point, the Germans would look the other way and ... *Bam*! Ryan would strike like lightning. He would take Diane and escape. Let the Zieglers dig themselves a giant hole like the fools on Oak Island, searching for treasure they might never find.

But Ryan knew gold brought out the crazies and the attention seekers. Since time immemorial, treasure had lured men out of their quiet, sedate lives to search the dry, stark desert canyons; the vast, rolling blue sea; rich, tree-studded valleys; and rugged, rocky crevices of the high mountains. Movies had been made, books written, and television shows dedicated to the search for treasure. Sane people turned into psychopaths just for the chance to hold a single gold bar.

Ryan knew he was no different. Searching for a lost trove of Nazi gold was the stuff that dreams and legends were made of. Now that he was on the hunt, he, too, had gold fever.

Ryan and Gunther shouldered into their harnesses while on the beach and then walked up the rocky channel to the edge of the blue hole. The brassy sun caused them to sweat as they stood staring at the almost clear water at the edge of the pool, stretching to a fathomless deep blue over the center, caused by the high transparency of the water and the bright white limestone surrounds.

The two divers sat on the craggy limestone, which dug into the flesh of their thighs through their wetsuits as they pulled on their fins. Ryan was the first to push himself off and sink beneath the water's calm exterior, until the air in his doughnut bladder pulled him back to the surface. Gunther slid in next, bobbing up to join Ryan while Hermann and Klein looked on from shore.

"Ready?" Ryan asked his new partner.

The German gave a curt, "*Ja*," then the two men lifted their power inflators and released the air from their bladders, sinking into the water. Ryan rolled onto his stomach, kicking with powerful strokes to glide along the sloping rock shelf toward the deep.

He felt a giddy elation as they headed down. Ryan was back in his element, exploring a pool he'd never been in before. As Ryan descended, he felt small currents buffer his body, pushing and pulling against him like waves on the beach.

Clearing his ears for the tenth or twelfth time, Ryan checked his depth gauge. They were currently at one hundred feet. The water darkened beneath them. He wanted to find the bottom, then turn and work his way up the slope, searching for gaps in the rock where the ocean seemed to surge through.

He glanced over his shoulder to find Gunther right beside him. The compact German was no more than five-eleven, wide in the shoulders, lean in the waist and hips, with powerful thighs built from years of swimming with fins and squatting heavy gym weights. He had short blond hair and blue eyes that matched the surrounding water. Ryan wondered if Gunther was as fanatical about Nazism as he seemed about diving.

Gunther popped out his regulator and grinned at Ryan, his white teeth flashing. With the reg back in, he gave Ryan the "hang loose" sign with his thumb and pinky extending from a closed fist. It seemed like the guy was enjoying himself.

When they reached the bottom of the hole, Ryan's depth gauge read 157 feet.

Ryan planted his feet on the sand floor and looked straight up at the sunlight glinting on the surface, then he slowly turned in a circle, taking in the steep cavern walls, the sloping wall formed of boulders the size of Buicks, and the large slabs of fallen limestone covered in decaying vegetation. The rockface appeared to have once been above ground, confirming the story he'd heard from James Andrews.

Exhaling a cloud of bubbles, Ryan motioned to his dive buddy that they would now ascend. Together, they kicked off the bottom. Checking his air, Ryan saw he had plenty in reserve and could easily make it to the surface if they didn't linger, but he wanted to do some exploring first, to find a spot to start the excavation of the gold.

Nearing the seventy-foot mark, Ryan saw a large gap in the rocks and swam toward it. He could feel the ocean surging through the crevice. Beside him, Gunther turned on his LED light, shining it into the darkness beneath the rocks. There appeared to be a tunnel, leading farther into the depths. Gunther swam forward, but Ryan grabbed him by the leg and hauled him backward.

The German spun, brow furrowed in question. Ryan tapped his air gauge and then motioned upward. Gunther consulted his own gauge, then nodded.

Ryan unclipped a spool of line from his harness and inflated the marker buoy with a puff of air from his spare regulator. Once the buoy reached the surface, Ryan wedged the spool beneath several rocks, and the two men headed up, making several safety stops on the way up to allow the nitrogen that had built up in their tissues to dissipate.

———

STANDING on the edge of the blue hole beside Hermann Ziegler twenty minutes later, Ryan explained the purpose of the marker buoy. In an hour's time, he and Gunther would make another exploratory dive.

"We should dive in teams," Hermann stated. "We can accomplish more together."

While Ryan didn't like the plan because he wanted to be the one to find the gold, he knew it was the most prudent way forward. Having two teams of divers would expedite their exploration and recovery time, as well as Diane's release.

Ryan also knew he had no choice. While he and Gunther had been underwater during their thirty-minute dive, the crew of the *Leopard* had set up a ten-by-ten canopy with a folding table beneath it, laden with the dive gear for

Hermann's team. More scuba tanks had been stacked in a small pyramid on the ground beside a large cooler.

Someone had also freed the three guards from the shed. They now stood at the ready at various intervals around the blue hole, armed with replacement UMPs.

After shedding his dive gear, Ryan walked over to the cooler and nudged open the lid. Encased in ice were cans of soda, bottles of water, and pre-made cold-cut sandwiches. Ryan helped himself to a sandwich and a soda before joining Gunther to brief *The Shining* twins at the table. Ryan could hear them now: "Come play with us, Ryan." He shivered. Hermann in a dress was a horrifying thought.

Ryan studied Klein, Gunther, and the Ziegler siblings. They all had similar facial characteristics, body types, the same thick blond hair and blue eyes. "Are you guys all related?" he asked impulsively. "Or is there something in the water you're drinking back in Germany?"

"*Ja,*" Klein replied. "We are *Lebensborn.* We are the chosen ones, meant to ascend to power and conquer the world."

Petra spoke sharply to the man in German. What she said, Ryan couldn't really tell, but to him, Germans sounded like they were screaming at each other even when having a normal conversation.

Klein smiled. "It doesn't matter what I tell him," he said to Petra in English. "He will be dead before we recover the gold."

Ryan stared right back at the German diver, not batting an eye. He had known from the moment he had swam out to the *Leopard* that he was risking his life. That was what Steve Carlton was paying him for, after all—to keep Diane safe and get rid of the ghosts.

What Ryan wanted was to have it all. Save the girl. Kill the ghosts. Get the gold.

CHAPTER TWENTY-NINE

Hermann and his dive buddy Klein returned from their exploration dive before Ryan and Gunther had completed their surface interval.

"The opening Weller and Gunther found extends well beyond what we could see," Hermann reported to his sister. "We pushed about fifteen feet into the cave, but it became incredibly tight. There is a gap beneath a large boulder, but we'll have to shed our gear to get through."

"What do you propose?" Petra asked.

Ryan listened intently to their conversation. Apparently, they were having it in English for his benefit.

"We need to stage tanks along the route," Klein stated. "It will mean a longer decompression dive, but it's the only way to make the push."

"What about rebreathers?" Ryan asked.

"We have them aboard the boat, but there's only enough oxygen and diluent to make two dives. Are you familiar with the Dive Rite Optima?" Gunther asked Ryan.

"Vaguely," Ryan replied. "I'm used to diving a rEVo III."

Normally, a diver trained and certified on each individual

rebreather model, even if two different models were made by the same manufacturer. While rebreathers operated on the same principle of scrubbing the carbon dioxide from a diver's exhalation and injecting oxygen into the system to rebalance the breathing gas, not all rebreathers were designed the same. Each had its own quirks and eccentricities that a diver needed to be aware of before entering the water.

"I'm an instructor for the Optima CCR," Gunther stated. "I will show you how to use it properly."

Hermann used a handheld radio to call the *Leopard* and arranged for two of the Optimas to be brought to the dive site. Twenty minutes later, a crewman arrived in the launch with the rebreathers and spare bottles of gas.

Ryan and Gunther shouldered the gear and walked back to the canopy. Klein was sketching the entrance to the cave and the fifteen feet to the restriction on the back of a laminated map, using a black marker on the white background. He would consult his wrist slate and then draw an overhead view of the cave along with depths and distances.

Gunther broke down the CCR training into short, quick bursts, acquainting Ryan rather quickly to the unique features of the Dive Rite Optima. Within another thirty minutes, the two men were ready to dive.

Ryan glanced at the drawing Klein had made, impressed with the thoroughness and the professionalism of the divers despite taking on an unvetted diver who was being forced to work under duress. But, then again, most aspects of commercial diving required one to work under duress. There was always a time crunch, ripping currents, freezing cold water, zero visibility, and a host of other factors to contend with.

Ryan tested the rebreather and slid into the water beside Gunther. They sank beneath the surface, slowly following the slope down toward the cave so Ryan could familiarize himself and become comfortable with his new diving apparatus.

Once they reached the cave entrance, Ryan could feel the flow of water pushing through the opening had lessened since his last dive. He noticed a trickle of bubbles coming from farther up the slope, indicating where Hermann and Klein had pushed into the cave and their trapped exhalation bubbles were slowly dissipating.

With a flash of the "Okay" sign, Gunther asked if Ryan was ready. Ryan answered with a "hang loose" sign. The two men clicked on their powerful dive lights and swam through the cave entrance.

The enveloping darkness was almost as complete as the silence. Ryan heard the solenoids click in the rebreather to release oxygen into his breathing mix with every breath he took. The computer constantly monitored his breathing and adjusted his gas mixture for the most optimal blend, meaning there was less buildup of nitrogen in his system and his dive would last much longer than on open circuit, where he would be limited by absolute bottom time and the gas reserve in his tank. Depending on the depth, he could spend hours underwater, the rebreather making minute adjustments to compensate as required.

Closing his eyes, Ryan listened to the water rushing past his ears; heard the pop of the electronics; the beep of Gunther's computer; and the scrape of a dive fin against the rock wall.

At the restriction, the two men studied the way ahead. They would have to remove their rebreather units and pass them through the opening, then swim after them and hope there was enough room on the other side to redon the outfit. Gunther motioned Ryan forward, pointing toward the hole.

With a weary sigh, Ryan wriggled out of his Optima and shoved it through the gap, careful to close the breathing loop before doing so in case he lost control of the device, and the falling weight ripped the mouthpiece from between his clenched teeth. The precaution was more to prevent the breathing loop from flooding than it was about control of the unit. If seawater entered the loop, it would chemically react with the soda lime absorbent and create a caustic cocktail that could burn a diver's lungs and cause death. More imperatively, once the loop flooded, the unit was inoperable.

Hermann had nixed the idea of Ryan and Gunther carrying spare safety bottles of gas because of the restrictions. If the rebreather stopped functioning, Ryan was dead.

Letting out a constant stream of bubbles from between his lips, Ryan wriggled into the cramped space beneath the boulder. Once he was beyond the restriction, he put his arms through the straps of the rebreather, so the tanks and scrubber hung from his chest. After opening the breathing loop, Ryan swept his dive light around the cave. The tunnel was narrower on this side. The divers would have to swim single file instead of side by side.

Ryan reached back through the restriction and took the reel from Gunther. It was standard procedure when swimming into a cave to lay a line. If something happened to his lights or equipment, or if the cave became silted out from the diver disturbing the particulate on the cave floor, the diver could grasp the line and follow it out of the cave. Small plastic arrows clipped onto the line marked the direction of the closest exit.

Ryan motioned for Gunther to wait as he pressed on ahead. He wasn't a trained cave diver, nor did Ryan have mapping skills like Klein, but he'd been on countless dives inside shipwrecks and penetrating a cave was no different than making his way to the engine room of a submerged vessel. He swam forward, using a frog kick to propel himself. Ryan noticed the water no longer pushed against him.

A glance on his depth gauge showed he was at ninety feet. The tunnel didn't appear to drop dramatically, but Ryan had descended twenty feet since entering the cave. The walls were not smooth, but rather constructed of boulders stacked haphazardly on top of one another, forming a loose funnel toward the bottom. With each probing sweep of his light, Ryan saw large crevices that dead-ended or led off into the dark.

Another thirty feet of line clicked off the reel as he concentrated on the main tunnel when, suddenly, the cave widened dramatically. Ryan saw the bottom of the blue hole beneath him in the beam of his light. He descended, looking all around, seeing large slabs of limestone had fallen from above to form the massive gap in the cave he now found himself in. Ryan felt like he was in a conical flask, descending the long neck toward a bottom that widened significantly.

From his position at the top of the cone, Ryan saw a small pile of boulders off to one side, but what caught his eye was the glinting of his light off the bars of gold laying in the sand just to the right of the pile. Forgetting about everything but retrieving the gold, Ryan dropped like a stone to the seabed, tied off the reel to a nearby boulder, and then picked up two of the gold bars. Their weight surprised him, but it shouldn't have. He'd held gold bars while recovering them from the sea before, but each time felt like the first. There was always the anticipation of discovery, the adrenaline of the first find, and the giddiness of showing the find to partners. Ryan had once likened the experience to getting that first kiss from a new date.

Standing on the cave floor, Ryan focused on the gold bar in his hand. He had completed part of the mission—he had the gold—but it still felt too easy. There was something not quite right about his push through the tunnel and into the cave. Swinging his light around, Ryan inspected the cave for a moment. His light paused on a skeleton trapped beneath a boulder, the jaw open, as if locked in a permanent scream.

When the water began tugging at him, Ryan suddenly knew what he'd forgotten about.

The water rushing into the cave had been the tide flowing through. Ryan's push past the restriction and down to the gold had come at slack tide. Now it was turning.

Feeling an immediate sense of urgency, Ryan pushed the two gold bars into a pouch on the rebreather's harness, then hurried to sling the Optima across his back in its proper position and cinch all the straps tight. It was going to be a long, hard slog against the current to exit the cave.

But none of that mattered.

As soon as the tide shifted and headed out to sea, the water rushing through the restriction sucked Ryan backward into the darkness. He tumbled head over heels, the dive light swinging wildly in circles as it twisted around on the lanyard attached to his wrist. He tried to take a deep breath but felt like the weight of the sea was crushing him. When his arm flashed in front of his face, Ryan got a glimpse of his depth—175 feet.

Ryan tried to right himself in the overwhelming current, afraid he would strike the back of the sea cave and be knocked unconscious. He twisted so he was facing the direction of movement, then spread his arms and legs like a skydiver steadying himself in the air. The trick worked and in the brief moment of his light flashing across the rocky cliff in front of him, Ryan knew he was going to hit hard and dove for the sand to protect himself. Instead of hitting the rock wall, he skidded across the sand, flipping head over heels again.

When he'd righted himself again, Ryan found he was facing into the sea cave. He got a grip on the light and saw the current had dragged him into another tunnel. Fighting to move back toward the gold, he realized the current was too strong to swim against. He was breathing hard and worried he would over breathe the scrubber, meaning he was putting too much carbon dioxide into the unit and that the soda lime wouldn't effectively remove it. Ryan wasn't sure how the canister system on the Optima worked, but, in the past, he had seen where channels had formed in the soda lime, preventing the rebreather from scrubbing the carbon dioxide and instead passing it right back to the diver. When the diver breathed in the elevated levels of carbon dioxide he would pass out. At this depth, a blackout would be fatal.

Ryan took a deep breath and slowly exhaled around the mouthpiece into the water, forcing himself to remain calm. He was sliding along the sand, being pushed by the current flowing through the gaps in the rocks and forcing him down this yet-to-be-explored tunnel.

After making a few more strong kicks against the tide, Ryan realized he wasn't going to make it back to the gold. Even with his kicks, he was going backward. It would be at least six more hours before slack tide allowed him to swim out of the cave the way he had come in.

With only one thing left to do, Ryan turned and went with the current. Suddenly, everything became easier. His body was no longer under constant pressure, his breathing shallowed, and a kick from his legs sent him speeding along.

As he swam, the question that nagged at the back of Ryan's mind was where this tunnel ended—would it pop him out into Exuma Sound, or would the water pin him to a wall and drown him?

There was no other option but to go with the flow and find out.

CHAPTER THIRTY

Glancing at the computers that controlled his Optima rebreather and monitored his gas supply, Ryan saw he had plenty of oxygen and diluent. He stayed low to the shifting sand that covered the hard limestone floor of the cave. With the current pushing him along, Ryan kept his legs slightly spread and his knees bent so his fins were wide and stable, controlling his balance. He had his hands folded together in front of him, the beam of his dive light focused into the dark tunnel ahead.

He guessed this tunnel had formed during the last ice age, around the same time as the blue hole on Big Darby Island. Back then, the ocean had been one hundred meters lower, and these unexplored formations had been above ground. Glacier runoff had eroded the limestone, leaving behind caves before the ceilings collapsed, opening the blue hole. Then, the oceans had risen and flooded the land.

Ryan felt like he was flying, just like that guy in the red underwear with the "S" on his cape. He wondered how far he'd traveled and was keeping an eye on the dive timer. It had been nearly ten minutes since he'd made the decision to go with the flow. He knew the average human could swim at approximately three knots with diving fins, and since he hadn't been able to swim upstream, he figured the water was flowing at four knots or greater.

After twenty minutes, he figured he'd gone about a mile through the tube. He still had plenty of gas in reserve, but there was no way he could swim back to the cave of gold now.

With each passing foot, Ryan wondered if he would exit the tunnel or drown to death when his gas supply finally ran out. At least the depth had held steady at 175 feet, but he was accruing significant bottom time, which meant multiple decompression stops on his way to the surface—if he even made it out of the cave.

Despite his attempts to remain levelheaded, panic tightened his chest, and his veins felt like spiders were crawling through them. He wanted to swim as hard and as fast as he could to find the exit of the tunnel or the end of his life, but he forced himself to take slow, even breaths. Panic had killed many divers, especially in overhead environments. Divers who had run out of air in caves had been found with bloody stumps for fingers from where they'd tried to claw their way through tons of rock to freedom.

What kept Ryan in check was constantly monitoring his electronics, concentrating on his slow, steady breathing, and remembering all the hours and hours of training he'd been through as a commercial, recreational, and military diver.

Years ago, after studying the deaths of other divers, Ryan had developed a personal diving philosophy: if there was air in the tank, then he could work out any problem he might encounter. That was the mindset he adopted now.

He used his fins to steer through the tunnel. At one point, he heard a low, keening sound coming through the water. After spinning in circles to see where the noise was coming from, Ryan found he was the one making it. He was absolutely terrified that his journey would end at a rock wall. His breathing and heart rate increased, amplified by the fear of being unable to escape the overhead environment.

Ryan wasn't ready to confront the grim reaper, but he had a plan. He would go out on his own terms. There wasn't enough gas in his tanks for him to wait for the tide to change and carry him back to the blue hole, and he doubted the Germans would attempt a rescue effort. So, Ryan decided that if he became pinned at the end of the tunnel, he'd slip off the rebreather and hold his breath until he no longer could, then he would inhale the sea and be at one with it.

In the back of his mind beat another tattoo: "You're not going to die. You're not going to die."

He screamed it into his mouthpiece, trying to drum up some courage, but dark doubts remained.

"I'm sorry, Emily," he whispered.

———

AFTER ANOTHER TWENTY minutes of stomach-tightening dread, Ryan felt the morbid fog lift from his brain. Hope swelled in his chest, to replace the fear that had lodged there.

In one of life's great ironies, he could see light at the end of the tunnel.

The swift current carried Ryan toward the brilliant blue orb. It made his eyes ache despite having had his dive light on. He clicked it off and clipped it to his harness, ready to grab the coral outside the cave entrance to keep from being dragged out to sea.

Unfortunately, the flow of water shot Ryan straight out of the tunnel like a cork from a champagne bottle. He arched his back, kicking hard for the undersea wall that extended in both directions as far as Ryan could see.

Ryan felt the current diminish as he moved to the side of

the cave entrance, closer to the coral-covered wall. Once he found a purchase for his hand on some bleached-out coral, Ryan took a deep breath and evaluated his predicament. He was out of the godforsaken cave and had a clear path to the surface, even though he knew that ascending immediately meant sudden death from the decompression sickness.

The rebreather's computer gave him a two-hour decompression schedule, with plenty of gas to spare if everything went according to plan. Outside the cave, the current was non-existent. The movement of the tidal water had produced a Venturi effect, where the speed of the water accelerated as it flowed through the restriction.

Slowly, Ryan began to ascend along the wall, his attention drawn to the colorful coral growing from the limestone and the rich abundance of marine life. He spotted trumpetfish, grunts, sergeant majors, larger snappers, and barracudas. Staghorn coral and purple sea fans provided hiding spots for tiny wrasses and parrot fish.

Moving no faster than thirty feet per minute to give his body plenty of time to off-gas any built-up nitrogen in his tissues, Ryan continued his ascent until he reached one hundred feet. When determining decompression stops, the general rule of thumb was to stop at half the depth for half the bottom time. While Ryan hadn't exceeded 175 feet, he'd factored in a safety cushion with the stop at one hundred. Now, he just had to spend thirty minutes hanging out, letting the rebreather feed him the optimal diving gas for the depth.

As Ryan waited, he felt his body begin to chill. The water temperature was eighty-two degrees Fahrenheit, much cooler than his body temp, but the water pulled the heat from his body faster than he could make it, despite the wetsuit's insulating properties. The adrenaline firing through his body during the long tunnel swim had ebbed, and now Ryan was aware of the onset of hypothermia. He clamped his teeth on the rubber mouthpiece and stiffened every muscle in his body as he held onto the coral wall, hoping to force the blood out of his core and into his extremities. Ryan kept repeating this exercise as he watched the minutes tick by with agonizing slowness.

In between tensing his muscles, Ryan cycled through the screens on the two computers, finding the electronic compass. He oriented himself with North, the wall being to his left, stretching out in a northeasterly direction. Visibility seemed to extend a couple hundred feet before fading into a dark gloom. As he watched a school of amberjacks, Ryan saw movement in his peripheral vision. A twelve-foot-long hammerhead swam out of the haze, its long tail propelling him forward in a never-ending hunt for prey.

Ryan felt naked as the shark loitered off the wall, cruising back and forth, as if sensing Ryan was an out-of-place visitor but not quite knowing what to make of the diver. If Ryan had been diving on open circuit, the bubbles would usually keep sharks away, but the rebreather barely made a whisper. The soundless operation of the diving unit allowed close encounters with pelagic wildlife and was therefore preferred by underwater photographers. Ryan huffed out a breath from around his mouthpiece, the bubbles billowing out. Mister Hammerhead eyed Ryan for a brief instant, then shot out of sight.

Once the Optima's computer beeped, Ryan began his ascent again. His body shivered uncontrollably as he made his way to his next stop, this time at the top of the wall, at sixty feet. He found a place to lie in the sand between two large coral heads, closed his eyes, and concentrated on controlling his body. Starting at his toes, he squeezed his muscles for ten-second increments, moving up his six-foot frame in slow, deliberate succession.

He wondered if Gunther had penetrated the restriction to

search for him. If he had, the German diver would have been caught in the same ripping current and subsequently washed down the tunnel. As Ryan hadn't seen his minder yet, he assumed he'd been left to fend for himself.

He prayed the Germans would wait for slack tide, giving him time to finish his decompression procedures and exit the water on the east side of Little Darby. If they thought he was dead, it was all the better.

Ryan had a new plan.

He would become the ghost.

Together, he and Scott would hunt the Germans to their deaths.

CHAPTER THIRTY-ONE

It took two more hours of hypothermic decompression stops before Ryan could slide out of the water and crawl up the beach. He lay in the hot sand, letting the sun bake his black wetsuit and take away the chill, but he still shivered from the heat loss. He needed hot liquids and blankets to wrap himself in so he could warm himself back to normal body temperature.

Once he'd collected his breath, Ryan shed the rebreather and made his way across the island. He hoped the Zieglers hadn't stationed guards near The Drifts Lodge, but just in case, Ryan darted from tree to tree, scanning the surrounding area before making a dash across the runway.

Reaching the small cabin that Alice and Rafi shared with their sons, he knocked on the door. Rafi opened it to find Ryan swaying on his feet, semi-delirious from hypothermia and dehydration. The Bahamian caught the American under his arms and dragged him into the small living room. Alice kept the place tidy, and everything appeared freshly cleaned, from the worn furniture to the dusted bookshelves.

"What happened to you?" Rafi asked.

"I've been in the water for almost four hours," Ryan croaked. "Got caught in an old cave, then the current took me out to sea."

Rafi guided Ryan into the bathroom. "Take a hot shower. I'll have tea ready when you come out. You was in de sea way too long."

Ryan nodded and reached for the shower knobs as Rafi closed the door. He stripped off the wetsuit and let the steaming water pound his naked body, then he sat on the floor of the tub and curled his arms around his knees.

Twenty minutes later, the hot water gave out. Ryan gathered himself and stood, shutting off the shower and using a fluffy towel to dry himself off. While he'd been in the shower, Rafi had brought Ryan's clothes from the lodge.

After Ryan had dressed, he asked Rafi, "Did you see any of the Germans?"

"Da people on de boat?"

"Yeah?"

"Not since dey got der people from de shed. Alice saw dem come."

Ryan nodded and followed Rafi to the kitchen. He sat at the table while Rafi poured him a steaming cup of black tea. Ryan ladled in two spoonfuls of sugar and stirred the concoction. Rafi watched the diver silently as Ryan sipped the tea.

"Your friend, he come soon," Rafi said.

"You saw Scott?" Ryan asked.

"He watch dose boat people. Dey very bad. He say you with dem."

"Do you know where Scott is?" Ryan asked, changing the subject. If he had to tell his story, he only wanted to do it once.

"He say he come soon. He better hurry. Storm come soon, too."

Great, Ryan thought. *More rain.*

———

By DINNERTIME, the strong tea and dry clothing had helped Ryan tremendously. His body temperature was back to normal, and he was ready to put his plan into motion.

Ryan had expected the former SEAL to return before darkness had settled, but Scott had yet to show. Keeping his fingers crossed that his friend was safe and hadn't fallen into the hands of the Nazi fanatics who had taken control of Big Darby, Ryan kept a close watch on the *Leopard* while staying out of sight in a room inside The Drifts Lodge. He feasted on another delicious dinner cooked by Alice and went to bed after drinking two fingers of rum to help warm him further.

The next morning, Scott still hadn't appeared. As predicted by Rafi, another storm front had moved in, and heavy rain had begun to fall. Ryan wasn't looking forward to going out in it, but he had a job to do.

After a filling breakfast and a report from Rafi that Hermann's crew had left the *Leopard* for the morning, Ryan donned his pack, having stashed it at the lodge before having Rufus take him to meet the Germans yesterday. He walked across Little Darby to where he'd come ashore after his harrowing swim last night and stepped lightly into RJ's waiting panga. The kid shot them around the end of the island, across the narrow channel, and slowed near where he'd dropped Ryan the first time Ryan had snuck onto Big Darby. Things had come full circle.

Ryan waded across the flats and walked up into the palm trees before following the rock wall up the ridge. He stepped carefully, placing his boots down where he wouldn't rustle dead palm fronds or snap fallen twigs.

The first place he checked for Scott was in the Green Castle, but he wasn't there. Ryan took a moment to recon the Germans' position. From the second-floor window, he could see the canopy set up over the dive gear and a team of divers entering the water. He wondered if the dive team had pushed through the cave and found the gold. Staying low, he glassed the area, looking at the guards. The Zieglers hadn't strengthened their defenses since Ryan had been there yesterday.

Of course, Hermann's team only consisted of six men and one evil female twin, plus another seven in the *Leopard*'s crew. Fourteen total adversaries. And they were all clustered around the dive site, except for Captain Haas and two members of the ship's company.

From the Green Castle, Ryan headed for Diane's tent. Once again, he found it devoid of life.

Stepping outside, Ryan glanced around, trying to figure out where Scott might be holed up. Ryan wished he could shout out his friend's name but knew that would only draw attention to himself and he wanted to remain unseen.

"Where are you, Scott?" he muttered.

From the tent, Ryan went to the spot where he'd hidden his weapons duffel. He uncovered it, relieved it was still intact, and set about donning the chest rig and checking his weapons.

Once he had everything adjusted to his satisfaction, Ryan began a search of the island for his absent friend.

CHAPTER THIRTY-TWO

Hermann

The first dive of the day had gone well. Slack tide had occurred just after 6:30 a.m. Gunther and Schuler had run a heavy-duty line from a stake at the canopy down through the cave opening discovered by Weller and Gunther on their first dive, past the restriction, and anchored it to the seafloor in the cave beside the gold.

When Gunther waded out of the water, he handed Hermann a gold bar plucked from a pile of others.

"There are many more," Schuler added, placing the gold bar he'd brought back on the table for Petra to admire.

"Any sign of Weller?" Hermann asked.

"None, sir, but it appears that the cave extends well to the east," Gunther replied. "It's possible the current swept him into it."

"Do you think he survived?" Petra asked gleefully.

"It's hard to say," Gunther replied. "If he's a skilled diver, he may have found a way out, but to me, it looks like the cave goes under Little Darby Island. I believe the current probably pinned Weller against the rocks."

Hermann began to pull on his dive gear. "The rope will keep us from drifting off, yes?"

Gunther nodded. "Keep your Jon line clipped to the main line, and you should have no problems."

"What about retrieving the gold?" Petra asked.

"It will take time," Gunther answered. "We'll have to pass it all through the restriction, plus our bottom time is severely limited by our open circuit operations. The way I see it, is that we drop quickly to the cave floor, fill a metal basket with gold bars, and bring it up using lift bags through the restriction. From there, we can guide it to the surface rather easily."

"How long will that take?" Petra asked.

"Depends on how much gold is down there," Klein said. "Hermann and I will do this dive while you time it, so we'll have a baseline to go from."

Petra clutched the gold bar while Gunther retrieved a stopwatch from his kit.

Hermann and Klein entered the water and followed the rope down to the cave. Klein carried a wire basket that looked like it had once been mounted on the handlebars of a bicycle. If there were as many gold bars down there as Hermann figured, then it would take a lot of trips to bring them all up in that basket.

Once past the restriction, the two men redonned their gear and descended as fast as they could equalize their ears. Hermann glanced at his dive computer. They'd been in the water for a total of fifteen minutes.

On air, their bottom time was less than two minutes, but Gunther had made the calculations, and the time it took to navigate the restriction on the way back up was equal to a five-minute decompression stop.

Hermann and Klein filled the basket in less than five minutes, stacking the bars on end, counting 128. Even though there was room for more, Klein stopped his boss from putting more in the basket. He attached the lift bags, but even fully inflated, they couldn't pick up the basket.

Klein began unloading bars until the basket lifted off the deck. They ended up with only seventy-two bars. The two divers guided the basket up to the entrance to the tunnel. They had to set the basket on a ledge, then deflate the lift bags to get them through the hole. The bags scraped against the roof of the cave and the basket stirred up particulate as it dragged along the bottom. With the tunnel rapidly filling with silt, the two men had to hold onto the guideline to know which direction to proceed.

When Hermann and Klein reached the restriction, they deflated the lift bags completely and rolled them on top of the gold. Klein peeled off his tanks and pushed himself under the boulder, then put his gear back on and reached back through for the basket. Together, the two men maneuvered the almost two hundred pounds of gold bars through the gap. Once through, Klein reinflated the lift bags as Hermann pushed himself under the boulder, then strapped himself back into his harness.

They glided forward, pushing the basket out of the cave before ascending the line. Breaking the surface, Hermann motioned for two of his men to assist them in dragging the basket to the shore. Seconds later, the two men swam out to where the divers waited and pushed the basket toward shore with the divers swimming alongside them.

"Forty-five minutes," Petra announced, making a show of clicking off the stopwatch.

Hermann shed his rig and sank into a chair, clutching a bottle of water. He was breathing hard from the long swim and from struggling with the basket. Klein was in no better shape.

"Two dives a day will take us weeks to recover the gold. If we could do more dives during the day, we could halve that estimate, but the current will be too strong to use lift bags," Klein said, dropping into a seat and putting his elbows on his knees.

"There's got to be an easier way," Petra reasoned. "Maybe we could blast open the restriction?"

"No," Gunther replied. "The boulder that forms the restriction is like a keystone. It's wedged into the original slide and holds everything in place. If we try to blow it, the whole thing will collapse on the gold."

"So, what then?" Hermann asked. "As Weller pointed out, I'm not trained in salvage diving. After making those last two dives, I understand why he wanted to work with a professional."

"Weller is trained on rebreathers and is a skilled diver, from what I saw," Gunther stated.

"Yes," Petra replied. "We've covered that. What are you getting at?"

"What if he took his chances with the tunnel? The current would have done most of the work for him. He could have swam out of the cave and be out there somewhere." Gunther swept his hand across the jungle, not knowing how right he was.

"Let's explore that tunnel," Klein suggested. "We have diver propulsion vehicles on the *Leopard*. We can scooter into the cave and find an exit. If it comes out somewhere in Exuma Sound, we can go back through the tunnel with a sled-like apparatus to retrieve the gold."

"How long until you can do that?" Petra asked.

Gunther checked his watch. "Next slack tide will be in

four more hours. That will give us time to off-gas and prepare our equipment."

"Then let's get it done," Hermann ordered. He glanced at the basket of gold bars. His mother was going to be so proud, but he realized he had a lot to learn about diving and treasure recovery. The next treasure hunting expedition, if there was one, would go much smoother.

A branch snapped in the underbrush not far away. Hermann's head snapped up. He surveyed the mangroves and wondered if Ryan Weller had indeed survived. An involuntary shiver coursed through his body. Weller didn't care about the gold. He wanted the girl, and he wanted them off the island.

It was a determined man who forwent the gold for his principles. From what little Hermann knew about Weller, he felt certain he was a man of conviction.

And he had the skills to hunt them all down and kill them.

CHAPTER THIRTY-THREE

Ryan

It was mid-afternoon when Ryan finally found Scott just off the main ridge, halfway between the Green Castle and the southern end of the island.

The former SEAL sat under a rocky outcropping. His left leg was straight out, but his lower right leg was bent at an unnatural angle. Ryan could see the anguish on his friend's face.

"What happened to you?" Ryan asked, dropping to his knees to assess Scott's broken leg.

"I got caught in the storm last night. I was trying to make it across the island before dark and slipped on the rocks up there." He pointed up the cliff. "I landed badly on my right leg and passed out. When I came to, I dragged myself under this outcropping." His breath hissed through his teeth as he fought a fresh wave of pain.

"I'm going to cut your pant leg and see how bad the break is, then we'll get you splinted up."

Scott nodded. "You got any water?"

Ryan took an unopened bottle from his pack and handed it to Scott before unzipping his medical blowout pack. He removed a pair of trauma shears and cut along the inside seam of Scott's pant leg to just above the knee.

"Good news. It's not a compound fracture," Ryan said, examining the leg.

"No shit, Sherlock. I would have bled out waiting for you to show up if I had a bone sticking out."

Ryan smiled grimly. "Sorry, I was busy."

"Doing what?"

Ryan explained the events of the last twenty-four hours.

"So, you found the gold?"

Ryan pulled one of the bars he'd picked up in the cave from his pack and handed it to Scott.

"Holy shit," Scott whispered as his fingers traced the *Reichsadler* engraved into the precious metal. When he looked up, Ryan was shaving the knots off two stout limbs with the knife he'd retrieved from Carlton's tent. "What are you going to do now?"

Pausing his work, Ryan said, "I had planned for the two of us to play Rambo, but now I need to get you out of here."

Scott grinned. "I can stay right here. You draw 'em in, I'll pop 'em."

"That's a plan of last resort. This broken leg makes you a sitting duck."

Scott considered that for a moment. "Where are you going to make your last stand?"

Ryan squatted back beside Scott's leg and laid his two sticks alongside it. "Okay. You ready for this? I need to set your leg and then splint it."

"You got any whiskey?" Scott held up a nine-millimeter round Ryan assumed was from his pistol. "I've got a bullet."

"No whiskey, just some rum." He dug through his pack and found the medicinal airplane bottle of Bacardi he kept there for emergencies. After Scott downed it, Ryan asked, "You ready?"

Shrugging, Scott put the bullet between his molars and bit down on the lead.

Ryan tried to make the adjustments to the leg in one swift motion, but it was tougher than he'd figured it would be. Scott wiggled and moaned, hands balled into fists and tears rolling down his cheeks from eyes he'd clenched shut.

"Hang in there, buddy. Almost done." Ryan pulled the pant leg down and then laid the two sticks along the broken tibia and fibula. Retrieving a roll of duct tape from his pack, he wrapped it around Scott's leg, trapping it between the sticks and holding the break in place.

"Are you done yet?" Scott asked, teeth clenched. "You're freaking killing me."

"Hold your horses." Ryan gave the leg a couple more wraps of tape. He sat back to inspect his handiwork. The splint started above Scott's knee and ran to his boot sole. The wrapped tape made his lower leg appear to be mummified, but it would hold the bones in place until they could get Scott to a doctor.

"Now, how are we going to get you out of here?" Ryan mused more to himself than to his injured friend.

"I'm not walking, I can tell you that," Scott replied. He drained the water from the bottle and crushed the plastic into a compact ball before screwing the cap back on. Ryan handed over another bottle.

"I can make a travois," Ryan suggested.

"I can't take that much abuse," Scott said. "Just leave me here to die."

"You'll starve to death before that leg heals."

"How about you get me up to the Castle and we'll make our last stand there? I can snipe the bastards at their camp and then send them running into a trap."

Ryan considered Scott's suggestion, his jaw muscles flexing. "I know these guys have taken a hostage and are probably willing to do far worse, but until they fire at us, anything we do will be in cold blood."

Scott snorted. "And you think they give two shits about you? They already told you the whole crew of the *Leopard* was expendable. Those freaking Nazis are going to do whatever it takes to keep that gold a secret. That includes putting a bullet between your eyes, not to mention your new girlfriend."

Nodding, Ryan rocked back on his heels and stood. He backed up a few steps, afraid the urge to stomp on Scott's leg would overwhelm him. Ryan didn't like Scott poking him about Diane. He surveyed the wilderness around them, hand on the grip of his KRISS Vector. It would be difficult to get Scott out. He had managed to fall in one of the most rugged sections of the island.

"Just what were you doing out here?" Ryan asked.

"I was checking on the GPR unit. I rigged some booby traps around it—just some simple trip wires with firecrackers attached, though this rain has probably ruined them. It's too bad we don't have anything stronger."

Ryan tapped his fingers against the receiver of his SMG. He considered Scott's suggestion that they lure the Germans into the jungle. "How about I get you to the Castle, so you have the high ground, then I go hunting."

"Isn't that what I just suggested?" Scott mocked, then his tone turned serious. "Look, Ryan, I know this isn't your forte. You like to do things nice and clean, but this is going to be trench warfare. Those Germans aren't going to just lie down and let you walk off with Diane and the gold—because I know that's what you're thinking. You can't lie to me. I've seen that look in your eyes before."

After a pause, Ryan replied, "You're right. I've been thinking this through. I think these guys work for a company called The Paladin Group. The *Leopard* is one of their vessels. I read up on them while I was trying to connect the dots. They obviously have enough clout to send a first-rate salvage vessel and a competent team of shooters and divers. These guys have deep pockets. If they're as deep as I think, then they'll send more men after that gold. From all the shit the Zieglers have been spouting, it seems The Paladin Group wants to spring a Fourth Reich on the world."

"Seriously?" Scott asked, leaning down to adjust his leg.

"What I'm thinking is that no matter how many men I kill, The Paladin Group will keep sending more until we're dead. Whatever we do, it has to be enough that The Paladin Group never bothers the Carltons again."

"There's no 'we.' I'm a sitting duck, remember?"

"I need your brainpower on this."

"First, you have to rescue Diane, then you figure out who the head of this Paladin Group is and contact them."

"Yeah. Maybe if I give them the gold, they'll leave the Carltons and Big Darby alone."

"That's the deal you have to make," Scott said matter-of-factly. "And if they don't take it, then you go scorched earth."

CHAPTER THIRTY-FOUR

Ryan fashioned a travois from several long branches and used a poncho to span the poles, lacing it on with paracord from Scott's backpack.

Once Scott was laid out on the travois, Ryan shouldered the load and headed for the Green Castle. Scott grunted and groaned with each bump.

They soon discovered a problem with using the flimsy poncho, as it kept catching on the passing rocks and roots and tearing.

"You got a suppressor for your rifle?" Ryan asked.

"Yep," Scott replied tersely.

Glancing over his shoulder, Ryan asked, "You got a suppressor for those groans?"

Scott flashed him the finger, but Ryan was too busy staggering up the slope to see it. The situation reminded him of hiking Greg out of a steep ravine in Puerto Rico after multiple gunmen had ambushed them and Greg had driven off the road.

Once he had Scott on level ground, the going was easier,

but Ryan had to stop to repair the seat of the travois so Scott wouldn't fall through. Halfway to their destination the poncho tore out completely.

As Ryan was trying to make repairs, Scott reached for one of the limbs. "Let's make these into crutches. I can make it from here."

Ryan found two branches of equal length and fashioned cushioned tops from extra pants and shirts that he and Scott had in their backpacks. He pulled Scott to his feet, and the injured man tucked the makeshift crutches under his armpits. It was slow going as the two men traversed the rugged terrain toward the house.

Scott had to rest often, the crutches digging into his armpits and his hands sliding on the smooth wood. On the last leg of the journey, Ryan looped Scott's right arm over his shoulder, and Scott hopped, one-legged, across the rough ground and up the back steps of the house.

"Take me upstairs," Scott said. "It's the best place to shoot from."

"And if you get bored, you can read Ellen Carter's autobiography."

Scott snorted out a laugh as the two men traversed the staircase. "You're a twisted individual, you know that, Ryan?"

"My wife likes to remind me on a daily basis."

"Someone should write a book about your exploits. This; the hostage rescue in Haiti; chasing Chinese Special Forces across the Caribbean after a stolen satellite. Sounds like a bestseller to me."

"It would have to be a work of fiction," Ryan said. "No one would believe this shit if we marketed it as a memoir."

"Yeah, you're probably right," Scott agreed.

Ryan eased his friend into the rocking chair he had used earlier when waiting out the previous rainstorm. Scott moaned as he bit back the pain. Ryan rummaged in his pack and pulled out a bottle of ibuprofen. "I've got this, or a morphine shot."

"I'll take the pills," Scott said. "The morphine will knock me out and I'll be of no use to anyone."

"Sounds like you've had personal experience with that."

The former SEAL grinned. "Once or twice. Now, you asked about the suppressor. Who do you want me to shoot?"

"Where's your rifle?" Ryan asked.

"In the old utility building. There's a small sump in there, full of water and muck. The gun case is in it."

Ryan went down the steps, scanning his sectors for threats with the Vector cradled in his hands. Even though most of the Germans were clustered around the diving canopy, that didn't mean the Zieglers hadn't sent out a roving patrol. He darted from the house to the utility building and found the sump behind the rusted hulk of the old generators.

Loath to stick his hand down in the dark liquid that had a rainbow sheen of oil across the top, Ryan found a stick and used it to fish around in the muck until he found Scott's waterproof rifle case. Once he knew where the case was, he worked the stick along the length of the case until he felt the stick bump over the handle. Finally, Ryan reached in and pulled out the case. Returning to the main house, he carried it upstairs and set it beside Scott's rocking chair.

Bending down, Ryan unsnapped the clasps. The Springfield M1A was Scott's go-to rifle for hunting and sniping. Based on the venerable M14, the Army had designed the rifle to replace a hodgepodge of infantry weapon systems after WWII. The M14 was accurate but heavy and was eventually replaced by the M16 after only ten years of military service. But the Navy had kept M14s aboard ships, and Special Forces had used them as sniper platforms. Scott had shot one when he was a SEAL and favored the M1A in civilian life.

While Scott examined his firearm and threaded on the

suppressor, Ryan went downstairs and retrieved a small table. He set it well back from the window in the second-floor bedroom, where Scott could use it as a shooting bench with a clear view of the *Leopard*.

"What's the plan here?" Scott asked.

"I'm going for the boat while everyone is busy at the blue hole. You shoot anyone who gets in my way."

"So, you want me to be the killer so you can have a clear conscience?"

"No. I want you to be my backup. I'll kill whoever I need to in order to get Diane back."

"Seriously, what's with you two?" Scott asked. "She has this ga-ga look on her face whenever you're around, and you get all jumpy any time I say her name."

"There's nothing going on between us," Ryan said flatly. "She's the principal. You know we do whatever we need to do to keep them safe."

"Yeah, I do," Scott replied, then turned even more serious. "Are you having an affair with this girl?"

"Absolutely not," Ryan stated.

"Just tell me what happened," Scott persisted. "That way, we can stop beating around the bush."

Ryan sighed and leaned against the wall, shoving his hands into his pants pockets. He scuffed at the floorboards with the toe of his boot, trying to decide if he should divulge his secret. Ryan concluded he should take it to his grave.

But Scott wasn't having it. He could see the gears turning in Ryan's mind. "Come on, man. I know you well enough to see that it's eating you alive. Just tell me."

Ryan decided it wouldn't hurt to share the secret if Scott could give him some advice.

Huffing out another sigh, Ryan nodded. "Okay. The truth is, we kissed." He held out his hand to keep Scott from saying anything because the big lug's mouth had dropped open. "We were talking, and she came over, sat on my lap, and kissed me. It startled me so much when I realized I was kissing her back that I stood and dumped her on the floor before running away."

"Classy, Weller."

"That's what happened," Ryan said defensively.

"Is that what you're going to tell Emily?"

"I hadn't planned to tell her anything."

"You're excellent at keeping operational secrets, but you ain't hiding that one. It's written all over your face."

Ryan didn't say anything. He knew he had to come clean with his wife.

"Look," Scott said, "my ex and I used to cheat one another just to piss each other off, but it still hurts knowing that someone you loved is out there fooling around with someone else. Come clean with her, dude. If you don't, I promise, it's going to affect your relationship. If I can read you like a book, so can she."

"You're right. I should tell her."

"Yeah, you should. And tell her it will never happen again."

"Because it won't."

"No. It won't," Scott agreed. "You're one of the good guys, Ryan, and if Emily can't see that, then she's a fool."

"Thanks, buddy."

"Don't thank me, yet. We're not out of the woods. Now, go get your principal. I've got your back."

"Okay. This is what's going to happen," Ryan said, and went on to tell Scott what he had in mind.

"That sounds reasonable, but you need a second diver."

"I know. I'd planned on you helping me, but that's not going to happen now. I'll just have to do it myself."

"First things first, get Diane, then go for the rest of it."

Ryan reached out his fist, and Scott bumped it.

"Be safe, brother," the sniper said as Ryan headed down the stairs.

———

THE FIRST PROBLEM was to get Diane. As long as she was being held hostage, the Germans could use her as leverage.

Once Ryan had her back in pocket, he could tackle the second problem, which was to get the gold, so he could use it as leverage.

Ryan crossed the island to the southern point and issued the prearranged signal for Rafi to come pick him up. It was just too taxing to swim the anchorage with all his combat gear.

While he waited, Ryan tried to plan out how he would take down the people on the boat. Last night, after Rafi had helped Ryan stave off hypothermia, Ryan had divulged the entire German scheme to the Bahamian. Rafi, interested in protecting his family, had agreed to help Ryan do whatever he needed to do to rid the islands of the radical fanatics. Now, Ryan was going to put that agreement to the test.

It wasn't long before Rafi arrived in the panga. Ryan laid in the bottom out of sight as Rafi navigated them around the southern tip of Little Darby and then up the eastern shore.

"Pull up to the *Leopard* and offer to sell them some fish," Ryan instructed.

Rafi motored them up to the salvage vessel, careful to keep the green hull of the larger ship between them and the island.

"De man has a gun," Rafi whispered as they came alongside, then he called up to the *Leopard* crewman, "I got de fresh fish. Ya wants to buy?"

"Go away," the crewman shouted.

The panga bumped against the steel hull. Ryan lay flat on his back, his Vector across his chest, ready to bring the SMG to bear. When the crewman came to the rail and looked down on the panga, Ryan saw the man sweep the boat with the muzzle of his UMP. Without hesitation, Ryan shot the man in the chest with a two-round burst, then he scrambled up the side of the bigger vessel and jumped aboard as the crewman sagged to the deck. He turned to Rafi and told him to hold fast while he went for Diane.

Ryan ran toward the *Leopard*'s superstructure, scanning for other threats, but saw no other crew members on deck. He opened the main superstructure hatch and transitioned from his long gun to his suppressed Glock. Slowly, he moved upward through the two decks to the bridge, where Haas sat in his captain's chair behind the wheel, sipping a cup of coffee. Ryan shoved through the door, startling Haas so badly that he dropped his mug. Coffee splashed across his white uniform pants before the mug shattered on the steel deck.

"How many people are aboard?" Ryan asked, leveling his pistol at the captain.

"Three," Haas replied, wide eyed. His demeanor suggested it wasn't a surprise to see Ryan storming his boat. "Myself, the first mate, and the cook."

Ryan nodded. There were only two left aboard now. "Let's go below."

The troubleshooter and the captain walked down the steps to the galley. Ryan used flex cuffs to secure the hands and feet of both the captain and the cook, then used dish towels to gag them. With the men secured, Ryan dashed through the ship to Diane's cabin.

He wrenched open the door and stepped inside. Diane had wedged herself into a corner of the room, her eyes wide with fear and her body trembling. Ryan figured he looked damned scary in his combat gear.

"We need to go," Ryan said, offering her his hand.

Gingerly, she took it, and Ryan pulled her to her feet. She hugged him fiercely. "I didn't think you were ever coming back. Petra said you were dead."

"Rafi is waiting in the panga outside. I need to get some equipment from the dive locker."

"I can help," she said, overcoming her earlier fright.

Ryan led the way to the locker. He grabbed a big bag and tossed in the last two O_2 and diluent bottles for the rebreather, then grabbed a big, military-style diver propulsion vehicle. He shouldered the DPV as Diane hefted the tanks, and they headed topside.

When they stepped into the bright afternoon sunshine, Ryan heard shouts in German coming from Big Darby. He and Diane ran to the *Leopard*'s rail and clambered down into the waiting panga.

Rafi had the motor running, and as soon as Ryan and Diane were aboard, they shot away from the *Leopard*. The burly islander made a wide circle around Little Darby, ferrying them to the western shore of Big Darby and dropping Ryan and Diane at the small dock there.

As Ryan climbed out of the boat, he said to Rafi, "Get Alice and the boys. Take them someplace safe."

The Bahamian nodded and opened the throttle on the ancient outboard.

"What's the plan now?" Diane asked as they picked up the gear Ryan had pilfered from the salvage vessel.

"I'm going to move the gold and blast the cave closed."

"*What*? Why?"

As they headed up the path toward the tent, Ryan explained about finding the gold and how he had been swept out to sea through the tunnel. "I'm going to move the gold into the tunnel so the only way to get to it is from the other end."

"It will take you a long time to move it."

"I know, but I want the Germans to think it's lost. If it's buried under water and rubble, they can't get to it. Once it's safe, we can negotiate with The Paladin Group to leave the island alone if I turn the gold over to them."

"Why not just let them take it now?" Diane asked. "Once they have it, they'll let us be, right?"

"I doubt it," Ryan replied. "As long as we know The Paladin Group was behind the salvage efforts, we're in danger. And after what just happened back there, I think they're going to come after us now. I killed one of the *Leopard*'s crewmen to rescue you. If I've learned one thing from dealing with people like this, it's that they don't give up. They'll keep coming for us until we're dead."

"Because we can point the finger at them."

"Correct."

"So, let them bring the gold up instead of you trying to move it. From what you've described, that's a lot of gold for one person to move. I've done some diving and have my advanced certification, so I know a dive like that, even on a rebreather and with the scooter, will take a long time."

"I know," Ryan said.

"Why can't Scott help you?" Diane asked.

"He fell from some rocks and broke his leg."

"Is he okay?"

"He'll be fine. I've got him stationed up in the Castle with his sniper rifle."

"He needs medical attention."

"*I know*," Ryan snapped. "I splinted his leg and he's got some pain medication, but we need to get rid of those Germans so we can get an emergency medical flight in here."

Diane shook her head in disbelief.

"I want you to go up to the Castle and stay with him."

"I'd rather stay with you," she replied.

Ryan fixed her with his stare. "I'm not putting you in danger by having you tag along."

They arrived at the tent and set their gear inside.

"There has to be another way," she insisted. "You're putting yourself in danger for no reason. Let's go to them, tell them to take the gold and leave us alone."

Allowing his frustration to show, Ryan asked, "Are you even listening to what you're saying? Those animals kidnapped you and held you hostage to force me to help them. They don't listen to reason. If they did, none of this would be happening right now. They're sick, dangerous people who will stop at nothing to get that gold and cover up any incidents that happen along the way.

"There's no dealing with terrorists. There's no trying to understand who they are and what they want, because when you come at it with that mindset, you've already lost. Terrorists don't care about feelings. They break shit and kill people. The only way to deal with them is by force. To get a bully to leave you alone, you have to punch them in the face to let them know you're not taking their shit anymore."

"And you think stealing their gold is punching them in the face?"

"Absolutely," Ryan agreed.

"And what happens after you punch them in the face?" Diane asked.

"They come gunning for me."

"Is that a wise plan?"

Ryan grabbed a bottle of water and took a long swig. "It's the only plan I've got."

"Don't do this, Ryan. Don't put yourself in jeopardy for me or for the gold or for whatever macho crap you're thinking about."

"I'm doing this for you, Diane, and your father. He hired me to get rid of the ghosts. It's time for an exorcism."

But Ryan was too late. The hunter had just become the hunted.

CHAPTER THIRTY-FIVE

Hermann

The handheld radio crackled to life with an emergency call from Captain Haas.

Hermann picked it up and answered, slightly annoyed by the interruption. He listened as the captain told the story of Weller's invasion of the *Leopard* and the subsequent rescue of Diane Carlton. His jaw muscles rippled under his cheeks as he fought back a wave of anger. It didn't surprise him that Weller had survived being washed out to sea, but it angered him that the man had taken the life of one of his team.

So far, they had avoided bloodshed, but Weller had upped the stakes.

"I was able to escape by cutting my bonds with a knife from the galley," Haas reported. "Weller took the woman away in a small boat driven by a native."

"Did you see where he took them?" Hermann asked,

glancing at his sister. She stood rooted beside him, hands on her hips as she listened.

"No," Haas replied. "I just freed myself and my first action was to call you," Haas replied.

Hermann set down the radio after thanking the captain for his report.

Turning to Petra, he saw her cobalt blue eyes had darkened. He knew that look. It was the determined focus she got when something didn't go her way and she would have to step up to fix it. He felt like a little boy under her gaze. He wanted to please her, but it seemed he could do nothing right. Hermann had signed on to this trip for the adventure, not realizing he would have to become a cold-blooded killer for The Paladin Group. It wasn't in his nature.

He had killers at his disposal, though. The men who comprised his team had criminal records, had been soldiers of fortune, or had killed indiscriminately in the past. He knew they had been assigned to him to do what he might not have the stomach for. As Petra stared him down, Hermann knew he had to order his team to kill. The gold was too important to The Paladin Group, and to his own future.

Hermann decided to throw them into the breach against Weller. They were six men against one. What could go wrong, other than what had already been done?

"Gather around," he ordered his men. "Klein, you will continue the diving operations. Take Bergmann to help support Gunther and Schuler. The rest of you are to spread out over the island. Two of you are to head for the tent camp, two to the Green Castle, and Artem, you head for the dock on the east side."

"And you?" Artem asked, eyeing the beautiful Petra.

"I will coordinate the mission," Ziegler said, stepping into Artem's line of sight. "Now, move."

The men scrambled into the brush, heading for their

various assignments, as Artem stared down Hermann. The two men had never gotten along. It had been Artem's team before Hermann had arrived—the fair-haired golden boy appointed by his mommy, as Artem had told him once.

It didn't bother Hermann. He had known men like Artem Kowalchuk all his life. They were men who envied him for his work ethic, his good looks, his mother's money, or his famous sister. It was time to prove his leadership and his worth to the team.

Petra laid his hand on her brother's arm. "I will go with Artem. I know how to handle him." She followed the Ukrainian out of sight.

Reaching for his UMP, Hermann checked the chamber to ensure there was a round in it, then shouldered into the sling. With the divers going in and out of the water, taking turns making the deep dive to retrieve the gold, they needed someone to stand watch over them and the collection of gold bars piled under a tarp near the tent.

Hermann was about to order Haas to bring the cook to shore so they could transfer the gold to the *Leopard* when he heard the opening volley of gunfire.

The hunt had commenced.

CHAPTER THIRTY-SIX

Ryan

B efore they headed for Scott's hide in the Green Castle, Diane changed into clean clothes. As they were about to step out of the tent, she stopped Ryan by placing her hand on his arm. "I wanted to say thank you for rescuing me," she said tenderly. "You know, before you run out there and get yourself killed."

"It's my job," Ryan said.

She bit her lower lip, then smiled. "When Petra told me you were dead, something felt like it had broken inside me. I didn't think I would ever leave that cabin." She paused as her voice cracked. "I didn't think I'd ever see you again."

He looked down at her searching blue eyes. "You held up well."

"No. Seriously, Ryan, thank you. I don't know how much longer I could have spent in that room. I was going crazy."

"Then you better stay out of sight, so they don't capture you again."

"Why are you being so stiff?" she asked, putting a hand on his cheek. "I'm trying to thank you."

"You said that already," Ryan replied. The warmth of her hand was causing his body to react to her presence, betraying his staunchness. He wanted to sweep her into his arms and kiss her again, but he was a married man. Supposedly, he was happily married, but these women who came into his life through his work had a strange effect on him. Maybe it was being thrust together under such dangerous circumstances that formed a bond of trust and respect, but whatever it was, he had to let it go.

Ryan forced himself to back away. One kiss was an accident. Kissing her again would be a willful act and one he couldn't explain away.

"Let's go. If we get separated, head for the Castle and find Scott. We'll regroup and move from there."

Ryan ducked under the tent flap and escorted his charge up the hill toward the Castle.

Halfway there, a burst of automatic fire peppered the trees at the edge of the path.

"Get down!" As leaves and twigs cascaded around them, Ryan shoved Diane toward the cover of the trees.

Once inside the brush line, he tried to determine where the fire was coming from. He lay on the ground beside his panting principal, one arm over her back to keep her rooted firmly to the ground. Ryan didn't need her jumping up and sprinting away.

"Stay with me," he whispered harshly. "No matter what. Stay. With. Me. I'll get you to safety."

Diane nodded, eyes wide.

"See that loop at the bottom of my vest?" he asked,

reaching around to his back to hook it with his thumb. "Grab it."

Diane seated her hand on the loop.

"Ready?"

"No." Her voice was shaky, and the adrenaline spike made her hand quiver.

"*Move.*" Ryan got to his feet, with Diane right beside him. He headed southeast, cutting across the island up the center ridge, with a plan to diamond back to the house, figuring the gunmen were watching the trail.

He could feel Diane's hand on the loop at his back, tugging reassuringly as he ran. If the weight was not there, Diane had let go and was not by his side.

More gunfire tore through the trees behind them. Ryan crouched as the incoming fire shredded more leaves and bark off the trees. As soon as the gunfire dissipated, he was up and moving again.

With Scott in the Castle and Diane by his side, anyone else moving around was fair game. Ryan saw a shadow dart through the trees ahead of them. Dropping to his knee, he raised his KRISS to shoot, but Diane slammed into his back, throwing him off-balance. By the time he corrected his aim, the shadow was gone.

Jumping up, Ryan made a ninety-degree course correction, heading straight for the Castle. He figured their attackers were trying to flank him. They needed to get to the Castle and secure the high ground.

Where the hell is my sniper?

CHAPTER THIRTY-SEVEN

Scott

Scott had known the shit was going to hit the fan the moment Ryan had shot the crewman on the *Leopard* while rescuing Diane. Less than thirty minutes later, the Germans were on the hunt, fanning out across Big Darby to find Ryan.

And they'd succeeded. Echoes of gunfire rippled through the air to the east of his position along the trail to the tent.

Scott stood. He had to change positions to provide covering fire. Trying to keep the weight off his broken leg and carrying the Springfield M1A, he hopped on one leg toward the window opposite the one he'd been using to overwatch the diving operation. With each thump of his foot on the floor, Scott feared he might break through the dry-rotted lumber or at least the jackals outside would hear him moving around and invade the house.

He cursed his luck at breaking his leg as he lost his

balance and accidentally put weight on the broken bones. Pain seared up his spine, causing his back to spasm. He dropped the rifle as he toppled over onto his side.

Wanting to scramble over to the M1A and check the optics, Scott was certain they were now way off zero, having been jarred in the fall, but the pain took his breath away and he could barely move. It was all he could do to make his lungs expand and contract. Having to concentrate on his breathing made everything else a peripheral activity, but his friend still needed his help.

Scott dug deep inside himself, searching for that special place in his mind where he went when his body had to function on its own and everything else operated automatically. He had found that tiny little box when he was a kid, after his father had left and his mother had become absent. It had been the place he had resided for weeks at a time during SEAL training, only letting himself operate at full capacity when the timing was right. The compartmentalization had served him well during his military career.

As he lay on his side, struggling to put the pain into another box, Scott thought back to those long days of Hell Week. He and the other BUD/S trainees had survived on minimal sleep, suffered hypothermia from the icy waters off Coronado Island, and had been covered in sand and mud and leeches and stink. Every step of the way, the instructors had told him to quit, and every step of the way, he had said no. He had locked himself into that mind box and refused to come out until they'd pinned a Trident on his uniform and sent him to his team.

His team. Scott took another deep breath, feeling the pain wash away as he found that special hiding spot in his mind. Ryan was his team now. Greg Olsen was his team leader. This shit was way more fun than the SEALs. He'd seen more action working for DWR than he'd seen kicking down doors in Iraq.

From below, Scott heard footsteps and men speaking in German.

Scott rolled onto his back, the stiffness of the splint making it awkward to move, then worked himself around so his legs were facing the bedroom door. He pulled the XD-M pistol from his hip holster and screwed on the suppressor before bracing the weapon against his bent left knee in a two-handed grip.

The stairs creaked as the two men made their way up them. Scott knew how they would come: one would duck around the corner and move into the room to his right, weapon ready, while the other would go left to clear his sector, adhering to standard room-clearing tactics taught around the world.

Scott strained to hear each footfall of the enemy, trying to predict where they were behind the wall. They had made it to the top of the stairs and were in the short hallway. The pistol quivered in his hand, the long suppressor adding cumbersome weight to the barrel. The DWR contractor tried to force himself to relax, willing his hands to be still, pushing the pain away.

The first man came around the corner. He wore the same cargo pants and bush shirt Scott had seen all the men on the Ziegler team wearing. No body armor. No helmets.

Scott's first round caught the man in the belly as he brought the XD-M off his knee. His second round hit the man in the sternum.

When the second German whipped around the corner, Scott's sight picture was still on the first man. As Scott transitioned the gun from one man to the other, the German brought his UMP around and pressed the trigger. A line of bullets tore up the floor to Scott's left, getting closer and closer as the man reconned by fire.

Scott put a round in the man's chest and the belch of fire from the German's UMP stopped. The bolt locked home on an empty magazine. The German reached for another mag in his back pocket, indifferent to the blood pouring from his wound. Scott shot him again, the round striking the man in the shoulder.

German Two dropped his UMP.

Instead of clutching his shoulder, as almost any injured man would, the guy pulled a tactical folding knife from his pocket. The sun glinted off the serrated blade. Scott felt a surge of hatred for the man. *Just freaking die already!*

He emptied the XD-M's magazine into the German's chest as the man tried to raise the knife.

German Two staggered backward and collided with the wall, leaving a bloody smear on the ancient floral wallpaper as he slid down it.

Scott heaved a sigh of relief. Three men down, counting the one Ryan had shot on the boat. Eleven to go. He now had two UMPs and a couple extra magazines for each to supplement his weapons cache.

He rolled onto his stomach and heaved himself up onto his good leg. He had found the sweet spot in his mind. His pain was compartmentalized, the adrenaline was flowing, and the bullets were flying.

Picking up the Springfield, Scott hopped across the room and stood at the window, bracing himself against the wall and putting all his weight on his left leg. He shouldered the rifle and peered through the scope. The optics looked unharmed, but he wouldn't know how far off center they were until he fired. Ideally, he would have recalibrated by shooting at a paper target and dialing the scope back in, but they were way too deep into this shit to call a time out.

A man appeared in the lane leading to Diane's tent. He was moving quickly toward the Castle, UMP shouldered, and firing into the jungle. Scott put his crosshairs on the man's chest and pressed the trigger.

The dude kept right on moving, oblivious to the supersonic round that had just passed by him, but Scott had seen the puff of dirt and dust where his round had struck the ground, and now had a general idea how far off zero the scope was.

Moving the crosshairs to compensate for the inaccuracy, Scott pressed the trigger again.

CHAPTER THIRTY-EIGHT

Petra

The German model caught up with Artem Kowalchuk near the Darby Channel dock. He turned to look at her, a sneer curving his lips.

"I knew you had the hots for me, Petra," the mercenary taunted, smiling conceitedly.

"You are my hero, Artem." Petra pulled a H&K USP Compact from a holster at the small of her back and shot the Ukrainian in the face. She had never liked the man, and now he could never touch her. Artem lay sprawled in the dirt, the back of his head oozing blood and brains.

Petra pulled a satellite phone from her shoulder bag and dialed her mother. When Katrine answered, Petra said, "We have a problem."

"I'm listening," Katrine said.

Petra explained about finding the gold and the difficulty in recovering it, then she told her mother about the troubleshooter Steve Carlton had sent to Big Darby, the steps she and Hermann had taken to ensure Weller's cooperation, and how Weller had been the first to draw blood.

"You must kill him," Katrine ordered.

"I agree. Hermann's men are hunting him down as we speak. You may want to send another team."

"I have one standing by."

"*Gut*," Petra said. "How soon will they arrive?"

"Tomorrow morning."

"Hopefully, we will have the situation in hand by then."

"I trust you and Hermann will do what is best for the organization," Katrine said curtly.

"We will, Mother." Petra ended the call, stepped down into the black inflatable boat tied to the dock, and motored across to the *Leopard*.

Captain Haas met her on deck.

"We must begin moving the gold from the dive site on board," Petra announced.

"I will get Tomas," Haas said.

"Bring him in your workboat." She pointed to the aluminum skiff tied to the rail at the stern of the vessel. "The inflatable won't handle the weight of the gold."

"How will we move it to the dock?" Haas asked.

"Do you know how to drive a track steer?"

"No," Haas admitted.

"I'll find a way," Petra said. "It will make transporting the gold from the blue hole to the dock much easier."

She left Haas and Tomas to prepare the skiff, climbing back into the black inflatable. Petra raced around the north end of Big Darby and beached the craft at the end of the runway. She pulled the USP from her holster again, running up the runway while dodging around the craters blown in the sand.

When she reached the heavy equipment, Petra tried to

open the doors on both the backhoe and the track steer, but they were all locked. She screamed in frustration. Putting her face to the plexiglass windows, Petra peered at the control panels and saw the empty key slots. She slammed a fist into the glass.

The crewmen that Weller had taken hostage had said the contractor had used the backhoe to move them to the shed. They'd also said the troubleshooter had someone aiding in their capture, but they'd never seen the second man. Petra suspected Weller had recruited a local to help him, possibly the same islander who had driven the panga that had delivered Weller to the *Leopard* to rescue Diane.

She wasn't fazed by the gunfire when it started. Petra figured the team had finally caught up with Weller and that they would soon corner him.

Before leaving the dive site with Artem, she had taken an earpiece and a radio. She inserted the earpiece, adjusted the bone mic in front of her lips, and switched on the powerful military-style comms device, then she started searching the tent for the keys to the heavy equipment.

Bursts of German greeted her as the two men who'd been sent to inspect the tent tried to corner Weller and his principal, using sporadic fire to drive them toward the Green Castle, where another team waited.

"They're headed for the Castle," one of the men advised. "Do you copy Team Two?"

There was no answer on the radio.

Petra stopped tearing apart the tent, her search for the keys forgotten as she listened as first Team One and then her brother tried to raise Team Two.

Unable to help the shooters, Petra returned to her search. She started dumping cans of food and cooking supplies onto the floor in her haste.

When she couldn't find the keys, a blind rage fell over her.

Petra screamed and cursed as she flung the contents of the tent about, desperate to find the keys and knowing her brother would falter in his quest to kill Weller and the woman. Despite all his rugged handsomeness and his *Lebensborn* lineage, Hermann was no killer. Petra would have to do it all herself.

Petra froze as the radio squawked again. "Sniper in the Castle! Sniper in the Castle!"

CHAPTER THIRTY-NINE

Ryan

Ryan and Diane broke from the trees and ran past the dead man sprawled in the dirt. In spite of his physical limitations, the former SEAL had found a way to stay in the fight, blowing a giant hole in the German's chest with his well-placed sniper round.

Scott had saved Ryan's ass once again.

Ryan felt Diane slow as they passed the bleeding German, the weight on his chest rig handle growing heavier. "*Move! Move!*" he shouted to her, glancing over his shoulder to see she was staring at the body.

Diane picked up the pace but was unable to match his longer strides. Ryan had to shorten his steps to compensate, but he didn't want to slow too much because of the other shooters in the woods. Bullets continued to chirp at the ground around them and smack into the trees.

Ryan veered toward the trees again, not wanting to go off

the beaten path to race over rocks and roots and through cobwebs. The sharp edges of the sabal palms had sliced the skin on his arms. Mosquitoes feasting on the oozing blood continued to encircle his and Diane's heads as they ran.

He wanted to make it to the Castle and gain the high ground. Ryan knew he and Scott could fend off the attackers and force them to regroup. And as they fell back, Ryan would creep into the woods and take care of the remaining Germans.

There was only one way forward once the bullets started to fly—and that was to kill them all.

Greed was a powerful motivator, and millions of dollars in gold bars provided incentive enough to commit murder. Once the bloodlust was up, it had to be met with force.

The tug of Diane's weight changed. She had tripped over a root, and as she fell forward, her feet entangled with Ryan's, taking them both to the ground. Ryan held out his hands to protect himself from the fall, trying to keep the barrel of his KRISS Vector from jamming into the dirt.

Rolling from his stomach to his side, Ryan tried to survey his surroundings, terrified one of the shooters would take advantage of the situation and easily kill them.

His worst fear came true as a lanky German stepped out of the tree line with his UMP shouldered and trained his sights on Ryan. The troubleshooter felt his insides go cold. For a brief instant, Ryan closed his eyes and asked Emily to forgive him for being stupid enough to kiss Diane and stupid enough to die on this crazy mission against a dark order of fanatics.

With his silent pleadings complete, Ryan's thoughts turned to survival. He tried to calculate the angles that would bring his attacker into the crosshairs of his overwatch. When he opened his eyes, he saw the German had moved closer. The man spoke in heavily accented English, but Ryan couldn't understand what he was saying. The man settled on shouting in German and gesturing violently for Ryan to dispose of his firearms.

Ryan gave the Vector a weak toss, and it landed just beyond the reach of his outstretched arm. His defiance must have incensed the German because he quickly moved to kick the rifle. With the Vector now farther out of Ryan's reach, the man stepped forward to grab the Glock from the holster on Ryan's hip. As the man straightened, a bullet smacked him in the side of his head.

When the bullet exited the man's head, it took with it a large chunk of the man's skull, exposing his brain. Slowly, the man toppled over, falling chest-first onto the dirt path, his vacant eyes staring right into Diane's. She kicked backward, screaming as she tried to escape the carnage.

Letting go of Ryan's chest rig, she jumped up, ran into the jungle, and vomited.

Ryan figured she would stay close by, so he quickly gathered up his sidearm and the KRISS SMG, then frisked the German until he found the radio and the earpiece attached to it. He had to rotate the man's head to remove the earpiece, and when he caught a glimpse of the exposed brain, Ryan added to Diane's pile of vomit.

Straightening and wiping his mouth with the back of his hand, Ryan looked around for Diane.

"Diane!" When she didn't answer, he muttered, "Where the hell did you go?" Then he shouted even louder, drawing her name out. "Diane!"

Again, there was no answer. Figuring she must have run off into the brush, terrified by the shooting and nauseated by the stench of death. Ryan felt it in his gut, too. He swallowed hard and took several deep breaths through his mouth.

He hoped she'd done as he'd asked and headed for the Green Castle, Ryan headed there himself, pausing to pilfer the radio and earpiece off the corpse of the first man Scott had killed. With radios in hand, Ryan sprinted straight up the lane and was out of breath by the time he arrived at the house.

Carefully making his way up the stairs, Ryan found Scott sitting in the rocking chair, staring through his rifle scope. Opposite him were two dead men, their UMPs stacked on the table beside the Springfield M1A.

"You've been busy," Ryan commented.

"Yeah. Saving your bacon."

"Thanks."

"Where's Diane?" Scott asked.

"I don't know. I'm about to go look for her." Removing the radios from his pocket, Ryan examined them. The controls were all in German, but he knew enough about the electronics to figure out how to change frequencies. He adjusted them both to a new setting before handing one to Scott. "I changed the frequency, so we should be good to go."

"Good thinking." Scott wiped the earpiece on the tail of his shirt before inserting it into his ear. He adjusted the bone mic while Ryan did the same.

"I'm headed for the tent," Ryan informed his friend.

"I count five bad guys down," Scott said. "That leaves the Twins of Darkness and that guy with the Nazi tattoo on his belly."

"How do you know about that?" Ryan asked.

"He took his shirt off when they were moving gold out of the basket after one of the dives. He's a real piece of work."

"Have you seen him lately?"

"No. Last I saw of him, he was headed for the concrete dock, but then I got sidetracked by Dumbass One and Dumbass Two back there—and then I had to save *your* dumb ass. Right now," Scott said, peering through the scope, "Hermann is still by the diving tent, and the divers are still doing their thing. What was your read on them? Do I need to plug them for you?"

"No. I think they're commercial divers caught up in this, like you and me. I mean, they could be mercenaries, but that wasn't the vibe I got from them."

"I'll keep an eye on them anyway."

"They probably know you're out here watching my six by now, so be careful."

"Same to you, brother."

"Well, we have the radios now. Holler if you need help. I'm going to look for Diane."

Scott glanced over his shoulder. "Happy hunting, partner."

CHAPTER FORTY

Ryan went down the stairs, pausing at the back door on the way out of the house to check over his SMG and pistol once more for dirt and debris that might impede their function. He used a cloth from his chest rig to wipe them clean and ensured their barrels were clear before loading up and heading out.

He ran straight down the path toward the runway, veering off to cut diagonally through the woods toward the campsite. Ryan hoped Diane had gone there, as he had no idea where else she could be other than wandering aimlessly around the island. Their plan had been to gather at the Green Castle, and he'd expected her to go there, but in the brief time he'd spent with Scott and during his weapons check, she hadn't turned up. He hoped she had not been captured again.

Hearing a diesel engine snort to life, Ryan stopped short, breathing hard. The only diesels Ryan knew about on the island were the bright yellow JCB backhoe and track loader. He took off running again. Sweat beaded and trickled down his back, collecting under his armpits and abrading his skin as his inner arms rubbed against the straps of the chest rig. The heat and humidity made everything unbearable. The mosquitoes chased him nonstop, and the sand fleas burrowed into his leg and arm hair, biting Ryan just to let him know they were there.

Arriving at the campsite, Ryan saw the backhoe was just lumbering out of sight around the turn to the path back to the Green Castle. The interior of the tent had been ransacked, and the keys to the heavy equipment had been dug out of the ground by the stove. He put his hands on his knees and breathed deeply, trying to catch his breath from the long downhill sprint over sandy soil and through the dense trees.

"Yo, Ryan," his earpiece squawked. "Looks like your principal is once again a hostage. Petra—shit, I keep wanting to call her Petra Verkaik. She was Playboy's Miss December 1989. Damn, she had some big—"

"Can it, Scott. What's happening with Diane?"

"She's riding in the cab of the backhoe with blonde Petra. Petra V was a brunette."

"You know an awful lot about that chick," Ryan quipped after a long drink of water from a bottle he'd picked up off the ground in the tent. He was psyching himself up for another sprint across the island when his gaze fell on the set of keys in the discarded plastic bag.

"What can I say, she was my first Playmate crush," Scott replied.

"Good for you," Ryan said. "Can we spend a little less thinking about Playboy and more time thinking about what's happening right now?"

"I think this Petra would look good as a centerfold as well," Scott said.

Ryan climbed into the seat of the track loader and inserted the key. He turned it, but the machine wouldn't start. "Come on, you piece of shit!"

"Put the safety bar down," Scott said, overhearing Ryan's muttering on the radio.

Ryan searched for the safety bar and found it in its vertical position. He slammed it down and twisted the key. This time, the track loader's engine started, and Ryan jammed the joystick forward, racing after Petra's backhoe.

The digital display screen showed Ryan that he'd reached the track loader's maximum speed of twelve miles per hour. It was a lot faster than walking and a lot easier on his body than running, plus the cab was air-conditioned, but it felt like he was moving in slow motion. The backhoe was outpacing him by almost twice the speed. By the time Ryan turned the corner from the landing strip onto the path to the Green Castle, the backhoe was almost over the hill.

"Where're they going, Scott?"

"Looks like they're headed for the dive site. The dude in the captain's uniform is bringing the *Leopard*'s aluminum workboat over to the dock."

"What do I do?" Ryan asked.

"Rescue the girl. Get the gold."

"No shit, Sherlock," Ryan said. "You've got overwatch. How do we make that work?"

"I can shoot out the tires on the backhoe."

"A possibility."

In a more upbeat voice, Scott said, "Or I can just plug everyone."

"Another excellent possibility," Ryan agreed. "But let's figure out something that doesn't involve having to hide more bodies."

"I've got the perfect solution. We just load them onto *Leopard* and scuttle it out in the Atlantic."

"I was hoping to nab that boat for myself," Ryan replied.

"Why? You going into business for yourself?"

"No, but I do have a plan for it, so let's refrain from putting any extra holes in her hull."

"I can't shoot the boat, I can't shoot the bad guys, and I can't shoot the equipment. What *can* I shoot?"

"Just keep your powder dry," Ryan said. "There will be plenty of shooting to come."

"Hot damn, I hope so."

Ryan rolled his eyes. He followed the tracks the backhoe had made where Petra had turned off the main trail plowed through the brush toward the blue hole.

The plan now was to just wing it. Diane was the priority. If that meant helping to recover the gold and loading it onto the *Leopard*, then that's what he would do.

"So, good news," Scott said into the radio. "By the way the captain is acting, he just found another dead body by the dock. I don't have a clear line of sight, so I don't know who it is."

"Could be a diver or one of the Zieglers' crew."

"They're down five men, plus the dude you shot. You realize I'm doing all the heavy lifting here, right?"

"Keep up the good work," Ryan said, stopping the track steer well back from the blue hole in the overhanging brush and climbing out. He proceeded forward on foot, cradling his KRISS Vector, ready for action. He added up the remaining German combatants. He figured eight: four divers, Captain Haas, the cook, and the Twins of Evil.

Ryan paused at the tree line. He had no clue what to do. He'd fantasized about running around the island à la Rambo, taking out the bad guys with Carlton's compound bow and dispatching them with fancy booby traps, but things had taken a few unexpected turns. The characters he'd pitted himself against had minds of their own and wouldn't let themselves be manipulated into his machinations. Diane being captured for the second time was proof of that.

He shook his head in dismay.

With a sharp *whack*, Ryan killed a mosquito on his neck as he watched the events playing out under the canopy. It was a little louder than he'd anticipated, but no one seemed to notice as Hermann and his sister turned to help the divers bring in the basket of gold. Despite seeing those same gold bars lying deep in the cave, and even carrying a couple away himself, seeing them sparkling in the sunlight was almost breathtaking.

The two standby divers, Klein and Bergmann, helped the Zieglers carry the basket as the scuba-equipped divers walked onto land with their fins in their hands, water streaming from their wetsuits and tanks.

After setting the basket on the ground beside the front bucket of the backhoe, the standby divers unloaded it into the bucket and then began gearing up to go into the water. Ryan figured the basket was the only thing they had that would fit through the restriction, which meant bringing up all the gold would take hundreds of trips in and out of the cave.

He knew his plan to slip in with the rebreather and move the gold into the cave was far-fetched. It would take him hours to move all the gold bars deep enough into the tunnel that rubble from the collapsing slope wouldn't cover them, and Ryan didn't have enough gas for his rebreather or time in his day.

Stacking the gold carefully under the watchful eyes of the Zieglers, Gunther and Schuler worked efficiently to move the gold from under a tarp to the front bucket of the backhoe. Professor Meyer kept a close tally on the bars, making marks on a clipboard.

Ryan moved his gaze from the gold to where Diane sat in a folding chair under the canopy, hands bound in front of her. He tried to play out all the angles, to estimate how the Germans would react, but he kept coming back to the same thing: there had been enough bloodshed over this gold. First, the lives of the original owners, then the crew of the U-boat, and now at least six of Hermann Ziegler's men had died on Big Darby. Ryan figured that the continued dispute over the gold would lead to the deaths of more men, including himself or Diane. He had to think about the safety of his principal and that of his friend.

It was no longer feasible to play Rambo. As Ryan tried to figure out his next steps, an idea popped into his mind. He'd stumbled upon the perfect way to extract himself from the situation and keep the gold out of the hands of The Paladin Group.

All it would take was a little luck.

CHAPTER FORTY-ONE

With a new plan formulated, Ryan wondered why the simplest solution hadn't occurred to him before.

He backed away from the trees and squatted beside the track loader. For a moment, Ryan thought he could drive it over to Scott, help him into it, and have him meet them at the dock on the western side of the island, but then decided he needed Scott on overwatch while he retrieved Diane.

He clicked the transmit button on the stolen comms unit. "You got eyes on Hermann and Petra?"

"Yeah, and your principal is being held hostage again," Scott reminded him with a touch of sarcasm.

"I know I'm sucking at my job, just watch my back," Ryan said. "I'm going out there."

"It's your funeral," Scott replied.

Ryan placed his submachine gun in the track loader's bucket and dropped his pistol, chest rig, and comms device beside it. He removed the pilfered gold bar from the magazine pouch and palmed it. He was loath to turn it over. It was worth about sixty grand, but Carlton was paying him a lot more for exorcising the ghosts from Big Darby Island and for protecting his daughter. At the moment, it was one of the few bargaining chips he had left.

With the gold bar in his raised hand, Ryan walked out of the trees and headed for the canopy where Hermann had established his dive operation.

It was Petra who spotted Ryan first. Without hesitation, she seized a UMP from the nearby table and aimed it at Ryan's midsection as he approached.

"I come in peace," Ryan assured them, shaking the bar in his right hand. "I picked this up while I was in the cave. I intended to bring it to the surface with me, but the tide changed, and I got washed out to sea."

"What do you want?" Petra asked.

Ryan looked past her to her brother. Hermann hadn't made a move for his own weapon, and he didn't look pleased at even being near his sibling. Turning his gaze back to Petra, Ryan said, "I'm going to leave this gold bar on the table and then Diane and I are going to walk out of here."

"*Nein!*" Petra shouted.

Gunther and Schuler had stopped stacking bars in the bucket to watch the drama play out.

Ryan edged toward Diane.

"You have killed our men in cold blood and interfered in our operation," Petra shrieked. "You must pay for what you've done."

"We've all paid the price on this mission," Ryan replied, trying to remain cool. "I'll take Diane, and we'll leave. Once you have the gold, you can leave the island and we'll all live in peace."

"You had your chance to leave," Petra said, her voice lowering to a menacing growl.

"I have a sniper watching us," Ryan stated. "If you pull that trigger, he'll put a bullet in your head, then he'll shoot your brother. We'll all be losers."

Hermann Ziegler stepped forward and placed his hand on Petra's UMP. He pushed the barrel down before removing it from her trembling hands. Her face turned red as she boiled with rage.

"Take her and leave," Hermann said.

"No! They must pay," Petra insisted.

"He's right, you know. We have all paid dearly on this mission." To Ryan, Hermann said, "The gold is what we want. Take *Frau* Carlton and leave the island until we're through."

"Will do. Where's the skiff you borrowed?" Ryan asked.

"We left it in the cove on Prime Cay," Hermann replied.

"Okay. We need a ride off the island. And I've got an injured man up at the Green Castle."

"The sniper?" Petra asked, still seething.

"Yes, the sniper. He's got a broken leg. Diane and I will take the track loader up to the house and then go down to the east dock. Captain Haas can take us across to Little Darby."

Hermann turned to his sister. "I'm going with him. Monitor the dive operation."

"You were *always* weak, Hermann," Petra spat. "I knew it and so did Mother. That's why she waited so long to bring you into the organization."

"Let's go," Hermann said to Ryan and Diane, ignoring Petra's ravings.

As Diane stood, Ryan untied the rope binding her wrists. She put her hand in his as they walked ahead of Hermann toward the track loader.

"Don't try anything dumb," Hermann reminded them. "I've got a gun on you."

"I would expect nothing less," Ryan replied.

———

AT THE TRACK LOADER, Ryan asked Diane to drive it to the Castle while Hermann pitched Ryan's SMG and chest rig into the brush. He then radioed Scott to tell him they were on their way, and not to shoot anyone.

Diane jumped into the cab, pulled the safety bar down, and started the engine. She backed the loader out of the trees, with her two passengers standing on the rear bumper. Skillfully, Diane maneuvered them back to the trail and then up to the Castle.

Once they reached the door, Hermann ordered Diane to shut down the machine and pocketed the key. "Where's your friend?"

"Upstairs," Ryan said, his arms raised to keep everything civilized.

"Let's go."

As they entered the house, Ryan called out to Scott. "Diane and I are coming up to get you. Put your guns on the table and Hermann won't shoot any of us."

"Copy that," Scott said.

Ryan led the way up the steps, staying close to the wall. When they were all in the room where Ryan had set up Scott's sniper bench, they found the injured man in the rocking chair, with his leg propped up a windowsill. His Springfield M1A rifle and XD-M Elite Tactical pistol lay on the table, actions open and magazines stacked side by side.

Ryan tossed Scott's backpack to Diane, then leaned down and caught Scott's right arm under his shoulder. "Come on, old buddy, let's get you out of here." He heaved Scott up onto his good leg. "This is going to be a little awkward, but it's the easiest way to get you out of here."

In one swift motion, Ryan scooped the bigger man up in his arms in a one-person carry and headed for the stairs.

Looping his arms around Ryan's neck, Scott puckered up

his lips and asked, "Should I give you a kiss as we cross the threshold?"

"Shut up, princess," Ryan grunted.

At the bottom of the stairs, Ryan leaned his back against the wall to stabilize himself and then walked through the back door and down the two steps to the sandy ground. He set Scott on his good leg and breathed a sigh of relief at having shed 235 pounds.

After Hermann gave her back the key, Diane climbed into the track loader's cab, started the motor, and raised the bucket to thigh level. Ryan backed Scott up to the bucket and helped him to sit down, then swung his splinted leg into the bucket. He climbed in beside Scott to cushion the ride while Hermann mounted the rear bumper again.

"I'm not too happy about leaving my gun on that table, Ryan," Scott said, just loud enough to be heard. "My fingerprints are all over those weapons and ballistics will quickly match my guns to the bullets that killed all those goons."

"I know. I'm not wild about it, either," Ryan admitted. "But this was the only way we could all walk out of here alive —or, in your case, hobble."

"No thanks to you. I wouldn't be in this mess if you hadn't taken this job."

"I told you to stay home," Ryan retorted. "I didn't twist your arm to be here."

Scott smiled. "No, but it was fun while it lasted."

Ryan rolled his eyes. *Nothing* about this little operation had been fun.

———

DIANE BROUGHT the loader to a stop at the dock. Hermann jumped down from the rear bumper and rounded the bucket, UMP dangling loosely from its sling.

Ryan helped Scott out of the loader and then he and Diane assisted the injured man into the waiting aluminum dinghy. Once they were seated in it, Hermann climbed down beside Diane. He put an arm around her and pointed the gun at her belly.

Hermann spoke to Captain Haas in German and then Haas started the boat's outboard. They motored south through the anchorage, past Lignum Vitae Cay, and around the south end of Prime Cay. He beached the aluminum workboat beside Diane's Carolina Skiff.

Ryan and Diane helped Scott aboard the skiff under Hermann's watchful eye. With Scott seated on the skiff's deck with a couple of lifejackets to support and comfort him, Ryan and Diane pushed the boat off the beach. Once it was floating, Diane swung a leg over the gunwale while Ryan continued to push the skiff into deeper water.

"Weller!" Hermann called. "Don't go back to Little Darby. Go south, to George Town."

"You got it," Ryan said.

Diane started the outboard, and Ryan climbed aboard. She aimed the bow at the cut in the reef, signified by deeper blue water surrounded by light turquoise green. Where the reef was just inches below the surface, the patches of water were dark brown, and in the extreme shallows, the water turned a pale yellow to reflect the sand.

"Are we actually going to George Town?" Diane asked.

"Yes," Ryan said. "Scott needs medical attention. If they can't set his leg there, then he can get a medevac flight back to the States."

Diane nodded, but Scott chimed in, "I could use a stiff drink, too. This damn boat is beating the shit out of me. You got any more of that Bacardi?"

Ryan slung his backpack to the deck and pulled out his

medical kit. He found the bottle of ibuprofen and handed it over along with the last bottle of rum. "That's all I've got."

"No smokes?" Scott asked.

"Why? You wanna burn one?" Ryan asked in surprise. He had never seen Scott smoke, but sometimes pain had a way of making a man crave things he didn't normally do.

"Just shut up and give me one."

Ryan found a pack of cigarettes and a lighter in his back-pack. He lit one and handed them over to Scott, who was washing down a handful of pills with the rum. Scott lit up and Ryan offered the pack to Diane, who shook her head.

"It's about thirty-five miles to George Town," Ryan said, tucking away the medical kit.

"Put the hammer down," Scott said, and Diane did, opening the Suzuki outboard to the max to skim across the smooth water.

Ryan exhaled a cloud of smoke as he looked north along the island chain. Once he had Scott taken care of, he was heading back to Big Darby—not to settle scores or right wrongs, but to make sure the gold never left The Bahamas in the hands of Hermann and Petra Ziegler.

CHAPTER FORTY-TWO

Two hours after leaving Big Darby Island, Diane pulled the Carolina Skiff up to a dock at the Exuma Yacht Club. Scott was in terrible pain from bouncing around in the boat but had suffered stoically, knowing there was nothing Diane could do to avoid it.

After tying off the lines at the dock, Ryan glanced around at the mass of anchored sailboats, most of them closer to Stocking Island, the barrier island that formed the protected harbor around one of the largest anchorages in The Bahamas.

George Town was known in the sailing world as "Chicken Harbor." The Exumas were a sparsely populated chain, and by the time cruisers arrived in George Town with its well-stocked grocery stores and medical services, they were usually ready for a break. From George Town, the next big jump was to the Turks and Caicos or farther down the notorious "Thorny Path" to the Dominican Republic or the Virgin Islands. The seas were rougher, and the passages required multiple days instead of mere hours. In light of this, many cruisers "chicken out" in George Town.

Most cruisers found themselves anchored in the harbor

for weeks longer than they'd planned before making the jump, while others decided they'd had enough of living on a boat and headed for home.

Ryan had been to George Town several times and had quickly fallen into the afternoon volleyball games, cruiser potlucks, and the slow pace of life in the easygoing town. One T-shirt Ryan had seen in the straw market reminded everyone of George Town's unhurried lifestyle, reading: "No one move, no one get hurt."

That wasn't the case for Scott. Each movement almost took his breath away as Ryan and Diane helped him over the gunwale and onto the dock. With Scott between them, his arms on their shoulders for support, the trio walked up the dock. At the entrance to the yacht club, they eased Scott into a chair while Ryan paid the dockage fee and called for a taxi.

Diane ran upstairs to the bar and returned with three sweating Kalik beers. They sipped them as they waited for the taxi, enjoying the cold beverages after only drinking luke-warm water all day on Big Darby.

When the taxi pulled up, the driver, a thin man with long dreads, wearing surf shorts and a muscle shirt with no shoes, helped lay Scott out on the back seat. As a result, Diane ended up sitting on Ryan's lap in the front seat. She looped an arm around his neck and used the other to stabilize herself against the center console as the driver careened through the streets, blaring his horn at every other taxi, golf cart, van, motorcycle, and bicyclist on the road.

The ride lasted a short six minutes before Dreadlocks pulled the cab to a screeching halt at the entrance to the Exuma Community Mini-Hospital. Like the rest of the island, there was no real hurry for Scott to be seen. Ryan agreed to pay with his credit card since the clinic didn't take DWR's insurance. Only then did the nurse take Scott through the swinging door to an examination room.

Before Ryan could follow, Diane put a hand on his arm. "I'm going to get two rooms at the Peace & Plenty. Come there when you have things straightened out with Scott."

Ryan nodded, then went through the door to find his friend.

The nurse was busy slicing off the duct tape and tree-branch splint. "How long has your leg been broken?" she asked in her island lilt.

"Two days," Scott admitted.

The nurse made a *tsk-tsk* sound as she tossed Ryan's contraption in the trash can.

"We were on an island north of here and couldn't get a ride down," Ryan explained, and the nurse made a note in Scott's chart.

The nurse left and was back in a half hour, splinting Scott's leg with a modern fabric splint with embedded aluminum stiffeners and Velcro closures. She bundled him into a wheelchair and took him to X-ray.

While Ryan waited for Scott to return, he walked outside to use his sat phone. He dialed Greg Olsen's number.

Greg answered with, "How's life in The Bahamas?"

"Ashlee ratted me out, didn't she?"

"She's a loyal employee, unlike *someone* who shall remain nameless but is on the other end of this line."

"So, here's the thing ... Scott fell and broke his leg. We're at a clinic in George Town getting it checked out right now. Is there any way you could send Chuck in the King Air to get him?"

"How much is this contracting job paying you? Greg asked.

"A nice round number plus expenses."

"Sounds like you're paying for the fuel and for Chuck's time."

"Fine with me," Ryan agreed, knowing DWR's chief pilot,

Chuck Newland, would jump at the chance to get in on the action.

"What about you?" Greg asked. "Are you doing okay?"

"I'm fine. A bit sunburned and mosquito-bitten, but otherwise unscathed. One other favor: do you know anyone in the Royal Bahamas Defense Force? Like, high-up?"

"I know a guy. Why?"

"I need their help. I've run out of options and using the RBDF is the best thing I can come up with."

"Break it down for me," Greg said.

Ryan told Greg the whole sordid tale, from being recruited by Steve Carlton to arriving in George Town, in less than seven minutes.

"I think your idea is sound," Greg conceded. "Let me make a few calls and get back with you when I know something."

"Thanks, Greg."

The two men said goodbye, and Ryan ended the call. He went back inside to find Scott hadn't returned to his exam room yet, so he found a soda machine and bought himself a Goombay Punch, a Bahamian-made soda that tasted like pineapple flavored with a hint of lemon. For Ryan, the soda was a bit sweet and left him thirstier than before he'd drunk it, so he filled the empty soda can with water from a nearby drinking fountain and then walked back to the exam room.

After waiting another ten minutes, the nurse wheeled Scott into the room. He now sported a fiberglass cast from his thigh down, with only his toes exposed at the end.

"Got a broken tib/fib, like we figured," Scott said. "Bones sheared at an angle, so while it's a clean break, it's not going to heal without surgery."

"He'll need to go to Nassau. We can arrange a medical flight," the nurse offered.

"No, thanks," Ryan said. "I have a plane coming to pick him up. We'll fly him to Miami."

"Very good," she said.

"We'll need a copy of his record," Ryan said.

"I can have that ready for you by tomorrow," the nurse replied.

"Good. I'll come back and get it. Can I take him to a hotel for the night?"

"No alcohol with the medication," she warned.

Scott rolled his eyes.

"Thanks," Ryan said and started pushing Scott out of the clinic.

"Don't I get a say in this?" Scott asked.

"I can leave you here, if you want," Ryan replied. "Diane got us a room at the Peace & Plenty. I'm sure the bed is much nicer there, and you won't get a cold beer here."

"Hooyah," Scott replied with the Navy battle cry. "Take me to the beer."

As the two men waited for another cab to ferry them to the hotel, Ryan's phone rang. Greg's name flashed on the caller ID.

Ryan answered with, "What's up, boss?"

"I talked to my contact in the RBDF. His name is Albert Sweeting. He's a captain in the Commando Squadron, the RBDF's Special Forces unit."

"I wasn't aware they had an elite unit."

"Now you know."

"'And knowing is half the battle,'" Ryan said, finishing the famous tagline from the *G.I. Joe* cartoons.

"Anyhow," Greg said, steering the conversation back on topic. "I'll text you Sweeting's number. He's expecting your call."

"I'll give him a shout as soon as I get Scott settled. He's got a broken tib/fib and needs surgery."

"Chuck will be there tomorrow morning with the plane," Greg advised. "I'll arrange for Scott to see a specialist when he arrives Stateside."

"That's great. Thanks for taking care of me on this one, old buddy."

"Did I have a choice?" Greg asked.

"No. Probably not."

Greg's tone turned serious. "You know I'll support you in whatever you need, right, brother?"

"Yeah, I do," Ryan said. "But I sense a 'but.'"

"There is, and I'm going to give it to you. I don't like you doing this shit alone. I know you took Scott with you, but from what you told Ashlee about this Paladin Group, they're heavy hitters. I'm worried about you being alone out there."

"I get it," Ryan said. "I need to go. Our ride is here." He ended the call before Greg could berate him further for being stupid. He didn't like it when Greg got overprotective. Ryan had known the risks when he'd signed up for this mission— maybe not the neo-Nazis and their fanatical goal of funding a Fourth Reich with the gold stashed on Big Darby—but, at the very least, the general danger of taking on armed men intent on driving away the Carltons at all costs.

Scott scooted into the taxi's rear seat backward, dragging his aluminum crutches after him. Ryan got into the front seat. With tires peeling out and the horn blasting, the driver managed to get to the Peace & Plenty without killing them or maiming any pedestrians.

Diane was waiting by the hotel's oval-shaped pool, a tall, fruity-looking drink by her elbow. She stood as Ryan and Scott approached.

Ryan couldn't help but notice she was wearing a bright red one-piece swimsuit, and Diane caught him looking. "You like it? I got it in the straw market next door."

"It looks good. I need a beer."

He pushed past her and headed for the bar. Once he had several Kaliks in hand, he returned to the table and handed the beers to Scott. "I've got a call to make. I'll be back in a bit. Then we'll get some clean clothes and some chow."

Scott tilted his beer in a toast.

Ryan walked away to find a quiet place to call Captain Sweeting. With Scott and Diane now out of the line of fire, it was time to set his plan in motion.

CHAPTER FORTY-THREE

The next morning, Ryan and Scott took a taxi back to the clinic, with Diane once again sandwiched in on Ryan's lap. She wore a new pair of khaki shorts and a blue blouse, while Ryan and Scott sported new surf shorts and T-shirts.

Once Ryan had the medical report in hand along with a copy of Scott's X-rays, they headed for Exuma International Airport.

Chuck Newland, DWR's longtime pilot, was already waiting with the Beechcraft King Air fueled for the return flight. He'd flown in earlier that morning and had turned the plane around quickly so he could get Scott back to the mainland as quickly as possible.

As Scott was about to get out of the cab, he opened his backpack, removed an old book wrapped carefully in a plastic bag, and offered the package to Diane. "Ryan found this in the fireplace of the Green Castle's master bedroom. I wasn't sure what was going to happen once we left the island, so I rescued it. It's the journal of Guy Baxter's mistress. It helped

Ryan find the gold. Hopefully, it will find its way back home. Keep it safe."

Diane took the journal and held it delicately, glancing between Ryan and Scott and back again. Clutching the book to her bosom with one hand, she squeezed Scott's arm with the other while beaming with delight. "Thank you so much. You don't know what this means to me."

Ryan helped Chuck get the injured man onto the plane and stretched out in one of the King Air's plush leather seats. The pilot had taken the time to remove one row of seats so Scott could ride comfortably with his leg extended.

Squatting by Scott, Ryan quietly asked, "You still got that gold bar?"

Scott's gaze drifted to his backpack. "Front pocket."

Ryan pulled out the gold bar wrapped in a gun cleaning rag and slipped it into his pocket.

At the airstairs, Ryan said to Chuck, "Thanks for coming on such short notice."

"I was just hoping to get in on one of those infamous Ryan Weller adventures again."

"Sorry, bud," Ryan said. "It's all over but the shouting."

Chuck grinned. "I can always drink margaritas and watch the *señoritas* while you do the shouting."

"Next time," Ryan promised. "Just get Scott back safely so he can get his leg fixed."

"Roger that. I'll buy you a beer next time you're in Fort Lauderdale and you can tell me all about it."

"Deal." The two men shook hands, and Chuck turned to button up the plane for takeoff.

Back at the taxi, Diane had moved to the rear seat, so Ryan jumped in the front. He told the driver, "Exuma Yacht Club."

He could sense Diane's questioning eyes on him but remained silent as the driver negotiated the twenty-minute

336 EVAN GRAVER

drive. Keeping his gaze out the window, Ryan felt his neck flush at the thought of Diane ogling at him. Once, he glanced over his shoulder and saw she was staring at the diary through the plastic bag, holding it like a long-lost treasure. He should have thanked Scott for recovering it as well. Ryan knew she was personally invested in the island's history as the new owner, and having such a valuable historical document would make her planned advertising scheme even more relevant.

The driver dropped them at the yacht club and Ryan paid him, adding a generous tip. The Bahamian drove away with a smile on his face.

"What now, master troubleshooter?" Diane asked.

"You're going to stow that book someplace. Does the yacht club have a safe?"

"I assume the hotel does," Diane said.

"Good. Have them put the journal in it so we can get going." Ryan checked his dive watch. "We have a meeting in fifteen minutes."

"Here?" she asked.

"No. At Government Dock."

Puzzled, Diane asked, "Why there?"

"Stop wasting time by asking questions," Ryan said, hurrying her. "Stow the book and let's go."

Diane huffed and headed for the hotel lobby. She was back moments later, confirming the hotel manager had locked the journal in his safe.

The walk to Government Dock took seven minutes. It was a busy place as a small interisland freighter had backed up to the concrete quay and was unloading shipping containers while commercial fishing vessels floated at the docks. Among them sat a SAFE Boats 25 Full Cabin marked with "DEFENCE FORCE" along the orange inflatable tube.

Several men milled about the boat in green camouflage fatigues, their black berets bearing the round gold logo of the

RBDF Commando Squadron. Each wore an olive-green bulletproof vest with a pistol in a thigh rig. Two of the men carried M4 Carbines.

As Ryan and Diane approached, a short, stocky man with captain's bars stepped off the boat.

"Are you Ryan Weller?" the captain asked.

"Guilty as charged. I assume you're Captain Sweeting?"

"I am."

"This is Diane Carlton," Ryan said. "She and her father are the new owners of Big Darby Island."

Instead of shaking hands with his new acquaintances, Sweeting clasped his behind his back. "I understand you have some information about an illegal salvage operation taking place in Bahamian waters."

"I do, but it's a delicate situation. Is there someplace we can speak freely?"

"On the boat," Sweeting replied.

"Preferably air-conditioned," Ryan countered. "The Peace & Plenty isn't far."

Sweeting turned to his men and issued orders for them to stay put while he accompanied his "informants" to the hotel. He handed over his vest but retained the pistol. "This better be good, Mister Weller."

"I can assure you, it will be," Ryan replied.

———

ONCE DIANE and the two men had seated themselves at a table in the Copia Restaurant, they ordered iced glasses of switcha.

"If you're comfortable enough," Sweeting said, "can you please tell me what this is about, so my men and I are not wasting our time."

"Thank you for agreeing to meet with me," Ryan said.

"Are you familiar with the legend about Sir Guy Baxter resupplying U-boats from Big Darby?"

"Everyone has heard of it," Sweeting replied.

"Good. Now, you're going to hear the rest of the story."

Sweeting sipped his switcha and listened in rapt silence as Ryan relayed the events that had taken place over the last couple of days on Big Darby Island. He finished with, "My plan to rid the island of the Fourth Reich involves you and your men."

Sweeting took a moment to process everything he'd just heard before asking, "What is it you want us to do?"

"I want you to wait until the Zieglers have the gold loaded aboard their ship, then swoop in and arrest them for salvaging without a permit in The Bahamas."

"And you have proof of this ... Nazi gold?" Sweeting asked.

Ryan unzipped a pouch on his backpack and removed an object wrapped in a cloth. He slid it across the table to Sweeting. The captain's eyes flashed wide as he unwrapped it, and he involuntarily drew in a raspy breath through his gaping mouth. Sweeting quickly folded the cloth back over the gold bar.

"Since the Third Reich is no more, by law, the gold passes to the current German government, giving them ownership," Ryan told the captain. "Neither the Paladin Group, nor anyone else, can claim it as theirs."

Sweeting nodded. "You're correct, but I'll have to take this gold bar for safekeeping."

Ryan reached across the table and picked up the bar. "I'll be with you when you stop the salvage vessel. I'll hand it over then."

Suspicion flickered behind Sweeting's brown eyes. "You are in violation of the law by keeping that."

"I know, but I don't know who to trust. Greg Olsen may have recommended you, but everyone has their secrets." Ryan had a few of his own, including one he shared with the woman beside him.

"I can assure you," Sweeting said, "that I would not have become a captain in the RBDF if I was on the take."

"That being said, let's agree to a handover at the time of the arrest. Now, do you want to see the situation for yourself?" Ryan asked. "Diane has a skiff we can use."

"Do these salvors know your vessel?" Sweeting asked.

"Yes," Diane confirmed.

"I think if we went charging up there in your RBDF boat, it would spook them," Ryan interjected.

"I agree. I know a man with a boat we can use," Sweeting said. "Meet me back at the dock in an hour." He stood and left the table, walking swiftly out of the dining room.

"*That's* your master plan?" Diane asked.

Turning to put his arm on the back of her chair, he asked in exasperation, "What do you want me to do?" Without waiting for an answer, he leaned in close so as not be overheard by the other diners. "Enough people have died for this gold already. We know of at least six just on Big Darby. There's probably a lot more we don't know about and never will. We need to let the RBDF handle it from here."

Diane crossed her arms and nibbled on her lower lip in thought. "And if things don't work out as planned?"

Ryan shrugged. "Then we hope these people disappear from our lives forever. The gold is what they wanted. As long as we stood in their way, we were liabilities."

Diane turned her head slightly, so their noses were less than an inch apart. "You'd better be right, Ryan Weller. Otherwise, you've failed at your job."

CHAPTER FORTY-FOUR

Albert Sweeting stood in the shade of a shipping container as Ryan and Diane crossed the blistering heat of the concrete quay comprising Government Dock. He had changed into blue shorts, a white polo shirt, and sandals. The RBDF captain was speaking into a cell phone with a finger jammed into the opposite ear to shut out the noise.

A ferry and the mailboat from Nassau had arrived at the same time. Consequently, people swarmed over Government Dock, all seeming to be in a hurry to get to their destination, some carrying bags full of swim gear for a day on Stocking Island and others hauling giant duffels of mail on their shoulders. Boxes, crates, and cardboard parcels rode on carts, were being packed into vehicles, or were carried by porters through the crowd.

Ryan waited until Sweeting ended his call, staying a respectful distance away so as not to intrude. The RBDF captain pocketed his phone and motioned for Ryan and Diane to follow him. They wound their way through the crowd, dodging a conga line of men unloading boxes from the mailboat, tossing them from one man to another before stacking them in the back of a truck.

At the edge of the dock, Sweeting stepped down into the cockpit of a mid-1980s Silverton sportfisher. Ryan judged it to be about thirty feet long. It was well maintained but getting long in the tooth, just like its owner, who Sweeting introduced as Tobias, a gray-haired Bahamian of indeterminate age.

The old man yelled for the mate to toss off the lines when the engines were running. Up on the flybridge, Ryan told the charter boat captain to head for Cave Cay. Tobias glanced at Sweeting, who nodded his assent.

Once in the channel, Tobias ramped up the throttles and the heavy fishing vessel stepped up on plane. They cruised north through the sparkling blue Atlantic, passing islands that stretched like vibrant green opals far into the distance.

TWO HOURS LATER, Tobias pulled the throttles back on the Silverton's twin Crusader engines. Cruising at twelve knots, they'd passed the Darby Islands and turned around just south of Cave Cay.

While Tobias and the first mate rigged fishing poles to the outriggers and prepared to troll back to George Town, Ryan and Captain Sweeting discussed what they had seen on the way up. The *Leopard* had moved offshore and, based on the quick sighting Ryan had gotten, appeared to be anchored over the mouth of the cave entrance.

"What's the ship doing so far from the island?" Sweeting asked. "You said it would be anchored by Big Darby."

"I think they've moved it out over the mouth of the tunnel that leads to the blue hole. That's what I would have done. They could build a platform using two diver propulsion vehicles and move more gold with them than with that little basket they were using."

"How long do you think it will take to raise the rest?" Sweeting asked.

"Hard to say," Ryan replied. "It depends on how long it takes to load the DPVs and bring them to the surface."

Sweeting rubbed his chin. "I don't have enough manpower or boats to keep a rotating watch on that salvage vessel."

"I think they're headed for Germany when they leave," Ryan said. "That means they'll run east, passing south of Cat Island. Can you get the RBDF to watch for the *Leopard* when she leaves?"

"A vessel that size has to have an AIS transponder," Sweeting said. "If she's transmitting, we can track her movements."

Ryan glanced at the instruments in the bridge console. They were original to the birth date of the old Silverton. He figured Tobias relied on his decades of knowledge about the area and didn't need fancy radar systems or chart plotters to navigate his home waters. "Too bad we don't know if she's squawking now."

"It will be easy to check once we return to George Town."

Tobias came up the ladder to the flybridge. "De lines be rigged. We catch de tuna and de dolphin." He turned to Diane and grinned. "Dat be de mahi-mahi for you, miss."

"I know what dolphin is," Diane retorted.

"Troll back along the drop," Ryan instructed, "but keep us clear of that salvage vessel we saw by Little Darby."

Tobias gave him a snappy salute. "I used to be in de RBDF when de captain was in de short pants."

Diane busied herself on her phone as Ryan and Sweeting watched Tobias get underway. They trolled along the wall but got no hits before they had to swing wide to avoid the *Leopard*.

"I FOUND IT," Diane announced, holding up her phone.

"Found what?" Ryan asked.

"The *Leopard*'s AIS, only it doesn't say '*Leopard*.' It says '*Sea Knight*.'"

"So, now that we know what they're transmitting, we can track them," Ryan said.

"It would be nice to know they have the gold aboard before I take my team out to stop them," Sweeting commented.

"No problem," Ryan replied. "Drop me at Little Darby and I'll keep an eye on it."

"Is that wise?" Diane asked.

"It's as good as we're going to get," Ryan reasoned.

"I agree," Sweeting added. "If Ryan were to get pictures or other proof, it would solidify our case in court. I'll need both of you to testify, if it comes to that."

Ryan nodded. "No problem."

Diane nodded, too, but Ryan wasn't sure she approved.

Sweeting turned to Tobias. "Take us two miles south of Little Darby and then reel in your lines. We need to make haste back to George Town."

"What's the plan?" Ryan asked.

"You have someone drop you on the island out of sight of the *Leopard* and find a place where you can watch it and not be seen. When they prepare to leave, you call me."

"Sounds good," Ryan said. In his heart, he hoped it would be that easy, but the reality of going head-to-head with the Zieglers again was hard to stomach.

If the Germans discovered him, there was every chance it would cost Ryan his life.

CHAPTER FORTY-FIVE

B ack in George Town, Ryan packed the Carolina Skiff with some food supplies and freshwater. He still had gear stored on both Big and Little Darby Islands and hoped he could recover a pistol or one of the H&K UMPs he had stashed earlier. It would be good to have a weapon, especially if the Germans discovered him.

"I'm going with you," Diane insisted.

"No. I promised your dad that I'd keep you safe. I let you get kidnapped twice. I'm not going to allow that to happen again."

"I can take care of myself," she said indignantly.

"Clearly not."

"Hey! I'm not a trained 'operator' like you are," she said using air quotes. "I got scared and ran the wrong way."

"I told you to hold onto my chest rig."

"And I let go. So what? Are you going to hold it against me for the rest of my life—or just the fact that I kissed you?"

Ryan stopped loading water jugs into the boat. "Look, Princess Di, this isn't about you. I'm trying to do my job."

"And failing miserably," she interjected.

"Fine. I suck. Whatever. But believe me, all I'm going to do is sit in the mangroves and get eaten alive by mosquitoes. Is that what you want to do? Just hang out at the Peace & Plenty and enjoy life, or better yet, catch a plane to Colorado and ride your motorcycles. Do anything but get into this boat with me."

"All right," she conceded.

Ryan didn't like the tone of her voice. "Toss off the lines, would you?" he asked as he started the outboard.

Diane threw the bow line into the boat, then trotted back to the stern line. Ryan engaged the drive, preparing to pull away as soon as Diane untied the line from the cleat, but no sooner was it in her hand than she jumped aboard the skiff.

"Diane," Ryan growled in warning, disengaging the drive.

"You need someone to drop you off. You can't leave my boat on the beach, or they'll see it."

"Okay. You've got a point," Ryan agreed reluctantly. "But you drop me off and come straight back here."

She rolled her eyes as she motioned with her hands for him to move out of the way so she could drive.

———

FOR THE SECOND time that day, they headed out of Stocking Harbor and drove north. Diane handled the boat with precision and all Ryan had to do was ride along.

When she finally turned into the cut between Bock and Prime Cays, Ryan stood on the bow to guide her through the shifting sand and coral heads into deeper water just north of Goat Cay. Ryan slipped over the gunwale into chest-deep water, wearing his surf shorts, a T-shirt, and water shoes to protect his feet. Diane handed him his backpack and the bag he'd packed with food and water.

"Are you sure you're going to be all right?" she asked.

"I'll be fine," Ryan replied.

"Where do you think you'll set up camp?"

"Probably on that little point that juts into Exuma Sound on the east side of Little Darby."

"Good luck." Diane backed the boat around as Ryan waded up onto Big Darby Island for what he hoped was the last time.

At the tree line, he glanced back to see Diane slowly motoring past the south end of Goat Cay. "Keep on going, woman," he muttered. "Don't cause me any more trouble."

Ryan wanted to sit in the mangroves, swat mosquitoes, and worry about absolutely nothing until he had to call Captain Sweeting on the sat phone and have him swoop in for the arrest.

He shouldered the duffel, its contents shifting awkwardly under the fabric as he walked. Crossing the island had become old hat, and he followed the rock walls and small paths down to the airstrip. The Zieglers had cleared the tent of all its food and water, and the only weapon Ryan could find was the compound bow and arrows left behind by Steve Carlton.

Ryan repacked the duffel, shoving his backpack into it before slipping his shoulders through the straps. With his hands free, he inventoried the contents of Carlton's bow case: a black PSE Stinger complete with fiber-optic sights, a stabilizer, and a wrist strap release aid with an index finger trigger, which helped the shooter gain accuracy over gripping the bow string with just their fingers.

He counted ten arrows, half with field points and the other five tipped with razor-sharp broadheads. After attaching the quick release quiver, Ryan loaded it with the five broadheads, then carried the other five arrows in his hand. Left in the case were the shotgun shells he'd dumped into it earlier. With no further use for the shells or the case, he shoved the case back into the hole he'd pulled it from.

Thus equipped, Ryan made his way overland toward the Green Castle, wanting to make use of its high vantage point. It would be easier than camping on a beach with no tent.

He spent fifteen minutes circling the house before approaching it. Ryan didn't want to walk up on a guard or step into a trap set by the Germans.

What he found turned his stomach.

The Germans had piled all the dead men in the kitchen. Flies buzzed around the bodies, and dried blood pooled on the floor. The bodies had bloated in the heat, oozing blood and puss and other nauseating substances from their bullet wounds.

Bile rose in the back of Ryan's throat. He ran outside to puke beside the old utility building. It wasn't the first time Ryan had seen a stack of dead bodies, but he hoped it was the last. When he closed his eyes, he saw the pile again and his gut spasmed. So much for hiding in the house. The stench was more than enough to drive him away.

Ryan went back inside and walked up to the second-floor balcony, at least he could get a handle on the enemy's position. From there, he could see men he didn't recognize standing around the canopy beside the dive site. They each carried submachine guns just like their predecessors. Even if Captain Sweeting didn't find any gold aboard the *Leopard*, being in possession of automatic firearms would still earn Ziegler and his men a stiff prison sentence.

Out to sea, the *Leopard* floated in choppy waters. He figured the divers were in the water due to the lack of activity on the deck.

He retraced his steps out of the house, avoiding the carrion flies and the stench by holding his breath. Outside, he shouldered into his duffel again and picked up the bow. At least he had something with which to protect himself against the armed men. With a grin, he tried out a new name, "Rambo Ryan."

The quickest way across to Little Darby, Ryan knew, was by boat, but without one, his only option was to swim. The shortest distance was between the concrete dock on Big Darby and the dock behind The Drifts Lodge. Not knowing whether there were armed men patrolling those docks, he headed south along the spine of the ridge again, then dropped east to the small point of land jutting out into the Darby Channel anchorage. From where he stood on the rocks, it was five hundred yards across the water, most of it less than five feet deep.

Ryan stepped down into the water and started wading, holding the bow above his head. In the middle of the channel, he could feel the current tugging at his clothes. He had solid footing on the sandy bottom and easily avoided being swept out to sea, but it took him longer than he would have liked to make the crossing. Fortunately, he didn't spot any boats coming or going between Big Darby and the *Leopard*, but that didn't mean someone hadn't spotted him.

Once he was on dry ground again, Ryan assessed his gear. Nothing had gotten wet except the clothes he'd been wearing, and they dried quickly as he walked along the dirt road that traversed the length of Little Darby Island. Just past the reddish-brown waters of the larger salt pond, Ryan took the fork in the road and headed east toward his destination.

The rocky outcropping projecting into Exuma Sound was a thousand feet long and five hundred feet wide. From the air, it looked like a whale's tail. Wispy ironwood trees sprouted from the thin soil, along with mangroves and scrub palms. Ryan stayed alert as he moved toward the edge of the cliff that dropped ten feet to the sea below. One thing about trouble in paradise was that the scenery was always good.

Ryan stopped dead in his tracks when he heard a twig snap to his left. He wished he had his trusty Walther PPQ pistol instead of the bow, but with a bit of luck, the Stinger would be equally effective. He nocked an arrow and clipped the trigger release to the tiny metal D loop forming the string nocks. Slowly, he drew the bowstring back, aiming the arrow where he'd heard the twig snap.

Another snap increased Ryan's heart rate. The twin rotary cams on the bow's limbs rolled over, and the heavy tension of the sixty-pound draw weight decreased by seventy-five percent so he could easily hold the bowstring to his cheek.

Through the pins of the fiber-optic sight, Ryan saw Diane Carlton step out of the thicket. She wore a black bikini top, green running shorts trimmed with white, and a pair of running shoes.

Ryan swung the bow a fraction of an inch to the left and snapped the trigger. The arrow embedded itself in a tree a foot from Diane's head.

"You almost shot me, Ryan!"

Ryan quickly closed the gap to avoid further shouting. "You're not supposed to be here, Princess."

"Stop calling me that!" she snapped.

"Stop doing the exact *opposite* of what I tell you to do," he shot back.

"I was about to say that I didn't feel safe without being near you until you deliberately shot an arrow at me."

"Because you need to take this shit seriously. Do you like being in danger?"

"No," she said glumly, then smiled wistfully. "But I do like being rescued by you."

"I'm not your knight in tarnished armor and you need to get over your desire to be rescued."

Diane stuck out her bottom lip and made a puppy dog face, then sucked her lip in and bit it seductively, almost as if she knew it was one of those trivial gestures that turned Ryan on. "But Daddy paid you to take care of me."

"And I wish I hadn't taken this job, so I would've never met you."

Diane puffed up her body as if she were ready to throw punches. "Take that back, Ryan Weller."

"I don't have time to play games, Princess. I have work to do."

"What? Stand over there on the ledge all day and watch the *Leopard* through binoculars?"

"Yeah, pretty much." He tugged at the arrow in the tree, then glanced around. "How did you get here before me? And where's the boat?"

"I left it with the caretaker on Goat Cay. When Daddy first bought Big Darby, he and I spent a few days making the rounds to all the neighboring islands to introduce and ingratiate ourselves with their owners and caretakers, kinda like you did with RJ when you gave him the pole spear?"

"It was the easiest way to get the information I needed," Ryan said defensively.

"Anyway, I left the boat at Goat Cay and swam across the cut since it was slack tide. I figured you would eventually show up here, so I walked over and found a place to watch the boat. Wanna see?"

Ryan shrugged, knowing it was of no use to argue. He was stuck with her again. As he tried to jerk the carbon-fiber arrow from the tree, the only thing he succeeded in doing was snapping off the shaft. He tossed the broken arrow on the ground at the base of the tree and followed Diane through the thicket to the edge of the cliff.

It was the perfect place to keep watch. The trees provided a nice backdrop to break up their silhouettes, and their shade provided a respite from the relentless tropical sun.

Leaving the bow hanging from a low tree branch, Ryan

returned to the spot where he'd dropped the duffel and carried it back to their new overwatch position.

"The mosquitoes are going to eat you alive in that outfit," he said to Diane.

"I have some other clothes in a bag. I keep some spares in the boat in case I get wet."

He tried not to stare at her and busied himself with digging out the binoculars from his backpack. Once he had them in hand, Ryan put them to his eyes and focused on the *Leopard*. He figured it was a mile out to sea, using dynamic positioning to hold her in place. As he watched, men swarmed the deck. They swung a crane out over the water at the stern of the vessel, and two of the men went over the rail.

The crewmen operating the crane raised a small platform from the water. As Ryan had suspected, the divers had constructed a rig from two DPVs to transport the gold. Once it was on deck, the two divers climbed up and began to hurriedly strip off their gear.

When Ryan had been aboard the *Leopard*, he'd seen a two-man recompression chamber, where the naked divers now headed. Other men picked up their gear, hung the dry suits on a rack, and began to disassemble the rebreathers on a small table set aft of the superstructure. Two more divers began to shrug into their own dry suits, preparing for another dive.

"Where did all those extra guys come from?" Diane asked.

Ryan glanced at her to see she had her own set of binos to her eyes and was also watching the action taking place on the *Leopard*. "I figured Ziegler called in reinforcements. With his entire team dead, he needed more muscle to retrieve the gold." He smirked. "Or to kidnap you."

"Funny. Real funny," Diane replied.

They seated themselves on the ground and took turns watching the salvage vessel through their binoculars.

"How long do you think we'll be here?" she asked.

"Let me consult my crystal ball. Oh, wait—I left it in my other pants," Ryan said sarcastically.

"There's no need to cop an attitude, Ryan. Like it or not, we're in this together to the end."

CHAPTER FORTY-SIX

An uneventful day passed with Ryan and Diane swatting mosquitoes and resting under a mosquito net Ryan had brought in his duffel. He hated being crammed under it with Diane, but nightfall brought out the biting insects. Being close to her was better than being bitten by all the bugs on Little Darby as they staked out the *Leopard*.

In the morning, they ate a simple breakfast of canned stew heated over a Sterno flame. They took turns staring at the boat, rousing one another when activity occurred on the salvage vessel's deck.

After eating boiled rice and canned tuna for lunch, Diane declared she was going swimming in the southern cove of the whale's tail. "No one will see me," she reassured Ryan. "The rock blocks the view of the ship, and those goons over on Big Darby have no idea that we're here."

Ryan shook his head. "I don't like it."

"When, dear Ryan, have I ever done anything you did like?"

After puckering up her lips and blowing him a kiss, Diane got up and pranced away, leaving Ryan alone on the rocky bluff, shaking his head and glowering at her impertinence. Her defiance seemed to have increased over the twenty-four hours, flaunting her body and his rules that would keep her safe.

Ryan watched the *Leopard*'s crew take another load of gold aboard and swap divers. He was timing the evolution. They were underwater for nearly an hour each time.

After two diving cycles had passed with no sign of Diane, curiosity got the better of Ryan, and he decided he should check on her. She was his principal for the duration, despite her opposition.

Crossing the whale's tail, Ryan stood in the trees at the top of the cliff. He had a clear view of Diane floating spread eagle in the cove of clam water, protected by the rocks from the surf raging in from the open sea. She wore only the black bikini, and the sun winked off the silver stud in her belly button.

Shifting his gaze to the cliff facing the main island, he saw a sea cave with a ridge of coral just beneath the surface of the water. The cave opening appeared to be about three feet higher than the water level, but he couldn't see how far it projected into the rock. It would be an interesting place to explore someday. Ryan added it to the list.

He took one last look at Diane, feeling like a Peeping Tom. Shaking his head, Ryan tried not to think about the kiss they'd shared. He'd kissed a lot of women, but there was something captivating about the one he'd shared with Diane. He couldn't put his finger on it, nor the reason why his mind kept reaching back for it. Maybe, he reasoned, he'd feel this way about kissing Diane until he was able to unburden himself to his wife. The word wasn't "captivating," he realized. The word he was looking for was "forbidden."

As he walked away, Ryan heard Diane scream. He raced

back to where he had last seen her to find two men with submachine guns horsing her out of the water.

Ryan turned, sprinted to their camp, and slung on his backpack. He then snatched the compound bow from the tree limb and grabbed the four remaining field point arrows. With nine arrows in total, he hoped they were enough.

Returning to the edge of the cliff, he saw the men had Diane between them and were leading her up the beach. He shook his head, wondering how he could have been so dumb as to let her get captured for a third time, but there wasn't time to contemplate either his stupidity or her stubbornness. There also wasn't time to ponder how these goons had found them. He'd thought they'd been careful to remain unseen, but something had given them away.

Ryan made his way along the narrow neck of land connecting Little Darby to the whale's tail, figuring the men were headed for the path that led from the beach to the central road. Instead of hacking his way through the dense undergrowth, the troubleshooter cut right and came out on the beach on the north side of the whale's tail. Once in the open, he sprinted along the edge of the water, wanting to get ahead of the men holding Diane hostage.

When he was abreast of what he thought was the southern end of the runway, Ryan cut left into the brush again. As planned, he was ahead of the two men and Diane. He squatted in the brush, breathing hard, trying to reoxygenate his body and calm his shaking muscles. Swimming laps around his boat, as he did most mornings, was excellent exercise, but running had always punished his body and Ryan realized just how out of shape he was.

In order to make his shots count, he needed to be as calm as possible. One tremble of his trigger finger or a tremor in the hand holding the bow would throw off his aim and the arrow would not find its mark.

You wanted to play Rambo. Now's your chance.

Ryan knelt in the brush beside the trail. He was still trying to catch his breath when the trio appeared. He nocked one of the broadhead arrows to the string and drew it back. Aiming carefully, he let the arrow fly.

As soon as he released it, he was nocking a second one. By the time he had the bowstring drawn and his thumb anchored to his cheek so he could see through the tiny peep sight in the bowstring, Ryan knew one man was down with an arrow to the chest and the second was using Diane as a shield.

He hadn't really used the sights installed by Steve Carlton and didn't know what distance each of the five pins corresponded to. Ryan had been using the old "point and shoot" method, but with Diane now being used as a shield, he had to be more careful.

Ryan aimed at the German's head and let the arrow fly. It went whistling past the guy's ear, making him duck. As the man reacted to the close call, Diane spun out of his grasp and ran into the brush. Ryan nocked a third arrow, whipped the string back, and let it fly. The arrow pierced the guy's chest, and he toppled over backward.

As he fell, the dead German's finger pressed the trigger on his UMP and unleashed the SMG's whole magazine on full auto. Ryan hit the deck. Fortunately, all the rounds went in another direction.

"Diane!" Ryan called in a whispered shout. "*Diane!*"

She didn't respond.

Ryan wondered where she'd run off to, then feared she might have been hit by a stray round. Creeping forward, he relieved one of the dead men of his pistol and thigh rig, strapping it to his own body. The gun was a H&K VP9, similar to his favored Walther. Now armed with a ballistic weapon, Ryan helped himself to spare magazines from the second dead man, then liberated both their UMPs. He set his new collection of firearms off to the side of the path, then pulled the two dead men into the brush before kicking sand over the bloodstains they'd left behind.

With his new implements of war, Ryan set off toward the whale's tail again, hoping to catch up to his principal. Diane had a bad habit of rabbiting on him. He needed a leash.

Ryan searched the area where he'd seen Diane disappear but found no sign of her. The gunfire would surely draw other Germans to their position, and he needed to corral his principal before they showed up.

At the campsite, Ryan caught up with Diane. "Are you okay?" he asked.

"No, Ryan. I am *not* okay. I'm tired of being kidnapped and I'm tired of seeing dead people."

Ryan thought about the stack of bodies in the Green Castle and wondered how she would react to them. "We need to move. All those gunshots will bring more bad guys."

As if on cue, they heard the roar of an outboard motor and turned to see the *Leopard*'s workboat heading for shore. Ryan put his binoculars to his eyes and stared across the water at the boat. It was loaded for bear with more armed men.

"Looks like company's coming," he said.

"I can't keep doing this," Diane griped, bent over, hands on her knees. "I wish I'd stayed in George Town."

"A little late for that now, Princess," Ryan said as he gathered his gear. "Get some clothes on so we can move fast through the scrub. That bikini won't protect you from much."

She pulled on shorts and a T-shirt. "My shoes are on the beach."

"Okay. Let's go get them."

On the way to get her shoes, Ryan dialed Captain Sweeting's number on his sat phone. When he answered, Ryan said, "Remember all those men we saw on the *Leopard?*"

"Yes."

"They spotted us. I've killed two of them already. We need help. Send your team. *Now.*"

"Copy that, Ryan. We're on the way."

Ryan ended the call and stuffed the phone into his backpack. Diane ran across the sand and slipped on her shoes, but before they could move off the beach, two men broke out of the trees with their weapons up. Ryan triggered a burst from a UMP, cutting down the first man and sending the second running for cover. From inside the trees, the man returned fire at Ryan and Diane.

Before Diane could bolt again, Ryan grabbed her by the shirttail and hauled her close, firing his submachine gun from the hip and dragging his principal toward the water.

"Head for the sea cave," he shouted, then let go of Diane to grip his weapon with both hands. His bullets must have found their mark because the incoming fire stopped.

Turning, he grabbed Diane by the hand and, together, they half-ran and half-waded through the water to the sea cave. Once inside, they moved as deep into the cave as possible, hiding in the darkness, water surging around Ryan's chest as he stood on the sandy bottom. The water was almost up to Diane's neck, and she bounced on tiptoes to keep her head above the waves that ricocheted off the beach and back into the cave.

Ryan tossed his backpack and his weapons onto a narrow ledge and showed Diane where to place her hand so she could support herself against the incoming tide.

"You picked a bad place to hide, Ryan," she spluttered.

"I think you're right. Let me check the area and see if we can get out of here."

Ryan moved to the mouth of the cave, but as soon as he

peeked out, bullets peppered the rocks above him and splashed into the water around him. He quickly withdrew. The last gunman must have survived and was now pinning them in the cave, hoping the incoming tide would drown them while he waited for reinforcements.

Standing to his full six feet, Ryan was slightly hunched over inside the cave with his head jammed against a depression in the rock, worn smooth over eons as the water lapped against it. The water was pouring into the cave as the tide rose.

Diane clung to the ledge with both hands, trying to keep her head above water. Bullets chipped off the rocky entrance and tunneled through the clear water, leaving swirling wakes of bubbles before their energy quickly dissipated and they fell harmlessly to the sand.

"I'm scared," Diane said.

"Me too, Princess," Ryan said gently.

Ryan had been in a lot of tough spots, but this one was beginning to feel like the worst of them all. The sea was unforgiving and trapped in the cave with no place to go, they would quickly succumb to it.

"You know, it's funny," Diane said, spitting out a mouthful of seawater. "I hated you for calling me Princess, but now it's quite comforting to know I have a nickname. I've never had one before."

"Happy to oblige. Now, maybe we should save our breath."

They fell silent, the water rising higher and higher. Waves lapped at Ryan's chin.

Diane tilted her head back to breathe. "I can't hold on much longer. My hands keep slipping."

Ryan leaned against the wall. "Come here."

She let go of the ledge and moved closer to him. Ryan pulled her in, and she wrapped her arms and legs around him.

"I'm sorry," Ryan whispered. "I made the wrong decision. I didn't keep you safe."

Diane pulled her head back to look him in the eyes. They were once more in the same position as the night of the kiss. "Thanks for trying." She tilted her head and pressed her lips to his.

Fearing he wouldn't live to see another sunrise, Ryan tightened his grip on her and kissed her back.

CHAPTER FORTY-SEVEN

The water continued to rise.

Diane climbed farther up Ryan's body and held her head against the rock ceiling, close to his. He wanted to keep kissing her, but since the last one, they'd been preoccupied with staying alive. The water lapped against his ears and smacked against the rocks, making it nearly impossible to hear anything happening outside the cave.

"Do you think Captain Sweeting is on his way?" Diane asked.

Ryan simply said, "I hope so."

He tilted his head, trying to hear something, a sound louder than what had been outside previously. Lowering his head below the water, Ryan listened to the sounds traveling through the waves. He had to block out the ringing of his tinnitus and listen intently, but it sounded like an outboard motor racing through the surf. Because of the way sound traveled through liquid, it was impossible to tell if the boat was coming or going from his position.

Ryan was about to surface for a second breath when he heard another sound—the distinctive bark of an M4 rifle. He lifted his head out of the water and said, "I think we're being rescued. There's someone out there other than the Germans."

"Thank God," Diane whispered, tightening her arms around his neck. "And thank you, too. I owe you my life."

"It was my job to keep you safe."

"I mean it, Ryan. I owe you everything. If I can ever repay the favor, please let me know."

Ryan was about to respond when he heard someone shouting their names.

"You hear that?" she asked.

"Yeah, I do. Let's get out of here."

Diane squeezed him with all her might with both her arms and legs, then kissed him again. "Good things come in threes, you know." Diane unclamped her body, took a deep breath, and dove under the water, swimming for the cave entrance with Ryan following close behind.

When they surfaced, Ryan saw several RBDF members checking dead or captured Germans—and a familiar face greeted him from the shoreline.

Wading out of the water, Ryan said, "What are you doing here, TJ?"

Truck Jackson Cab had joined Ryan on his last adventure to Haiti and had quickly become a part of the team. When the five-foot-eight former Navy boatswain's mate wasn't aiding the DWR crew, he was guiding fishermen in the Florida Everglades.

"Greg thought you might need some help, so we steamed over on *Dark Ocean* to aid Captain Sweeting."

"Diane, this is TJ Cab," Ryan said. "He's one of my coworkers at Dark Water Research."

"Glad to meet you, TJ," Diane said, extending her hand.

"What's with all the black smoke?" Ryan asked, pointing east at the dark column rising straight into the air.

"Oh, yeah. I guess your fascist friends lit that abandoned house on Big Darby on fire."

Diane sank to the sand and put her head in her hands, sobbing.

"What's with her?" TJ asked.

"Diane was planning on remodeling the Green Castle into a bed and breakfast," Ryan said.

"Oh, *shit.* I guess it's going to be a complete rebuild. Sorry, Diane."

"Come on, Princess. Let's get out of here." Ryan put his hands under her arms and eased her to her feet.

Diane wiped the tears with her palms. "I guess I've got my work cut out for me."

———

THE YELLOWFIN CENTER console used by *Dark Ocean*'s crew as a runabout, dive tender, and fishing boat sat just off the beach with Dave, one of the ship's crew, at the helm.

"TJ, can you help Diane into the boat?" Ryan asked. "I need to get my bag out of the cave."

"You got it, boss. Come on, Diane."

Ryan swam back into the cave and found his pack had washed off the ledge and now lay on the sand. He ducked down to retrieve it. The UMPs were still on the ledge, and he carried them out as well, making his way through the surf to the Yellowfin. Ryan dumped his gear into the boat, then pushed it backward into deeper water. Dave spun the wheel and headed for *Dark Ocean.*

Ryan looked back at the idyllic island setting and thought of the terror and intrigue that had come with his latest mission. It had cost the lives of men and changed him somehow. Every mission had some effect on him, but this one had been different. He focused on the black smoke billowing into the sky and wondered if setting fire to the Green Castle had been the Germans' way of disposing of the bodies they'd piled inside. Shifting his focus to Diane, who was also looking at the smoke, he saw she was pensive.

She noticed him staring and knuckled a tear from the corner of her eye before smiling at him. He felt sorry for her. She had seen death and destruction up close, and this ordeal, he knew, had changed her too. One couldn't help but be changed after being kidnapped and seeing men die in battle.

Ryan wanted to gather her in his arms and hold her close, tell her everything was going to be okay. Diane was a strong woman. She was a survivor like him. Instead of moving to her, he stayed where he was, holding onto the T-top and sitting on the gunwale. He turned his attention toward the sea where *Dark Ocean*, DWR's flagship, lay a respectful distance from the swarm of RBDF boats surrounding the salvage vessel, *Leopard*.

Dave pulled them alongside the rear platform of the yacht support vessel converted to Greg Olsen's personal offshore office. Not only was the vessel equipped with state-of-the-art dive equipment and salvage gear, but it had also been converted to allow Greg to access almost every space in his wheelchair.

Once Ryan had helped TJ tie off the Yellowfin to the big cleats studded into *Dark Ocean*'s deck, he tossed his gear onto the support vessel, then stepped across to help Diane come aboard. She looked somewhat bedraggled from their harrowing ordeal, and Ryan knew he looked the same.

Waiting for them on the aft deck were Steve Carlton and two of the people Ryan loved most in this life. Greg Olsen sat in his wheelchair with his arms crossed, wearing a pair of khaki cargo pants and a DWR T-shirt. Emily stood beside him, wearing white shorts and a green tank top over a sports bra.

Ryan felt his heart rate increase at the sight of her, as it always did. From the moment he'd met her in the lobby of Ward and Young, the insurance company she had worked for at the time, he'd been infatuated with her. They had been through so much together. They'd weathered real storms in their sailboat and storms in their relationship, but they'd been married for over a year now. Surely, they could weather a kiss—or three.

Scott's words about how keeping his transgressions a secret would affect his relationship came back to him.

Ryan bumped fists with his boss. "How's Scott doing?"

"He's good," Greg replied. "They took him in for immediate surgery and put a titanium rod down through his tibia to hold everything together. He should be back to normal in six weeks or so."

"Great. I was worried about him."

Ryan then hugged his wife, holding her tight. He buried his face in her blonde hair, smelling the familiar scents of her shampoo and sunscreen.

Emily squeezed him. "Okay, sailor, wait until we get back to the room before you start feeling me up."

"I'm just glad to see you," he said, stepping back to hold her at arm's length. "I love you."

Emily laughed. "I love you, too." Then, seeing the seriousness in his eyes, she asked, "What happened out there?"

He clenched his jaw muscles, wanting to blurt it all out, but took a deep breath and relaxed. "It's a long story." He turned and beckoned Diane over from where she stood with her father. "Emily, this is my principal, Diane Carlton. Diane, this is my wife, Emily."

"I've heard a lot about you," Diane said, shaking Emily's hand and smiling self-consciously.

"It's nice to meet you," Emily replied. She glanced at Ryan, and he could see the worry in her eyes, almost as if she could see what had transpired between him and Diane. Or maybe he was projecting?

"Let's get you into a hot shower and some clean clothes," Emily said to Diane. "Then you and Ryan can tell us all about your adventure."

Ryan felt his gut tighten as he watched the two women walk away. Despite their physical differences, they both had the same mental toughness.

Carlton walked over, hands in the pockets of his dark slacks. "I'm glad to see you're alive, but I'm not sure this qualifies as a successful job, son. I might have to deduct for damages."

Ryan could hear the jocularity in the man's voice and withheld the biting comment he wanted to dispense. Instead, he said, "Yeah. Sorry about the Castle."

"The way that fire is smoking, I'd say it's a total loss," Greg chimed in.

"Be grateful," Ryan said. "That place was a death trap."

"What do you mean?" Carlton asked. "It had good bones. It could've easily been fixed up."

"The last time I was in there, there were six bodies stacked up in a pile in the kitchen. Let it burn."

"Bodies?" Carlton asked, his tone and posture rigid.

"Don't get squeamish on me, Steve," Ryan said. "You knew how this could end up. You don't send out a troubleshooter and expect to keep your hands clean."

The billionaire nodded. "You're right. I just didn't expect the body count to be so high." Carlton seemed to relax, but Ryan could tell he was still worried about the implications of the dead.

"I think the RBDF will exonerate us of any wrongdoing," Ryan said. "Now, gentlemen, if you'll excuse me, I want to shower and change." He took two steps then paused, snapping his fingers. "Oh, by the way ... I left your bow on Little Darby somewhere. I shot two men with it."

"Good God, man," Carlton stated in shock.

"It was them or Diane. I chose Diane."

Ryan turned and walked away, leaving Greg and Carlton to stare at each other and wonder exactly what had happened on the Darby Islands.

CHAPTER FORTY-EIGHT

Over a steak dinner that night aboard *Dark Ocean*, Ryan and Diane told the whole story, with Greg, Steve Carlton, Emily, TJ, and Captain Sweeting listening in rapt silence.

Sweeting had come aboard after the capture of the German salvage vessel. He informed Ryan the crew were being held on multiple charges including salvaging without a permit, transporting illegal salvage, and possession of firearms. In addition, each person who hadn't checked in with Customs would receive a ten-thousand-dollar fine and up to five years in prison.

Ryan cut into his steak and took another bite of the medium rare New York strip. He chewed thoughtfully as he listened to Sweeting's account of apprehending the Germans aboard *Leopard*.

"In addition to the Ziegler siblings, their mother was on the ship," Sweeting said. "She'd come to oversee the recovery of the gold and bring in more divers and hired guns. Speaking of gold, when can I expect you to hand over the bar you have?"

Ryan pulled the gold bar from his pocket and shoved it

across the table. Greg intercepted it and looked it over. The gold was as shiny as the day the Third Reich had minted it. After examining the bar, Greg handed it to TJ, and the group passed it around the table.

"Imagine the history of this bar," Steve Carlton said, holding it reverently before handing it to Sweeting.

"Our prime minister has reached out to the German government to inform them of the gold's recovery," Sweeting stated. "My boss, the minister of national security, has asked me to sign a contract with Dark Water Research to dive on the recovery site, and ensure all the gold bars have been brought to the surface."

"We'd be happy to do that for you," Greg said.

"I have a contract here." Sweeting held up his phone. "To whom should I email it?"

Greg gave his email address, and his phone chimed a moment later. He read through the proposal and set the phone down. "Everything looks good to me, Captain. We'll start in the morning. Ryan and Dave can make the first dive while my other divers fly in."

"Excellent," Sweeting replied. "Now, I have other business to attend to, if you'll excuse me."

Ryan stood with Sweeting and escorted him to the aft deck of *Dark Ocean*. While they were waiting for the RBDF boat to pick up the captain, Ryan asked, "What are you going to do with the *Leopard?*"

"She's been seized as evidence and will be auctioned off to the highest bidder."

Ryan asked, "Can I ask you to give me first dibs?"

Sweeting smiled. "I'll need to speak to my boss about that, but I don't see why we can't come to an agreement."

"Thank you, Captain." Ryan extended his hand. "I appreciate all your help."

"It was my pleasure, Mister Weller. If you're ever up in Nassau, look me up. I'll buy you a beer."

The RBDF Safe Boat floated out of the darkness and Sweeting hopped aboard.

Ryan stood with his hands in his pockets, watching the boat's running lights disappear into the distance. He breathed in a deep lungful of salt air and exhaled heavily.

"That was a big sigh," Emily said, startling him. "Want to tell me about it—and why you're buying a salvage boat?"

Ryan heaved another sigh. He had to tell her about Diane. "Look, there's something I need to say. I'm going to apologize for it right now, up front."

"What is it?" she asked, placing a concerned hand on his arm.

"Well, two things. The first is that I should have called you to let you know what I was doing." Closing his eyes, Ryan tried to formulate the right words for the next confession. He clenched his jaw muscles together. There was no need for a story or a long running narrative because it boiled down to one simple thing. "And I kissed Diane."

Emily looked out to sea, watching the calm, undulating waves roll in the distance. "I know. She told me."

"Are you mad?"

"Oh, believe me, sailor, I am one *pissed off* woman. You kissed someone else."

"I know. I know. It was an accident, and it was all *my* fault."

At that moment, his wife did the last thing Ryan expected. She laughed.

"What's so funny?" Ryan asked defensively.

"You, groveling."

"I'm trying to apologize."

Emily continued laughing. "Diane told me you dumped her on the ground and ran away. She said the look on your face was priceless, like you were a scared little kid who'd got caught with his hand in the cookie jar."

"I'm glad you find it funny."

"It's *hysterical*—but I'm still pissed."

"It won't happen again," Ryan said sincerely. "I promise."

"It better not. I remember you promising to forsake all others, too."

Ryan had no witty comeback. Emily was right, and she had every right to be mad. The first kiss was an accident, but the other two were purposeful. He had wanted to kiss Diane then, but not anymore. He wanted Diane off the ship and out of his life.

Emily slipped her arms around her husband's waist. "Ryan, thank you for telling me. It would have been hard to look at you if you'd kept it a secret while I knew the truth. I don't think I could have ever trusted you again."

"Can you trust me, now?"

"I forgive you," Emily said, "but that doesn't mean I fully trust you right now."

"I'm sorry I broke your trust, Em. I'll do whatever I can to earn it back."

"How about you start by telling me why you're trying to buy the *Leopard?*"

"I want to give it to Travis Wisnewski."

"Really?" she said, surprised.

"It was my fault that the *Peggy Lynn* got torpedoed out from under him and now he and Stacey are stuck working on whatever boat DWR assigns them to. It would go a long way in making amends with him."

Emily rose on tiptoes and gave him a quick kiss on the lips. "I love you."

EPILOGUE

Two months later
Nassau, The Bahamas

Ryan walked out of the sprawling yellow, three-story Treasury Department building with a copy of the *Leopard*'s bill of sale and the boat's title in his pocket.

Captain Sweeting had arranged for the sale of the salvage vessel right after the indictment of Hermann and Petra Ziegler, their mother, Captain Haas, and all the members of their team as co-conspirators. The trial had made international headlines, letting the world know exactly where The Bahamas stood when it came to justice.

Waiting in a cab were Emily and Travis and Stacey Wisnewski. Ryan hopped in the front seat of the minivan and showed the address of the marina to the driver.

From the back seat, Travis said, "I appreciate the all-expenses-paid vacation, Ryan, but what's with the mystery tour of the island?"

"Just wait," Ryan replied.

Ten minutes later, the pavement turned to dirt as they passed a row of commercial docks. Old fishing vessels and decrepit freighters rode low in the clear blue water between the commercial docks of Arawak Cay and the mainland of Nassau. Most of the island had been paved and occupied by industrial docks of Nassau Container Port, with its vast sea of shipping containers, ship-to-shore gantry cranes, trucking facilities, and freighter wharves. The other half of Arawak Cay had been created when Nassau Harbour had been dredged in 2009 to expand the cruise port facility. The dirt from that project had created another forty acres, expanding the original island in 1969 from seventy acres to 110. This new land had yet to be paved over and the roads were still rough dirt tracks full of potholes and weeds. Trees had sprouted up to provide shade for the dockworkers, fisherman, and tourists who frequented the island.

As they approached the address Ryan had given to the taxi driver, he pointed to the green hull of the salvage vessel with its forward white superstructure and yellow cranes mounted to its low after deck. "Stop us over there."

The cabbie halted where indicated. While the others disembarked, Ryan paid the driver. Leading the way to where a security guard lounged in the shade of a tree, Ryan produced his paperwork and showed it to the lethargic patroller. The guard glanced at the boat title and then looked at Ryan's ID, before nodding toward the boat.

"What the hell are we doing here, Ryan?" Travis asked, becoming increasingly annoyed.

"Just wait," Ryan replied with a mischievous grin.

"I don't like it when he smiles like that," Stacey said. "What's going on, Emily?"

Emily held up her hands. "I've been tasked with keeping a secret."

"I'll explain everything in a couple minutes," Ryan said. "Let's go aboard this boat." He pointed toward the gangplank leading to the *Leopard*.

Travis went first, admiring the *Leopard*'s lines and the well-equipped deck, though some of the gear had disappeared since the last time Ryan had been aboard her. He didn't know if the Bahamian government had confiscated it or if the locals had appropriated the gear for their own needs, but there was nothing that could be done about it now.

They toured the vessel's interior spaces, examining the engines, the berthing, the shiny stainless appliances in the galley, and various other compartments on their way to the bridge.

When they were all finally gathered in one spot, Ryan laid the boat title on the instrument console along with a bill of sale made out to Travis Wisnewski for the sum of one dollar, although Ryan had no intentions of making him pay. He produced a pen and signed his name in the appropriate spots, then handed the pen to Travis. "Sign there and there, please."

"First of all, what am I signing?"

"I bought this vessel from the Bahamian government after they seized it from the Germans. You might have read about it in the papers. Anyway, I'm giving it to you. I know it can't or won't replace *Peggy Lynn,* but it's my way of trying."

Travis cocked his head.

Ryan could see the gears turning in the man's head. "Just sign the damned papers, Travis."

"You know I hate your guts, right?" Travis said.

"Yeah. I know. I don't really care, either. Just sign the papers and take the damn boat."

Travis threw down the pen. "*Uh-uh*. No way. This has got to be a trick."

Ryan handed the papers to Stacey. "Talk some sense into your husband. I didn't buy round-trip airline fare for you guys." He took Emily's hand, and they left the Wisnewskis standing on the bridge of their new boat, looking dumbfounded.

As Ryan and Emily walked out of the superstructure onto the aft deck, Emily asked, "Think they'll take it?"

"Would you turn it down?"

"I'm not a commercial diver," she countered.

Ryan shrugged. "I can only lead a horse to water. I can't make them drink."

"And if they don't sign?"

He grinned. "Then I guess I have to decide which boat to sell."

"Easy," Emily said, hooking a thumb over her shoulder. "That one."

They were about to step down the gangplank when Stacey called for them to wait. She ran down the exterior steps from the bridge and wrapped Ryan and Emily in a huge hug. "Thank you! Thank you! Thank you!" she cried, her entire body humming with intensity.

Travis came down slower, approaching tentatively. He held his hand out to Ryan, who shook it once Stacey released him from her bear hug.

"Thank you, Ryan. I don't know what I did to deserve this but after the way we left things in Mexico, I figured you'd never speak to me again."

Ryan squeezed the younger man's hand. "You've put up with all my shenanigans over the years and I had one coming. You gave it to me. Let's put it in the past and forget about it."

With a broad grin, Travis said, "You got it."

"Go and enjoy your boat. If there's anything you need, just call."

Ryan and Emily left the Wisnewskis on the *Leopard* and walked back toward Nassau. He felt good about handing the boat over to his old friends, even if it had cost him every penny Steve Carlton had paid him and then some.

The Bahamian government had compensated DWR for retrieving the remaining gold from the sea cave, and the German government had paid Ryan a finder's fee since he was the first to dive on the gold, which he'd generously split between the crewmembers and divers aboard *Dark Ocean*.

Diane Carlton had returned to Big Darby to begin clearing away the debris of the old Green Castle, planning to start her new life on the island.

With a smile, Ryan squeezed Emily's hand. It was good to be by her side, even if he was on a short leash.

"What are you grinning about?" Emily asked.

"Everything, baby," Ryan said. "Everything."

ABOUT THE AUTHOR

Evan Graver is the author of the Ryan Weller Thriller Series. Before becoming a writer, he worked in construction, as a security guard, a motorcycle and car technician, a property manager, and in the scuba industry. He served in the U.S. Navy as an aviation electronics technician until they medically retired him following a motorcycle accident that left him paralyzed. He found other avenues of adventure: riding ATVs, downhill skiing, skydiving, and bungee jumping. His passions are scuba diving and writing. He lives in Hollywood, Florida, with his wife and son.

To see more of his biography please visit the about section at www.evangraver.com

Made in the USA
Middletown, DE
26 December 2022

20466661R00215